Praise for the novels of Jacqueline Navin

The Princess of Park Lane

"*The Princess of Park Lane* is a sensual and charmingly written love story." —*Romantic Times*

"Delightful." —*The Best Reviews*

The Bliss

"One of the most romantic heroes I've read all year. Don't miss this exciting tale."
—Lisa Kleypas, *New York Times* bestselling author

"By turns, raucously humorous and achingly poignant, but always wonderful . . . an excellent storyteller with a deft touch for characterization, dialogue, and plot."
—*Affaire de Coeur*

"A delightfully entertaining love story."
—*Historical Romance Reviews*

"Refreshing characterizations. Loved every minute."
—*Rendezvous*

"Pure Bliss." —*Midwest Book Review*

"A very pleasant way to while away a chilly evening."
—*BellaOnline*

continued . . .

Meet Me at Midnight

"Gripping . . . drew me in completely."

—*All About Romance*

"Proves how talented Jacqueline Navin is . . . Five stars."

—*Midnight Book Review*

A Rose at Midnight

"Her books are gifts to be treasured. Fantastic! Five bells!"

—*Bell, Book and Candle*

"Exhilarating . . . she plots like a master." —*Rendezvous*

The Flower and the Sword

"Strong characters . . . a dramatic, tightly woven plot . . . superb."

—*Rendezvous*

"A beautifully written tale. Fantastic!"

—*Bell, Book and Candle*

The Heiress of Hyde Park

Jacqueline Navin

BERKLEY SENSATION, NEW YORK

THE HEIRESS OF HYDE PARK

A Berkley Sensation Book / published by arrangement with the author

PRINTING HISTORY
Berkley Sensation edition / August 2004

Cover art by Tim Barrall.
Cover design by George Long.
Interior text design by Julie Rogers.

For information address: The Berkley Publishing Group,
a division of Penguin Group (USA) Inc.,
375 Hudson Street, New York, New York 10014.

ISBN: 0-425-19778-6

BERKLEY SENSATION™
Berkley Sensation Books are published by The Berkley Publishing Group,
a division of Penguin Group (USA) Inc.,
375 Hudson Street, New York, New York 10014.
BERKLEY SENSATION and the "B" design
are trademarks belonging to Penguin Group (USA) Inc.

PRINTED IN THE UNITED STATES OF AMERICA

10 9 8 7 6 5 4 3 2 1

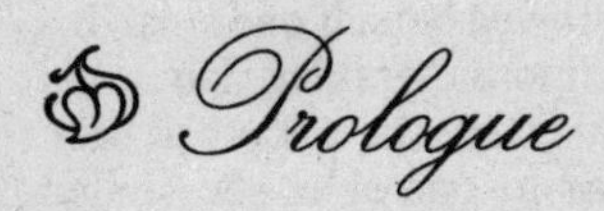

Prologue

In her boudoir, Lady May Hayworth stretched like a cat. Pushing away from the small escritoire she used for her research, she put the papers she'd been reading aside and rose to give full extension to her knotting muscles.

Looking at the tall, rangy man stretched out on the divan, she smiled. Robert's eyes were closed, his naked chest rising and falling with the deep breathing of sleep. He still wore his reading glasses, an anathema perched on the end of that chiseled nose. The sharp angles of his cheekbones wore a slight flush, his sensuous mouth slack and without tension. She fought the urge to kiss him, a self-indulgence quickly tamed by a rush of tenderness. She hated to wake him.

He was such a gorgeous man. His coloring was swarthy. She teased him sometimes about having Spanish blood, whereupon he would utter caressing words in that language—how exactly did a stable owner speak fluent Spanish?—as he played the Latin romancer. Half the time it reduced her to giggles, which was something for a woman of her age, which was five and forty this spring—and the other half of the time it reduced her to trembling clay.

They'd been lovers for nearly a year, but while the secret

liaison had yielded a comfortable and intimate relationship, there was more unsaid between them than there were truths spoken.

Robert Carsons was the owner and operator of an upscale stable here in London, a man who worked with his hands. She was the daughter of an earl. Between them lay insurmountable differences, but they were less to do with the disparity in their current social positions than they were with the secrets between them.

Strolling quietly to him, she allowed herself one small indulgence. Threading her fingers into the graying hair at his temple, taking care not to touch his skin, she smoothed back the thick lock. Cocking her head to one side, she smiled again, and whispered, "Who are you, Robert Carsons?"

She was no fool. She'd always known Robert's past was steeped in fine breeding and money. His blood was as noble as hers. It wasn't just the languages he spoke or the cultured accent he slipped into during their quiet evenings together that gave him away. It was in his bearing, his pride, his occasional arrogance. Mother had always lectured that good breeding showed. And so it did, even with weathered skin and callused hands. But why the charade of a common stable keeper, she had no idea.

It was something they had talked about only once. It had led to a frightening quarrel that May had feared might mean the end of their relationship. Lady May, who was not without a healthy dollop of pride herself, was forced to let the matter drop once they'd reconciled, for she had been deeply shaken by the idea of losing this man she had come to love.

After all, she had her secrets as well.

So they had called a truce between them—no questions, no pasts, only the present. And it was a lovely truce, filled with passionate nights and long philosophical debates and silly times that left her laughing until she gasped for breath.

She started when he cocked one eye open and grinned. "Are you going to stand about all day playing with my hair?"

"You were awake the whole time!" she exclaimed. She

slapped him on the shoulder, but he caught her hand and pulled her down onto his lap. Locking his hands around her waist, he held her pleasantly imprisoned.

"Are you finished with the journal?" he asked.

"It will be years before I am. So many names. My brother was a profligate and a scoundrel unmatched. Therefore, this task of finding those children he left behind after all of his numerous affairs is a daunting one."

"Well, at least Michaela is satisfactorily settled."

She bristled. "You keep bringing up the subject. I have admitted, haven't I, that I was wrong about Adrian Khoury? The two are quite happily married. Now I am on to the next project."

"Who is it, a son or daughter?"

"Another daughter. Wooly was quite fond of the mother, a Judith Nash. He writes about her in the most glowing terms. He missed her when she severed their affair, one of the few times the woman was the first to leave. Imagine, Wooly pining so. He was even over the moon on the name the mother chose for their child. Trista Josephine."

"Mmm," Robert responded, winding a tendril of her hair around his finger.

"You aren't listening at all."

"I am listening, I promise. The woman charmed Woolrich. That's a lark." He buried his nose in the curve of her shoulder. "Daughter named Trista. A romantic name for so practical a woman to give her child."

She settled into the warmth of his chest and sighed. "Why do you say she is practical?"

"Because she sent Woolrich away."

"He asked her to be his mistress, but she wouldn't."

"No. Some women aren't like that. They have sensual natures but overdeveloped consciences. A pity. I am most grateful that you are not thusly hindered."

"With a sensual nature?"

His hands roused a response that belied this, and he chuckled. "Certainly not. I meant an overdeveloped conscience."

"Well, of course. Don't you think that is why I am doing all of this fairy-godmother nonsense, going about finding these lost lambs and bestowing upon them their inheritance, making certain they are all right and well taken care of—things my lighthearted but tragically unconcerned brother should have done."

"And you are determined to find every last one," he said.

"Indeed, I shall, but this one is proving quite stubborn. Upon the death of the mother, she continued at the house where she grew up as a paid companion to the fourth Lord Aylesgarth's widow for a few years, but then she all but disappeared."

He laughed again. "You love the thrill of this little hunt, the joy in the giving. And family. You feel for these children."

Even with the delicious pressure of his lips just behind her ear, she could manage to think clearly enough to grant him this. "Family is everything," she murmured. "And these lost nieces and nephews are all the family I have left to me."

May fleetingly wondered about him, about his family. Did they know where he was? Did they care? Perhaps they thought him dead.

Did he think of them at times, miss them?

Forbidden though it was, the curiosity that burned inside her pressed against her throat. She swallowed it back, turning her face to his for his kiss.

At times like this, when dangerous thoughts came, it was best to lose herself in the one thing that could banish all thought, all care. She gave herself over to Robert's kiss, and forgot her quest for the lost Trista Nash for a while.

Chapter 1

There was an excellent reason why Lady May Hayworth's inquiries on the whereabouts of Trista Nash had gone without result. The girl, who was now a woman of three and twenty, no longer used that name. She went by the name of Trista Fairhaven. It wasn't a legal name, but no one ever checked these things. Just like no one knew that her status of widowhood was an equally fabricated fiction.

On this afternoon in early spring, in a bustling workroom at the rear of a posh milliner in London's West End, she rushed about the tables strewn with netting and feathers, giving orders to Betty.

"Goodness, child," she exclaimed as the grinning girl finally brought the correct spool of ribbon from the row along the wall, "if you do not move more quickly, I shall have to wrap you in the stuff"—she feigned a severe look as she pulled out an arm's length of bright purple grosgrain and wielded it threateningly—"and tickle you for every moment you kept me waiting."

Betty stuck out her tongue. Trista pretended to be shocked at such outrageousness.

"Betty, are you finished with your lesson?" Mrs. Hines,

the milliner shop proprietress said as she propelled her large girth into the room. "I'll not have you neglecting your education."

Betty, the youngest of Mrs. Hines's two daughters, gave a pout, but it was only a token one. She was a happy child. No one took her kindly, bossy, overbearing-but-well-intentioned mother too seriously. However, they didn't disobey her either.

"No, ma'am."

"Then do so right this minute, thank you. We will await your return after you've written your letters. See to it."

"Are you certain she said a nest?" Trista asked Mrs. Hines doubtfully, turning the brown thatch of twigs over with a grimace. They had gotten an order for a hat by one of the richest duchesses in the city, but the woman had only one thing in mind—to draw attention to the money she spent on her clothing. As a result, the order was so outrageous, so ostentatious, it was difficult to build the monstrous headdress without flinching.

"Indeed, she did," Mrs. Hines replied with a flourish of her expressive hands, "and none of your artistic touches on this one. Oh, your taste is too fine. I should have your cousin do it. Luci!"

"I promise to be flamboyant," Trista replied, laughing. "And to exercise as much poor taste as I can muster."

"Then use more tulle, dear," Mrs. Hines gushed, pulling yards of the stuff off the bolt. "And what about these cherries?"

Trista groaned. "Maybe you *should* have Luci do this."

"Or Betty," Mrs. Hines said with a conspiratorial wink. "Ah, I know it wreaks havoc with your sensibilities to have to ruin high-quality materials, but this is the burden of an artistic eye. Learning to balance business with aesthetics will stand you in good stead when you and Luci purchase the shop. I can hardly wait to wallow in the waters of Bath, and I swear I will not spare a single pang of conscience for you buried in swaths of ribbons and feathers—"

"And birds' nests," Trista said, holding up the offending

object. It was affixed with a hook on the bottom in order for it to be secured to the hat whereupon the duchess had specified a plumed bird be placed atop the thing so that its brightly colored tail feathers trailed down her back. Her Grace, upon placing her order, declared it would be "spectacularly breathtaking," a description to which they all privately agreed but with rather a different meaning.

"What is the first order of doing custom, dear Trista?"

Looking down at the gaudy mélange she'd created, Trista squared her shoulders. "The customer's wishes must come first. I do know it well. But I do not have to like it."

She sighed, resigned to her task. Trista hoped this criminal misuse of good materials would not spoil the excellent reputation of the shop, for soon it would belong to her. It was what she'd worked for, stingily saving every farthing for Andrew's future. Her son was, and always had been from his birth nearly five years ago, her utmost priority, and seeing to his security was her most cherished dream.

The tinkle of the bell from the street door sounded, signaling a customer had entered the shop. Mrs. Hines hurried through the curtain separating the workroom and graciously appointed outer regions with the tireless enthusiasm with which she always greeted customers.

Working in silence for a while, Trista considered she was making good progress. She was actually pleased that she had minimized the atrocity. Possibly.

"A couple of swells just came in," Luci said, rushing to her side. "With two ladies, and I use that term loosely since one is showing her bosom in broad daylight. Oh, well, it's quite a bosom. It seems one of the women lost her hat. It was blown off and crushed under a carriage wheel. Her companion is buying her a new hat to replace it, and Dina is in a tizzy."

Dina, Mrs. Hines's eldest daughter, presided over the showroom. "Dina is always in a tizzy," Trista said. "Now hold that securely while I tie the ribbon."

"No, she's in a tizzy because of the man. You simply have to see him. He's fabulous."

"Hand me that thread."

"Aren't you the least bit curious?" Luci squinted at the creation growing at an alarming rate on its stand. "Oh, dear."

"Is it that bad? I thought I might have saved it."

"You are good, but not that good, cousin. Come here," Luci said, picking up the hat while jerking her head to the mirror.

"Oh, no," Trista said, laughing.

"It is only fair," Luci urged, and positioning Trista in front of the mirror, ceremoniously placed the complicated headgear on her head.

"You look like a duchess!" Luci declared with a laugh.

"Of Hades, perhaps."

"Well, it is an absurd piece. Imagine if we could dismiss that ruff."

Trista turned her head this way and that, seeing the possibilities. The base of it was, as all Mrs. Hines's hats were, made of good stock and fit well atop her curling cloud of soft, pale hair. She never took time to do more with her hair when working than to twist it back into a very loose knot, leaving tendrils to twine into gentle corkscrews around her face, but even this unkempt style did not detract from the elegant dip of the brim.

She fantasized how she would save it. The shape did wonders to accentuate her eyes, which were gray and large and quite alluring underneath. The shape of her nose, a bit pointy, a bit pert, and her prominent chin were complimented by the impudent angle. It was a riding hat, smart and deserving of little ornamentation, merely a ribbon, perhaps a single plume.

Dina stuck her head into the workroom. "Trista, where are you? Luci— Oh, there you are. What the . . . ? Trista, that hat is simply horrid. Are you trying to frighten our customers away? Oh, bother, I have no time for your silliness, get me that hat you've just completed for the Countess Dufrenay. Quickly. A gentleman is here and says he will pay thrice the price we charged the countess. Then we can make another up for the countess later. They are in a hurry."

Neither Trista nor Luci thought to tell Dina to fetch it herself. She never stepped foot in the workroom. The showroom was her domain, and she presided over it like a despot. Luci went to get the hat.

Glancing over her shoulder, Dina said, "Do you see him? He is simply gorgeous. Of course, he's insufferably arrogant, coming in off the street and expecting us to produce a hat for his companion, but I must say he did it in the most charming way. I could hardly believe it when my mother told me to do it. Well, a man like that, one simply makes allowances, doesn't one?"

Through the small doorway, Trista did indeed see a man. He was very tall, with dark brown hair worn rather roguishly long and tied in a queue. An unruly forelock spilled onto a high brow, an intelligent brow.

She took a step forward, her mouth going slack as shock rippled through her body. A slow curl of excitement crooked itself around her stomach.

He looked so familiar. He reminded her of . . .

His eyes fixed on her. She felt the painful rattle of her heart in her bosom. Time stopped, her mind stopped. She was all instinct now, as alert as a deer facing a bowman in a glade.

His eyes widened. Then he did something strange. As dumbfounded as she, he stared, motionless for a moment, then raised a single finger as if to beckon her.

Roman. My God. Roman.

And he'd seen her.

She mewled, stumbling backward as if not trusting herself to keep from rushing forward to the befuddled summons he had given.

"My goodness, what are you doing?" Dina snapped. "Where is that Luci? Trista, please take that ridiculous contraption from your head. If our customers see you, it will frighten them off."

Bless Dina—solid, practical. Her voice cut through the haze.

"What?" Looking about, Trista was somewhat surprised

to see herself here in the shop's back room. Around her were snippets of ribbon and tufts of tulle blowing like dust motes against her hem.

Mrs. Hines's shop. She was still here. For a moment . . . for a moment, she'd been back at Whitethorn.

Whipping the hat off her head, she threw it on the table.

"Be careful with that." Dina peered at her. "Why are being so clumsy? It is not like you. Trista? Where are you going?"

"I am ill," Trista said as she ran for the back door. She almost ran into Luci, who had just emerged from the closet where they kept the completed hats out of harm's way and as dust-free as possible before they were picked up.

"I found it!" Lúci exclaimed, then grunted as she quickly sidestepped to avoid her cousin, who raced by her to grab her shawl and slam through the door leading to the alley.

"Give that to me. See to Trista; she is sick," Dina said, taking the stylish hat, one of Trista's finer creations. She blew the tiniest accumulation of dust from it as she walked back toward the front of the store, muttering, "Probably the shock of seeing herself in that dratted hat that did it, Lord knows."

"I say, Aylesgarth, what's got you?"

His friend slapped him on the shoulder.

Roman Aylesgarth, the seventh Lord Aylesgarth, absorbed the blow without so much as blinking. It was nothing compared to the one he'd just been given.

He could have sworn he'd just seen Trista Nash standing inside the curtained room wearing . . . a bird's nest on her head.

Dear Lord, he hadn't thought he had overimbibed last night, but he must have.

"You look like you've seen a ghost." Raymond chuckled. Roman frowned at him, forcing himself to stop looking at the curtain that had been abruptly drawn over the apparition. A ghost?

"What is it, Roman?" Raymond asked, concern in his voice.

I've just seen the only woman I've ever loved.

He'd not say that. Raymond would have laughed. Anyone would have. How well it was known that the cold and debauched Lord Aylesgarth did not love. He played, he lusted, he toyed, he ran in circles that made a demon wince, he didn't give a damn. If he loved anything, his reputation would have it, it was his team of perfectly matched horses, his fine, swift phaeton, aged whiskey, cured tobacco after, and a pair of accommodating thighs belonging to a pretty, docile lass who understood his loathing of attachment. He was a terror and didn't give a whit about it. Terrors did not love.

But perhaps they had, once.

"I thought I saw someone I knew."

How paltry those words, signifying nothing of import.

"A woman, eh?" Raymond said, his humor restored. He gave Roman's back another clamp and was rewarded with a glare that left him clearing his throat. "I'll just go see if Annabelle has chosen her hat."

Roman didn't hear him. He was moving toward the curtained doorway. For some reason he was angry. If it was indeed Trista Nash back there, how dare she hide from him.

"Excuse me," the shopkeeper's daughter said, coming to block his path. "May I help you?"

This girl's color was high. He was used to women getting flustered in his presence. It was a nuisance most of the time, the kind of thing his cronies alternately admired and rode him about.

"I wanted . . ." To go back there and search for someone. He straightened, trying to clear his head. "I thought I saw someone I knew. I . . . Does a Trista Nash work in this shop?"

The woman opened her mouth to answer, but the *swoosh* of the curtain being flung back startled her out of it. Another woman, dressed in a simple cotton work dress, stared up at him. She had the hat on her head he had seen Trista wearing—or no, he must have been mistaken.

"No. A Trista *Nash* does not work here." She dipped into a shallow curtsey. "I am Luci Miller, my lord. I am sorry to have startled you."

Her hair wasn't the same, this one being a darker blond and no wild curl to it. Her eyes were blue, not the gray he remembered so vividly. But the height was approximately the same, and from a distance, his eyes had probably deceived him.

The shop attendant looked at Luci, then back at him. "I am sorry, my lord. Is there something I can get you?"

"Oh, Ally!" a female voice called. He closed his eyes against the grating voice. It belonged to Raymond's plump wife, Marian. She had taken to calling him Ally—a shortened form of his surname and title, Aylesgarth. It deepened the automatic dislike he had felt upon their first meeting. Grudgingly, he turned to her.

"What do you think of this one?" Turning her head this way and that, she struck a pose. Behind her, Ray laughed.

Roman didn't understand his friend's affection for the woman. She talked far too much, and too loudly. He supposed Ray did, as well, so perhaps they were well matched. They were recently married and had come to London on their wedding trip. Roman and Marian's sister, Annabelle, had met through the couple and found a mutual attraction, enough to sustain a passably pleasant series of evenings and afternoons, a respite from the boredom Town life had become for him. They were often a foursome, but the association was becoming tedious.

He went over to join them, wondering what in the world had made him think Luci Miller was Trista Nash. Was it merely the suggestion of her hair, the pale impression of her form? Not that he didn't think of Trista. He did so. Often. But he wasn't prone to chasing about thinking he had seen her.

Perhaps, he thought slyly, he had seen her.

It defied reason, and yet he couldn't shake the feeling of

excitement buzzing in his veins, the subtle expectancy that danced along his nerve endings, rippling along his flesh like a gentle wave of heat. His body, he realized, felt like it was ready to run, tense and taut. To race after a fleeting image, a memory? Or a real person?

God, he *was* bored—that had to be it or else he wouldn't be indulging in such fanciful thoughts. The day was turning out to be less than amusing. Ray was pleasant enough, but Marian plucked at his nerves and Annabelle was . . . ordinary. Disappointing. Women inevitably were these days.

He paid for the hat, and went first to hold the door. As they filed through, he looked back at the curtain and saw the woman Luci watching him anxiously. And the knot in his stomach gave one last, great wrench, as if something were very wrong.

He always trusted the knots in his stomach.

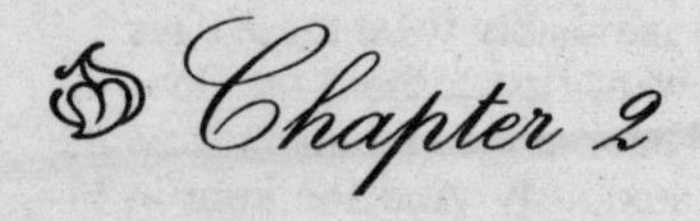

Trista sat in the small parlor of the modest house she shared with Luci and Luci's husband, David, in a respectable, if not exactly ultra-fashionable, neighborhood. It housed the four of them comfortably—Luci, David, Trista, and her small son, Andrew.

Trista looked at her cousin. "I suppose I have a great deal to explain."

Luci's face was kind and full of expectation. The sound of splashing water carried from the kitchen where the tub was set. Their one maid and cook, Emily, was keeping an eye on Andrew who was enjoying his bath, splashing through reenactments of naval battles from the Vikings to Lord Trafalgar with vigor.

David Miller was in the small room that he used as his office. Since losing his job at a bank, he spent more and more of his time here, reading medical texts, which fascinated him. Unfortunately, he often imagined himself suffering from many of the maladies about which he read.

Thus, both males of the household were occupied in their favorite pastimes, leaving the women to talk.

"I first laid eyes on Roman when I was six years old."

Trista's voice was soft as a picture came to her mind's eye of a boy, all legs and arms, perhaps a bit too thin, then, with a nose that did not yet suit his face, and round, wary eyes. Roman as he had been then had inspired equal parts romance and fear. Seeing him again today, her reaction had been no different.

Luci rose and took out two glasses and filled them with wine, a rare indulgence but certainly called for this evening. Handing one to Trista, she lifted hers briefly in salute, then sipped.

Trista stared at hers for a moment as she wrestled with her thoughts. "There is a long history there. As you might guess by my revealing to you the truth about Andrew."

"I take it from the fact that you do not wish to see him that he doesn't know. . . ."

"About Andrew. No. He knows nothing of his son, not even his existence." Trista let out a long, heavy breath. "How could I tell him? If you knew the story, knew what a fool I had been then . . . You must think so ill of me, to learn of all the lies, the way I've deceived even you."

Luci made a face and gave sort of a shrug. "I only wish you had told me. Though, I understand. When I think of what it must have been like for you to bear an illegitimate child after all you went through yourself, I can quite guess how much it tormented you."

Never, never could Trista have envisioned that she herself would give birth to a child outside of the blessing of marriage, for she had tasted the hardships of bastardry in the early years of her life. This was precisely the reason why she had taken such drastic, and perhaps not completely truthful, measures to protect her son.

"I hated lying, but, Luci, if I didn't tell Andrew, then I certainly wouldn't make a fool of him by telling others. Do you see? It was my secret alone."

"Then, Captain Fairhaven? Did he exist at all?"

"Only in my imagination. I had to have a husband, you see, for Andrew's sake. A fictitious one was all I could conjure."

Trista stood suddenly, her hands clutched at her waist. "It must seem impossible to imagine me of all people being so reckless as to fall prey to a man. But I was a very different girl than the woman I have become. Not so cold as this, nor as wise." She pointed her finger at Luci. "I blame Mama in part."

"Your mother! What did Aunt Judith have to do with it?"

"She fell in love with Roman first. When she first took her post at Whitethorn Manor, she refused to think ill of him. We were so happy to be there after all we'd been through, barely escaping living in the streets, and Mama was determined that it was going to be wonderful. And then we met this beast of a boy, and she insisted he had goodness in him. It was too romantic, and I fell prey to the notion as well.

"I should have trusted my first instinct. The day I set eyes on Aylesgarth, I made up my mind that he was a most disagreeable boy. Oh, he was sad, of course. Even I could see it. I remember him so clearly. Wild, stifled, as arrogant as the devil himself, and rather as nasty as old Nick, too."

"I recall her letters to my mother." Luci smiled. "He gave her quite a run about. I was of the impression she tangled with him on a few occasions."

"She was the only one he respected, and he did listen to her although he did not have to. You see, his father had left their home to live in London, abandoning him and his sister to a mother who . . . well, it is unkind to speak ill of the dead, but the Lady Aylesgarth had a fondness for anything in bottles. Laudanum, sherry, wine.

"She was a very unhappy woman. While Lord Aylesgarth ran rampant in London with his mistress, the two of them openly living together and blissfully happy by all reports, his wife languished in her misery, tainting everything in that house, including her children. It was rather a pitiful place, for all of their money. Those two, Grace and he, were the most pathetic children I have ever encountered."

"No wonder it tugged at your mother's heartstrings. He was as he was because of his unhappy home."

"Aylesgarth as a boy was hell on wheels, not one to sit

and sob into his tea. He was twice my age when I came to Whitethorn, sullen and as unlikeable as a troll. Except trolls are ugly. He was beautiful. Even awkward and bony, with his hair wild because he refused to comb it or use pomade, he was gorgeous."

Luci sipped her wine thoughtfully. "Did you like him, then?"

"It was impossible to like him, and yet . . . somehow it was equally impossible not to. Oh, he was a rotter to me in the beginning. He pestered me, told me the house was haunted by a headless ghost that ate children. He stole my dessert, put insects in the nursery to frighten his sister and me, laughed at us and—worst of all—called us babies."

"What a horrid boy!" Luci laughed and Trista smiled at the memories, not really wanting to but not able to stop herself.

Roman had been a storm blowing into the house, anger and resentment whirling like hurricane-class winds around him. But he had been exciting, impossible to ignore, an enigma even to her child's brain . . . or perhaps it was her heart that was affected, even then.

"He was monstrous. But Mama said I must be kind to him. I didn't dare disobey Mama."

Luci followed her with her eyes as Trista paced around the room. "Yes. Aunt Judith had a way about her. Gentle, but formidable. So, tell me, when did you decide you adored him?"

"It was several months after we arrived at Whitethorn. He'd forever be taking off into the woods for long periods of time, sometimes igniting the entire household into a panic until he'd return, belligerent and defiant, as if all the fuss was a supreme bother and completely unnecessary." She sighed, and suddenly her hands would not be still.

"So, this one time when he appeared after one of his long absences, he found his sister and me fighting over a doll Mama had saved up her wages to buy for me. Grace was jealous of it. Of Mama, I think, more than the doll. She had dozens of dolls, but she wanted mine. You see, her mother never noticed her much. I could never get angry at Grace.

She didn't have Aylesgarth's fire, and without any attention from her mama, she simply faded."

"Your mother's heart must have been touched by that one as well."

"Mama was very kind to her, but Grace resented me all the same. And she really hated me for getting that doll. She tried to take it away from me and in the tussle, the doll's china face was smashed. Ruined. That was when Aylesgarth found me, weeping like the baby he'd called me so many times."

"That must have pleased his lordship. He liked to see you unhappy, you said."

"You see, that was just it. Instead of laughing at me as he might have done, he seemed to take pity on me. He was gruff of course, but he said kind things that made me feel better. He told me I was a brave girl who'd taken none of his nonsense so he couldn't see me weeping over such a thing as a broken doll. I told him it had been a present from my mama, and he changed then. He seemed to understand."

Luci sat forward. "How interesting. So there is a heart indeed beating in that broad chest of his."

"It was considerably less broad at the time, but, yes, it would seem so. But wait, it is even more puzzling." She paused, surprised to feel the sting of tears in her eyes. "He brought the doll to me the next day. He had persevered with the overwhelming task of gluing back the shattered face. I tell you, the result was something hideous to behold. But somehow, it was so dear. He had tried very hard to make it look well."

Luci's face showed her interest. "How extraordinary that he would do such a thing."

"From that moment on, he was my hero."

"He sounds so lonely." Luci's voice was wistful.

"He did have one friend. A partner in crime, more like it. Jason Knightsbridge. He lived in the village. They were infamous. They'd run the fells together and find all manner of trouble."

"Did he say anything when he gave you the doll?"

"Not really. Well . . . he only mentioned that his mother had said she would purchase another doll to replace mine, or give me one of Grace's as punishment to her, but he had told her that it wouldn't be the same, that money couldn't fix some things that were broken." It still bemused her, such poignant insight from this boy.

"And he was right, wasn't he?" She looked at her cousin. "Oh, no, Luci! You are charmed, too, aren't you?"

Luci nonchalantly addressed herself to her wine, "It's a charming story."

Trista sighed. "Yes, I decided he was wonderful, too. But, Luci, he wasn't." She added darkly, "That wasn't the last time he fooled me. Oh, he was no longer a monster, but neither was he the angel I wanted him to be. Those impulses to do good, when they come upon him, never amount to much. This one brilliant flash of noble nature seemed to prove all Mama's theories about his true goodness, and it fed my illusion of him for a long time."

"Aunt Judith didn't suffer many fools. Tell me," Luci said, rising to bring Trista her glass, "did he *never* fulfill your high esteem?"

Staring into the liquid, Trista grimaced. "No. In the end, he did not."

Luci was silent. "I suppose the rest of it is fairly predictable. You grew up and . . . things happened."

"I'll explain, so perhaps you will understand. Perhaps I will understand as well. As you know, Mama stayed on after the children no longer needed a governess, for Lady Aylesgarth liked her and so she was hired to be her companion. When Mama died, I took her place in that employment. I was sixteen, old enough. It was logical, a secure job. But . . ."

Luci's sharp eyes conveyed empathy with those empty years.

"I was rather lonely," Trista admitted. "And I suppose being shut up in that house with Grace, who disliked me, and Lady Aylesgarth, who was barely coherent half of the time, I was quite vulnerable when the wild, handsome son of the house returned home from University."

She looked out the window, seeing not the neat houses lined up in the square, but a place back through the years and the young man who'd exploded life into her dreary existence. "I was already half in love with him, you see. It was the doll, that one aberrant gesture that stuck in my head. It colored everything."

"You fell in love."

"I was fated to. Mama used to say that I was kissed by fairies, that some children are and it means they are meant to find great love. She herself had found she did not want this, but that I was my father's daughter, and that Lord Woolrich was a passionate man with a great heart. It was my destiny, then, to find one man with whom I would spend the rest of my life, loving completely."

Luci gave a small laugh. "Your mother was the most practical woman I ever met. I simply cannot imagine her saying such a fantastical thing."

"Mama did have a romantic side. I had a sense those years of waiting for something wonderful to come to me. And it did. It was like I'd been dormant, ready for him to come and find me, breathe life into me."

She sighed, her fingers restlessly picking at lint, moving over her skirts, brushing and smoothing as she thought back to times she'd forbidden herself to remember. "I don't expect you to understand how it was. It seemed to me then that he had been struck by the same bolt of lightning as I. We were grown up, and those feelings were no longer innocent ones, but real, with all of the implications of adult attraction, and . . . I suppose I am just trying to rationalize. I was just a stupid girl who fell into the same trap as a thousand other stupid girls before me."

"I do understand. The man . . . well, he is . . . hard to ignore. And as you say, quite understandably you were vulnerable."

"Oh, more than that, Luci. I was duped. He lied to me. Oh, I know it is ridiculous that I believed him, but he promised me nothing less than marriage. I believed him! I know how ridiculous that sounds to us now, but we are women who understand the world, and lords do not marry servants. But then, oh, then I was a child who believed in dreams, who believed in him and in infinite possibilities, and that the world was mine. Do you see now how it was? I thought he was going to be my husband."

Luci bowed her head. "I do understand, Trista, truly I do. Tell me, then, if you were so much in love with each other, why did he leave you?"

"His father returned to Whitethorn and told him he had to marry. He did so reluctantly, I know that. His family required money, and the cure for that was for him to marry an heiress with a great fortune. And I was not, of course, an heiress. I was his mother's paid companion."

"Oh, darling, that is wretched. He betrayed you. You trusted him, and you were all of, what, eighteen? And he . . ."

"I was seventeen. He was twenty and four at the time. It was right before his mother died that he wed his heiress, and then the irony was that his father's death followed quickly afterward. A coincidence, merely. This was not a case of a spouse unable to live without the other. Lord Aylesgarth lived very well without poor Lady Aylesgarth, happily if the rumors were right, right here in London with his mistress. His son, as it turned out, had the same view of women. He wished to have me and his wife in the same manner as had his father."

"The cad! And to think I admired him, thought him handsome. Well, handsome is as handsome does—our mothers taught us that."

Trista smiled at this uncharacteristic show of spleen. Luci's rare outbursts of temper were so incompatible with her usually placid and cheerful self that it was odd to see her vehement.

She said, "I refuse to say I am ashamed. That would be a grave insult to Andrew. Rather, I am embarrassed by my lack of judgment. I will not say I am sorry, either. Regardless of what happened, I could never regret it."

"Because of Andrew, I know," Luci said.

Yes, because of Andrew. The child was her life, her world. But also . . . and this she would never admit, but also because she'd been alive once, truly alive.

Luci frowned at her cousin. "Oh, dear. What could it have been to see him there, in the shop like that today?"

What was it like? A nightmare, a dream. It didn't seem real at the time. But now, it was all too real. Because she couldn't shake the feeling that she was in danger from him somehow. But what could he do to her now?

The moment the brave thought came to her mind, she knew the answer. Andrew. She feared Roman not because he'd broken her heart and abandoned her, but because he was Andrew's father.

"It was . . . disconcerting," she said, and finally took up her glass, reasoning that she could not be expected to talk if she were diligently sipping her wine.

She was rescued, however, from having to answer any more questions by the entrance of David. He had a book in his hand and flourished it with a grim smile. "I found it! Listen to this."

"Oh, dear Lord," Luci moaned, all but smothering the exclamation behind the back of her hand. "What is it, dear?" she asked more pleasantly.

"Listen to this, listen to this. You know how I told you my heart kept skipping all the time. Like this . . . beat, beat, beat, *thump,* beat, beat, beat, *thump*?"

"I thought I explained it is from your overwhelming love of me, my darling," Luci said sweetly. She exchanged a repressed smile with her cousin.

"Very clever, my sweet. But I've found it here. This Dr. Harcum has written about that very thing. And you will never believe what he says. He writes, 'The rhythm of the heart is of fragile constitution, for at any moment the humors of the blood can be out of harmony.' And here, here he says, 'Hearts are of a mercurial nature.' There, haven't I said that, Luci? Haven't I always said hearts are funny things, unpredictable things?"

"You have, my love," she said.

"Indeed," he agreed, basking in his triumph. Flipping through the pages, he added thoughtfully, "And he has a great deal to say about sniffling. Phlegm, you understand, is produced when the balance of fluids is overtaxed."

"You do not have sniffles," Luci said, losing her patience.

"But I think I do, dear." He sniffed experimentally. "I'm feeling a buildup, I think."

Trista kept her head down, terrified that her dear cousin-in-law might see her smile. It wasn't funny, not really, but since David had been dismissed from his post so as to make way for one of the trustees to put their nephew in his position he had been preoccupied with his health.

Luci was understanding. She had confided to Trista that she believed David was only distracting himself from his real worry by reading. Unfortunately, he was concentrating far too much on medical texts.

"You are not having any such thing. Go on with you, and fetch Andrew out of the bath for us. It is time for his story."

This was the one thing guaranteed to move David—Andrew. He adored the boy, and he loved to regale him with long, spirited stories.

David headed toward the door. "In keeping with the lad's current fascination with water, we are in the midst of a rousing, if rather tame, version of the *The Odyssey*. I left out Circe. Sexual imprisonment is hardly a theme for a young mind. Don't want to blight the boy's emotional growth." He exited with a waggle of eyebrows that had Luci both shaking her head in disapproval and laughing.

At least David still had his sense of humor. Trista had often marveled at her good fortune. About the time David lost his position, she and Luci decided to try to purchase the hat shop. They had been able to save money by all living in one household. Fortunately, it also meant that Emily could keep Andrew during the day, and David had begun Andrew's tutoring during his free time. It had turned into an ideal arrangement.

But today, after seeing Roman . . . No. Not Roman. She

had made up her mind not to think of him that way. Aylesgarth from now on.

The disturbing feeling that something had shifted, that all this peace was coming to an end, and that it had not been meant to last, merely a lull between two episodes of major importance in her life, churned underneath Trista's breast.

She was being silly, oversetting herself like this over such a small matter. What would it matter to him if he had seen her? She had been but one woman in a long line of women who had temporarily amused him. How like her own father he had proven to be in the end, caring little for the spoils he left behind. And her fears for Andrew were most likely for nothing. A mere by-blow, as they called unwanted children in his circles.

She knew this well enough. For she was one.

"Are you all right?" Luci asked, laying a hand on Trista's shoulder.

"Fine, really," she answered. "I am tired."

Luci watched her closely. "I should say so. It has been an eventful day. You should get some sleep. We have to get to the shop early tomorrow and finish that masterpiece. The duchess expressly requested it be ready for the Minton lawn party, and that is the day after tomorrow."

"Very well, then. Good night, Luci. And thank you."

"Good night, Trista." They embraced lightly, simultaneously giving the other a peck on the cheek in the French fashion, a legacy from their mothers who had been sisters and very affectionate. "Pleasant dreams."

Trista's dreams that night *were* pleasant. She dreamed of warm brown eyes laughing and a man's hand on her naked waist.

She dreamed of Roman.

No, she thought as she stretched the sleep from her when dawn broke. Aylesgarth. She must not think of him as a man, as Roman. She must regard him evermore as that which he had chosen to be. A title.

* * *

Lord Aylesgarth rapped upon the door to his sister's home. The head footman opened the door, and he brushed the man aside as he stepped inside.

"Tell my sister that I am here," Roman said tightly.

The servant was a stiff man who enjoyed his power very much. He also never broke formality. Roman disliked him, and he disliked Roman's casual dismissal of protocol.

"Very well, my lord. Come into the entryway while I see if she is at home."

"Of course she is at home, man, she never goes anywhere. She has a touch of our mother in her, enough to squirrel away when she should be out among live human beings. Good God, open those drapes, will you? It looks like a tomb in here."

The servant refused to give any reaction. "Very good, my lord."

Roman took himself in the direction of the parlor located down the hallway. Grace's voice called to him from behind. "If you are quite through bullying poor Foster, you may come to the library, Aylesgarth. I have decided, since you already know my habits too well, that I am at home today, though in no mood for your temper."

He turned to see his sister standing in the doorway to the front parlor. She was tall, like him, and thin like him as well. She had dark hair, shiny and straight. Right now it was pulled tight in a simple style. It wasn't the most flattering coif, but Grace was more practical than fussy in her approach to fashion. She had a straightforward prettiness that suited this. Although seven years his junior, she had a seriousness about her that made her seem older than her years.

"Then blasted don't provoke it," he griped, stalking back to the front of the house. She smiled, tolerant of his outburst, her dark eyes twinkling as he entered the room.

To his surprise, the footman had opened the curtains as instructed, lighting the dust floating in the air so that the parlor looked like a muted fairyland. Grace, dressed in dove gray that was fashionable enough to be not quite somber, but only just, moved gracefully to a chair.

It always surprised him how beautiful she'd grown. She'd been a gangly child, and disagreeable to boot, but time had made her tall and lithe, with an ethereal quality that could sometimes seem aloof, even snobbish to others. This was nothing close to the truth. Grace was timid, but she put on a brave front. She was his only kin, and though she looked nothing like him, for they favored opposite parents, he deeply felt the bonds of kinship.

"Don't you have servants to clean?" he groused, beating a cushion before lowering himself into a seat.

"I keep as few of them about as possible. People annoy me."

"I will have a cuppa, if you don't mind. You do have a cook, or do you turn the spit yourself in the late afternoons for your supper?"

She gave him a patient look and rang a small bell. "No need to be cruel, especially when I am always so welcoming. I even have shortbread, your favorite."

"You are too thin." He looked his sister over critically. "And you are pale from too much time indoors."

She was not disturbed by his complaint. "Pale complexions are the fashion."

"Pasty, you mean. I don't like it. I don't think the city suits you, Grace."

He could not help mentally comparing her fashionably wan appearance to the sparkling vibrancy of Trista. As soon as he registered the disloyal thought, he immediately cursed himself for it. That was cruel of him, but it did not make it any less true that Trista had always far outshone his reserved sister. As children, the two of them together had seemed like a diamond and a shadow.

Grace had been a lonely child, like him, but of a different constitution. It rode heavier on her, their sad home. It made his stomach twist with conscience to think of how many times he'd shouted at her to leave him alone. He'd craved solitude, escape, and being a boy, he was allowed the freedom to seek it.

Would it have cost him so much to take his little sister with him every so often?

It was unlike him to indulge in regrets, and he didn't frolic in memory. It proved too painful by half. But today he was in a pensive mood, and recollections long buried seemed to seep rapidly through his mind, taking him unawares and giving him the most extraordinary thoughts.

Had he seen Trista or had it been a figment of his imagination?

"And you are too grumpy by far," Grace said.

He grinned. "It is good to see you."

"But it isn't fondness that brings you, or else you'd come by more frequently."

"I visit," he said defensively, still feeling the sting of guilt.

"But you never stay long. Is it because I depress you? Ah, don't bother to respond. I can see that it does."

"Not you. This place. How can you live where *he* did? With *her*?"

She shrugged. "Because *he* was our father, and *she* was merely a mistress, the sort of woman most men keep. I daresay you've even kept a few yourself, haven't you? What should I care about what happened all those years ago, after all? They are both dead. And Mother, too."

"You huddle in the dark as she did."

"I like my solitude, yes. I prefer to read."

"Do you ever go out on visits?"

"I have few friends," she defended. "I daresay you would not approve. They are not the gay sort you favor."

He curled his lip. "Intellectual sticks." He leaned forward. "I cannot tell you how many times I am asked about you. I do not know why you shun society for these dullards."

"I find them interesting. Much more so than the vapid types so abundant in the beau monde these days, and everyone running to balls and musical evenings and the theater and such, all in a desperate attempt to attract a husband. And they are always judging everyone." Her face grew shadowed.

"There's a capital idea. A husband."

She looked horrified, and a spot of color flamed on her cheek. "To steal my freedoms and bore me to tears. No, thank you."

He shrugged. Why was he arguing with her? She lived a contented, if not exactly brilliantly happy, life.

She did what she always did when he made complaint of her, which was to turn her head just so and make her face blank, saying in a voice edged with warning, "You are growing tiresome. I fear I am destined to displease you."

He was instantly sorry. He had only said what he had because he worried about her.

She saved him from having to reply by changing the subject. "I've read in the rags you've been running with cousin Raymond."

"He's good enough companionship. Why do you not come out with us?"

"No," she answered quietly. "I know my ways annoy you. Leave me in peace and cease growling at me."

"I am not a dog, and I do not growl."

"You do. It is most unbecoming."

He gave her a long, meaningful look. "Perhaps I have something to growl about." He waited a heartbeat and followed this with, "I thought I spotted Trista Nash the other day."

"Trista? Here in London? But, I thought she was dead."

"You assumed she had died when I couldn't find her."

"But where did you see her?"

"At a milliner's shop. She was in the back room. She was . . . she had this hat on. With a bird perched upon it, and fruit. And flowers."

She looked at him in horror. "You were drinking."

"Not that day, but the night before."

"Good God, you've got the alcohol poisoning. Do you remember Mother? She used to see mad dogs when she came off the spirits."

"I do not have any such thing. I saw her. Or at least someone I thought was her. They said she didn't work there, and another woman who looked slightly like Trista came out with the atrocious hat upon her head, and I thought I might have been mistaken. But it doesn't . . ." He trailed off, making an ineffectual gesture with his hand. She remained silent, and he finally finished, "It *felt* like her."

Grace's face set in stubborn lines. "She haunts you, doesn't she? I don't know why you just don't forget her."

He reclined, crossing his legs so that his left ankle was resting on his right knee. "Neither do I. It would be the logical thing to do."

"You are nearly thirty, Aylesgarth. Not young any longer."

"Positively ancient," he muttered miserably.

"What I meant was, you should be more in command of your emotions."

His response was a dark, slightly threatening look of which she took no mind.

The maid wheeled in the tea cart and Roman and Grace addressed themselves to it. "Excellent shortbread," he commended, taking a second.

Grace smiled. "You always made a pig of yourself at the sweets. How is it you are not as plump as a partridge?"

"Because I go out among the other inhabitants of our city. I walk, I stroll, I ride, I dance. These things you should try, Grace."

She gave a snort, the kind ladies saved for exasperating brothers.

He shrugged. "I was thinking about the house, about those days. I wanted to know"—he paused here, on uncertain ground—"if you ever thought about them."

"They were unhappy days. I try not to, but, yes, I think of them."

"Do you remember Miss Nash?"

Grace lowered her lashes. "Yes. I remember her."

"She was a great lady." He said this quietly, with emphasis.

"She was kind, yes. To us, she seemed very gracious. Now, if you are going to ask me if I think of her daughter, the answer is a resounding no. She was a conceited child who had the audacity to think herself better than us. Imagine, brother, she pitied us, always looking at us as if she were the young miss of the house and we were her servants. I know it pained you not to be allowed to marry her, but I swear, it would have been a disaster if she'd succeeded in doing so. It was always what she wanted, you know. You felt so bad after it all, but you did nothing wrong."

He was silent, his teacup half raised to his lips, staring off.

Grace said, "I can't believe seeing her—or thinking you did—would overset you this way."

He put the cup on the saucer with a clash. "It hasn't overset me." He rolled the tension from his shoulders. "It just has me thinking."

"About Whitethorn. It is just a house, Aylesgarth. It isn't haunted or anything."

He pursed his mouth. Then why had he been visited by ghosts? Many ghosts, which were all the same woman, but of different ages.

They were so vivid in his mind. Trista impossibly young, her hair loose and long, the fair ringlets making her look like a tiny nymph. She'd caught him blubbering once, he'd forgotten why. He only remembered her hiding, watching him, and as embarrassed as he had been to be caught in a weak moment, it had made him feel some succor to have her close by.

And younger, staring at him fiercely when he'd taunted her, souring his fun with those silent, wounded looks.

But most of all, he remembered Trista as a woman, smiling with the sun spilling on her hair, lighting it into golden flame as it had been when they went to the abbey, where the half-fallen walls provided shelter, privacy. There he'd kissed her for the first time. She'd trembled in his arms like a rabbit. He'd been a man, an experienced man, and yet he'd shaken like a smooth-faced boy to have such a privilege, and had felt that kiss to the very core of him.

Other ghosts crowded his mind, as well. Trista with her

large gray eyes wild and accusing, weeping, shouting. Trista leaving him.

And him standing there like a dolt, watching her go, refusing to believe she really meant it. His pride swelled and engulfed him, and he'd told himself he hated her. She'd betrayed him, playing games to get him to do as she would and forsake his duty.

But it was no game. Would he have done anything differently had he known she was not bluffing? Would he have gone after her, given in?

He didn't think so. Not then.

He realized Grace was speaking. "Pardon?"

"I said, we were certainly not the only unhappy children in England. We weren't beaten or brutalized. I knew a girl at school who had terrible nightmares, poor chit, because her father regularly took a strap to her. We were lucky."

"You are right, of course." He looked broodily about him. He did hate this house. He had never been able to be completely comfortable within its walls. That is why he had given it to Grace and taken another house for himself.

"Well, I cannot be glad for this pensive mood, and most especially if it was brought on by that . . . by Trista Nash," she said. Sighing, she added, "However, if it brought you to my doorstep, then perhaps we can turn it around to a more pleasant end. Would you stay to dinner?"

He said he would and suggested they play cards. They did. He did something that night that he had never done before. He let her win.

Chapter 3

Andrew was the picture of his father, the same lazy wave to his hair, the same hint of a downward slant to his eyes that made the elder appear appealingly in need of consolation. There was the strong chin, too, which they had in common, and the soft upward curl in the corners of their mouths.

All of these Trista inventoried as she sat with her son. She'd been doing that now for four days, not able to stop herself from thinking about Aylesgarth, from fretting over the small face, which, as she'd been recently reminded, was astonishingly reminiscent of the harder, older version she had looked into for the first time in nearly six years.

"I want a ship for my birthday, like Ulysses's. I want one exactly like it. Can I sail it on the lake in the park, Mama?"

"You have not asked properly." She ruffled his hair. It was soft, thick for a little boy. She loved him so much, it sometimes hurt to look at him.

"Please, can I have a ship for my birthday?"

"Please *may* I?" she corrected. He rolled his eyes and mimicked, "Please *may* I?"

"Dearest Mother," she went on.

He smiled. "Dearest Mother."

It was an old game, each phrase getting more and more ridiculous. She took her turn. "Most glorious and spectacular person in this entire world with whom I am so happy to be her son."

He giggled. "Most . . . goriest and tackspackular person in the entire world and I am happy to be my son."

"And who I will always love and worship beyond any other and wish I could kiss all day long."

"Oh, no, I am *not* saying that!"

He fell on her, dissolving into laughter and she crowed. "Then I win!"

"That isn't fair, you said 'kiss' and you promised you never would."

"Well, it always works to make you get all giggly, and then I win." She prodded his ribs with a few tickles, renewing his laughter. It was a pure expression of the complete, uncomplicated joy of childhood, bubbling up from his toes. It always made her happy to hear it.

"Can I go out to the garden?" His eyes sprung open. "Oh! Oh! Can I put a pool in the garden when I get my ship? Then I can play with it there. Oh, please, Mama. Please. I'll even kiss you."

"Such sacrifice. We shall see. I can hardly imagine what we would do about all of the mud you'd be in, but I'll speak to Aunt Luci and Uncle David."

"Oh, thank you! I know they'll say yes."

He was probably correct, Trista thought as she watched him race out. She was still smiling rather stupidly—a permanent fixture to her face in the presence of her son—when she realized she should get dressed into her working clothes. Today was Tuesday and she did not usually go in to the shop on Tuesdays, but she had agreed to come in this afternoon so that Mrs. Hines could take care of some errands.

It was late, however. She hated to ruin her dress, one of the few she had splurged on since she had started saving for the milliner's shop, but there simply wasn't time to change. Calling upstairs to David, she told him she was leaving. She checked in the kitchen with Emily. "Andrew is in the garden, did you see him?"

"I saw him," Emily said, not stopping her peeling of a small pile of potatoes. "He passed through here not a minute ago, and take a look."

Trista peeked at her son, who was busy lining up soldiers in the dirt, and sighed. "Why is it boys are forever getting so dirty?"

"It's what boys do," Emily replied with a shrug. "It's a good thing he likes his bath."

"What do you think of a pond in the yard? He wants one in which to sail the ship he's requested for his birthday."

"Goodness, what will that child dream of next? He does have an imagination."

"He does, but it seems to be exclusively naval."

"Well, that comes from his papa, Captain Fairhaven, I'm sure," Emily said, nodding her head as she rinsed the potatoes in a bowl of water.

Trista's bright smile wilted. "Yes. Good-bye, Emily. I'll be home for supper."

"Good day, Mrs. Fairhaven. Will you be taking the cart?"

"It's a fair day. I'll walk."

"Should I call Young Stuart to take you?" This was her son, a man in his second decade and engaged to be married, who suffered being called Young Stuart to distinguish him from his father, who was known at only two score years of age, as "Old Stuart."

"He was sweeping the front stoop. I'll fetch him on my way out."

The company of Young Stuart passed a pleasant stroll along the London streets. He conversed amiably, mostly about himself, as they negotiated the glut of traffic and lorrie wagons teeming in the streets. She smiled and nodded, making appropriate noises of interest as he told her of his plans with the fine Betsy Church, his intended. As no response was required of her, it was easy to drift off, thinking of Aylesgarth.

She had been so shocked to see him the other day, she

hadn't thought to look at the woman he was with. Was it his wife? She'd never met her, so she wouldn't recognize her even if she had taken note. Whomever it was, he was probably devoted to her. He'd have to be to go to so much trouble to replace a crushed hat. Had marriage tamed the wild boy? Had this heiress he'd married done with her money what Trista couldn't with her whole heart?

Perhaps, he loved her.

Upon arriving at the shop, Young Stuart tipped his hat and said he'd be back at six o'clock for her.

She entered the shop, calling out a cheerful greeting. Strange. It was so quiet.

"Hello?" she said, taking out her hat pin and laying it, the hat, and her shawl in the corner. She smoothed her skirts, looking about. Where was everyone?

"Mrs. Hines?" she called, heading toward the curtain. As she reached it, it was abruptly snatched back, and a wide-eyed Dina stood in her path.

"Trista. I'm sorry."

"Sorry? What is it? What has happened?"

"He wouldn't leave. Mama made a slip, and he's been sitting there all day."

"What do you mean? Your mother fell? Is she all right?"

"She is talking about me, Trista," a male voice said.

Dina squeaked and jumped as a masculine hand appeared on the edge of the curtain. Trista stared at the signet ring, a family crest that was very familiar to her. She'd seen that hand with the ring too many times, dreamed of it, remembered the feel of it on her skin as vividly as if she'd just been touched.

The curtain drew back, and Aylesgarth stood before her.

"And the slip was of the tongue. She told me the truth about you."

Trista gasped. She stared, speechless, breathless, into the steady dark eyes that pinned her as effectively as a butterfly trapped in a glass display.

"You must forgive her. She did not realize you didn't wish to be identified. So, when I returned and asked after you, this young lady tried again to deny it, but her mother, not knowing the ruse, gave up the game."

"He's been sitting in the gentleman's chair all afternoon, just waiting."

Mrs. Hines rushed toward them, her skirts crackling. "I don't want any trouble, young lord, or I'll call the constable." She waved her chubby hands imperiously. "I don't care who you are."

His look was gentle amusement. But he gave her a slight bow. "I am the Lord Aylesgarth, madam, as I stated when I came in. I simply wish to speak to Miss Nash."

"I told you, this isn't 'Miss Nash.' She's Mrs. Fairhaven to you."

His eyes shot to her, flickered a moment. "Mrs.?"

She still couldn't speak. So she nodded, a shaky, half-formed incline of her head.

"Trista, is it all right?" Mrs. Hines's plaintive face bore her concern. "I *will* call the constable, you know, if you wish."

"No. It's quite all right. Lord Aylesgarth is an old friend." The words creaked out of her, but they gained strength. She even managed a smile.

"Then will it be inconvenient if I go on with my errands?"

"Please do, Mrs. Hines. There is nothing to be alarmed about. Go ahead, Dina. You may go to the showroom as well. I'm certain Lord Aylesgarth will be . . ."

Leaving soon, she had meant to say, but she made the mistake of glancing at him, and the words died in her throat. Just this morning, scarcely an hour ago, she had looked into a miniature of that face.

"Hello, Miss Nash," he had said on that sunny afternoon when he'd burst into his mother's boudoir where Trista sat reading from a book of essays, Lady Aylesgarth listening with her rheumy eyes staring into space.

He'd ridden all the way from the far village across the fell, where the stagecoach had left him off. He was wind-blown, his hair wild, and his face stung red-brown. His eyes sparkled, loving the surprise he was giving them. It had been years since he'd been home last, and they'd had no word to expect him. Nevertheless, here he was, materialized like an imp set on bedevilment and too pleased with himself by half for the shock on their faces.

He had tossed the greeting to her casually, his gaze lively and quick as he took in the place, but as he strode into the room he did a classic double take, his eyes narrowing in that way he had when he was intent, and he turned to give Trista his attention.

Again, this time his voice deeper with a sultry sort of pleasure, he said, "Why, hello, Miss Nash."

He had changed from that day when she had first seen him as a grown man. His forehead was now slightly lined, and creases bracketed his mouth, grooved as if cares had worn them there. His eyes had fine lines fanning out from the corners, and his hair, though still unruly, was darker. He used to roam out of doors, of course. London had no doubt tamed him. He probably spent more time roaming in bedrooms these days.

"You are married?" he said, advancing into the workroom. He stood in the middle, shrinking the place with his broad shoulders and long, lean man's body.

"Widowed," she said, giving him her shoulder as she searched for some silk to begin her work.

"When did you come to London?"

She felt a sharp pain in her throat, as if the lies were going to hurt to speak them. "After my husband's death, I came here. My cousin had a position here and thought she could get me one. As you see, it worked out nicely." She couldn't help but add with pride, "We are saving to purchase it. Probably, if all goes well, I will be part owner in two or three years."

He moved to stand at the other side of the table, his eyes holding her in the most uncomfortable manner. She had forgotten how he could look at a person like this, leaving one feeling stripped, laid bare for his perusal and evaluation.

"Why did you run from me the other day?" he asked.

"I didn't run from you," she snapped. The flush of embarrassment, of reaction, of fear was making her intolerably hot. "I . . ."

"You saw me and you ran. When I came to look for you, someone else was there. She told me you didn't work here, and I doubt she would deny it unless directed to do so by you."

"Actually, I didn't direct her," she said, feeling childish and defensive and angry that he could do this to her. "I suppose she saw I didn't wish to speak with you and made her own choice. Besides, she knows me as Trista Fairhaven. My . . . my married name."

"If your name was Mary or something else of the common sort, I might believe a misunderstanding took place, but women named Trista aren't so common." He took a step forward, and she took one back. "I've only known one."

"Perhaps she thought you said Patricia. I've had that mistake made."

"Perhaps. You still haven't said why you ran."

He wasn't going to give any quarter on that, so she shrugged. "I didn't wish to speak to you, obviously. What would be the point, really? It has been a long time since we knew each other, and I thought it would be awkward."

"I see." His eyes flickered over her, taking her in from head to toe. She was suddenly conscious of her hair, which she'd taken no more care with today than any other day when she planned to be in the workroom, but she sent a silent prayer of thanks heavenward that her dress was one of her favorites.

"There's a coffeehouse just down the street. Come with me. I want to talk to you."

A flush of pleasure rippled through her, even though she shook her head. "I cannot. I only just arrived, and I have to get my work done."

"It's all right," Dina chirped.

Trista was horrified to find her and her little sister gaping from the doorway. "I'm sure I can handle things," Dina said with a conspiratorial look at Aylesgarth. "You two knew each other before, I had no idea. But this is wonderful. I thought there was some trouble, the way you reacted before, Trista, but I don't see why you should not spend the afternoon catching up. If it is work that keeps you, don't even think of it. I can see to things here. You are not to worry."

Roman's look was sly. He relished this intrusion, giving her a look of triumph. "I think Miss Hines has switched sides."

"Well, I was under the wrong impression before," Dina explained, flustered as she spoke directly to him. He did that to women, got them stammering and batting their eyes to disconcert them and have his way. "It is her day off, and having an important visitor from her childhood should account for something."

He turned to Trista, his eyebrows hiked high. "Coming in on your day off. How industrious. I can see why you inspire such loyalty from your employer."

Trista ignored him, turning to Dina with a tight expression she prayed the woman would have sense enough to read. "I promised your mother I would come in today so that she could see to her errands."

"But it is a slow business day. I can take care of things, and we don't have any pressing orders. I insist. I promise I will tell Mama it was my idea."

"There," Aylesgarth beamed, "it is all settled. Thank you, Dina."

"But—"

"It is only coffee," he said.

Seeing herself neatly pinned by the opposition, she excused herself, rushing into the water closet in the rear to make a hasty adjustment to her hair. God, it was hopeless, but she managed to pull it a bit tighter, and the aid of a comb and bit of water smoothed the few tendrils that refused to be caged in pins. She had no need to bite her lips or pinch her cheeks, for her color was already high. Checking her dress, she caught herself and dropped her hands.

What did it matter if her appearance was completely

dreadful? She was acting as much of a ninny as Dina had. She wasn't trying to attract the man, for goodness sake.

But a woman's vanity didn't follow along the lines of logic. She gave her hair one last quick pat, fixed her hat to her head and jerked it down to a rather jauntier angle than she usually sported, and slipped in the pin to secure it. Then she squared her shoulders, breathed in a deep, cleansing breath, and let it out again before stepping out and bestowing upon him her most aloof, unconcerned look as she gathered her shawl and announced she was ready.

Coffee, she told herself. It was just a coffee.

*"Tell me about yourself," Roman said, leaning on his el*bows.

She lowered her eyes, avoiding him, frustrating him.

This was a new Trista, someone completely different. He'd known kind Trista, and passionate Trista, and scathing Trista, and laughing Trista. But demure, mysterious Trista was a novelty.

He could hardly expect her to be the same after all of this time. Life had a way of happening to a person, altering their brain, and their hearts. Nor could he expect her to welcome him. Their parting had not been a pleasant one.

But why was it she seemed . . . cold? Closed to him.

That he had not felt before.

"There isn't much to tell. I work in the hat shop. I plan to purchase it—"

"That much you've already said." He was anxious, impatient. He wanted to reach across the small table and take her hand in his. He wanted to demand to know if she'd thought of him in the intervening years, who this Fairhaven man was, if she loved him, if she mourned him, and if she did, did she grieve as much for a dead husband as she had for him . . .

And why had she left?

"Otherwise, I have a very boring life," she said.

"How long have you been a widow?"

Her eyelashes swept down. "A very long time."

He said nothing more. He found silences sometimes forced others to fill in the breach, offering more information than they cared to offer in order to avoid the awkward moment. He could be formidable at manipulation if he cared to be.

But Trista only sipped her coffee and, after a moment, raised her eyes to his. They were the most extraordinary gray, light and misty most times, such as now, but when her emotional state was roused, her pupils expanded, turning the gentle orbs to steel. He remembered suddenly how they'd bore into him when they made love, transfixing him so that he couldn't look away. He jerked, physically affected by the jolt of rippling pleasure that went through him.

He was the one who looked away. "I am sorry to hear of it."

God, what a liar he was. He didn't even know the man and he could dance for joy at the fact of his death. There was no possibility for him with Trista—she could barely look at him. They'd settled the matter between them long ago. And yet he was jealous.

"Lady Aylesgarth is dead," he said suddenly.

"I knew," she said. "I got word after I left from a few friends in the borough."

"Not my mother. I meant my wife."

"Oh." She was disconcerted. "I am sorry."

"Yes. It turned out that with her death, I was disinherited from her father. She grew to dislike me and turned him against me. He blamed me for her unhappiness, and I was left without a farthing, apart from the dowry settlement upon occasion of the marriage. Isn't that funny?"

"Funny?"

"Ironic, then. Or perhaps tragic justice."

"It seems tragic to me in the fact that the woman died," she said, her nostrils curling the way they did just before the storm clouds gathered in her eyes. "I can see you mourn her deeply."

"I regret her passing, but I cannot say it devastated me to lose her. We were not close."

"Were . . . did she . . . are there any children?"

He watched her for a moment. "No. It was a good part of why we were estranged. In her estimation, the lack of children was my fault. The problem, she was certain, was not with her. That would be a flaw and Therese was sublimely reassured that she had none. She was the high-strung sort, having been spoiled to unbelievable heights by her parents. Her death was attributed to my failure to give her a contented life."

"How did she die?"

"Influenza. She passed swiftly, within a week. There was no time to call her family. That was what was so hard for them, the suddenness and not being able to be there."

"But their reaction is most irrational if they think you were to blame," she said, and there it was, a glint of the old compassion. She used to look at him like that when he was a boy and she was only a winsome scrap of a girl. He should have dismissed her as unimportant, the daughter of a servant, and he had at first. But she had held her head high and looked at him with pity, and instead of despising her as he'd wanted to do, he'd been drawn to the tiny soul that could see good in him when not a single other person had.

Had he been hoping to see that look? Perhaps. Lord knew it wasn't his style to go about beating his breast and plying his troubles like wares.

"They needed someone to hate. They are that sort, and I suppose one can let it go considering they lost a daughter. I might not have found Therese pleasant companionship, but they loved her to distraction. It was dreadful for them to lose her."

She nodded politely. "So do you come to the city often?"

"I live here now. Grace has the house in Hanover Square. I bought another in St. Giles Crescent."

"How nice." She finished her coffee and began to gather her reticule. "This has been most pleasant. Thank you. I wish you the best of luck."

He came to his feet so quickly he knocked over the chair. "Allow me to see you home."

"Oh, I couldn't."

"You can't walk the streets alone. I insist."

She gave him a scathing look. "I am not a pampered miss, my lord, nor am I a lady of your class. I am a widow and a working woman. I can wend my way home without harm to my reputation."

"But what of footpad and thieves," he said, following her as she walked briskly toward the door. "London is an unsafe place, ask anyone. Why, just yesterday I read in the papers of two women who were robbed right near Charing Cross, in broad daylight."

She said firmly, "I cannot tax your kindness any longer. I will see myself home."

"I am going to follow you, Trista." He grinned, seeing how irate she was.

"You never could stand being denied. You complain that your in-laws spoiled their daughter. Spoiled indeed—you were the one who was always having to get your own way."

She allowed him to open the door, and he thought, *Then why is it I got so little of what I wanted?*

He felt as if he had emerged from a cave, so bright was the sun as he fell into step beside her, taking the post nearest the street, as a gentleman does. She gave him a nervous glance and kept her stride.

"I cannot imagine what you might have wished to accomplish in us speaking," she said. "But if it was merely to refresh yourself of my status, then I hope our coffee together has supplied you with that information."

She was telling him that he should not, under any circumstances, entertain the thought of their resuming their relationship.

"Do you ever think about the old days, Trista?"

She stiffened immediately, her step quickening. "No. Never."

"Even sometimes? Oh, every so often. In the spring, perhaps."

They'd parted in the spring, and she flustered at this mention. It got her vinegar up. That at least had not changed. Her eyes clouded and the delicately curved nostrils flared spasmodically as she spoke.

"I do not dwell on memories of unpleasantness, something my mother taught me."

He'd forgotten how stirring the sight of her inflamed was. He could barely repress a smile, although he didn't take her temper lightly. "She was always a wise woman."

"Yes. And she told me looking backward can only lead to dissatisfactions for which only I will suffer, and I've suffered quite enough."

That melted his vigor. At last she was drawing her dagger and taking a jab at him. A well-placed and highly effective one. "And that is because of me?"

"Not only you," she said, her eyes darting nervously. He used to be able to read her like one does a printed manuscript, but no longer. "I lost my husband, which was a far greater loss."

That one went for the heart and found it. He jerked his head and laughed, as if it had not bothered him a whit, and feared he gave himself away. "Of course you mourn this Fairhaven fellow."

"He was a Captain, and a great man. I accept *all* my losses, and I accept that I am alone now. What I require from others is to not make my position untenable by creating any scenes at my place of employment and leaving me to live my life in peace, unmolested. I would imagine that would be a reasonable request, and not impossible to honor."

"You want me to leave you alone."

"I believe I have been trying to make that point since you came into my shop."

He strode in silence, mulling over his warring reaction. He couldn't blame her. It might gall him, but he had no hold over her. What could he say—no, I refuse to leave off because I feel like I've found something precious that has been mislaid for years. I want to shout, swing you up in my arms, celebrate? He certainly would say no such thing, and she would not welcome it if he did.

He might forever think of Trista as his. She belonged to

him from childhood, the ethereal angel who had quietly crept into his mundane life. With no fear, she'd slipped a delicate wedge into the cracks of his brash façade, and slowly opened him to life. To feeling.

But she wasn't his Trista. That was done, gone. Had he thought differently—considered that they really might have picked up where they'd left off? No. Hoped, perhaps, but that was a fool's game. Still, he was a fool enough to have wanted something of what he'd lost.

They turned off Marylebone toward Camdentown, and he frowned, wondering at her circumstances as they headed for that section of the city, which could at best be described as modest. However, before they'd gone too far up Albany, she turned off to a small square facing Regents Park. The row of houses were neat and well-kept.

She looked everywhere but at his face as she turned toward him. "I think we should say good-bye here. Thank you for walking me. It was pleasant to see you, but . . ."

"But don't get any wrong ideas."

"I think it best." She cast a nervous look up the street.

What was she so afraid of?

"I would feel better if I see you to the door," he said. He found himself perversely unable to let her go.

She was twitchy. Her arm shot up, pointing to the first house on the end. "It is only that one right there. I can surely manage that far without fear of being accosted."

Seeing she meant not to budge, he got his back up, almost savoring the challenge. He was a prideful fool, or so it had been said on more than one occasion, and no less so now with his heart hammering in his chest and his brain rattling inane things he wanted to say, such as, "When can I see you again?"

An alarming realization jarred him, and for a moment he was as breathless as if he'd been punched. She didn't seem to want to be seen with him. Was it because she was involved with another man and didn't want to have to explain him? Someone she hoped to marry who might not understand her strolling about London on the arm of a former lover?

It would explain her demeanor, her skittishness, vagueness, downright hostility. She was afraid, perhaps, that he would spoil something important to her.

The bitter thought brought his spine in line. He realized he'd been an absolute fool. He'd begged and scraped, taking her reluctance as residual resentment over the past that he might charm his way clear of if he applied himself to the job. He'd deluded himself because he simply couldn't think that . . .

"This was a mistake, I think," he said. He executed a bow. "I thank you for tolerating my folly. I am always rather stupid when I run into old friends. Sentimentality is a fault of mine. Good day to you, Mrs. Fairhaven. I hope you have a long and rewarding career as a milliner shop owner. I shall send all my custom your way."

Trista was baffled by his abrupt change in manner, but she knew she had moments in which to make her escape and she should do so without delay. She turned on her heel and marched into the square.

Trepidation grew with each step. Would he come after her, would he watch her? She headed for the house on the end, the one she had indicated. Thinking she should be fetching her key, she pulled her reticule open and as she searched among the handkerchief, the purse with a small amount of change, and the tiny scent pot she kept inside, she hazarded a glance back to the corner.

He was gone.

She stopped in her tracks, her head falling back as she breathed an enormous sigh of relief. Dashing behind a tree, she waited, just to make certain he would not appear again. When a few minutes had passed, she slipped out and hurried down the driveway, back to the mews that butted up against the rear gardens of another, far less expensive row of homes.

When she entered her house through the kitchen door, Emily looked up, startled.

"Lord, Mrs. Fairhaven, what are you doing coming in the

back door like a scullery maid? I thought you were set to work this afternoon. Is it the fever? Your color is high."

"No. I decided to come home. Where is Andrew?"

"Having his lesson with Mister David. But, madam, how did you know to come home?"

"Why? Is something wrong?"

She had already taken three steps toward the stairs when Emily stopped her. "No. The little master is fine. It is the lady who is here for you. I told her you would be out until supper, but she said she's been searching for you for so long, she was most anxious to see you and she would just as well sit in the parlor if I didn't mind and wait for you to return. She's there now."

"A lady? Who? Searching for me?" On the heels of Roman's predatory pursuit of her this afternoon, this raised a mild prickling of gooseflesh.

Emily showed her the card. It was inscribed with the name Lady May Hayworth. Scrawled in a flourishing hand was the personal message, *I would be most grateful if you would see me at once.*

The name didn't jog any recollection. Who was this woman, and why was she so desperate to speak with her?

Intrigued, Trista headed for the back staircase, calling over her shoulder, "I'll sneak upstairs and freshen up. Please go tell her I have returned and will be with her shortly."

Lady May was not a snob, not strictly speaking, but she did have her standards, and this house was definitely below them. It was clean enough, but the shabby furniture and faded draperies were really atrocious. The architecture was so plain—not a neoclassical touch in sight. It existed as a Spartan example of puritanical taste, which to her mind meant no taste whatsoever. She supposed that was the point. The roundheads—thank God they had been overthrown—had nearly destroyed the glory of England with their ridiculous pretensions of holiness.

What of cathedrals and soaring columns holding lofty galleries that brought to mind heaven? What of cupolas and domes, such as the ones housing breathtaking art in the Vatican and Florence, Paris, and Venice? Surely the best of what man could do was a true tribute to God.

She had gotten herself so worked up—but it was always that way when she was put to mind of Cromwellian policies—that she was startled when the woman entered.

"Goodness," she said, placing a hand on her breast. It fell upon a soft array of pink feathers. She was fond of both the color and the frothy adornment, separately and in splendid combinations, and often wore fashions sporting these trademarks. "You gave me a start."

"My lady," the woman said, sinking into a deep curtsy.

May felt she might weep. It had been like this when she'd found Michaela Standish, but then Michaela was the spitting image of Wooly, and it had been like looking into the past and seeing him again.

Ah, but never mind. Here was another of her dearest brother's lost children, and another beauty.

"Are you Trista Nash?"

She had the loveliest eyes. Not Wooly's, not even in their shape. But her blond hair, all those curls, why she could be her very own daughter.

"Yes." She held up the card May had given the maid. "Do I know you?"

"No, my dear, but it is my deepest wish that we will become friends. You see, I am your aunt. I am sister to the Earl of Woolrich, your father."

She went ghostly pale. May rushed to her. "Perhaps you should sit down. I know it must be a shock."

Under her guidance, Trista sat. May patted her shoulder. "Did your mother tell you about us, Wooly and I?"

"Yes, but I . . . I didn't expect to find you, indeed to ever meet you. I assumed that the family wished nothing to do with Mama, or me."

"Oh, poor dear. You must forgive your papa. He was not good about responsibility. He was not a bad man, however, just a rather frivolous one."

The way her head came up sharply to catch May's eye

gave her pause. "Your father was a lover of women, a lover of fun," May explained. "He never had bad intentions, and this you must understand. He never told me about your existence. It was not out of malice. It was simply something he considered what occurred between himself and his . . . well, your mother, to be private."

"You never knew? But then . . ."

"How did I know to look for you? That part was simple. You see, my dearest brother passed on just over a year ago and his journals came into my possession. Perhaps it was wrong of me to read them, but I missed him so. I took a peek and found them to be detailed accounts of his adventures, and their result."

She smiled tremulously. "I am one of the results, I assume?"

"You are. Now the difficulty came in finding you. I have spent a good deal of time in pursuit of a Trista Nash, not knowing that you had married and were under your husband's name. All accounts of your whereabouts cease several years ago. My solicitors didn't know of your marriage. I shall have to speak to them to sharpen their detecting skills, as there remains much more work to be done after you."

"You mean, there are other . . . results?"

"Of course. I have already found one of your sisters. I cannot wait for you to meet her. But tell me, did your mother prepare you for this in any way, did she speak of your father to you?"

"I knew his name, knew they had been in love."

She seemed at a loss. May laughed softly to ease her discomfort. "Oh, he did love her. He adored her, according to his diaries. It was not a mere dalliance. He wanted to set her up in her own house, become her protector."

"But she refused to be a kept woman," Trista said. "She took me and went into service as a governess. She met him in the park, you know, and because he was behaving so badly, she marched up to him and scolded him terribly. He told her she was the only woman to chastise him."

May laughed, delighted. "I am certain Wooly was in love on the spot."

"I suppose he was, because he pursued my mother vigorously after that, hounding her until she agreed to see him. Eventually, his boldness, the daring of him, and the excitement of having a nobleman's attentions won her over. She thought she might be in love for a time, and it was serious. But she grew disillusioned."

"Ah." May nodded. "It was just a passing infatuation for her, then."

"I do not mean to insult you, but Mama told me he showed no ambition nor caring about anything beyond his amusement. He refused to be serious, and she had a serious side that, in time, yearned for discussions and exchanges of ideas. It wasn't that he was empty-headed, it was simply that he didn't have the vaguest notion why he should bother to think. He had too much fun misusing his time and resources, and she grew contemptuous of him until they finally parted."

"How sad for dear Wooly. He was what he was. And after all, it is no different than most of his class. It is simply what gentlemen do."

"Yes, that was what Mama said." She didn't add that her mother had tacked on one extra word as that which gentlemen did. Nothing.

"It broke Wooly's heart. You see, he was quite taken with the idea of making their relationship permanent. But your mother did not wish that life. More's the pity."

"Why do you say so?" Trista asked sharply. "She did not wish to settle for a life of a mistress. And she did not love him anymore."

May was taken aback. "Why, simply because we might have known each other, then. I would have at least been aware of who you were, and we wouldn't have missed all of this time together. But I mean to make that up to you. You must call me Aunt May as Micheala does. She is your half-sister, the first of Woolrich's children whom I found just last year. She is wonderful, and you are going to love her. Oh, look at you. You are in shock. This is all too much, isn't it?"

"I've never known anyone from my father's side of the family, never thought to meet them. I think Mama and Lord Woolrich thought it best to make a clean break of it when they parted."

"I know it was unjust to you to cheat you of your family. But I would very much like to make it up to you now."

"Indeed, your efforts are most welcomed. I am glad to know you. It is dear to me to know my father's relatives."

"Oh, thank you, dear. I quite agree with the importance of family and all of that, but actually I was referring to another very large and very tangible difference. Your inheritance."

Bless her, the lovely young thing was speechless, nearly uncomprehending. May laughed in delight. "Why, didn't you guess? You are the daughter of a very wealthy earl who had no legal heir. The entailments passed to a cousin, a dreadful man, let us not talk of him, but dear . . . his fortune . . . Do you understand what I am saying? You are an heiress."

Chapter 4

Roman did not keep his promise. He went back to the shop. It took a week and three days until he couldn't stand it any longer. It rained that day, and he stood across the street, where he had positioned himself under a sputtering lamppost. While he was getting pelted by the downpour in the dark, a boy came along with his bell atop a long pole and snuffed out the flame.

He gave Roman a bold look, as if wondering if he was up to no good. Roman dug in his pocket for a few shillings and tossed them to him. The lad grinned, touching his forelock. "G'day, gov'na," he said, grinning to show off two missing teeth.

An hour later, Mrs. Hines arrived, followed by her daughters. The woman he'd seen that day who'd worn the hat rushed right by him, ducking under the canopy outside the shop and brushing the wetness from her before dashing around the back to the workroom entrance.

The lights were lit, the front door unlocked, and the shop was opened for business. He watched, waiting until lunch. Afraid to leave his post for fear of missing her, he suffered his growling stomach and the steady drip of cold rain off the brim of his hat and down the back of his collar.

"Don't you have enough sense to come out of the rain, boy?"

This was spoken by an extraordinary miniature creature perched on the back stairs, the ones he was in the middle of climbing at two in the morning after having snuck out to smoke a stolen cigar with Jason. They'd gotten caught in a downpour and he was squishing as quietly as he could up to his room to find warmth, dryness, and the comfort of his bed to ease his roiling stomach and aching head. He was feeling hellish, already vomiting twice from the cigar. How did men smoke those things?

He eyed this intruder crossly. "I am a lord, or I will be, you know," he'd told her in a voice as frigid as his nose, "and you will not call me boy. I am not a boy, anyway. I am a man."

"You aren't. And I know who you are. You are the young master of this house."

"And you are the new governess's child. What are you doing running about in your nightdress at this hour? Look at you. You've a hole in the skirt, for goodness sake. Are you a beggar?"

Huge gray eyes had shifted in color, matching the iron-hued clouds that had dogged the sky all day. "I will mend it in the morning. I don't have very nice clothes because we've had troubles. We aren't poor," she clarified, "but have just come out of a bad spell. Things will get better."

She recited this as dogma, as if it were oft repeated to explain their sorry circumstances. Her mother must have told her this.

"You are barefoot. Don't you even have slippers?"

"I often go like this. I like it. It feels good."

A surge of antagonism made him say, "You look like a witch. A young witch. You had better take care. They will burn you at the stake you know."

This would have reduced Grace to tears, and effectively won his objective, which was to get this annoyance out of his path. But this tiny chit simply blinked and said, "Why did you stay out in the rain? It is rather foolish. You will catch the ague."

"I often do. I like it. It feels good."

She'd given him a dry look, as if she thought him silly. Him! He'd teach her. A dollop of his best medicine for curing pests and she'd steer clear of him in short measure.

It had taken him longer than expected. Twelve years, to be exact, but he had finally managed to drive her away for good.

His feet were soaked. He stayed until six, when the shop closed, watching each woman filing out. No Trista. Perhaps, he thought as he went home, it was her day off.

He returned two days later, sending a boy in at midday to ask for Trista Fairhaven. He came back with the message that she no longer worked at the shop. When he looked up, he saw the woman who worked with Trista in the back room, the one who resembled her a bit, staring at him from the window.

A week later, he went to the house, the one on the end of the row where he had walked her. They didn't know a Trista Fairhaven. She certainly did not live there, he was informed stiffly by a doubtful butler who sniffed the air as if detecting a whiff of spirits to explain this aberrant caller who kept insisting he speak to someone who did not occupy this residence.

Dejected, he went to Grace's house, craving company, which was a change from the past.

Noticing immediately something was wrong, Grace asked, "What is it Aylesgarth, what has happened?"

"She's gone," he said, sitting heavily in a chair. A cloud of dust rose around him. "I've lost her. Again."

Grace gave him a level stare. "Brother mine, she was never yours to begin with. Forget her."

Trista's life was transformed. In one day, all of her worries, her anxieties about Andrew's future, her business prospects, the daily struggle to make something of herself so that she could hand that something to her son . . . vanished.

She was a wealthy woman. It took days, perhaps weeks, for this to fully settle in her brain. Every time she thought of it, she became giddy all over again. If Lady May weren't with her, prodding her and advising her, she might not have ever fully grasped the full impact of how her inheritance had made it possible for her to have a completely different life.

A new life, a better life for Andrew, and security and peace of mind for her.

She might have squirreled her fortune away, but Lady May would not hear of it. She pressed Trista to purchase a fashionable house near Hyde Park. Once Trista saw it, she could not resist.

It was a gorgeous four-story town house with a parlor in the front for formal company, a cozy den for family only, which sported a mullioned bay window and marble mantel with a huge pier glass hanging over it. There was a kitchen and a morning room, a dining room, servants' quarters, several bedrooms, most with their own water closet, a music room, a study, a small conservatory in the back of the house that led to a lavish walled garden complete with a domed folly that made the lushly landscaped retreat look as if Aphrodite might materialize any moment to frolic there.

"But I should go ahead with my plans to purchase the hat shop, and then think about investing in—"

May waved off her conservative logic. "You cannot be accepted in polite society if you are in trade. You must look beyond your hat shop now, darling. Your prospects are much broader. When you set up a household in Mayfair, you are making an investment in your future."

Her future was Andrew's future, and so Trista had acquiesced. She bought the house *and* the hat shop, but the latter was Luci's domain now. Mrs. Hines retired and Dina made a surprise move in offering to be Luci's new partner.

Without employment, Trista had to adjust to a new life. She was a woman of leisure, or at least she would be once the redecoration and refurbishing of the house was completed. It gave her great joy that Andrew loved his new house, the only drawback being a bit of distance from his beloved uncle David, but the couple visited often.

May was about constantly. The gracious lady had been delighted to learn she was a great aunt. She took to the boy immediately, and Andrew loved her back with a startling acceptance that stunned Trista. But then, it was impossible not to adore May. The woman was infectious with her enthusiasm and her boundless energy.

Very soon after the Hyde Park house was purchased, a minor chimney fire at Aunt May's Park Lane home caused damage to the first floor. May, reluctant to impose, was finally convinced to move in with Trista after her niece confessed that she could use the help in setting up the household—she had never run a house this large.

"But, my dear, of course. If you need me, I will most certainly help you," Aunt May had responded, and the rest, to Trista's mind, was a blur.

First, May insisted that the staffing be seen to. Trista had brought Emily and Old Stuart and Young Stuart with her. They were like family to the boy and she did not want him to lose them. A legion of other staff were hired, as well. May employed a head footman, two underfootmen to work alongside Young Stuart, a cook, and two maids. Emily was promoted to housekeeper and Old Stuart took to the stables, grateful to be away from the tumult in the house. There were some bumps along the way, but mostly they all transitioned well. Her quiet life was now a bustling one, filled with decisions and demands and countless tasks, all of which she enjoyed immensely.

As the materials for the house were ordered, wall hangings, window treatments, fixtures, and the like, she was also under strict orders to see to her wardrobe. Lady May's exclusive modiste, the brilliant Madam Bonvant, agreed to take her on and she was astonished at the results. She looked sleek, frail, and fashionable in the delicate muslins and rich silks draped so artfully on her slender frame.

How had this fairy-tale happened? she wondered at

times, when she would walk through this grand residence, which by some miracle belonged to her. Or perhaps when she chanced to catch herself in the mirror, beautifully coiffed and wearing a fine gown. Some nights, as she watched her son drift off to sleep and she felt her heart full of hope for his future, she wondered if it could all be true.

"You are my fairy godmother," she told May once as they pored over dress sketches.

May blushed furiously. "Really! You were doing just fine for yourself when I found you."

"Fine, yes, but nothing like this."

For the second time, her life had been completely and inexorably altered. She was now, through Aunt May's patronage, invited to all the season's major events. Not as a debutante, of course, as everyone considered her a widow. That and the fact of her somewhat advanced age saved her the pains of a proper Season, but she was not without admirers. Her dance card was quickly filled at balls, and she never lacked for a gentleman willing to fetch her punch or hold her plate while she selected refreshments from the buffet.

"Are you happy, Trista?" Aunt May asked her as they rocked sleepily during the carriage ride home after one evening spent dancing until dawn.

"Oh, Aunt May, I am most assuredly the luckiest woman in the world."

Her aunt beamed. "I cannot wait for you to meet your sister. When she arrives home from her wedding trip, I am going to get the two of you together immediately."

And she *was* happy. Happy and amazed, and so mindful of her good fortune. If she had moments of melancholy thinking of Roman Aylesgarth, she quickly dashed them aside. She refused to dwell on him. She'd conquered that part of her life many years ago. It had been difficult, nearly devastating, but she had gone on—at first with difficulty, yes, but now she had a new life, filled with promise that things would be easier for her. Roman was her past. Now she had a spectacular future.

She was very certain she finally had her life very nicely in hand. And then came the night of the Linhope Ball.

*"Have all of your dances been promised?" Lady May won*dered, adjusting a feathery ruff encircling her neck.

Trista consulted her card. "I refused Colonel Harmon and Lord Billingsly because I simply couldn't imagine dancing four dances in a row. But I have promised the former I would sit with him at supper and Lord Billingsly has vowed to call upon me this week and take me for a drive in his new landau."

"And?" Lady May said leadingly.

"They are all pleasant men, but there is no interest."

"Ah. Well, the Season is still young, and then there is the summer and all of those house parties to go to, not to mention the waters at Brighton or Tunbridge Wells. Plenty of opportunity for fun. Now, smile. You look ravishing. Lord, how your father would weep with pride. I see him in you, you know. But it must be your mother's eyes."

"Actually, my mother had blue eyes, but my aunt had gray eyes like mine."

"They are lovely. Your features are exquisite, and my maid has done your hair perfectly, although Madam Bonvant deserves the credit, for she gave precise instructions on what would go with that dress. She always knows. You look like a regal Diana. Enjoy being beautiful, Trista, enjoy being young. Enjoy being at a ball, among some of the most amusing—and wealthy—people in London."

Trista ran both hands down her skirts self-consciously. Tonight was one of the largest, most exclusive balls of the season so far, and she was right in the middle of it, with a full dance card, no less. This had to be an evening out of someone else's life—but then, she'd had that sensation quite often of late.

She felt quite beautiful in her dress, which was the latest style, the French Empire cut the Empress Josephine had made all the crack in Paris before the war. The high-cut waist was wound with ropes of faux pearls, the softly folding skirt left to billow down her long legs and float around her ankles. Her bodice was shockingly low. The color, mint green, did something to her peach-tinted skin. In this, Madam Bonvant was a genius. She knew which colors suited, and her eye for what style most become a particular figure was impeccable.

Madam had instructed her to have her hair dressed in a pile of curls, à la Grecque, as the ladies called it, and gave her another rope of pearls to be woven into it. Her borrowed jewelry, tiny pearl drops at her ears and a single-strand choker of pearls around her neck, were real, however. She kept touching them, nervous lest she lose them. They were warm against her cold fingers.

Lady May caught her nervousness and smiled. She was about to say something, no doubt to comfort and reassure her, but her attention was diverted by a man coming up just then.

He bowed low and May smiled at him. "Lord Charbonneau, how lovely to see you."

His eyes shone as he rose, and his smile was unmistakably sly. "I am the first to catch you tonight, I think. And just so, as I have been awaiting your arrival."

"May I present my niece," May said.

Lord Charbonneau was polite, but it was clear his utmost wish was to take Lady May to the parquet for her first dance. He made this request immediately after the introductions.

"Oh, I couldn't possibly, my lord. We've only just arrived, and my niece is new in the circle. I wouldn't dream of abandoning her."

"Don't trouble over me," Trista said, "I know a few people here, enough to mind myself for a spell. Besides, I was about to fetch a punch, which, judging from the line I see from here, should keep me well occupied. Go ahead, please."

May paused. "If you are sure."

Beside her, Lord Charbonneau, of a moderate height and pleasant face, waited a bit impatiently. He might look mild, but in this Trista sensed he was deceiving. He badly wished to dance with her aunt and would not be put off.

Trista laughed. "Go on. I shall be fine."

Lady May smiled, and as she turned to Lord Charbonneau, she paused, frowning at someone in the crowd. As her aunt was led away, Trista glanced at whom had caught Aunt May's attention.

She was surprised to see a very familiar face. And he was looking back at her.

The blood drained to her toes, leaving her cold and incapable of the slightest motion. The last thing she was prepared for tonight was to find herself staring at Lord Aylesgarth.

Into her mind flashed the insane thought to flee, to hide behind May's diminutive form if she could, to avoid this man at all costs. But her feet could not move.

His sardonic gaze as he approached was a mockery of the usual pleasantness one expected to see between old acquaintances. He reached her, and held out his hand.

Without thinking, she laid hers in it, moving like a mechanical toy wound by a key. He didn't take his eyes from her as he bowed over it most carefully, as if he, too, could not quite fathom what was happening.

He said, "Mrs. Fairhaven. You manage to turn up in the unlikeliest of places."

Her heart began to hammer, sending the blood to her head so swiftly that she was light-headed in an instant. She managed to say something, and dip her knee slightly.

Through his fine white glove, through hers, his touch burned. She could detect a faint hint of spice about him, a masculine scent as he drew her a step closer to better converse without being overheard.

"How ever does a hatmaker find herself on the guest list of one of Mayfair's most exclusive parties?"

"My aunt," she said. She tried to pull her fingers from his grasp, but he held her firm.

"Is this a masquerade? You are quite the Cinderella."

She yanked harder, and succeeded in freeing her hand.

"My aunt," she said, emboldened by indignation. "Lady May Hayworth. I am here with her."

He was still confused, frowning doubtfully at her.

"You knew my father was the Earl of Woolrich. Well, his sister has chosen to acknowledge me."

"I see. What a surprising development. One moment sweating in a London shop, the next dancing at the home of the Duke and Duchess of Linhope. You look very well. Indeed, wealth suits you, as does your good fortune."

The path of his eyes left her quaking, with what emotion she couldn't hazard a guess. This man seemed to bring them all to a fever pitch.

She opened her fan, fluttering the ivory fronds between them, more to create a barrier than any sort of cooling wind. "If you will excuse me, I have promised this dance."

She made it as far as a tiered fountain before he cleverly used the large obstruction to corner her. He did so smoothly by simply placing his large body in the path of where she intended to go.

"I won't excuse you. I am a tad put out with you, *Mrs. Fairhaven*."

She stopped, alert. Why did he say it like that? What did he know?

"I never cared for being duped. You should have remembered that. I went to the house you took me to when I escorted you home. They'd never heard of you, by either name."

Oh, that. She did not relax, however. "I just purchased a home," she said evasively. "It is near the park. Across from it. You can see the park from the front window, actually."

She was babbling. She shut her mouth with a snap of her jaw to stop herself from making more of a fool of herself.

"Did you? How very exciting. But it still doesn't explain why you directed me to the wrong house. And do not say I mistook you. You fidget when you fib. It gives you away hopelessly."

"Well, I suppose the obvious answer is that I didn't wish for you to know where I lived." She caught Aunt May's eye, who was straining around the broad shoulders of a man standing between them to keep an eye on her.

The sight of her gave Trista confidence, and she realized she wasn't helpless against a powerful peer of the realm any longer. Although she was not precisely his equal, she was not a servant in his mother's house, and she didn't have to entertain his rudeness.

She tossed back her head, and with her most scathing expression in place—enhanced recently from having observed her petite but very commanding aunt—said, "I do not require being excused, then, if you insist on being rude. Good evening, my lord."

She made to step past him, but his broad-shouldered form effectively cut her off from the rest of the room. Still, his stance was casual, not threatening even while he disallowed her retreat.

"You are giving me the cut?" he responded, his voice full of incredulity.

Oh, if she could simply leave him like that, gaping like a landed fish. But she couldn't get around him.

"Has no woman cut you before? You forget, my lord, that I have known you for twelve years, and exposure over a period of time can develop an immunity, which is exactly where I find myself. Immune to you."

"But you haven't exposed yourself to me in quite a while," he said drolly, and over her gasp, he added, "And for the record, I don't believe you are as immune as you wish you were."

"You were always insufferably stubborn. And had an unsupportably high opinion of yourself. I'd have thought you'd outgrown that. Why are you smirking like that?"

"I was just thinking."

"And what were you thinking?"

"That the lady doth protest too much."

She snapped her fan closed and lifted her chin. "You are a conceited man," she managed, mindful to keep her voice down. Over to her left, Aunt May was still watching without seeming too obvious.

Leaning forward, which was a mistake as it afforded her a dizzying noseful of a most stirring masculine scent—yes, now she remembered how wonderful he always smelled—she angled an arch look at him. "I learned a long time ago that your failings more than exceed your attractions. And while other women may grow faint at your impressive physique and dashing manner—which you trade on as easily as a cobra trades on its gaudy scales—I find it a sad replacement for the qualities that I have grown to value in men. Of which you have none."

He sighed. "I see I have not increased in your esteem through the years. Yes, yes, I see that the sight of me clearly leaves you quite cold. Except—look see! Your color is up, my dear. I recall vividly how you would flush in the throes of passion."

"Are you suggesting . . ." She couldn't say it. Her kid-covered hand groped for the edge of the fountain for support, her fingers dipping into the water. She snatched them out, unsettled.

"Oh, please, Mrs. Fairhaven, my meaning is not so base as you intimate. Just look at your indignant chin jutting out at me. No, I meant the passions of anger."

He didn't, and they both knew it. "I think you should take yourself off," she said haughtily. "You are annoying me mightily, and I would not like to cause an uncivilized scene."

"But I have come to beg a dance." He executed a flourishing bow, an exaggeration of that gesture of respect. Several people around them took note, giving them a long look, alert for any gossip. They were slow to turn back to their own business.

Through tight lips she said, "As it happens, my dances are all promised."

"I don't believe you. You are fidgeting again." He lifted an index finger and wagged it at her.

"Then you are calling me a liar. Very nice. That is twice you've insulted me tonight."

"I never said lie. Prevaricate, deflect, and avoid. And yes, you are not above an outright fib, as you've amply demonstrated. You have not promised all your dances; I would be willing to wager on it."

"I have," she said, taking the card dangling from its ribbon tied around her wrist and waving it at him with a grin full of triumph. "I have had more requests, in fact, which I have had to turn away."

What was she doing? He was provoking her as easily as he had when they were children. But he could prick her spleen like no one else she'd ever known and she couldn't help herself.

She might have been nine and he fourteen, back in the days when he could taunt her to tears.

"Really? Well, aren't you the splash. Let me see the card, then."

She withdrew it. "No. I need not prove anything to you."

He smiled knowingly. "I see. Very convenient, this."

"Really. Oh, here, take a quick perusal. I am not fibbing."

He took the card with a dubious look. Pursing his lips, he glanced at it for a long time. "I see I am incorrect. My apologies. You are quite the rage, it would seem. Congratulations."

Taking the card, he held it out over the water swirling at the base of the fountain and before she could think to do anything about what he clearly intended, he dropped it in.

She blinked, incredulous, shocked, and very angry. He simply looked at the card, the ink lifting, floating, smearing within a few seconds of being immersed. "Oh, dear," he said *sotto voce*.

She might have known. He'd been a wretched boy; he was now a wretched man with no less mischief and malice.

Lifting her gaze slowly, she said, "If you think this will win you a dance, then you have forgotten much about me."

"I have not underestimated your stubbornness. All I ask is that you be reasonable. We are at a ball, you find yourself suddenly and unexpectedly available for a dance, and so it would seem a practical solution for us to take the floor. Come. I do not bite. Or, as you may recall, only in private and you quite liked it."

"Do not talk of such things." She fumbled with her fan,

searching desperately to find a way past him without drawing attention.

He sighed. "You have known me for a long time, Trista. I would think you would be aware of how pointless it is to resist me. Oh, not my charms. I seem to be losing my touch in that department. But there still is my 'indomitable will,' as my poor tutor used to say. Come. What is one dance?"

"If I gave in to you, you would consider yourself the victor here."

"I ask for a dance, not for your flag. And I am practically begging you. In fact, I propose to go down on a knee in a moment if you do not relent, so assuage your pride with the sight of me panting like a puppy for the privilege of just one simple dance."

Seeing she was effectively cornered, she gave him a haughty nod, which pleased him immensely. Before any of her promised dances could be called in—Lord knew what Roman would do if confronted by one of the men whose names he had eradicated from her card—she went with him.

She would appease him and then make good a quick escape.

They took their positions for the quadrille. She cursed her luck. Why could it not have been a country dance, which involved the entire group? The quadrille broke the units of dance down to four, furnishing plenty of opportunity to talk.

And touch. She placed her hand over his and waited.

"How did your friend like her hat?" she asked in the awkward silence.

"She liked it very much. Mrs. Hines does excellent work, and Annabelle was taken with the artistry. Yours, I suppose."

"I don't know if it was mine or Luci's. We both do the design work. Or did. It's her shop, now."

"You say that as if you miss it, and here you are dancing in a mansion. You are a puzzlement, Mrs. Fairhaven."

The music began, and they turned to face each other. She sunk into a pretty curtsy, and he grinned at her while folding into an elegant bow.

She took his arm again for the promenade. "I do not mind hard work," she said.

"But you prefer being rich. And a woman of leisure?"

"In part. There are advantages, of course. So, is Annabelle a serious interest?"

He gave her an assessing look. The dance took them apart, and it was several moments before she was returned to his side.

"That was interesting," he said dryly. "My new partner apologized for her clumsiness, claiming her bunion was aching."

The comment was so unexpected, she burst out in a giggle.

His eyes went soft, and his smile followed suit. "What were we talking about . . . oh, Annabelle. I was escorting her for the afternoon, for the week, actually, while my cousin and his new wife, Annabelle's sister, were visiting. It was not a serious acquaintance. But it is good of you to be interested."

She swallowed her denial, knowing he would accuse her of "fibbing" again, which she would be. Yes, she was curious about him.

"I had heard tell of you from time to time over the years," she said in a studiously casual tone, hoping he wouldn't guess how she'd devoured tidbits that had come her way. "You have been enjoying London, but are not well-known for . . ."

The ladies gathered in a circle with their partners outside the ring. Then it was to the left, face partner, then to the right.

When they went back to their foursomes, she finished. "Your love of society."

"I am not antisocial," he stated calmly, "although it is true that I've dedicated myself to other amusements. I find them so much more soothing."

Like gambling at Whites, she had heard. He was known for his uncanny luck. And women. Mostly women.

"So, what are you doing at a ball?"

"Why I heard tell of a Mrs. Trista Fairhaven having hit

the scene, and I simply had to find out if it was possibly true."

"You came because of me." She clearly communicated that she did not believe him.

"Do you doubt it? See. I do not fidget when I say it. Therefore, I am telling the truth."

"But you always lied well, Roman," she said.

She'd called him Roman. She'd promised herself she wouldn't do that, wouldn't even think of him as Roman.

To cover, she said quickly, "So you heard I had come into money. As I recall, your first heiress did not prove as profitable as you had hoped—"

His brows forked into a tight vee as he interjected, "As my father had hoped."

She ignored him. "Are you seeking another heiress?"

"Do you think you are the only woman in the room with money?" he countered with a scoffing chuckle. "Or even the only woman with money with whom I've had a past 'friendship,' my dear?"

"Ah, so you admit it, then. You have taken a string of lovers since we parted."

"No, of course not," he replied, his voice low so as not to be heard by those close, but dripping with enough sarcasm to set her teeth on edge. "I joined a monastery and have observed the chastity of a monk." His look hardened as they circled each other, hands joined. "And what of you?"

"I entertained a brief career as a Cyprian. My lovers are legion."

They paused, sizing each other up, so intent that they missed the next step.

Trista hurried to take her place, scolding herself for allowing him to goad her so well. She burned to vent the emotion clogged in her throat.

But there was a crowd about her, close enough to notice something amiss, and she didn't want to draw attention. It would do her ambition for her son no good if she showed herself poorly to the polite world.

"This is not the place," she said, determined to terminate

this disastrous conversation. Even better, this stupid dance. "I've forgotten the rest of the steps. Excuse me."

"Then I will call on you."

"Do not dare," she warned. "I will not be home whenever you call."

He followed, his voice low and rough in her ear. "If you force me to extreme measures, I cannot answer for any damage to your reputation. It isn't my intention to humiliate you, but I will not be stayed." His lips curled, setting in a determined line. "I will see you in due time. Perhaps I will give you an opportunity to miss me first. Until then, have a pleasant evening, Trista, and don't think to hide. I've found you twice. I'm beginning to gain confidence that the fates are on my side."

"Go to the devil," she said sweetly, and brushed past him to join her aunt.

May was thoughtful, watchful. "Who was that?" she whispered. "I do not believe I know him, but his face is so *familiar*. I cannot place it."

"Do not worry. He is merely some no-account wastrel. I am sorry I allowed him to coax me into wasting my time. Now if you will excuse me. I need that punch more than ever."

May said, her keen gaze sweeping assessingly over Trista, "You had better make it champagne. It will settle your nerves."

Chapter 5

It was a damp day in April, a trifle overcast but there was a promising light under the clouds where the wind was blowing in clear skies after several days of rain, and Trista took the opportunity to take her son to the park. Luci had arrived this morning bearing good news about David. She came along to give Trista the details.

"Lady May's recommendation made all the difference. Lord Peterson was very impressed at David bearing the kind regard of such an influential lady. I swear, your aunt knows everyone!"

"She is amazing. And she is the most generous person I've ever met. It genuinely delights her to make others happy. So, did David get the job?"

"You haven't heard the best part. Oh, this is rich! When Lord Peterson heard of David's qualifications, he not only hired him on the spot, he handed him an armful of files and asked him how soon he could straighten out the accounts."

"But that is extraordinary!" Trista exclaimed happily. "I assume David is thrilled."

"He came home last night and immediately shut himself into his study. And when I asked him about it this morning, he said he'd worked until three o'clock in the morning, and was up with the dawn to finish. He barely took time for breakfast before rushing off to the bank. And when I warned him to take care with his heart—I had to tease him, I couldn't help it—on account of hearts being funny things and all, he sniffed and informed me that occasional bouts of productive work were actually good for the humors. Imagine."

Trista laughed and gave Luci a big embrace. "Now you shall long for the days when he was about the house more often."

"He plans on being very busy. It couldn't come at a better time, actually. I am so frequently at the shop. It is going very well, by the way. Dina is so much easier to get along with now that her mother is gone, and Betty, well she was always a dear."

"Mama," Andrew called, "can I sail my boat?"

"Stay close. Not the big lake. Try this little one, here."

He frowned, clearly displeased, but obeyed without argument.

"Speaking of dears," Luci said, beaming at Andrew, "what a good boy he is."

"He is. Nothing like his fa . . ." Trista cut off abruptly. "Let us catch up with Andrew on the banks. It's slippery there. I want to be closer."

Andrew raced along the bank, keeping pace with his boat. He was running too far ahead.

"Wait there," she called, and Andrew stopped.

They paused at the lane that wound through this end of the park to let an open landau pass. Andrew retrieved his boat, and began to walk back to her.

Everything happened so quickly then . . . it was merely a series of alarming impressions—Andrew heading back to her, the landau with two passengers. In the carriage, she noted a lady's hat of very good quality and Roman reclined comfortably with his arm slung on the back cushion, behind the woman.

Beside her, Luci gasped, her hands gripping Trista's arm painfully.

Seconds ticked by, and every one of them lasting a year. She was acutely aware of being out in the open, no place to hide. And Andrew. Andrew who could *be* Roman a score and five years ago, so obviously an Aylesgarth that only one glance from his father would cleave her world wide open.

And then it passed. The landau drove on and Roman never looked over. He saw neither her nor his son.

Andrew said, "Hurry up, Mama!" and turned to run back down to the pond's edge. Luci and she crossed the lane and headed across the lawn to a bench where they could sit and watch over the boy.

It was a long time before Trista spoke. "I know you do not approve of me keeping Andrew a secret from Aylesgarth."

"I do not judge you, Trista."

"But you do not think it was right of me to do."

"I believe Aylesgarth has a right to know that he has a child."

Trista took in a long breath and let it out in a rush. "All men are not like David, Luci."

"What does David have to do with this?"

"David loves you. And he is not . . . one of *them*. The noble class . . . they are different. Look at my father. He loved my mother, loved her so much that he suffered greatly at her loss, but he accepted the situation because he was an earl and she was a governess. And me . . . he never even saw me. It is only Aunt May's conscience, her need to have all of us little reminders of her beloved Wooly that has brought me this fortune. My father did not care whether I was getting on well."

"What does that have to do with Aylesgarth?"

"The two of them are cut from the same cloth, through and through, I guarantee, Luci. Do you know that my mother refused to be Woolrich's mistress? She risked complete ruination by going off on her own with me. Oh, he offered her a settlement, but my mother refused to take it. She told me it made her feel like a . . . like she would be less than herself if she accepted the money."

"I loved your mother, Trista, I surely did, but she had her ways, and they were hard ones sometimes."

"She had to be strong, God knows. After a few years of struggling in menial jobs, she answered an advertisement for a position in his London house. It was Roman's father's house. Given her education and refined manners, he saw fit to send her to Kent for his daughter, and me along with her. We were desperate for that position, for a home and bread in our bellies. That was the fate Woolrich left her to, going on to other women, other pleasures without a thought to what he had left behind."

"I still do not understand," Luci said patiently, "why this reflects on whether Aylesgarth should know of his son."

"When Aylesgarth was told he must marry his heiress, he did not stand up to his father and tell him he had promised to marry me. Instead, he offered me a somewhat lesser privilege." She drew her features into a grimace. "He asked me to be his mistress."

"Oh, I see. And this makes him like your father?"

"It makes him like all men of his class. He did not care for me. He was a lord, and I a servant, the same as my mother and Lord Woolrich. Why would the existence of a child have mattered to him?"

"So you never told him because you thought he wouldn't care, that he would shirk his responsibilities? That is too simple."

"I didn't tell him because either that or . . ." She sighed. "Or worse. Perhaps he would have taken an interest. Then he would always be part of my life. If he knew we shared a child, his patronage of us would brand my son a bastard. No. What I did was far better. It wasn't perfect, it wasn't fair, but it was the best I could do. I invented Captain Fairhaven and Andrew became a legitimate child."

"Except that it is a lie."

"Roman was off with his new bride, loaded down with

her fortune to have sons and heirs and never worry about either of us again."

"Mother! Aunt Luci! Look at her go!" Andrew cried, clapping his hands and jumping up and down on the bank as one of the ships caught the wind and took off across the water.

"Mind your feet in the mud," Luci told him. "She's a swift one, I'll say!"

"You are a wonderful sailor," Trista called encouragingly.

"Like his father." Luci said this softly, and Trista shuddered. "That is why he loves sailing so much. He believes his father was a captain. He feels it is a part of him."

"It is better than him thinking his father was a scoundrel who played loose with his mother, and doesn't care a whit about him. I should know."

"Yes. I suppose you should."

They fell silent for a space. Then Trista said, "I'm not so certain, you know. About Andrew and Roman. I wonder if I've made a terrible mistake. I never felt the loss of Woolrich in my life too keenly. But perhaps it is different for a boy."

"Would you ever consider telling Aylesgarth now? I mean, you've met up with him again. It could be that destiny is providing an opportunity for Andrew to know his father."

"Oh, God. If Roman should learn now of what I did, he would hate me beyond measure. His marriage left him with nothing. He might even try to take Andrew. And I can give Andrew everything now. With Woolrich's money and Lady May's influence, I can provide a fine education, make him a part of the most exclusive circles of the *bon ton*. Tell Roman—not a chance, not even the slimmest. It would be inviting disaster, and therefore no matter how much of a wrong it is against Roman, I must think of Andrew first."

Luci made a small noise of protest.

Trista rushed to defend herself. "I mean, what could he do except muddy things? Why should I tell him, and ruin everything?"

She was grateful her cousin did not state the obvious.

* * *

May sipped her morning coffee in the family's parlor at an hour when everyone else was taking their luncheon. She'd slept late, her mind keeping her awake with suspicions and worries she didn't know how to address. Her relationship with Trista was delicate. Despite the many pleasant hours they'd spent in each other's company, they hardly knew each other. And Trista was so different than Michaela. Michaela had been like an awakening colt, ready and anxious to tear into the meat of life. Trista knew her own mind, she'd lived, been married, had a child to care for. She was more measured, more cautious, and as a result, so was May.

The sound of the intruder startled her, causing her to spill her coffee into the saucer as she clattered it down.

Robert strode into the room.

"Goodness, but you move silently," she said, her racing heart skidding to a halt. "You nearly stripped my nerves."

"But that is precisely what I mean to do," he said, striding without pause to take her into his arms. "You've never complained before."

She laughed and kissed him. He held her tight, keeping her with him. His mouth moved slowly, igniting an immediate spark of excitement in her breast.

"I miss you."

"Silly, you see me—"

"Not as often as I want. You have been very busy of late, and I cannot come and go as easily here as I did in your town house. When will it be ready for you to return?"

"Too long."

Pleasure was thick in his voice. "So, you missed me as well?"

"Wretchedly. How did you get in here?"

His look shifted into a baleful expression. "It is not a simple matter, I can tell you. God help me, I am too old for such follies. Which reminds me, when you leave to return to Park Lane, you must tell your niece about the basement window, the one back by the coal shoot. It doesn't latch properly."

"But I had my footman check the premises thoroughly before Trista purchased . . . You?"

He shrugged. "A man has got to improvise. This is too much talking by half. Come here."

"You have that look in your eye, Robert. It bodes ill."

"Then why are you smiling?"

"Because I like it when you bode ill." She slipped beside him. Her eyes were hungry for the sight of him. At her home, Robert came and went discreetly with great frequency. Few were the nights that he didn't share her bed. Where he lived when he was not with her, she had no clue. She'd quelled all curiosity, all feelings of possession. With Robert, more than what they had was not possible.

His eyes drifted to the gaping vee of her wrapper. She had only a chemise underneath, made of sheer lawn and trimmed with prim little ribbons. Pink.

"Your dishabille indicates you were expecting me."

"I always hope," she said. Her hands went to his hair, feeling the crispness of the springing waves. He dipped his head, kissed her deeply.

"I think you willed me here. Admit it. Your thoughts made me abandon my customers and trot over here like a well-trained hound." He rubbed the side of his cheek down the column of her neck as his hand slipped inside the opening of her dressing gown, cupping her.

"You can't mean to do this now," she said, struggling at first, but quickly subdued when he grazed her excited flesh with a slow caress. "Come back tonight."

"I cannot wait until tonight. Sometimes the door to the basement is bolted and I am thwarted."

"I'll arrange to have it left open. Not . . . now. I must dress."

"Are you going out with Charbonneau?" His voice held a certain tightness that on another man might have been mistaken for jealousy. But Robert being jealous of Charbonneau was as absurd as a gazelle envying the grace of a baboon.

"Actually, yes. Why?"

He withdrew his hand. May breathed a sigh of relief and gathered her strength to sit up, but she had underestimated his passion, and his determination. His expression grew fierce, and she had the sense that he was restless or unhappy.

"What is it?" she asked him.

"It chafes," he said.

"What?"

"Having only the nights. I know we swore never to speak of it, but there are times when I abhor this half-existence we share. And it has grown so much less since your moving here. Too much less."

She was exhilarated by his words. "I hate every moment parted from you," she said sincerely. "But you are silly to be unhappy over Lord Charbonneau."

"He is in love with you."

"But I . . ." I love you, she'd almost said. But they'd never spoken of love. It was one of the many things they avoided, which was so silly, really, when both of them knew all too well about hidden truths.

Instead, she said, "But I do not love him. He is merely an admirer. I've had them before, and you know they mean little to me."

"That is good." His eyes raked down her, lingering once again at her gaping neckline. She felt her breasts tingle in response, the sensitive peaks pearling, aching for his touch.

He dropped his head into the curve of her neck. She heard his contented sigh, and almost relaxed, thinking him tame until she felt the touch of his long, strong fingers along her leg. She knew his intention, and was torn between excitement and horror. Or perhaps a heady blend of both.

"Trista is only over at the park. She can return any moment."

"We will hear her in plenty of time."

He was doing things, wonderful, wicked things with his clever fingers that left her helpless. She panted into his mouth and he chuckled.

A sound brought her up, flailing against him, but he didn't move, and he didn't ease the pressure between her legs.

"That's the front door. Go, quickly."

"But what if she comes in?" Robert said, grinning. "She would find me here, and you . . . like this . . . looking too delicious to believe. She would know what we are doing. It makes it much more exciting, no?"

"No! I would be mortified."

His lips sank into the curve at her throat. "The fear heightens awareness," he murmured, brushing lightly along fevered skin. He moved so that his chest dragged across hers, exciting her breasts, bringing her to the brink of exquisite pleasure. "It boils the blood to unbearable heat. It makes your skin feel too tight, and just when you think you're going to burst, your bones melt under the force of the heat."

Her hands wrapped around his wrist as her back arched. She felt the force, she felt the heat. "This . . . Robert, I can't . . ."

"You can."

Her head thrashed. She gasped helplessly. "They are coming."

"No, darling." He chuckled. "You are coming."

Violent waves swept up her body, bursting into a series of ecstatic spasms. She bit her lips to keep her cries from escaping. When the storm ceased she closed her eyes and fell back, her lungs working like a frantic bellows to restore her lost strength.

Robert's voice close to her ear said, "Ah, May. You are going to ruin me some day."

He rose. She didn't open her eyes. She didn't wish to watch him leave.

It was getting very painful, watching him leave.

When she heard the sounds of pattering footsteps—these would be Andrew's—running past the parlor door, she pulled herself upright and adjusted her dressing gown.

It was not a full minute later that the pocket doors were pulled open. Trista and Luci entered, still wearing their light cloaks and gloves.

"It was glorious out there," Trista exclaimed as she removed her hat and patted her hair. "The wind is up and there's a nip in the air, but the sun is bursting through, or trying to. April is so fickle . . . Aunt May, what are you doing with the window open?" Trista exclaimed. "It's still too chilly, and you are only in your wrapper."

May stood. She looked about, as if not knowing what she was about. "I . . . I was overheated." She blushed, groaning at her choice of words.

"I can see that. Your color is too high. Are you feeling well? Oh, goodness. Your lip is bleeding."

Her eyes flew wide and she touched her mouth. "I . . . bit it by accident, I suppose. Don't you hate that? Actually, I think I need to lie down. I am feeling . . . ah, peaked."

Trista stared after her aunt as she nearly fled the room. She and Luci exchanged a puzzled look.

The house near the park was not a mansion. It was a towering town house, consisting of three Palladian style stories and a row of dormers under the eaves. It had a wrought iron fence around the front garden and a classically ornamented façade. It was a beautiful place, and Roman had to admit to himself that he was impressed.

There was no trouble finding this residence. Trista Fairhaven had come out to the beau monde. She was no longer anonymous. She was the acknowledged niece of one of the *ton*'s most celebrated members.

And so she could hide no longer.

He raised the iron knocker, and was shown inside. Fully prepared to be turned away, he was anticipating this very thing so intently that when he was told to wait in the formal parlor, he was taken by surprise.

He found himself in comfortable surroundings. Her taste had certainly evolved. This room was stunning. Perfect. She had probably been tutored, he imagined. Again, he was surprised at the wealth it indicated. It made him feel uneasy.

It was an indication of just how new, how different everything was these days.

A movement by the open pocket doors drew his attention, but all he saw was a dark head by the latch accompanied by the rapid retreat of running feet. He stood, thinking he might go take a look. He'd heard she had a son. Everyone knew about her and he'd listened to every bit of it, absorbing each detail, weighing it.

He wondered about the boy, and found himself jealous again, thinking of the child she had shared with Captain Fairhaven, that shadowy, heroic figure she had loved after him. They'd married and produced a baby in short order. It must have been a great love.

When Trista appeared in the doorway, it startled him out of these thoughts. She came into the room with a confident stride, a composed face, and a chip on her shoulder the size of Gibralter.

"It is kind of you to call on me," she said after the pleasantries were established. "Although you take the burden of old acquaintance too far. Our association is in the past. It has no place in either of our present lives."

He struck an indolent pose and perused her with his laziest stare. "Is that why you saw me without any fuss? To tell me that?"

She inclined her head like foreign royalty. "You know it is true. We need to understand each other, and end this now."

He was suddenly angry. He had never been very good at controlling his temper. He'd never had any discipline with that hot, stinging feeling. It had driven him to do the things that had won him the reputation as little Lord Terrible.

Now, as a man, he'd not had the same struggles. He'd grown, matured, no longer given to fits of temper, but when he was with Trista, the past and the present clashed in a violent storm, blurring everything he thought he knew about himself, all he'd thought he had long since changed.

He rose and went to the window where yards of watered silk hung in rich folds and puddled gently onto the floor. "Do you know what I miss about the past?"

He saw her spine go stiff.

"I miss the fells. Midsummer Eve, do you remember?"

"No," she insisted, picking up the bell, and giving it a

sharp ring. "Where is Belinda? I told her to bring the tea immediately."

She was so lovely. Her hair, soft as spun silk, gleamed in the gentle light. His hand flexed, wanting to feel its texture again.

"Midnight, do you remember Trista? We danced like pagans."

"I don't recall," she said, fidgeting.

"You had drunk wine for the first time, and you were quite tipsy. You were very charming when in your cups that night. You kicked off your shoes and lifted your skirts to your knees—"

"Roman, please!" she cried.

The effect of hearing her say his name was like a knife clear to his heart. Roman, please. Roman, please love me, please stop all this nonsense and hold me.

That was what he longed to hear, he realized.

"I do not wish to talk about the past," she insisted. "It is very painful to me. I made up my mind a long time ago to put it behind me, and I will not traverse those unhappy trails for your amusement."

"Were they so distasteful to you?" he asked. "I doubt it, for you enjoyed it at the time, as I recall."

Her eyes blazed. She did not move a muscle, but he saw the way her hands gripped the arm of her chair. "I enjoyed it too well, for you could be very diverting when you wished to be."

"So you are not as immune as you claimed to be at the ball? How heartening."

"I do not underestimate you, Roman. You've lost none of that power. It is rather dangerous, and I've lost my fascination with danger. I am a woman, now, not a fool of a girl. A bit wiser, and more than a bit more pragmatic. Even cynical. If you do not cease, I will have you removed, and you can do what you like, cause what scandal you will." Her voice climbed, nearly hysterical, "but I will not have it, do you understand?"

She sat as straight in her chair as if she was a schoolgirl

strapped into a backboard, her hands white-knuckled on her lap. He felt the familiar rush of regret that came always after one of his verbal lashings.

He took his seat again. "Very well. What should we talk about, then?"

"Nothing. Why will you not see we have nothing to say to each other? I had wished to be civil to you, but that might prove impossible. Oh, I recall how you are when you feel yourself denied. I remember how it tears at you, and you rail like a madman. But please, try to understand my side. We can have no friendship between us."

"This placating tone is nauseating. I prefer you as you were a moment ago." He leaned forward slightly, his eyes pinning hers. "Passionate."

Her eyes flared wide. "I wish to speak to you reasonably, so that you may see there is no advantage of our initiating any sort of friendship. *Any* sort."

"Are you afraid of me?" he asked, amazed.

She flinched, giving everything away in a split second before she ducked her head.

She had said nothing, but he knew the answer. It made him sorry, suddenly, and helpless. Was there nothing he could do to change her mind?

He had to change her mind.

A faint ring of voices brought her head up. Somewhere in the house, her son was laughing. She appeared alarmed.

"I had to marry her," he said abruptly.

Her eyelids fell heavy over her eyes. She froze. "I know. Can we not discuss this?"

"My father . . . you know . . ." Ah, but there were still things he could not speak of. "It wasn't like it was with us. Therese was not a true wife. Marriage for a family such as mine, it is a business arrangement. You know this. She was nothing like you."

"No, she was a lady, and she was an heiress. That was what was required, Roman. You know, I can appreciate now, with the passage of time, that perhaps you were trapped as much as I by what happened. I know neither one of us was happy."

"I proposed a solution."

"That I become your mistress, yes. I suppose it was a solution to you. Your class thinks nothing of such arrangements."

"I hate when you do that—my 'class,' as if we are a different species."

"It is the way of the noble to consider themselves a breed apart. Above other men, above morals even. But I was just a simple commoner. You can't imagine that I would agree for you to enter into a marriage blessed by God and church while taking me as your mistress. It is an abomination of morals, of what is right, a perversion of love."

He wanted to howl with frustration. That he couldn't deny the basic logic of what she was saying, and that he was deeply insulted by the reasoning applied to that logic, twisted like a knot in his gut. "Oh, yes, we altered beings with titles and money are so very different from the common folk. Please tell me, Trista, now that you have found yourself to have the blood of a noble in your veins, how have you changed now that you are one of us? No, I see you still cling fast to your plebian morality.

"You always acted as if I'd insulted you with my offer. So many other women would have done it, and been glad of it. But not you, not Trista Nash, by God. You were above the cut. Such arrogance, but I suppose you couldn't help it. After all, it is quite true that you were unlike anyone else. Before or since, I've never met your like or your equal. I suppose that is part of why I can't seem to let you go."

She didn't look at him. "You've proven yourself amazingly adept at letting me go."

"I didn't let go. I never let you go."

"You did, Roman. You gave me away for a fortune."

"All right, damn it. I did what I had to do. It was a mistake. Oh yes, I make them occasionally. But I don't repeat them."

Tea arrived, but by that time, he was spent. What had he

come here for, anyway? He'd not thought about that. All he'd done was savor the idea of another meeting, another confrontation, another time in her presence simply because not seeing her again was a possibility not to be entertained.

With little conversation, she poured out and he stirred in a dollop of cream, the sound of the spoon scraping the cup almost mesmerizing. He pondered his own folly.

He had this ridiculous, sentimental, and completely uncharacteristic notion that providence had brought her back into his life, that they would somehow resolve it all, take back what they'd lost.

But that wasn't really going to happen. It was only now becoming tragically obvious that he had deluded himself rather stupidly, and as a result, miscalculated completely the entire situation.

He placed his teacup on the small table between them and stood. "You are quite right. This was not a good idea. I don't know what I was thinking."

Halfway to the door, he paused. "The other night, you seemed to be under the misconception that I was not well-off financially. I only say this because you speculated that my interest in you was due to your recently becoming an heiress. I do not wish for you to believe this. Although Therese's family withdrew the shares in their family investments that were promised to me, I still had her dowry, which was sizeable. I invested it, and if you've heard of my reputation as you say you have, you know I have been known to have good fortune . . . in some areas. In short, Trista, I do not need your money. I am wealthy beyond your inheritance, beyond thrice what Woolrich gave you. I live modestly. I find myself not exactly miserly, but I cannot help but be frugal. You see, I have a purpose to amassing money and am rather obsessed with preserving it. Can you guess why?"

He paused for effect. He supplied the answer after a heartbeat. "Because one day I might have a son, and I do not want him to have to make the choice I did. He will be free to do what he wants, see who he wants, go where he wants. Marry whom he wishes."

Again, the faint sound of a child's voice drifted to him, and he saw Trista's lips tremble. He felt a dangerous welling of emotion of his own, and thought he better get the hell out of there before he did any more damage to his ravaged pride.

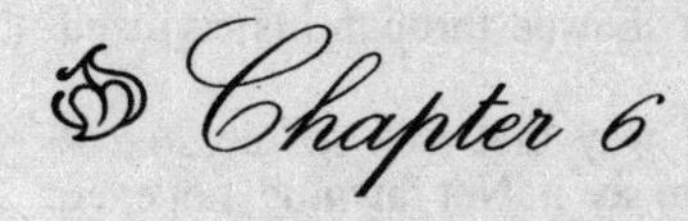

Chapter 6

Lady May didn't mention Roman's having paid a call, but Trista knew she was curious. She appreciated the restraint. Eventually she would have to tell her something. Before she could come to it, however, Michaela Standish Khoury and her new husband, Major Adrian Khoury, returned to London after an extended trip abroad.

The sight of her half sister was shocking. She'd seen pictures of their father, and Michaela resembled him to a degree that was uncanny. Her thick, wild curls were chestnut, her eyes the same exotic shape and haunting green as Woolrich's famous ones.

She and Michaela became instant friends. She learned that Michaela, too, had been plucked from ordinary life by their mutual fairy godmother.

"Bosh!" Lady May exclaimed, hearing herself referred to thusly, waving her hand and fluttering the feathers on her sleeve.

Major Adrian Khoury, Michaela's newly wedded husband, smiled, his eyes going soft as they rested on his wife. "You brought her to that ball the night we met. Do you remember, Michaela? It was rather a remarkable introduction. I know I shall never forget it."

Michaela gave him a repressive look as she flushed. "I seem to recollect it as well."

The major chuckled and let off his teasing. He was a quiet, intense man, Trista found, not what she had expected. She had heard of him, of course. Not many did not know of the legendary Major Adrian Khoury, for he was a war hero of some note. He was not brash or stoic, but a soft-spoken man with a core of steel that showed through his civilized exterior.

He adored Michaela in a way that was so moving, it brought tears to Trista's eyes to see it. Not fawning, not even overtly affectionate—although a sly touch or glance might be exchanged when they thought no one was looking—they had an understated connection that could be felt most keenly.

They were so in love, so unapologetic about it, not caring a whit that it was simply not done to hold such affections for one's spouse. How she envied them.

She inevitably thought of Roman. She hated herself for being so weepy and weak and tried her best to ignore this very unflattering trait in herself and keep her thoughts on steadier ground.

And yet . . . it haunted her that he seemed different. Perhaps he'd changed. She certainly had, why not him?

She was afraid to fully believe this. There was no question that she was susceptible to Roman. His one glance could melt her, a raised brow made her tremble. She was still wildly attracted to him. No other man had ever had this effect on her. From the time he'd crossed her path when she'd been six, he'd been her world.

He was her weakness, and she must guard against it. For Andrew's sake.

Later that week, the three Woolrich women were escorted by Major Khoury to attend Lady Viola Carraway's afternoon tea party. It was their first outing together. Lady Viola was one of Lady May's dearest friends, and may have been excited about the afternoon. Yet, upon entering the elaborate rooms of the Carraway mansion, she stopped dead in the hallway.

"Oh, dear," she said as they handed their spencers to the footman and straightened their skirts. May peered into the parlor with an expression of disgust. "It is that Withrow woman, Lady Viola's sister-in-law. Had I known she was visiting, I would never have accepted the invitation. I cannot abide her society. She is the worst snob. Her sour face is not what I am in the mood for."

Major Khoury stepped inside and whipped off his cloak. "Is there some problem?"

"Oh, never mind. Just keep your wits about you, ladies, and make certain they are sharp. You might need them." She arched a brow at Major Khoury. "Do you have a bayonet with you by chance?"

He sighed. "I am afraid I do not."

"More's the pity. Ah, well, dear friends . . . into the breach." Sweeping into the room, smile in place, she glided toward her hostess in a flourish of feathers. She set the room alight as she entered it, eliciting a round of gleeful greetings.

Michaela and Trista exchanged amused glances. "She is good," Michaela said.

"I see that," Trista replied. "I can only hope one day to learn a quarter of what she knows about people."

"You do not do so badly," Major Khoury said, pausing between them with both arms crooked. "Ladies?"

They went in behind Lady May.

Trista was stunned to see Roman was one of the guests. He sat with a female companion in a pair of chairs in the corner.

He knew she was here, for he glanced at her, nodded, and turned away. His message was clear. He was respecting her request to keep his distance.

It was difficult not to notice how good he looked. His dove gray coat and pale-lemon waistcoat were of soft brushed wool. She looked at his companion, whose back was to her, and was relieved to see she was a dark-haired woman. That meant she was not the "Annabelle" Roman had brought into Mrs. Hines's milliner's shop. The momentary relief turned into a stab of renewed jealousy. Then, just who *was* she?

Her curiosity was not appeased. In a moment of boisterous talking while everyone was presented, Trista missed the introduction, having been diverted by a gallant Lord Nevers taking too long to bow over her hand. She would have pulled Aunt May aside, for her aunt had greeted Roman warmly and been introduced to the lady, but Lady Viola ushered the women quickly into chairs, robbing Trista of the chance.

Her stomach twisted hotly as she observed the way Roman and the dark-haired woman were the only ones off by themselves, close enough to enjoin the conversation, but separate, as if they desired a bit of privacy.

Who was she? She had her head bent forward, enough so that a good portion of her face was obscured. Her attention was all on Roman, and he was basking in it like a tom in a patch of shining sun.

The woman's hair was rich and classically designed and the fleeting glimpse of profile showed a fine nose and strong chin. Trista's heart sank. She was certainly handsome.

Lady Viola was a dear creature, perhaps in her late fifties yet the type of woman who retains some of her girlishness in her giddy, breathless way of talking, in her emphatic gestures, and her effusive, ingratiating manner. She fussed over her guests, striving to create a pleasant atmosphere.

Michaela and May knew most of the others and were comfortable immediately. Trista watched them with admiration. The major, she noted, made a tactical retreat, standing by the big bay window with the men as soon as the pleasantries were concluded.

It was an amicable atmosphere except for Lady Withrow, who soon turned her greedy eyes to Trista.

"So this is your neice," she said to May.

It was an open secret, which was to say it was generally known but not overtly acknowledged, that Trista was her father's bastard daughter. Lady May had assured her it was no trouble to acknowledge the connection in her case, that these sorts of family alliances at the top echelons of the ton were "done" all the time. It was the influence of the family, not the legitimacy of the heir, that counted, she said. Trista had found this to be true enough.

But there were some—Lady May urged her not to give them a thought—who still made much over the matter. The scandal of it thrilled them, and they nitpicked cruelly. With one look at Lady Withrow's beadlike eyes and straight, lipless mouth, Trista knew she was dealing with one of these.

"Where is your family from, dear?" Lady Withrow wanted to know.

"Kent," Trista replied.

Lady Withrow waited expectantly for her to elaborate. Trista stared back and smiled, hoping she appeared as empty-headed as a bird.

The conversation moved on. Lady Withrow was disgruntled at having been thwarted.

Trista could hardly have cared. She was too acutely aware of the male presence over her left shoulder. It was like an enormous heat came from him, singeing her skin through her lovely sprigged muslin, setting her nerves tingling along the side of her body.

It must have affected her concentration, for it was only when she heard Aunt May repeating her name several times that she realized she was being addressed.

"Oh, excuse me," she said quickly. She pressed a hand to her temple, as if this action could still her thoughts. "I am afraid I am still unused to these hours one keeps in the city. We were out very late last evening and I am a bit under the snuff, as you say."

Lady Withrow's eyes glowed, as if she'd been waiting for just this opportunity. "Well, of course, you were in trade, dear. You must be used to waking at the crack of dawn. The hours kept by society must be taxing. It does take some getting used to."

Trista froze, her drink halfway to her lips. There was a

shocked hush, and everyone was looking at her. Her eyes sought her aunt.

May's face altered, her soft, feminine features hardening with imperceptible movement. She opened her mouth, but it was Michaela who spoke first. "Do you patronize Mrs. Hines's shop, Lady Withrow? It really is top drawer—you should go. It is so rare to find designers these days who understand fashion and don't simply allow their customers to pile as much plumage as can be managed because it makes it look expensive. So many people take their money so very seriously, and it makes them act in the most idiotic manner."

The major made a strange snorting sound from over in the corner. He also seemed to be having a difficult time keeping a proud smile from his lips. Michaela looked at him and gave him a jerk of her eyebrows.

If Lady Withrow understood the insult, she didn't let on. "As in all things, finding quality is difficult. One is forever coming across upstarts and impudent people who would tout themselves as on level with their betters without benefit of good breeding."

May nearly came up out of her seat, yet once again she was preempted by another voice. This time it was Roman who cut in, and the sound of his soft, masculine tones in the discussion brought everyone up short.

"Good breeding. I hear so much talk about it these days, and yet see so little evidence of it."

Lady Withrow smiled and he inclined his head to her in acknowledgment. She purred, "Indeed, my lord, I have rarely heard it put with such good sense."

He muttered an apology and reached in between the cluster of chairs set out around the tea service, picking a shortbread biscuit from the tray. "Why, thank you, Lady Withrow. But I doubt you have gotten my meaning correctly. I have no prejudice against those encumbered with titles. I myself toil under the burden. But I have noted that true quality is sometimes a scarcity among the most thickly pedigreed. Do you know, Lady Withrow, that people actually equate social standing with social worth? Imagine. Ah, well, there is simply nothing worse than a shallow wit."

Everyone was silent as he took a nibble of the biscuit, chewed, then stated, "I believe you've demonstrated that quite succinctly."

Lady Viola chimed in. "Oh, I dare say, that is so true what you say about titles. They used to mean honor, but they do not account for anything any longer. Why, do you recall Lord Gerrenfod? He was a louse. His poor wife—how she suffered him, I do not know—she told me in confidence . . . oh, perhaps I should not say anything, then."

She turned to May to advise her on this cloudy conundrum. Lady May patted her hand. "Your point, dear Viola, is so expertly made, I think you need not trouble your conscience further. I believe we all knew Lord Gerrenfod well enough to infer the comparison."

"Oh, thank you, dear." Viola's gratitude turned to bemusement as it dawned on her she didn't understand at all what May might have meant.

Just as quickly as he had appeared, Roman faded back to his corner, taking his seat with his silent companion. He must be mightily devoted to her, for while the other men guffawed by the window, he sat tamely by her side.

It was only a fortnight ago that he found this inconstant man at Trista's doorstep, dogging her at dances, making himself out to be some long-suffering and frustrated suitor, and here he was, in puppylike devotion to this new woman.

Vindication surged upon her with a vengeance. She knew he had not changed! His character was most certainly *not* improved since he had played so lightly with her deepest affections. And more was her relief that she had not told him about his son. How would such a fickle heart care about Andrew, about all the Lady Withrows in England who would peer down their noses and scoff? He wouldn't.

"Trista, dear," Lady Viola said, "I hear your son is quite the charmer. Your aunt dotes on him. How is he doing in his new home?"

"He is well, thank you for asking. He loves the park, and being close to it is a great treat."

"Will you be sending him to Eton or to Harrow?"

"I . . . haven't decided."

"Well, which did his father attend?"

"Oh, yes . . . Ah . . . em . . . Harrow, I think."

"Does the boy now have a tutor?"

"Not at present. He was getting instruction, but he is still young and some things are still not yet decided upon."

"I am sure he will wish to follow in the exact footsteps of his father," said Michaela, who knew nothing of what she was starting. "He is the most delightful boy. All he does is play with his boats. You see, he wishes to be a sea captain. His father, of course, was one."

"Oh, he was? Was he killed in the war?" Lady Viola wished to know.

"Captain Fairhaven?" Lady Withrow boomed, taking an interest now that names were being bandied about. "I know the Fairhavens of Surry, was he related to these?" She tapped her chin with a chubby finger. "Although I do not recall them losing a son. What was his given name?"

Oh, God. What name had she concocted for the man? She couldn't recall! She'd told Andrew a heroic tale of his father going down with his ship while saving the lives of his crew, but such a tale as that would have made the papers if it were true, so she couldn't tell the ladies this. They would know she was lying right away.

She began wringing her hands on her lap as her mouth worked.

"Can't you see she does not wish to speak of him?" Lady May covered Trista's trembling hands and faced Lady Withrow once again. "It is still too painful."

Lady Withrow was not exactly in charity with Trista's aunt. Their dislike for each other was not unbridled, but neither was it hidden. She glared at her now, not settling for May's excuse. "It has been quite a few years, I am told. The boy is, what, five years old?"

"She loved him very much," May insisted. "It takes a

great deal of time to recover. After all, they had nearly a year together and then he was lost at sea. They were so very devoted."

Misty-eyed Lady Viola said, "Oh, you poor darling."

She saw that she was bouncing her knee, and stopped. Before she could help herself, she glanced at Roman, fearing the guilt was apparent on her face.

He had noticed the knee, too. His eyes held challenge and question.

"Did you see how she snubbed me?" Grace hissed as they queued up to the buffet table.

Roman held her plate, ignoring the comment and hoping his sister was not working up to one of her fits of pique.

She had recently confided that it was for fear of attacks of anxiety that came upon her when in public that she had taken to staying at home. She was afraid others might witness the profuse sweating, trembling, and breathless confusion that came upon her. Her heart raced so fast, it ached, and she feared she would collapse, but the surgeons—all five whom Roman had called in to find what was the matter with his sister's health—had detected a strong heartbeat without any of the signs of illness.

It was then he understood the nature of Grace's complaint. It was her nerves. His worst fears had been confirmed.

He refused to accept this condition, to consign her to a life like their mother's. He found he cared deeply for his sister. He hadn't always been cognizant of this. But it was Grace to whom he turned when his world had imploded upon seeing Trista again. It occurred to him that despite the distance that he'd placed between them over the years, she was still the one who knew him best.

Well, one of two women who knew him best, and the other one being the reason he had sought out the familiarity of a sister who needed his help to overcome this infirmity.

They had visited the garden of her town house first, and by keeping up a steady stream of conversation, he had managed to keep her outside nearly a quarter of an hour. Next, they took a stroll along her crescent. Then to the park at its center. Each victory gave Grace courage, but it was only his constant attentiveness that enabled her to accomplish her goals. He'd calmly talk to her, drowning out the panicked thoughts in her head, and eventually she was learning to ignore them.

Even with her excitement at her progress, it had taxed his powers of charm greatly to convince her to accept this invitation to Lady Viola's tea party. She had agreed only with his assurance that he would not leave her side the entire time and that he would make a quick excuse and get her from the place the moment she felt her heart race or her thoughts tumble over catastrophic thoughts.

He was feeling rather pleased with himself at this new dedication to good works. He had even turned down an afternoon in Annabelle's bed—a pastime that, lately, had not filled him with as much anticipation and interest as it once had—to be here, holding his sister's hand, so to speak.

It seemed a stroke of bad luck to have Trista present. It made Grace skittish. As for himself—God she twisted his insides just to look at her. Was she so great a beauty? He could never tell if she were truly as gorgeous as she seemed to him. She was simply the most incredibly beautiful woman in the world to his eyes. At each turn of knowing her, she'd fascinated him, from the ethereal child with wise, knowing eyes that saw too much to the gangly, angry girl he'd teased mercilessly, to the breathless creature he'd come home from University to fall in love with, to the wild, spitting she-cat who'd left him, refusing to understand the limitations of the world and blaming him for its unfairness.

"She did not even look when we were introduced," Grace said, darting a glance toward the women. "I suppose she thinks herself my better, now that her father's family has chosen to acknowledge her. And do not tell me she didn't see me. I haven't changed all that much, have I?"

"She was lying," he said softly. He wasn't even certain

Grace heard him. "Her foot was jerking about like a rabbit under her skirts."

"I am taller, I realize," Grace said. "And my light hair has darkened. Could it be she really did not know me?"

"She doesn't like to talk about her son, or her husband."

Grace realized they were having two completely different conversations. "Oh, bother. I do not wish to spend the day discussing Trista Nash—or Fairhaven, for that matter. I should not have come, perhaps. I am feeling most uncomfortable."

"She did not snub you," Roman assured her, surprising her that he had been listening after all. "Eat something. I will not allow you to give in to your inclination for retreat."

"I cannot eat." She sounded horrified.

"Then put something on your plate and push it around while I eat. If you make a spectacle of not partaking of the food, your hostess will be offended."

God, he was a selfish creature, no better than the wild boy who'd plagued the neighborhood. He cared about his sister's nerves, yes, but he cared more that she not demand that they should leave. Trista . . . he had to find a way to speak to her, alone.

Because she'd *lied.*

The certainty ate a hole in his chest. It throbbed as his mind worked on ways to get her in a private enough situation that he was able to speak with her.

These things could be done. He was a master at maneuvering social situations to suit him.

"Her aunt is ridiculous, with all those feathers," Grace sniffed. "What a silly woman."

Roman gave his sister a warning look. "I believe Lady May has the most elevated reputation, Grace. Have a care who you say such things to. Most people adore her."

This did not please her. "I wish to leave, Roman. You must take me home at once."

"Why? Because Lady May is wearing pink feathers?"

"Of course not. Seeing . . . *that woman*"—this, of course,

meant Trista—"has overset my nerves. She is a plague to me, and always has been."

"The woman inherits a few thousand pounds a year and suddenly she can chase you from your own circle?"

Grace stiffened. Some things were so dependable, it was almost too easy. Grace had the Aylesgarth pride, the same as him.

Her eyes grew canny. "You used to manipulate me easily when we were children, but I've grown a bit more sophisticated since."

He waited, for despite her quick insight into his machinations, she didn't seem inclined to leave. Perhaps she wasn't as sophisticated as she wished.

But then, emotions like lust, jealousy, rivalry . . . these were fairly basic.

In the end, they did not leave. The opportunity he was looking for came just as everyone settled down with their plates. The terrace doors had been flung open, and several of the guests went out to sit at the table and chairs set up out of doors. It was all very informal, people busying themselves of little knots of men and women, and within this interweaving, he managed to have Grace seated next to Lady Viola, who was an adept hostess, and the very kind Mrs. Blenheim.

She was nervous but she didn't balk. This left Roman free to roam, but it was not to the terrace or to any of the seats left indoors he headed, for Trista had excused herself moments earlier and gone to the back of the house, toward the water closet. It was a simple ruse. How often had he waylaid her when she was a child, leaping out and frightening the wits out of her when she was walking alone at Whitethorn? Then later, as her lover, he'd sweep her into an empty room just to hold her, smell her, kiss her longingly, and promise that he would sneak into her room later on that night.

He shook off the disturbing memory, feeling a most unwelcome rise of heat. He was not about seduction . . . well, he supposed he would if it were possible. For the moment, however, he wished some answers.

He was not completely without sense. He knew this absolutely mindless need to ask her about her husband—*why did she lie?*—was completely illogical. But he was determined to do it.

He had no right. Yes, yes, and it was insufferably arrogant of him to presume to demand answers from her about her life . . . But he'd still do it, because he had to. Very simple, very clear.

He moved stealthily down the hallway to the threshold of an empty room to lay in wait for her. He didn't even have the grace to feel ridiculous. He was far too excited for that.

When she passed, he reached out a hand to span the narrow passageway and effectively block her path.

"Boo," he said.

She closed her eyes, as if in deep disgust. "I cannot believe you would do this."

"Why? I used to do it all the time."

She opened her eyes. The storms were there, gathered into intense pinpoints of steely gray. "Have you grown up so little?"

"In some ways, no. I never could stand being thwarted. I still do not like it."

Cocking her head to one side, she studied him. "What happened to the contrite man beating his breast in my home a few weeks past? I admit, I very nearly believed it, but here is the brash one returned. I must say, your sincerity did not last very long."

"I didn't lie to you that day," he said, stung.

"That is an elegant touch, the way you hold yourself, as if you've been insulted."

She tried to push past him. He didn't let her. She settled back and glared at him.

He sighed. "You are heartless, do you know that?"

"I have a heart," she defended, lifting her chin. "It is not kindly disposed toward you, however."

"Then it is a hard one. A callused heart."

She glared at him. "Do you know how calluses form? It begins with tender, unmarked skin that is abused, overused, misused. A blister forms. Quite painful, swollen and tender to the touch. But as the blister heals over time, the callus forms as a protection against the future."

"Very clever. I had forgotten how spry you were with words."

"I am sure you lost track of any singular quality of mine in the intervening years. No one could blame you. All those women—why it would make greater men than you confused. Which reminds me, shouldn't you be getting back to your . . . whatever she is."

"Sister," he supplied. "So you did not recognize her."

Her eyes flared wide. "That was Grace?" She seemed to deflate, her indignation draining out of her, leaving her sheepish and unwilling to meet his eyes. "I did not know. I thought . . . My. She has changed quite a bit. She is so lovely."

"Dare I hope you might have been jealous?"

"You forget yourself," she admonished, wincing at how much she sounded like a prig to her own ears.

"I didn't forget so much." He moved just slightly closer, his voice lowering. "For example, I vividly recall the scar on your thigh. From when you were eight, and you fell climbing the fence. I was the one who ripped my shirt and tied a bandage around it, and it turned into a great adventure. I got whipped for ruining the shirt and you got bread and water for climbing the fence."

"Which you dared me to do."

He shrugged. "I was a devil, which you knew full well. You, however, were a preternatural child who should have had better judgment. You usually did."

"I never seemed to manage to hold my own with you. You could goad me into anything."

"I don't recollect goading. Coaxing, yes. Cajoling, definitely." His eyes grazed her, softening, as a demon's smile played on his lips. "I especially remember cajoling. I was good at that. Perhaps because I enjoyed it too well."

He braced his hand on the wall, so close to her ear that he might have lifted a thumb and traced the outer curve.

"I might," he said, his voice lowered to a purr, "be able to coax you still."

"I doubt it."

"You sound unconvinced. Just as I am about the matter of you beloved husband."

"I can hardly care," she told him flatly. But she wouldn't look at him.

"Your eyes are darting about most furtively, Trista. I have to ask myself . . . why?"

"It is none of your business, that is why. Now, if you do not wish to cause a scene, then move aside."

"You will not cause a scene," he said with confidence. "Tell me about the good captain. Where did you meet him?"

"In a village where I ran to get away from *you*. I cannot fathom your sudden interest. You cared little enough for my well-being when Captain Fairhaven came to my rescue, so why all the curiosity now?"

"Captain Fairhaven? Is that what you called him?"

"He was a captain," she stammered.

"Yes. And his name was Fairhaven. Most logical. But in bed, did you also call him captain in the throes of passion?"

"I will not answer that."

"No, I don't imagine you would. Not with someone who remembers the breathless way you said *his* name over and over again in those rushed, heady moments just before you reached climax."

She pushed against him. She would have slapped him if she could. If she had, it might have done more good than her ineffectual shove. All that managed to do was raise his smirk to a higher level of mockery.

He said, "Forgive my forwardness, but I simply have to know. Darling Trista, your knee gave you away just now, bouncing like a child's pony at a gallop. You never did answer what Captain Fairhaven's Christian name was. Did you know it, after all?"

"Of course. It was Andrew."

"Andrew. You named your son after him."

"I named my son after his father—is that so unusual?"

"Did you call him Drew? Andy? No, don't look over my shoulder. No one is going to save you this time."

"You said you would leave me alone." She sounded plaintive, almost desperate. "I have done nothing to provoke this disrespect."

"Oh, but you did, you see. You lied." He stepped closer. "And, I admit, I've been maddeningly curious about this man, this Captain Andrew Fairhaven. I am even more curious why he is such a secret. You refuse to speak of him, even to those sympathetic matrons who are slavering to hear the romantic story."

"It is no secret. He was my husband. His loss is still very painful to me."

"You seem surprisingly angry for one so aggrieved. Grief, my dear, turns down the corners of one's mouth, not this white-lipped grip you've got your lips pulled into. It saddens the eyes, not brings them to a fever with pent-up fury. It makes one gray, soft, and you are all fire and full of color. Why, look at your cheeks! But most of all, Trista darling—"

"Stop calling me that!"

"—it saps one's strength, leaving one limp and defeated under the terrible burden of mourning one so dear. Here, we come to that knee again, bouncing away in fidgeting splendor, giving you away."

"You are obsessed with my knee!"

"Not just your knee, darling. Your ankle, oh, and your foot. I distinctly recall the graceful curve of your foot, and the neat little toes all lined up so prettily. I was partial to your waist, as well. It was so tiny, it amazed me. And I loved your shoulders. Like a statue . . . Oh, yes, I was fairly obsessed with them. You had a wonderful back, and your neck could occupy me for hours."

Her mouth worked silently for a moment before she could produce any sound. "You are depraved."

"Ah," he said, grinning, "so you remember our trysts as

well. Yes, I was depraved, and you used to love it. Tell me, was Captain Andrew Fairhaven adventurous in the bedroom?"

"Do not speak of him. You disgust me."

"Oh, that was good. Indignation that I would besmirch his memory . . . except any man would wish his loving wife would remember his skill in lovemaking, so trust me, we do him no dishonor. There, now tell me. Did he know how to touch you to make you pant in that delicious way you had, with half-formed words spilling out of your mouth in a tumble because you were so gone you couldn't even remember how to speak?"

She stared back, mute, and he was fairly confident it was because she had no capacity for speech. This pleased him, and he pressed on.

"Did you dig your nails into his back? I thought I would bear the scars forever. Not that I minded. And biting—God, I still can feel those tiny, sharp teeth of yours sinking into my shoulder just at the moment when you lost control."

"Stop it," she said. "You are—"

"Yes, depraved, I know. Do you remember—"

"No!" she cried sharply, loud enough to get his attention. The shock of it, of what he was doing—what the *hell* was he doing?—brought him up short.

She looked ill, facing him now with an expression that did not satisfy even his cruelest part.

"No, Roman. Stop it now. I don't remember. I never remember. And I never want to."

He brought his head up, shaking loose of her scent. Was it scent? It was spell, then, conjured from scent, and sight, too, and memory, and terrible, terrible wanting.

Moving back, he felt appalled. She'd lied to him. She lied. About Captain Andrew Fairhaven, and he'd gone a bit mad, because that man had been to her what he was not allowed to be.

How he hated Captain Fairhaven. It didn't matter that he didn't know him, didn't matter that it made no sense, that the man had done nothing wrong against him. It only mattered that he had married Trista, and given her a child.

Pain twisted so hard, he gasped, and in that weakened moment, he heard a rustle of skirts and a breeze wafted across his hot cheeks. She escaped, moving past him, and he let her go.

And still, his mind pulsed with obsession. Andrew Fairhaven. Captain . . . sea captain, army captain? Who was he? Why was Trista being so mysterious—was it love, loss? No. He wasn't being stubborn. There was something wrong here. He knew her too well to believe this was all some profound show of grief.

His instincts told him something was there, something deeply secret, and very, very important. And damn it, he was going to find out what it was.

Chapter 7

May laughed softly as Andrew played before her, marveling at the little boy's imagination. He had constructed a makeshift shelter he had concocted for his horse. Three others were positioned in the intricate pattern of the carpet, which were representing various spots in his make-believe world where the horses spoke to each other and had incredible adventures.

He leaped up to press a chestnut mare into her hand. The painted wooden figures had been her brother's when he'd been a boy. She'd thought of them recently and made a present of them to Andrew. Now, he wanted her to play.

"Pretend you are thirsty and you need a drink of water."

Propping the horse on her knee, she made her voice high. "Oh, I am so thirsty. I wish I had a drink of water."

Andrew raced to find the black one with the white star on its forehead. In a voice deepened to show heroism, he said, "Here is water, Misty. Take a drink."

May made slurping noises and Andrew giggled. "Oh, Thunder," she said on a sigh, "that was so wonderful. Thank you."

He was delighted and raced off to get Blade, the gray

horse, when he stopped in his tracks. They were in the front parlor, the formal parlor. They'd come in here rather than the family's drawing room in the rear of the house because the pattern on the carpet was apparently more conducive to a make-believe world. They could hear the knocker from here, and it was that sound that froze him. As the head footman came to answer it, Andrew ran to the pocket doors, which had been left open, and peered around the corner.

May watched him, curious as to why he would behave so. When the caller entered, a gentleman whom they had met at a rout recently, little Andrew craned his neck to see who it was. The man left his card and exited quickly, and the boy ran to the front window, watching him leave.

"Andrew," May said gently, "come here to me."

He trudged on his short legs across the room to stand before her, his head down.

She patted the seat beside her. "Here."

He sat down. She put her arm around him and gathered him close. She expected him to stiffen, perhaps even resist. He was profoundly averse to anything smacking of romance, even eschewing fond pecks from his mother most times. But he wrapped his arms about her and buried his face on her ample bosom.

May smiled and stroked his hair. "Who were you expecting?"

"I didn't want the bad man to come," he said, his voice muffled.

May gently eased him away to hear him better. "Now, who is the bad man?"

"That tall man who came to see Mama. She doesn't like him. He made her cry."

He turned a suffering look toward the door. He looked so small and furious. May felt her heart swell. "I don't want him to come here anymore," Andrew said.

May stroked his silky hair, troubled. She had no doubt the man of whom he spoke was Lord Aylesgarth. Trista always had a strange reaction to that man whenever they met at a society event, and she'd mentioned he'd called on her. Had he made her cry?

Her interest was piqued. She'd recognized him when they'd been at Lady Viola's as the man she had thought she'd known at the Linhope Ball. But she had never met him before that. It was odd. She was usually so good with faces.

She pressed a kiss to the boy's hair. "I shall speak to your mother about it, how is that?"

His grip tightened. "I want her to tell him to go away. He shouldn't make her cry. I don't like him."

"I know." She cuddled him again, waiting until he inevitably pulled away. It was always too soon, and her arms felt empty and aching.

She had never had children of her own. Her marriage . . . that memory brushed painfully against awareness. She immediately suppressed it.

Her marriage had borne nothing but suffering. No children. And in a way, that was a blessing.

"Do you wish to play some more?" she asked him.

He shook his head, looking down at the horse figures scattered at his feet. And it was just then—that gesture—that made it clear. The way he pulled his mouth just so, the angle of his head, and suddenly what had been glaringly obvious was unsheathed and staring her in the face.

"Oh, Lord," she muttered, collapsing back into the seat. In silence, she watched Andrew gather up his toys and walk to the door, trudging in that endearingly earnest way he had.

She sought Trista immediately. She was in the back garden, overseeing the placing of ornamental shrubs. Since her days indulging her creative impulses at the milliner's shop had come to an end, Trista had turned to horticulture as a hobby, and was in the midst of overhauling the garden.

"Indeed, I could use a moment to catch my breath," she said when May asked if she might wish to come in for a glass of lemonade. Pulling off the rough work gloves, she brushed off her skirts and came in.

"What is it?" Trista said, seeing her aunt's face.

May simply replied, "Come inside." She waited until

they were seated in the family's parlor, a pitcher of lemonade sweating before them. "What I have to ask you is a delicate question, Trista. If I am wrong, then I come alarmingly close to calling you a liar. And yet . . . I don't think I am wrong."

Trista's expression was closed. It was almost mulish. This was one of the few things that brought to mind Wooly in this child of his. Whereas Michaela was completely Woolrich made over, both in looks and temperament, Trista was a mystery. May supposed she was like her mother, whom she had not known except through Wooly's diaries. From these she gleaned Judith Nash to be headstrong, proud to a fault, gentle, bright, and intensely private. All of these characteristics were aptly applied to her daughter.

May drew in a breath, wondering if she was about to jeopardize their relationship by asking what she must. "Is Lord Aylesgarth Andrew's father?"

Trista's mouth opened, slackened by shock. She blinked once, then looked away.

"Do not be afraid to tell me the truth. I will not betray you."

She took a long time to respond. "How did you know?"

"I looked at your son while Lord Aylesgarth was in my mind, then marveled at my own stupidity, for he is the picture of the man. When I first set eyes on Aylesgarth, I thought I knew him. I realize now it was the resemblance to Andrew that gave him the impression of being familiar."

Trista's face crumpled and her hands began to wrestle with each other. "Oh, dear. Is it so obvious? I thought it might only be clear to me." She looked desperately about the room, as if searching for someone or something to come to her aid. "This brings great fear to my heart, Aunt. What if Roman should find . . ."

"He does not know," May stated.

Trista shook her head. "It is all very complicated, Aunt May. But, no, I never told Roman that Andrew is his son." Her head dropped.

"I do not know what happened in the past, of course,"

May said carefully, "but it does seem to me that Lord Aylesgarth is more than a bit . . . taken with you. I could have guessed your association had been a close one from the way he has been pursuing you."

"He wishes to renew our relations, but I most certainly am not interested in such a proposition." At seeing her aunt's dubious expression, she explained, "Oh, he seems the civilized man, and he certainly has an appeal. But he lied to me, he betrayed me. He seduced me. He promised himself to me in order to get me to . . . to take advantage of my feeling for him. He then married an heiress."

May looked back at Trista calmly. "But that is the way things are done—"

"Then he suggested—no, *begged* me to become his mistress."

May sighed, taking a moment to straighten the folds of her skirt before speaking. "I know how that suggestion went with your mother from Wooly's diaries, and I don't suppose you were too flattered by the offer, either. But, darling, it is not a betrayal for a young man with responsibilities to propose such an arrangement."

"And what of Andrew? He would be exposed as illegitimate. You see the stigma I contend with as Woolrich's byblow. He would face the same."

May drew up her petite frame. "No one dares speak against you."

"Not openly, but you cannot stem all the innuendos, the stares."

"There was curiosity, yes, and talk at the beginning. We both knew there would be. There will always be small-minded people who will use any flaw, real or imagined, to hold over someone else in order to make greater the sense of their own importance."

"But that is exactly my point. I am accepted because your influence in society is so great. But there would have been no one for Andrew, for at the time I didn't dream you or any of my father's relations would bother with us."

May held up her hand to still Trista. "Yes, I see you felt

you had no choice. Then. But what of now? The man deserves to know he has a son."

"Oh, please do not say that. Don't you think that very thought is constantly in my head?"

"Well, then—"

"But can I trust him? He is a man who does what he wishes, no matter what the effect. He has no discipline, and often has no regard for those he might hurt."

Aunt May wore a look that testified to her less than complete belief. "I saw no evidence of a wicked character. Trista, can it be that, given your past, which is long and deep, I know, you cannot be completely . . . well, *objective,* my dear?"

"I know him better than any other person on this earth," she said, then paused, groping for words. How could she explain Roman? She didn't know where to begin. He was a man she admired in many ways, but he ignited within her a deep, abiding certainty that he was indefatigably dangerous.

"He is spoiled, given to temper . . . He is often thoughtless." She added weakly, "He might hurt Andrew."

"Andrew? Or you?" May waved her hands impatiently, dismissing the question. "I think he hurt you very deeply in the past, and you've made the mistake of thinking that you must always be self-sufficient, self-contained. You are fiercely independent, Trista, which is not a fault by any means, but it is not always best to shut others out. Some people were not meant to be alone. Your mother was comfortable that way, I imagine, but you . . . why look at how it torments you."

Trista ducked her head. "My mother used to say the same."

"You have to make a decision to trust again. Will you live all of your life alone? Oh, Trista, believe me when I say that I know what it is like when the past seems to take over one's perception. I almost influenced Michaela against Adrian because of my own past when terrible things happened . . . well, it isn't important now, but it was a lesson to me about not letting your skeletons get in the way of seeing things as they truly are."

She sat down with an ungraceful plop. "You think I should tell him?"

May was silent, but Trista knew. She twisted away, no longer able to bear her aunt's patient gaze. "I had been thinking that, too. My conscience plagues me day and night. But, Aunt May, he is so inconstant, and I hardly know which side of him to expect. One time he is thoughtful, another time angry . . ."

"Ah. Men such as he do that when they cannot have their way. It is not in their nature to bear frustration. They are men of action, and they will always fight for what they feel in their heart belongs to them."

"I do not belong to him, by his own choice made years ago. But you are correct in how you describe him. He was always incapable of accepting what he did not wish to be."

"He is a strong man, a powerful man. This frightens you."

Sighing, Trista said, "I wish our paths had never crossed again."

May reached out and took her hand. "You must do what is right, Trista. Things have changed. You do not wish to hear me say this, but I must speak. The man has a right to know."

"I know. I do know." Trista braced herself and faced her aunt. She said, "I will think about it, I promise. But I have to think of my son."

Under the benign gaze of Lady May, a thought echoed, as if she were reading her aunt's mind. Not only *her* son.

Roman's son.

On Thursday, Roman passed Trista, flanked by her aunt May on one side and her half sister, Michaela Khoury, on the other as they rode in the park. Michaela's husband, the rather famous Major Khoury, steered his horse smartly close to the flank of the mare his wife rode.

Trista looked fashionable, riding in the saddle with an

air of comfort that impressed him. She had three plumes sticking out of her hat and her waist cinched so tightly in the expertly tailored jacket his hand itched to span it.

She did not even glance his way.

The following Monday, he passed her and Michaela on Bond Street when he was escorting Grace to the shops. Beside him, his sister made a disgruntled noise.

The two parties paused and greeted each other stiffly, but pleasantly. Trista was dressed in some purple thing. He wouldn't have normally noted a lady's dress except that she looked exceptionally fine and her hair as bright as spun sunshine in the daylight. Her hands wrung nervously as she apologized to Grace for not knowing it was her at Lady Viola's tea party.

"You are so different," she said. "I can hardly believe it is you."

"I am taller," Grace said flatly, bordering on ungracious. Her hand, clutched in the crook of Roman's elbow, dug into his flesh even through the light wool sleeve.

Trista tried to laugh. "No, not just that. The years have been very kind to you, Grace."

But such compliments couldn't thaw Grace. At Whitethorn, Trista had often complained that she could never please his sister, and it was apparently still true.

On the Friday nearly a fortnight after that, he glimpsed her at a cotillion. She turned away, and he stewed on the snub, fighting with his temper. He remembered flushing her dance card before and entertained visions of doing so again, but would only humiliate himself.

She didn't want him.

He was frustrated, blocked, thwarted.

Nothing he could do was going to make a difference. He was only making it worse, trotting after her in all his bullying glory to do his worst. Alas, she refused to be terrorized into loving him again.

He danced with Grace, who clung to him, and he took her home early because she had an attack of nerves. He suspected she had spotted Trista.

The following day, he went to visit Annabelle, thinking what he needed was a woman. It had always had remarkable healing properties in the past, ones he and his friends often enumerated with delight. Instead, he realized he was as interested in accompanying her to bed as he was in learning how to needlepoint. He broke it off with her instead, relieved when she took it well.

He saw Trista at the theater that evening and thought he was going to go out of his mind.

And then, on Tuesday next, a letter arrived that changed everything.

It was short, to the point, and absolutely explosive. He trusted the man who'd sent it, but it was important for him to see for himself, so on Wednesday he left London, riding east into Hampshire.

On Saturday, he was able to speak to the parson himself, a Mr. Cordry. He was a middle-aged man, rail-thin, with sparse light-brown hair, and the spry, jerking manner of a ferret. He was kind, however, and helpful. Roman's inquiry seemed to intrigue him, and he took at once to scurrying around his office, pushing his spectacles back into place, for they were wont to slide down his short nose, and pulling book after book down off his shelves.

"Here we have it," he said, finding the right volume and opening it. He showed it to Roman. It was a registry of marriages from the fall of the year he had requested, each printed carefully with all the particulars—date, time, witnesses, etc. Roman flipped through the book, examining every page closely until he was finished.

No mention of a Trista Nash and Captain Andrew Fairhaven.

He sat back and pressed his thumb and forefinger to the bridge of his nose, counterpressure to the tension building there.

Mr. Cordry appeared sympathetic. "Now, mind, my lord, all of this was before my time. I recently came down from Northumbria. Couldn't take the winters there. Cursed cold."

Roman felt a profound disappointment. The Bow Street

Runner he had hired to investigate Trista had found she had gone to live with her cousin, Luci, and Luci's husband, David, in the village of Kenneth in Hampshire after leaving Whitethorn, but he could not get a fix on the dates and the exact sequence of her whereabouts.

It was curious, this sudden pressing need to know, to understand all about her romance, her marriage to Captain Fairhaven. How did they meet? Where?

That blasted knee, at Lady Viola's tea . . . bouncing away, worming doubts and curiosity into his mind. What was it that had sent her into paroxysms of nervous fidgeting? Something there . . .

His man had been unable to find a record of marriage in any of the predictable spots between Kent and the Hampshire hamlet. Had Trista gone some other place, someplace he didn't know, couldn't guess? He could hardly comb all of England searching for the elusive Captain Fairhaven.

She had married quickly after leaving him, he knew that much. He could imagine her, raw and vulnerable after their parting. They'd said vicious things to each other.

She'd hated him, accused him of trying to make her his whore. . . . It still made him sick to recall her tears and fury, how implacable she'd been, how utterly immutable to him. And he'd lost his temper. He'd said things he hadn't meant.

He had no idea they were the last things he would say to her for six years.

"Even if I didn't trust my memory, I trust these books. I keep them meticulously, as did my predecessor. He was a good man, very thorough. You should have seen how organized this place was when I came here."

"He is retired?"

"He died. An ailment of the heart. But I do know Mrs. Fairhaven came to live with her cousin after she was widowed. I distinctly recall reading she wore black to the fall festival, which we hold on All Saints' every year. The parson's wife made mention in her journal of how she made even that drab color look good at the country dance held in the evening."

He passed a volume to Roman. It was a journal of sorts. "Oh, go ahead. It's not the personal sort of thing one might expect. It's about the village, the people, the church, and the general happenings. More like a chronology."

"You've read it?"

"Indeed. It was incalculably valuable when I arrived in familiarizing myself with the people and the customs hereabouts. I have read it most thoroughly. The dance was the first chance the local folk got to get a good gander at Mrs. Fairhaven. The neighborhood, you understand, was somewhat curious. Small communities make much of visits and new arrivals and such. I am certain it is much the same in Kent."

"Indeed it is. And this was in November, then."

They'd parted in the early days of August. Hot temperatures, hot temper, and words that created a gulf that he could not breach. He felt a flash of guilt. He had been so sure of himself, that he was in the right. It had proven precious little comfort.

"Yes, indeed. None of us asked her about her dead husband, of course. Miss Luci had asked us not to, and it was all so raw and new for the poor dear. And then, it was not long after that when it became obvious she was increasing, and my wife said we should all just concentrate on helping her as best we could. Of course, Netty Welpole was a gossip, and she always had a question about the child, but no one allowed her to say much to Mrs. Fairhaven. We all just wanted to help her and her child."

He frowned. "The child?"

He had not given the boy a thought in all of this. It was possible this was just a bit too painful, the thought of her loving another man, having his child, peering into a tiny face and seeing reminders of a husband lost years ago. A constant reminder, more so as he grew and became more the man his father had been.

But now, his mind fixed on the boy. And a deep sense of disquiet stirred, like wind picking up, the first inklings of a storm. "But she'd been widowed for how long?"

"No one knows. I told you, they didn't ask any questions about the captain, it wouldn't have been right. She was so bereaved."

Yes. He'd seen for himself her act of deep grief, so effective at discouraging questions.

Mr. Cordry went on, "But he couldn't have been gone so very long." He went to his desk to retrieve another book, and after a moment of floundering with the pages, he showed Roman the birth registry for Andrew Michael Fairhaven. "His son was born March twenty-fifth of that next year, and that was only five months after Trista arrived here."

March.

His pulse jumped, ticked like a clock wound too tight.

"Which year?" Roman snapped. He peered at the finely printed name, the date, reading it over and over and over.

For it was wrong. It was wrong somehow, but he couldn't figure out exactly how it was wrong, but that *was* because his blood had stopped flowing.

His breathing ceased. He blinked, staring, thinking, disbelieving, then finally his body revived and air rushed into his lungs and his heart began to race and blood thundered in his ears, deafening him with its sound.

It was obvious, of course, so obvious he couldn't quite grasp it, not for a long, long time.

March. March.

"My lord?" Mr. Cordry asked. He leaned forward, concerned. "Lord Aylesgarth? Are you quite well?"

"What time are your guests arriving?" Robert asked.

Lady May turned her face up to his, presenting a very unhappy mouth to be kissed. "Soon enough," she murmured. She sighed contentedly and settled in against him. "I should be getting dressed, but I don't wish to move just yet."

They were in May's small suite, having a lie-in among the mussed covers strewn over her bed. It was not exactly the wisest thing to do, but May had seen that Robert, who usually never complained, had started making disgruntled comments about how they never spent any time of consequence together, and how tired he was of the sneaking about in the night.

He had groused, "I had my fill of such adventures in my youth. I am too old for this."

Two things alerted May to the fact that he was seriously put out. The first was that this was the second time he had mentioned his age—not so very advanced at five and forty as he suddenly seemed to think—and the other was his reference to his past. This he rarely did. So she had taken the comment to heart and suggested a relaxed morning.

She knew he liked spending long, lazy hours in May's company, and she adored the quiet times, the silences that were companionable and cozy, and his strong male presence in the room. Simply having him about was a comfort to her.

They had shared the pot of coffee and stack of newspapers that had come up on the tray May had taken from her bewildered maid, whom she had met at the door, unburdened, and shooed away hours ago. Draining the last from her cup, she turned the page.

"This was a wonderful idea. We should do it more often."

Robert peered over his reading glasses. "We would be doing it often enough if you hadn't allowed that idiot to talk you into getting your walls repapered."

She turned the page. "The smoke had ruined the old paper. And it smelled."

"Yes, in the room with the chimney fire. What of the rest of the house—did that also need redoing?"

She shrugged petulantly. "Well, you can't have new wallpaper in just one room. Once you are having a home made over, it is expected that the entire place will be refurbished."

"Such a lavish undertaking. Not that I care a whit on the expense, as it is your money to do what you will. What bothers me is that it takes too long," he said, flicking his paper to punctuate his annoyance. "I am too—"

"If you are about to say 'old,' Robert, then I beg you to stop. You are young, and virile and handsome and I sigh with wonder at your scaling such heights—figuratively, of course—to see me. This inconvenience will not last forever.

Now shush. I am trying to finish this most scathing article by Lawrence Flatbush."

"That man is a menace." Robert paused to read the political cartoons, then chuckled as he turned his page. "He loves to expose those in power without thought to the morality of what he does. It is all in the sensation he can stir. It sells a good number of newspapers, I know, but why does he have to dress it as if he is after justice? It is ridiculous."

"I am scandalized that you would say so. He is a hero. He backs up all of his accusations with facts and these have been held up, even in a court of law." May put aside the article and rose. "Last week, a man in the Exchequer was convicted of the very crimes Flatbush put forth in that series last fall about false bond sales. Because of Lawrence Flatbush, many people were saved a fleecing."

Robert glanced up from his paper. "I don't suppose anyone but the brilliant Flatbush had an inkling about what was going on. Don't you see, May, he merely gets his cue from the investigators, then jumps upon their parade and takes all the credit."

"You know," she said on a sigh, "sometimes I think you wait to see what I say, then take the opposite tact. You enjoy these verbal battles far too much."

"No to the first, and yes to the second." He rose and gave her a quick kiss and a grin, then dressed.

She donned a simple day dress and tied her hair up. It was time for him to leave, and it was going to be tricky with the servants about and apt to come upon them at any moment.

She checked to see if the way was clear, and brought him downstairs without anyone seeing.

"We have a dilemma," she said, pausing in the hall. "The cellar is out, as the window lets out on the street. During daytime, that is just too much of a risk. The back entrance is out—all the servants are milling about there."

"The garden should serve," he said, directing them to the library. They slipped inside. "I'll use this door to the terrace and scale the fence." He winced at the thought, but didn't mention his age. "I already scouted this possibility although

I never used it before. I didn't wish to leave the door unlocked behind me. Here, come give me a proper good-bye."

May meant to allow him only a quick embrace to say farewell, but it was so warm, so lovely in his arms that she leaned into him a bit and lay her head on his shoulder. She closed her eyes, filling up on the tangy spice of his scent and the secure way his muscled chest bore the weight of her against it.

"Perhaps," she murmured, "I shall call off the wallpaperers. The second floor does not necessarily have to be done. And it is all taking such an inordinate amount of time."

Chuckling, Robert smoothed her hair. "You have what you like. It is a temporary inconvenience—"

May smiled, waiting, but he did not finish his sentence.

"Oh," a voice said from the doorway, and May looked up to find Trista staring at her.

May moved quickly, taking a step back.

Trista said, "I was just looking for Andrew. We are to go to the park." She hovered in the doorway, reluctant to enter. Her eyes kept darting to Robert.

May responded, her voice false and light. "Oh, Trista, this is Mr. Carsons. He has the carriage house down in Hanover Square, you know, the one near St. George's? It's quite the best in London."

"How do you do," Trista said and Robert bowed.

"We were just talking . . . about carriages. I was thinking about a new landau. The one I have is fine, of course, but I thought it might need replacing."

May grasped for self-composure, but she couldn't stop shaking, although she wasn't sure why. A rational part of her wondered if it would be so terrible just to tell Trista about Robert. It wasn't what she or Robert preferred; they'd always kept their affair discreet, but it would hardly be the end of the world. Nor was she embarrassed. She wasn't the type of woman to apologize for what others might think.

But her emotions were another matter. There came over her a sense of panic that was completely illogical.

Was it protectiveness? Robert and all of his secrets were

more vulnerable to unwanted attention than she. He had taken great pains to avoid being noticed for what he was.

She waved her hand jerkily to the door, smiling a smile that probably wasn't fooling anyone. "He was just leaving. Thank you, Mr. Carsons. I will think over the things we discussed and send my man round with my decision."

Robert regarded her with eyes half-closed in scrutiny, and she felt uncomfortable. But it was Trista who concerned her. She was watching closely.

"If you go back to the kitchens, then someone can show you the way out," she said. He stiffened.

What was wrong—she was only playing out the charade. He might rile at being treated as a servant, but it was his farce, not hers. In his dealings with his prestigious clients, he had always carried himself with dignity, never bowing or scraping, but he'd been careful to show proper deference. She couldn't understand why this situation would put him out so.

Then she realized that *she* had never treated him as anything less than her social equal.

Realizing her mistake, there was nothing she could do, not even when he gave her a little bow, not a courtly one but the rough sort that men of his station performed for their superiors, and touched his forelock, that ancient gesture of fealty, which was meant to mock her.

His eyes blazed and she saw the injured pride in him as he said, "G'day, ma'am."

She wanted to call him back immediately. She'd insulted him gravely. But Trista still watched. Rooted to the spot, she stared a moment after Robert, then spun on her heel. "I think I shall go get dressed. Mr. Charbonneau is coming for me in less than an hour."

She didn't see Robert's step pause, his shoulders twitch. But she heard the slam of the door a moment later.

Chapter 8

The arrival of Lord Aylesgarth to the house by Hyde Park was met with a small furor. Luci, who happened to be visiting, kept the restless man occupied in the parlor while Trista escaped upstairs.

Trista found herself clumsy and breathless as she rushed to change her dress and tidy her hair. To say she was shocked when his name had been announced was an understatement. She'd been nearly flattened by the fact that he was once again at her door, begging audience.

There was no reason to fear him, that was what Luci had told her. But she knew better. There was always something to fear from Roman, especially where Andrew was concerned.

When she entered the parlor, she saw Luci had arranged for the tea already. She was seated, and Roman was lounging in a wing chair to her right. His long legs were stretched out before him, and he was playing with a gold coin, which he kept twirling about his fingers absently.

His posture was full of insolence, his face checked anger, and the way Luci sprung up from her seat when Trista entered spoke volumes about his mood.

Oh, Trista knew him like this. No one could do bad manners like Roman.

She plastered a smile in place and went inside, gushing some nonsense about being delighted to see him and how lovely it was that he'd visited them—how long *had* it been?—when he cut her off.

"Your poor cousin has been trying to coax me into civil conversation, and I was forced to tell her that I am not a gentleman, in the sense that I cannot abide prattle when I have something of consequence on my mind."

Luci's wide, anxious eyes swerved from Roman to Trista, filled with abject appeal. Trista was immediately sorry for subjecting her to Aylesgarth while she got her courage up.

He rose rather abruptly, more like unfolding himself as if he had springs in him, a tiger in a box suddenly set free. "I hope you will not take offense, but I would like a private word with Mrs. Fairhaven."

Luci stuck out her stubborn chin. "I am not at all certain that would be proper," she replied.

Dear Luci, she was nearly shaking in her boots, for Roman was absolutely fearsome when he was like this. Trista herself had never been affected by his show of temper, although she'd watched others cower before him most pitifully.

"I will see him, Luci, thank you."

"Perhaps," Roman said, speaking slyly as Luci crossed the room, "you might occupy yourself with the boy. He is about, is he not?"

"He is at his lessons," Trista said quickly.

Roman paused, letting the silence pulse in the room for several beats before moving. He went to a table and lifted a small toy boat. "He might need this when he is through. No doubt he left it behind the last time he played in here. I suppose he sneaks off and plays in here where it is quiet. I used to do the same thing. Isn't that odd, that we would have this in common, or perhaps it is something all boys do."

A storm was about to break. It was best she face it alone. "I have no doubt the latter is correct. Boys love to create their little worlds of competition and mastery, I suppose." To Luci, she said, "You may excuse us. I will speak to Lord Aylesgarth on my own. Thank you."

But she was not out the door when Roman called to her sharply. "Mrs. Miller!"

Luci started and swung around. "Yes, Lord Aylesgarth."

He held up the toy. "For the boy. You mustn't forget it. He might be looking for it."

"Oh. Oh, of course." She came and took the toy from his fingertips, and he smiled at her, a cold smile.

"Thank you. And tell young Andrew . . . well, tell him to take better care with his playthings. It is the curse that we males of the race struggle with, losing the things that matter the most to us."

Luci cast a puzzled glance at Trista, who shrugged and motioned with a slight jerk of her head that she should go.

When they were alone, Trista squared her shoulders and faced him. "I don't suppose you are interested in refreshment."

"Whiskey if you have it."

"I was thinking of tea." She indicated the tray.

"A waste of time. Come to think of it, the whiskey wouldn't help, either."

"Why have you come, Roman?"

"Ah. Yes. Well, it is a delicate matter."

"Stop toying with me. You have a very distinct purpose, and I wish to know what it is."

"And cheat myself of this lovely moment? I think not. I am owed some compensation for what you have done to me, don't you think?"

Her heart skipped a beat. "What do you mean?"

"I am curious," he said, ignoring her question. "About that most important male in your life."

He's going to ask about Andrew! she thought, and the floor under her seemed to dip.

"You know who I mean," he taunted, approaching her with a satanic grin.

She opened her mouth, and a part of her collapsed inside, resigned. But no voice came forth.

"Captain Fairhaven is who I am speaking of, of course," he said.

"What?" She was too surprised to hide it.

"Yes. The good Captain Fairhaven. Was he a war hero? I wondered about this, you see. It rankles, because he was such a better man than I. He had to be, as you married him after you left me. I recall how determined you were when we quarreled that last time at Whitethorn, how brave, the color high on your cheeks and your eyes that marvelous steel color they deepen to when you really mean business. We had been at it for days before that, and then that last time, you were so cold. I felt the difference in you. I suppose I knew then that you were lost to me."

He is asking after Captain Fairhaven. He is merely jealous.

"And so I have come to wonder if it was something else that gave you strength to end it. Had you already met your husband? Because if you had, then it would explain everything."

He bent his head, and his voice softened. "I could never understand how you could leave me like that. We had gone round and round about this issue of my marriage, and then one day you were gone."

"There was no point to any more discussions. You were set on your marriage for gain. I was set on not becoming your mistress. We had reached an impasse. I left."

"Yes, yes, but the abruptness of it was what always bothered me, Trista. Yet you left everything behind, every last trinket in your little room, all your clothing, even your handkerchiefs. And no good-bye. I admit, that stung."

"I was afraid that you would not allow it to rest. I thought a sudden parting like that would be the only way to break off."

"Ah. So no Captain Fairhaven at that time?"

"No."

"You met him later."

"Yes, I did. When I went to visit Luci, who took me in."

"I see." He nodded, thoughtful. "I suppose I can understand it now that you've explained it. And you were right to take off without a word. I might have kidnapped you and held you against your will had I known what you planned. I was hopelessly in love with you. I wouldn't have given you up for anything."

"But you did." A feeling of coldness took over now that she was remembering. "You did as your father asked, and he asked you to marry an heiress."

"It was an impossible choice. Did you know how I agonized over it?"

She blinked. She'd not troubled herself with thoughts of his end of it. Her difficulties were quite enough to occupy all of her imagination.

Soon after she'd found out Roman was to marry another woman, she'd discovered she was pregnant with Andrew, and she could spare no sympathies for Roman after that; all of her focus had to go to providing a future for her child, and that meant lying her way to her child's legitimacy.

"I didn't think of that," she admitted.

"No," he purred. "That was quite unfair of you, I thought. It eases my soul that you did not find refuge with your dashing Captain Fairhaven until after you'd left me."

"Must we discuss this again?" she cried suddenly. She had a rather strange feeling out of the blue. He was playing with her. His tone held a touch of mockery, his eyes the glint of dark mischief.

She knew that look from old.

"What? Us? Or your precious captain? Because I know how it pains you to speak of him. I have seen evidence quite frequently that you discourage even the most casual of questions regarding him. The poor man, forgotten so quickly. Well, I suppose it is what happens when one is a made-up person. I mean, fictitious personages cannot expect to be hailed and regaled, can they?"

The room gave a twist, a sudden alteration of orientation. She swayed, caught herself. "What did you say?"

"I said he wasn't real. You made him up." He took exactly three steps, three precise, purposeful steps to tower over her. "And the reason you left without telling me was that you panicked. You found yourself with child, and you fled. Now. Tell me I am mistaken, Trista. I shall watch to see if you lie."

Her knees buckled and she felt herself go, then his hands were on her, holding her up, then she was against him, feeling his warmth, his power.

"Open your eyes, Trista, and look at me. Don't be such a coward."

She obeyed him, pathetic and defenseless. She gazed up and found his face hard, his mouth tight.

They stared, their noses nearly touching. Then his lips parted as his mouth went slack and all the hard edges of him softened. In his eyes, a desperate light animated the deadness that had been there before, and his hands clutched her differently.

"Trista," he murmured, and bending his head slightly, he brought her closer still. He hesitated, and she could feel his muscles strain as impulse battled against will.

She dug her fingers into his strong shoulders. Her head was swimming with shock, and with this nearness. How strange that her impulse was to bury her face against his chest and hide, when it was him she was hiding from.

He was built like a blacksmith. Men of his quality were long, elegant figures, cultivating a fey appearance to conform to the fashions set by the elegant dandies of the day, but Roman was solid, hard. Yet he put all those dashing figures forever to shame. No man could match him, nor the feeling of utter permanence, of power, of consequence. He moved lower, closer, and his lips found hers.

It was a hungry kiss, deep and long, and she felt as if she'd come home, which was so strange in the midst of his pronouncement. She wanted to cry, but whether this was caused by the realization that he knew about Andrew or because she was locked in his arms, she couldn't tell.

Emotion overwhelmed her. The relief of an unburdened

conscience, the thrill of his nearness, the tart fear of what he would do now, sharpened each nerve until she thought she would shatter in his arms. Somehow, her bones held tight, and drew on his strength and passion.

She caught his face gently in her hands, the rough-smoothness of his cheek—yes. She remembered the silken texture of his male skin, taut and firm, hard muscle and bone underneath. She'd never kissed another man, never touched one. She'd never wanted to. This man was all she'd ever craved. Time shifted out of existence and she loved him. It only took one kiss, and all that had happened to tear them apart was erased. Gone.

He pulled her away from him, and she looked up, bewildered and sad to lose the beauty of the kiss, and she saw his face shift again into coldness. She made a small sound of protest as he shook his head, fighting with himself as much as fighting to deny her the comfort they had just shared.

He stepped back, and she stumbled on unsteady legs. Although the support of his tall frame was gone, his hands were there to guide her, but they did not linger. He steered her to a chair, and she sank into it, head bent.

It was painful to look at him.

He'd hate her. Proud man, he'd never understand, not ever. For lying to him, for taking away his son, he'd hate her forever, and only now, after his kiss and the realization that he was still the only man she wanted, did she realize how great a hurt it was.

With an effort, she tilted back her chin and faced him again.

He was so handsome, and still vulnerable for all the thunder in his face right now. He said in a strong, quiet voice. "Fetch him to me."

Oh, no. He couldn't mean . . .

"He doesn't know," she stammered.

"I will see him. He must be told, of course, but you may do that. I have no desire to punish the boy. You will find the right time to do it gently. However, for today, I *will* see him."

She shook her head mutely. This was not to be tolerated. They must talk, the two of them, before Andrew was brought into it. Bringing him before Roman . . . it was too sudden, too quick . . .

She should have told him when she'd first realized that he deserved to know, and then *she* would have been in control of the situation, but she'd cowered from it and now she had no choice.

"Trista," he said, "bring me my son."

"Who told you?" she asked.

"I will answer your questions later. I am sure you have many of them. I, too, have a great many things that I wish to know. But now . . . I wish to *see* him."

"Do not hurt him," she blurted. The moment the words came from her lips, she saw him recoil. "I meant only that you are in a mood and that you should have a care about being gruff."

His eyes glittered. "I did not ask any direction for when I view my son."

Her trembling had changed to violent shaking. She picked up the bell to ring for the maid, and dropped it. She had to kneel on the carpet to retrieve it, nearly falling when she did so for her legs were still water. All this he watched dispassionately, but there was no malice in him. Only a dreadful, implacable coldness.

She rang the bell and presently, a maid entered.

"Sandra, please send my son to me. I wish him to meet Lord Aylesgarth."

Sandra disappeared, unaware, of course, that she was bringing the young master of the house to meet his father. Despite the obvious resemblance between the boy and Lord Aylesgarth, one would have to be alerted, as were Aunt May and Luci, to piece together the relation.

The silence was awful. She bit her lips to keep from weeping, feeling like a ninny to sit here and battle tears. What an ineffectual idiot she was. Disaster approached with the unlikely sound of Andrew's new shoes clicking smartly on the marble in the foyer.

She lost her nerve, and stood, drawing Roman's gaze. Her son was just outside the door, and she didn't know what Roman was going to do. This revived her.

She only had time to say, "Please!" before the door opened and the boy came in.

"Mama?" Andrew said. He came straight to her, but his eyes were on Roman. They were wary, large and luminous. Roman's eyes in that little face looking at Roman, and now, with the two of them in the same room so that she could look from one beloved face to the other, it was astonishing how similar they were.

Roman did nothing. He said nothing. Nor did he move, except that his hand at his side lifted. She could see a palsied flutter as it floundered for a moment, finding purchase on the edge of the table beside him. But he didn't shift his weight to it, or move other than to track the little boy with the measured slide of his gaze.

"Mama?" Andrew said again, his soft little boy's voice hitched up just a bit.

"This is Lord Aylesgarth, Andrew. He has asked to speak with you."

"I know him," Andrew replied, his tone conveying his distaste.

Roman watched this, took it all in—the boy, the face, the mood, the angry eyes leveled at him. After a moment, he said, "Hello, Master Andrew."

"Hello," Andrew said, for she'd taught him to be polite. But it was a grudging greeting.

They stared at each other, unaware or uncaring of the awkwardness of it. The boy remained belligerent, the man . . . Roman's expression was raw.

She placed a hand on Andrew's shoulder. "Where are your manners?"

"I said hello," he replied. He twisted to look back at her, his eyes sharp as they peered into her face.

"It was Lord Aylesgarth who found your little boat. Did Aunt Luci give it to you?"

He didn't seem impressed. But he murmured a thank-you under his breath.

Trista was puzzled. Andrew was normally outgoing and not shy with strangers at all. He had taken to Lady May right off, and the new staff were constantly finding the little boy in their midst, eager to tell them his imaginary adventures or coax them into a game of draughts. But he was very unhappy with this interview, and there was no mistaking the looks he threw Roman's way.

"I want a biscuit," he said. He pointed to the tea tray. Before Trista could correct him he corrected himself. "May I please have a biscuit?"

Trista looked at Roman, who gave a slight nod. "Go ahead. Let us take a napkin and make a tiny satchel, then you can take the treats with you. You may go back to your lesson."

The boy went to the tray and began heaping selections into a cloth napkin. This motion seemed to release Roman from his frozen state, for he spoke again. "Do you like boats?"

Andrew shrugged. "I like them. My father was a sea captain."

A slight pause. "Yes. I recollect that now."

"I'm going to be a sea captain one day," he said, bunching the edges of the napkin together clumsily.

"Here," Trista said, intervening, "you'll crush them. Let me."

Andrew snatched his little satchel of goodies and fled from the room.

"Andrew!" Trista admonished, and took a step to follow the child and bring him back for a proper farewell, but Roman held up his hand. She flushed hotly, at once embarrassed by her son's bad manners—she'd taught him better and couldn't imagine what would prompt him to such rudeness—and the fact that Roman had, in that one curt command, taken his role as father, overriding her impulse to call Andrew back.

She almost disregarded it, but she didn't dare.

No. She didn't dare.

He stared after the boy, and in the protracted silence her thoughts were given ample opportunity to flourish into awful possibilities as to what Roman was going to do next. When she could stand it no more, she asked him.

He looked at her, his eyes focusing on her as if he only just now recalled she was in the room. He turned his back and strolled to gaze out the window.

"The boy must be told in time. Until then, I wish to be given an opportunity to visit him, get to know him so that it will not be a shock. He is mistrustful of me. This cannot continue."

"If you come to the house, are observed with the boy, there will be . . . speculation. Is it your wish to claim him openly as your bastard?"

She spoke this last word with enough vehemence to snap his head around. He glared at her, angry, in pain.

She didn't blame herself, even if she'd done him a grave wrong. She'd protected her child. She'd saved Andrew from the taint of illegitimacy, something she knew plenty about. She was not going to stop now.

"You have kept him from me for five years."

"And I would have for five more or for all of his life to save him what I knew as a child. It is not a treasured thing to be illegitimate."

"You are hardly in your mother's shoes," he said dismissively.

"Yes. Recently, I became an heiress. I am redeemed. I have money, good blue blood in my veins that comes with connection to power so that I need never fear being cast out to the street to starve. Except that the scandal of it would follow him all his life, and I would do anything to protect him from all that would hurt him."

"How noble you are," he said scathingly. "If you are trying to make me feel sorry for you, it will not work. You did this because you hated me. You stole my child from me."

"He is my child."

"Do you forget how he was made?" he said suddenly,

taking a bold step forward. "Do you forget those long, lazy nights without sleep when we played with passion and pleasure? I assure you I do not, so if you are claiming sole responsibility for the boy, I will challenge you, for I can recollect distinctly that I was there. Those memories have not vanished, for they were of some import to me. He *is* my son as well, a fact you've conveniently forgotten."

"I only have to look at him to be reminded," she snapped, then whipped her head away, sorry she'd said it.

His voice changed. "Did it bother you, that he takes his looks from me?"

"No." It was an honest answer. She would not elaborate.

He crossed the room and gathered his hat and gloves. "I wish to acquaint myself with him, so if you could ease the transition, it would be wise. I will not be kept away by pouts and sullen looks. I am his father, and one day he will know it."

That imperiousness was back in his tone. She knew he took refuge in being obnoxious, as he'd always done as a boy when his back was against the wall. By the level of his objectionable arrogance, she could always measure his discomfiture.

"I need time," she said.

"You have a week." He pulled on his gloves. "I've been kept from him quite long enough."

"What do you intend?"

He paused. "I don't exactly know. I am more oriented toward what I do not intend, and that is to be kept a stranger in my son's life any longer. We can discuss his education and other matters when I visit."

"I have made those arrangements. His tutor—"

"But these decisions are not yours alone any longer, are they?" He gave her a tight smile. "I will arrange to have an allowance put aside for him. My solicitors will contact yours with the details."

"That is not necessary," she said, and he leveled a quelling look at her that stifled the protest quickly.

He was headed toward the door when he paused, his hat

in hand, framed in the doorway. Without turning around, he asked in a voice much softened, "Did you . . . did you think I would not want him?"

"Things were very different then, and I was . . ." Young, foolish, naïve, afraid.

No excuses. She would not explain, or plead with him . . .

Oh, but she couldn't resist. "What else could I have done? Continue as your mistress as you had wished? Then he would have been openly known as your child, conceived and born out of wedlock. That I would not have. You knew well enough how it was for me."

"You were always safe at Whitethorn."

"No, Roman, I did not think you would wish to give me the kind of protection I required. You were to marry, you had your new wife to give you children. It didn't seem possible that there could be a good way to bear out the situation, so I thought it was best Andrew and I make due on our own."

"And now, recently meeting me again here in London? You kept him from me all of this time."

She sighed, shaking her head to convey her regret. "I thought of telling you, agonized over it, truly I did. But it was done, and it is not such an easy thing to undo."

He nodded, but she doubted it was in agreement or understanding, but simple acknowledgment that she had given some sort of answer. He did look at her then, his gaze tight with a scrutiny that was not kind.

"I liked to flatter myself that I knew you, knew you so well you could never deceive me. It was conceit on my part. I was wrong, it seems. You are a good liar after all."

He left then, and she stood for long moments, sucking in great lungfuls of air, hoping the oxygen would chase the queasy feeling in her chest.

Chapter 9

The house was like a house in mourning. Sitting with May and Luci in the sunlit conservatory, Trista battled the constant hiccups of panic as they discussed Roman's visit.

Luci asked, "Do you have any idea how he learned about the boy?"

Trista shook her head, then sighed. "Lies are flimsy things. There are a million ways for him to have found the truth. Roman cannot let go of something once it gets in his blood. He would not have let the matter rest, and I'm afraid my own silliness put him wise to something being amiss. I should not have averred so poorly when asked about the captain . . . I should have had a ready story and spoken . . ."

May reached out and grasped her hand. "I am not without power, you know. He is merely a lord, and not mighty here in the city."

"No. That is not what I want. After all, he is in the right, isn't he? I should have told him, you said so yourself."

"Perhaps you would have, in time."

Trista thought about that. She rather thought she would. Even his finding out in such a fashion was a relief. The worst had happened, and she was going to cope with it.

"I think he will be very gentle with Andrew," she told the other women, "although Andrew is against him. I don't know why."

"Oh, dear. I am afraid that little monkey overheard you and Roman one afternoon and took a dislike to the man because he had upset you." She looked to Luci, who said, "You know how he is."

"Of course." Trista let out a protracted sigh. "He gets that stubbornness from Roman, of course."

Luci and May exchanged a look. Seeing this, Trista demanded, "What is it?"

"I rather think it is you who gave him that trait." Luci laughed. "You are as bullheaded as . . . well, a bull."

"I've had to be!" she defended.

"Perhaps," Lady May said diplomatically. "The issue here is not what was done. No one can argue with the concerns you had for Andrew, and as we all love him, we want him to be safe, and happy, and a good future secured. What *is* at issue is what is to be done. Do you know, Trista, what Lord Aylesgarth plans?"

Trista shook her head. I know he is hurt and angry."

May nodded. "Naturally. Men do not like their power usurped. They take it as the natural order that they make all the decisions, and you made a most fundamental one in taking your son off to raise by yourself. It will take some time before he is able to forgive you."

"I don't think he ever will."

"Trista," Lady May said, her voice slightly admonishing, "if you do not wish for Lord Aylesgarth to judge you, you must not judge him."

"But I know him, you forget."

May gave her a cryptic smile. "*Knew* him, my darling. There is a difference."

Those words played in Trista's mind, and perhaps they had a hand in the dream she had that evening. Or it could have been the storm.

There'd been a gale like that that last night she'd spent with Roman, before she knew she was with child, before she knew it would be the last time they'd make love. In the dream, she found herself back in that small room at Whitethorn.

Around her were her belongings. Her self in the dream hardly noticed them. They were ordinary, things she'd looked at so often they were not remarkable, but a part of her that wasn't in the dream catalogued each one.

There was the fan her mother had given her for her seventh birthday, the doll Grace had broken, a fistful of shriveled wildflowers that Roman had presented to her when she'd been ill for a week with influenza. The books that had been her presents for Christmases past were lined neatly on a shelf. She'd long outgrown the simple stories, but she looked at them from time to time when she wanted to remember her mother and the strong, animated voice reading to her by candlelight.

She became aware of the sound of the wind, the rain pelting the small window, and turned in the bed, clutching the soft coverlet, one of the extravagances Mama had finagled since becoming Madam's companion.

She snuggled deeply in the comfort of the bed. How contented she was. She liked it here. It was the only home she'd ever known. She was in love, happy. She wanted nothing to change.

Then, Roman stirred and she realized he was in the bed with her. The crisp crackle of lightning made her cower into him and he chuckled, drawing his arms around her.

"You are very rude to wake my pleasant sleep," he said softly.

She breathed his scent, squeezing shut her eyes to block out the blaze of the violent atmosphere beating against the house. She felt frightened, although she usually loved storms. The feeling of fear seeped out of the dream, drenching Trista's sleeping form in sweat.

"Nothing can hurt you," Roman said, no longer laughing at her. He kissed her, and she fell back, limpid and willing to be taken to the edge of the world.

"It will always be like this," she whispered into the dark.

He kissed her again. He looked at her, his eyes soft and filled with emotion. His hair was mussed from the bed, his mouth slack and swollen from kisses and bites. He toyed with a lock of her hair, and the feel of his fingers tangled in the strands made her eyelids droop in lassitude.

And then they weren't in the bed. In the way of dreams, the setting changed suddenly and they stood facing each other out on the open fells, atop a pile of rocks they had made their own place. Roman said, "Something has happened. I must marry."

She knew he did not mean her.

"Someone my father picked. I've only just met hcr. She's rich, boring, stupid, and plain as pudding. The most important thing on the list is, of course, the first, for the family needs money."

And then everything was black and oily. She saw nothing, heard only his voice as she wandered unmapped places of her dream. "Nothing will change, Trista. We will still be together. It will hardly matter."

He was there before her again all of a sudden. He grinned, held out his arms. And suddenly he was falling away. In the dream, distance was flooding the space between them, and she had to shout her words to be heard. She heard them ring hollowly, as if a great vacuum had swallowed the both of them whole. "But you said you wished to marry me."

He said something, but she could not hear him. He was almost gone.

Her mother's voice rang clear, and she turned to see her sitting next to her, surrounded by the blackness that had torn Roman and her apart.

Men of quality are different than we are, Trista. The money, the status, it is more important to them than love, and they don't understand what really matters. They only understand power.

Not Roman, Mama, she'd thought so many times as she'd lain with him, laughed with him.

But her mother only shook her head, then turned to the void where Roman had been.

Roman went alone to visit his son. Grace had wished to come. He promised her that after he had the opportunity to know the boy better, get him feeling at ease, he would bring him round for an introduction.

He had known, but not shared with her, that the boy hadn't taken to him very well. How furious the little face had been, mulish and so startlingly like his own that Roman had been dumbstruck. He'd wanted to go down on his knee and take the small stranger in his arms. He'd wanted to shout at him to wipe that arrogance off of his face this instant, that he was in the presence of his father, and damn it, he was to show respect.

Neither of which was probably an effective means of winning a reticent child.

He blamed himself for the boy's aversion to him. He had to have looked severe, stricken as he was by the heady experience of looking at his own child for the first time. He had frightened the boy, made him wary.

He was determined to do better. It could not be difficult to win a child with what he had planned today.

Children were simple, uncomplicated—at least, children who had good homes were. Weren't they?

He was hopeful that Andrew would prove pliant in time. Trista always knew the love and devotion of her mother. Therefore, she would have been a good mother to Andrew, and so it would stand to reason that the boy would be secure, well-tended, not apt to bad temper as Roman had been. He had himself been a boy neglected, mistrustful and angry. But Andrew had not had these disadvantages. It should be easy to win him to his favor.

With these optimistic thoughts, he rapped upon the front door. They were dashed within moments of being shown into the front parlor.

Trista came in, dressed in a peacock day dress that was so flattering he momentarily forgot he was here for the child.

He simply stared, and his pulse, already elevated by the excitement of his mission, began to race swiftly.

She was so very pretty. Soft and feminine, each curve beckoning his gaze. The only thing about her that was not becoming was her expression. It was not welcoming.

"This is a terrible idea," she said.

"I asked that Andrew be made ready by one o'clock. It is nearly that time. Is there a problem, an afternoon rest period I didn't know about, a punishment that precludes him having an outing?" His voice was clipped, covering the slight waver he was sure only he could hear. "If so, I have to insist this excursion take precedence. I have waited a long time."

"He is not ready."

"Then I will wait." He lowered himself into a chair.

She wrung her hands. "You do not understand. I don't mean he's not ready in the sense . . . what I do mean is that he does not wish to go. I told him that you were a friend and wished to take him out for a special day, a treat, but he refuses. He doesn't understand. You are a stranger."

"If the boy balks, it is from good sense. Of course I am a stranger." He paused, drawing out the last word and was rewarded with the sight of her embarrassment staining her buttermilk complexion. Yes, he wasn't above a dig or two. He was not going to overlook what she'd done to him.

"Which is the purpose of this outing," he went on. He addressed himself to removing his gloves. He hated wearing the things. "My remaining a stranger cannot be allowed to continue."

"Then call on him here at the house. I will bring Andrew in to speak with you. We will introduce him to you gradually."

"No. This house is your home. He will not accept me here." He didn't know how to put into words what his instinct told him. He was the intruder in every aspect—in the house and in the family.

"You will frighten him by taking him away, and then it will not serve your purpose to having him relax, get to know you."

"My objective is not to become his friend," Roman pronounced, "but to bring him to acceptance of me as his father. This I will do. However, I do not wish to incur his resentment. I have decided to handle this delicately, giving much deference to the boy's feelings, but I will not be stayed. Do not mistake me, Trista."

She was disconcerted, anxious. A mother's worry, he saw, and something tight and warm twisted in his belly. He was not angry.

He said, "Why don't you come with us, then? It will make it easier on the boy to have you along."

"I thought you wished to spend time with him alone."

He pretended to shrug off the changing of his mind. The idea of her presence was oddly comforting. He was nervous about taking the boy, the truth be told. After all, Andrew *was* his son. His only child. It wouldn't do to have the boy despise him.

"I shall await you," he pronounced imperiously, as if the matter was already settled.

She nodded, her soft curls bobbing. Her cheeks, high with color, glowed and she almost smiled, so relieved was she, and he wanted to hold her, tell her it was going to be all right.

When she returned, it was with Andrew. The boy looked at Roman resentfully. He had to swallow hard against the pain lodged in his throat. Why did he dislike him so much? Was he this unfriendly to everyone?

"You remember Lord Aylesgarth," Trista said with forced cheer.

The little boy bobbed his chin.

Roman met Trista's distressed look, and donned a smile. "Of course, he's a bright boy and not likely to forget me. Let's be off, then. Enough dawdling."

He had tried to sound off-the-cuff and jovial, but it had come out much too commandeering. The boy lowered his head and trudged after his mother, his hand firmly lodged in hers.

As he took them to the waiting carriage, it struck Roman

what a poor idea this was. Mother and son walked comfortably together, and he left to be the outsider.

Today was meant to change that, but it only seemed to make it all that much more apparent that he was not part of their happy, self-contained little world. He had no place with them.

Oh, Lord, he thought miserably, here I am again.

*The first indication that the afternoon was going to be a dis-*aster was that Andrew did not so much as ask where they were going. Surely, any child would naturally be curious, even a bit excited, one would dare hope. The very fact that he did not do so pointed to his aversion to the outing.

The second was that when Roman presented Andrew with a box with a large red ribbon upon it, Andrew only stared at it.

"Go on," Roman said, his voice a bit rough. "It is for you."

Andrew looked appealingly to his mother. "Open it," she said, sounding pleasant, but making her eyes convey her meaning that she meant it as a command.

Andrew pulled off the ribbon, opened the tin box, and stared without expression at the neatly lined carved wooden soldiers.

Roman pointed to them when Andrew didn't say anything. "These are the Horse Guards. Major Khoury was a member of the Horse Guards. See, this one"—he picked up one with a particular design to the painted uniform—"is exactly like the major."

Andrew continued to look at the gift, not touching. "I have toy soldiers."

"But these arc special." Trista could have kicked herself for interfering but she couldn't help herself. "You liked Major Khoury, do you remember? Would it not be interesting to have these, since they are like his regiment?"

He shrugged.

Roman grinned. "If they are not to your liking, I shall

take them back to the toymaker and select something else. My guess is a boat would be assured to make you smile."

He said it heartily, with no trace of bitterness. This surprised Trista.

The third indication of Andrew's sullen mood was the way he slumped down in his seat. When he pulled out one of his small toy boats and concentrated on them, making noises as he played and paying no attention to the adults, Trista knew he was not going to give the slightest measure.

Roman did the exact worse thing. He tried to engage the boy in conversation.

"What subjects do you enjoy with your tutor, Andrew?"

It was unthinkable that that boy wouldn't answer an adult, although it was clear he would have liked to ignore the question. He kept his eyes on his boat and said, "Arithmetic."

"Good at numbers are you?"

There was a noncommittal motion of the shoulders. It could have been a yes or a no.

Trista said, "Andrew is already able to count all the way to one hundred."

"Two hundred," Andrew corrected. He unstuck his gaze and slid it to her, as if taking her to task silently for underestimating him.

"That is an excellent accomplishment."

"And he can do addition and subtraction." Trista hoped this would prod Andrew's pride to show off some skill. At least he'd be speaking. "Would you like to do some figures, and show Lord Aylesgarth?"

"I don't feel like doing numbers," Andrew said, "my tummy hurts."

Roman looked instantly alarmed. "Is he ill?" He shot bolt upright, as if ready to throw open the door and summon the surgeon at a moment's notice.

"He is fine," Trista assured him.

"I'm not fine. My tummy hurts. I need to lie down."

Roman pinned a panicked look on Trista. "He isn't going to retch, is he?"

"Don't give him any ideas," she said drolly. "Andrew will be fine once he sees where we are going. Ah, where are we going, Lord Aylesgarth?"

"To the park, I thought. Not Hyde Park. I am sure you go there quite often, and I thought that something new might be of interest. We can go down to St. George's, where I had heard there may be ballooning today. I thought this might interest Andrew."

"Does it have a pond?" Andrew asked, showing enthusiasm for the first time.

Trista explained, "Andrew likes the water to play with his boats."

"I am going to be a sea captain," Andrew announced.

Roman paled. "I see. Well, I don't know if it does have a pond. But we . . ."

He trailed off, for the brief flare of animation had disappeared and Andrew sank back into the cushions, deflated.

"Andrew," Trista said pleasantly, pausing with a clear signal to her son that she expected him to look at her. "Ballooning sounds quite exciting. Don't you agree?"

He made a sour face, as much as he dared, but bobbed his chin. An affirmative.

"I think it sounds just wonderful," Trista said, but it was too late. Roman stood, flipping up the hatch on the roof. At his full height, his head and shoulders cleared the opening, obscuring him as he spoke to the driver.

While he was doing this, Trista, who was sorely vexed with her son, took the toy boat from Andrew. At his indignant expression, she said quietly, "You will have it returned when your manners improve."

Roman settled back. He expelled his breath, and Trista watched him swipe at his hair, a sign that he was exasperated. Beside her, the small boy did the same.

They went to Hyde Park, their carriage one of the few in the The Ring. It wasn't the fashionable hour for seeing and being seen, but that was not why they were here.

"There's the pond," cried Andrew, who had perked up when he saw where they were headed.

"You didn't have to do this," Trista said. She wished he hadn't. Somehow, it felt wrong to see him defeated so soon.

He ignored her. "That's not a pond. It's the Serpentine. It is a veritable lake."

Andrew looked at him askance. It was the first time Roman's voice had not been tentative when addressing him.

They alighted and Andrew stood poker straight and told Roman that he had enjoyed the drive very much and thank you, after which his mercenary motive became apparent when he begged Trista to return his boat.

She wouldn't have, but she didn't want Roman to know that she had tried to intercede, so she fished it out of her reticule and handed it to him. "Yes, here it is."

"May I go—"

"Yes."

Roman strode after him. He hadn't been fooled, however. She had seen his eagle eyes taking in the exchange.

She sighed and followed. For some reason, Aunt May's observation that perhaps her claim to know this man was not as accurate as she would think popped into her mind. She had known him well in the past, but this was six years later. Could he have changed? He seemed different.

And then, sometimes, he was exactly the same.

They walked along the bank, the man and the boy separated but somehow synchronized, so that when the boy paused, the man did. When Andrew hunkered down with his boat, Roman bent and picked up some rocks.

She stood and watched him examine them, turning them over, weighing them. Those that passed muster, he slipped into his trouser pockets, ruining the smooth lines of the well-tailored garment.

Her eyes filled, a surge of memory hitting her so hard she couldn't bear it. She'd seen him just so more times than she could think, choosing his stones.

Then he took the first one, curling the index finger of his right hand around it and with that peculiar stance—shoulder to the lake, half-crouched—he whipped it with a flick of his wrist. The stone flew, hopping once, twice . . . all of five times before plunking into the depths of the Serpentine.

Andrew looked up.

Roman took another rock out of his pocket and made ready. He released it in that powerful spurt of energy that used to fascinate her, but this one was a dud.

He muttered a curse, and she smiled at the determined look on his face. Fishing in his pocket, he pulled out something that was not a skipping rock. Trista couldn't see what it was, however, although she was intrigued, for he seemed to wish to stuff it back into his pocket out of sight, giving Andrew a furtive look as if to make sure he hadn't seen it.

The next rock he produced brought an eager grin. He really got himself set and released it with flourish. Seven skips. He was quite pleased with himself.

"How do you know how to do that?"

Andrew had addressed the question.

"I used to go to a pond when I was a boy."

"Did you sail boats?"

"Sometimes. I skipped stones, fished, taught myself how to swim. My best friend, Jason, knew how, but I would have been damned first before I'd ask him to show me."

"Lord Aylesgarth," Trista clucked, "such language."

"Oh." He was startled, not realizing what he'd said. He looked at her, sheepish, and the look was impossibly familiar.

He showed Andrew the sorts of rocks to look for—flat with some weight to them so that they really flew when you threw them. Andrew hunted with him, finding a few Roman deemed worthy. Trista noted that he didn't patronize the boy, rejecting most of the selections. But Andrew didn't grow discouraged.

When it came time to throw them, Andrew said, "No, thank you," and turned back to his boat.

Trista sat on a bench, watching them and thinking of all the ways it could be different right now. And yet, she didn't regret a thing. Not having had her secrets. And, strangely, not having them found out.

Roman came to sit with her. They didn't speak. They watched Andrew together for a long while.

"What was he like? As a baby."

"He was always wonderful. Very curious, very energetic. He has a temper."

"It stands to reason, given his heritage." She didn't know if he meant himself or her, but it wasn't worth pursuing. He was right. Either way Andrew looked to his ancestry, he could find a proud and sometimes haughty legacy.

"I mean, what sorts of things did he do? What did he like, what did he wish for?"

"He had a morbid fascination with insects when he was two. He collected them for a while the summer before we came to London, and I would have to take him on long walks of discovery so that he could find new specimens for his collection. He made great ceremony of the collecting, the supplying of each pet insect with a comfortable home, providing food, and then at the end of the day we would release them all because he was worried their mamas would miss them."

He laughed, and she joined him.

"Thank goodness that is at an end," she said.

"He loves boats." Roman squinted into the sun.

"And horses."

"But boats because of his father, the sea captain. I assume he has been curious about his father."

"He has wished for information, yes, and I've told him what I thought he could understand. His father could not be with us because he was a sea captain and was lost at sea."

"Perhaps that is why he wishes to become a sea captain himself. To find his father. He might have taken you literally in the man being 'lost' in the sea."

"I had not thought of that. The interest in ships and his father is rather recent, after coming to London. David, Luci's husband, used to teach Andrew through his books, and the ones about ships and sailing on the sea were always a favorite. They would pore over them together, and David, who is wonderful at telling stories, would embellish everything into a yarn about pirates and captains, etcetera, and I suppose that was what made the entire prospect of his father being this heroic figure so appealing."

Roman nodded. "It's in a boy's nature to look up to a father, and I suppose an absent one is all the more enticing."

She remembered how fiercely he idolized his own father, whose yearly visits to Whitethorn caused such excitement. The Lady Aylesgarth would rouse herself from her bed to inspect the house and, often under Mama's guidance, begin to take an interest in her appearance.

The entire house came alive with activity, but none was so changed as the young lord. Roman would be in a perpetual state of agitation. Yet, woe to anyone who suggested that this was due to his happiness at the imminent arrival of his sire. He'd deny it to the grave, insisting that he cared nothing for the old man's visits. But he did. It wasn't until he was older himself that Roman admitted it.

The visits were short, a few weeks sometime in the warmest months of the year. They were always disappointing. Lord Aylesgarth didn't enjoy the country. He didn't enjoy his wife, and the fondness for his children, which caused him to rain emphatic attention on them for a short period, soon was spent.

When he'd return to London, and his beloved mistress, Lady Aylesgarth returned to her bedroom, crisis having been met and the façade sustained so that her husband did not know the shameful truth of her addictions. Grace, who was the most unchanged by these visits, was relieved and kinder in these days, but Roman threw himself into exile, taking off to the vast forests and fells, keeping away for days at a stretch.

Trista had seen the loneliness, the yearning on his face. And now, she knew instinctively that the idea of his son pining for his own father, though he be a fictitious rival, upset Roman.

"Don't imagine it is the same. I have told him much about you," she said.

He was shocked and she realized what she had said. "No,

not by name. I didn't wish Andrew to know you by name, not until he was older."

"You intended to inform him about me?"

"Yes, indeed. I appreciated very much the information my mother was able to give me as a child about my father, even as unflattering as it was. I know that Andrew will be very angry with me, and I will face that. But as he was a baby, I couldn't tell him the truth and ask him to lie to the world. He wouldn't have understood and it is certainly not something I wanted to teach a child, how to get away with deception."

She shrugged, playing with the seams of her gloves. "It was my hope that he would understand when he was old enough to be given the facts. In the meantime, I tried to be as honest with him about all the questions he asked about you. When he asked me where his father went to school, I told him Harrow. When he asked me where his father came from, I told him about Whitethorn—the place, the house, all that went on in it. I did not name it, of course. But he knows all about it."

"You told him about Whitethorn?" He shook his head slowly, digesting this.

"He asked about your family. I told him of Grace. He wanted to meet her, but I explained that she was a lady, and very busy with her life and that maybe she would come visit us some day when she found time." She smiled as her gaze fell on her son. "He took it in stride, and didn't ask again. He assumes the matter settled."

"And . . ."

"I told him about you, Roman. His Captain Fairhaven is you. He knows about all the things I knew of you. He absorbed it all."

"Is he bright?"

"He has an interesting mind. I said earlier that he was curious. Of course, I've no other child to compare him to, but he does seem to have an inordinate need to know how things work. He asks some of the most incredible questions, and I have to take books from the lending library to look up the answers."

This pleased him, and she thought she noticed his chest puff up with pride.

Andrew ran up to them just then. "I saw a toad."

"Oh, don't touch it!" Trista exclaimed, leaping to her feet in sudden alarm. "Where was it?"

"Show me," Roman said, already starting down to the bank. Trista followed tentatively, her eyes scanning the grass for signs of the wart-ridden creature.

"Here!" Andrew called joyfully, and Trista started, emitting a small yelp when she saw a brown lump leap into the air. Andrew ran after it at full speed.

"Don't!" she called, thinking the boy was too close to the edge.

She closed her eyes and uttered a small prayer. She nearly didn't make it through the insect phase. God help her if Andrew developed an interest in toads.

Roman hunkered down and pointed to the thing, explaining something to Andrew she could not hear. It leaped again, and he shuffled over, keeping pace as it made its way to the man-made lake. She heard him say, "Come, Andrew. You can watch him."

Andrew glanced over his shoulder to see if she was coming. Trista knew he wanted her, but she could not consider getting any nearer to the toad. Just the thought made her shiver in revulsion.

He ran back to her side, forsaking the fascination of the toad, and slithered onto the bench, wiggling into place and taking out the boat from his pocket. Slumping down, he began to make motions with it, adding swishing sounds as he lost himself in an imaginary nautical world.

Trista sighed. She looked back to Roman. He was on the bank of the Serpentine, skipping rocks by himself.

Grace eyed the miniature of her brother. Little Andrew eyed her back.

"You may call me Lady Grace," she told him. The sight

of that solemn little face was doing strange things to her heart. It was impossible that she would feel this pull of affection at this, her first sight of him. He was a stranger, for all he looked like an Aylesgarth, and the child of Trista Nash.

Behind him, Roman stood silent, his face dark. She could read the pain in the lines around his eyes, the furrows that bracketed his mouth drawn down in a frown.

This was his son, and yet the boy could not abide him. She was infused with a renewed anger at Trista for this. Because of her, her brother's son did not even know him.

"It is lovely to make your acquaintance," she said, addressing the boy.

"You're pretty," Andrew said.

The baldly stated compliment was unaccountably flattering. Perhaps it was because the little boy said it so frankly, as if it were simply obvious and delightful.

She had not had anyone tell her she was pretty in a long time. Or ever?

"Thank you." Her voice sounded stiff. "You are very kind to say so."

He smiled a moment, then seemed confused by this formality. It was impossibly awkward. She was not usually good with children, but something about this one—most likely the uncanny resemblance, which was having the most startling effect on her—made her wish to try.

She added, "You have quite made my day, young sir."

He brightened, his smile renewing. He looked so much like Roman as a boy that the years dropped away as she looked into his face. She had to fight a ridiculous urge to go down on a knee and draw him to her.

This was Trista's child, she reminded herself. She had been prepared to feel that fully at this meeting, but all she could see when she looked at him was her nephew, her family.

Roman stepped up, placing a hand on the boy's shoulder, then dropping it when he shied away. "I wished to present young master Andrew to you. We are off to the park, for a quick ride. Then I am to return him to his mother."

Grace was suddenly cross. She did not wish to have her nephew taken away so soon. "You will have tea," she announced. "And no arguments. Come Andrew. Do you like treacle tarts?"

Indeed he did. But by the sly look he shot over his shoulder to Roman, he liked her bossiness much better.

She caught Roman's gaze on the lad while young Andrew sat with his confectionary treat. It hurt to see the suffering, the wanting so plainly on his face. She made up her mind, then, determined to be of some help.

"Andrew, perhaps we might play a game. If you do not mind, we might send word to your mama that you will stay a bit longer than planned. It is up to you, of course, but I was of a mind to play some chess. Or draughts if you prefer. You do like games, do you not?"

"Oh, yes, I do. Thank you." He smiled at her, a sloppy smile that did nothing to detract from his charm. Something in her chest tightened. She realized with a shock that she was in love. So quickly.

And by the look of him, this child of her brother and her enemy was already quite fond of her, as well. Imagine that.

It was her first indication that life had some surprises yet in store for her.

Chapter 10

It occurred to Trista that if Roman was better prepared for his visits, if he was aware of the things Andrew enjoyed, it might improve matters. She wrote these down and posted them to his address.

Not long afterward, a message arrived requesting the honor of escorting Trista and Andrew to Vauxhall Gardens on the upcoming Saturday. It surprised her, the surge of excitement when she read it, and she told her son the news in a breathless voice.

"We are to go to Vauxhall, Andrew!" she cried. She'd always wished to go.

His eyes lit, catching her excitement. "Hurray!" He jumped up and down, clapping his hands, then stopped. A puzzled frown crossed his features and he asked, "What is Va-ha?"

She laughed gaily, pronouncing it again slowly. "It is a pleasure garden, which is to say it is where people go to have fun. They have delicious ices and ham that is shaved so thin, it is a marvel, and fine chickens to eat. You can dine out of doors. And it is very beautiful, with all kind of exhibitions and shows to see, acrobats and magicians and the magic lantern that shows pictures on a screen."

His eyes widened. "Is Uncle David coming?" he asked. "I want him to see the magic lantern and the acrobats."

"We'll have to see. Lord Aylesgarth has asked us. I'll send him a message and ask if he minds Uncle David and Aunt Luci coming with us."

The joy disappeared from Andrew's face. "Why does *he* have to come?"

"It was his idea. Andrew, you must stop this terrible behavior with Lord Aylesgarth. He wishes to be your friend."

A stubborn look was his response.

"I know you think he upset me one time when he came to call. He and I were very good friends a long time ago." She chose her words carefully, determined not to tell her son any untruths—the ones she had been forced to tell were bad enough—but also not wanting him to guess the relationship between Roman and herself. Her mother's instinct told her it was too soon.

"He knew your grandmother, and she liked him very much. When he was a boy, oh, a little older than you, my mother thought he was a very fine lad."

He screwed up his face. "Why did she think that?"

Sighing, Trista asked, "Can you tell me why you dislike him so?"

"He looks at you funny," he blurted. "I don't like it. He wants to take you away."

Trista rocked back in her seat, astonished at this. "That is nonsense. He very much wishes to be your friend."

"Well, he can't be. I'm Uncle David's friend."

Trista pondered her options. She could insist, and would under normal circumstances, that the boy either change his manner toward Lord Aylesgarth or he would not go on the outing, but as the objective was to foster better relations between Andrew and Roman, this was hardly the course of action to take. Andrew's behavior so far was not so much unmannerly as it was telling. He wasn't comfortable with Roman. In fact, it seemed he was afraid of him.

She shrugged her shoulders, adopting a mild attitude. "Well, you are missing a fine friend, I can tell you. I mean, the way he skipped those stones was absolutely amazing. They seemed to fly like veritable birds over the water. And it could be handy to have someone who is not afraid of toads along when at the Serpentine."

But Andrew only looked at her, still uncertain. She saw she was not going to persuade him no matter what she said.

Lord save her from stubborn men.

Luci and David did go to Vauxhall. Trista suggested it as this would ease Andrew's fears at first. Roman agreed.

There was some male nonsense about who was paying for whose admission, with Roman insisting they were his guests and David refusing to allow this. It was a matter of great import with both men. David, flush with his new job and wanting to be bountiful, versus Roman's pride.

With a shocking lack of tact, Roman tired of the argument, pushed David aside, and laid the money down to the clerk. He walked away, counting the matter settled.

David sniffed in agitation, taking out his handkerchief. He coughed tentatively into it, then paused, listening to his chest to determine if he could hear any rattles. It was a bad sign. Luci hooked her arm through his and whispered, "You'll get him next time, dear."

They exchanged a conspiratorial glance and went off in their own direction. This was at Trista's request, to keep Andrew from tucking himself close to his uncle in order to avoid Aylesgarth.

Andrew's hand squeezed Trista's as she followed, not Luci and David, but Roman. She ignored him, pulling him along with her. Roman waited for them, falling into step, and they proceeded up the Grand Walk, an avenue lined with elms.

For all her years in London, Trista had never indulged herself with a trip to Vauxhall. Every penny she had earned that she didn't absolutely need to spend had gone into savings for her part of the milliner's shop. How strange that those days of penury would seem so long ago when they were only a few months in her past. And what irony that although her finances could now permit her to bring Andrew to amusements such as the pleasure park every night if she wished, she hadn't thought of it until Roman suggested it. Her mindset just wasn't one that contemplated opportunities for leisure.

Beside her, Andrew strolled with his eyes large and luminous in the clever lights hung among the trees. They were ghostly, fairylike, and the entire atmosphere inspired wonder. Roman glanced down, then caught her glance and a pleased smile pulled at his lips.

She wanted to throw herself in his arms suddenly, for a rush of contentment seized her. It was only now she realized how much she'd been looking forward to this. She felt like a traitor, disloyal to Andrew who had not wished to come and whom they had to trick by telling him his uncle David would be with him.

But her son wasn't suffering. He was quickly caught up in the excitement. "Look, Mama!" he cried, pointing to a puppet show.

They paused and watched the play. Trista grimaced at the violence, but Andrew hooted and Roman presided over them, their benefactor beaming at his success. He was thinking that Andrew having a good time would mean a thaw in his attitude.

She herself was hopeful, but when they left the small stage, Andrew once again hugged her side.

"We'll take the South Walk," Roman said. "Look down toward the arches. There are three of them in a row, and beyond them you will see the famous painting of the Ruins of Palmyra. It is so realistic when viewed from afar that it has been known to fool the unknowing into thinking there is an ancient city in the middle of London."

"The Ruins of Palmyra," Andrew muttered in awe. Trista doubted he had any sense of what a ruin was or where and when Palmyra had existed, but it sounded so exotic that even his five-year-old brain couldn't miss the excitement.

They turned down the wide avenue, passing venders and stalls. The crowd was not thick, so they were able to view the painting in all of its wonder.

"It's so gorgeous," Trista said breathlessly.

Roman seemed pleased at her reaction.

"We can take one of the temples for our supper. There are tables for dining al fresco."

"That means eating dinner outside," Andrew said.

"That is right. I will arrange a feast."

When they were seated under the Romanesque shelter, Trista observed, "You seem very familiar with the place. Do you come often?"

He shrugged, and knowing him so well, her jealousy flared at his avoidance, thinking it meant only one thing.

And, knowing him so well, it was exactly what he intended.

Still, she couldn't keep herself from asking, "Have you brought other women here?"

"Yes. Are you jealous?"

"Yes."

"Good." He grinned and she made a face at him. "But this is the first time I've asked one to bring her son."

"Well, then I can feel special."

His gaze was warm on her, and she marveled at her cheek. Somehow, their old banter had come back for a moment. In this enchanted place, it seemed possible to tease him.

"I want to show you the Dandy Horse," Roman said when they were finished. "It is a new invention, a rather ingenious device for a single person to ride upon."

He took them to a vendor who had several odd-looking wheeled devices hitched to his stall. Roman paid him and took the largest one out of its dock.

It had two tall wheels, very thin, like carriage wheels that were assembled in tandem to each other so that there was a seat in between them, and what Trista thought must be a steering device attached to the front.

"Why, it's extraordinary. What did you say it was?"

"It's a velocipede. See, you operate it like this."

With a push of his powerful legs, he propelled it forward into an empty area of the avenue, and with deft twists on the column ascending from the front wheel, maneuvered it about. He might have looked ridiculous except Roman could never seem so. Instead, he appeared masterful, gliding gracefully on the absurd contraption and making her envious of his careless aplomb.

Andrew grew excited despite himself. It really was a marvel, and no boy would fail to be impressed.

"You've had a spot of practice," Trista observed, a sour tinge in her voice.

"I've ridden a few times," he said as he passed her, circling after another push of his feet.

"No doubt all those previous times you've sampled the pleasures of Vauxhall. Do women ride the things as well?"

"Not unless they wish their skirt shredded to pieces in the wheel spokes."

"Oh, then I suppose all of your companions had to wait while you sped about."

He grinned knowingly as he steered the thing up to her, and with a sudden planting of his feet, brought it to an abrupt halt. "Ah," he said, and seemed very pleased. Then he turned to Andrew. "Would you like to try it?"

"Oh, yes!"

"No!" Trista said.

"You mustn't overprotect the boy," Roman scolded, undaunted.

"It is much too dangerous."

"No more so than climbing on a horse. Come, Mrs. Fairhaven, you cannot begrudge the boy a simple pleasure. Look see, I shall get him one of the smaller ones meant for children and hold on to the back to keep his balance just so. I'll run behind so he doesn't fall. No harm could come."

She didn't like it. The strange-looking machine made her nervous. "I don't think so," she said. "There are other amusements." Her tone made it clear her decision was definite.

She expected him to protest. Having been well acquainted

a long time ago with Roman's inability to be denied what he wanted, she was ready for a barrage. Instead, he looked pathetically defeated. She might have been fooled, except he put a bit too much emphasis on his sad eyes.

He sighed. "Well, Andrew, that is the end of it, then. Your mother has spoken."

Andrew looked so disappointed she thought for a moment he would weep. His accusing gaze was leveled at Trista when Roman—oh, the opportunistic wretch—sidled beside him at that moment and put a companionable hand on his shoulder.

Andrew did not move away.

Trista glared. "You did that on purpose."

He looked innocent, which was a feat for Roman. It was difficult for a man with a square jaw and jutting cheekbones, whose face was all hard lines and masculine contour, to look so guileless. "Is that a yes?"

What an exasperating beast he was. "One quick turn, and you hold him the entire time," she conceded, knowing even as she spoke that it was a mistake.

"Done! Here, Andrew, straddle the seat like so. Now you saw how I did it. Do you think you could manage the same?"

Andrew said yes, but that didn't encourage Trista. He would have agreed to anything required to give him a turn on the velocipede. He rushed through Roman's instructions, nodding to everything that was being told him without hearing a word of it. Trista knew he didn't know what he was doing, and was about to intercede when Roman's voice grew stern and he told the boy that if he wished to ride, he had to attend.

This, surprisingly, Andrew did. He repeated back the directives Roman gave him. Trista didn't know what was more surprising—Andrew's receptiveness or Roman's patience.

When it was time for him to try it, Trista put her hand to her mouth, biting down hard as Andrew wobbled.

"Catch him," she called.

"He's fine." Roman's voice was filled with the kind of disgust boys might demonstrate when learning that girls don't appreciate that absolutely fascinating nest of blood-worms they've discovered.

Andrew didn't fall. He made a warbling circle, his steering jerky. Roman gave him some pointers on how to manage better, but the second time around, the velocipede tilted dangerously.

Trista stifled a cry. Andrew tumbled from the seat, but Roman was there, catching him by the back of his little coat before he hit the ground. The velocipede was in his other hand, and he looked like Hercules, balancing all dangers with the greatest of ease.

Andrew wriggled out of his grasp and hopped upon the velocipede again. "Once more," he commanded. His tone had not softened toward Roman, but at least he was speaking to him, albeit only when it served him to do so.

"That is quite enough," she called.

They ignored that and Andrew went around again. Trista felt a twinge of annoyance that they would unite against her. She didn't like this Dandy Horse. It seemed . . . unnatural to be propelling oneself about at such speeds without much control, but Roman—of course, that reckless maniac liked anything that was wild and dangerous—was having a time of it, as was his son. Not even winded, Roman trotted after the boy, giving an extra push without seeming to while he kept the machine upright, and this provided Andrew with an exhilarating ride.

They finally ceased tormenting her, and Andrew climbed down. "Did you see, Mama?"

"I saw," she said, accepting his little body pressed against her.

Roman grinned, triumphant.

The rest of the evening was anticlimactic after such an adventure, but it passed pleasantly. They bought ices and strolled along the lanes, observing an exhibit or pausing to watch a show. When they reunited with David and Luci, Andrew slipped his hand into his Uncle David's and strolled away from Roman and Trista, talking excitedly about the Dandy Horse.

They headed home soon after, piling into the Aylesgarth's carriage, which fit all of them with only a modicum of scrunching. After taking David and Luci home, Andrew curled into Trista's side. He was half asleep by the time they arrived at the house at Hyde Park.

"I'll take him," Roman said.

"I'm used to carrying him," Trista replied, but stopped when she saw the intent expression on his face as he gathered the little boy into his arms. She didn't protest as he bore his burden up to the nursery.

Andrew looked so small cradled in his father's arms. Roman's face was stone, betraying nothing. He lay Andrew in his bed and stepped away as Trista sat on the edge and peeled off his shoes and socks, undressing him down to his undergarments and slipping a nightshirt over his head.

When he was tucked in tightly, his bedclothes swaddled around him, she kissed his forehead. He squirmed, sighing lightly in his sleep. Coming to her feet, she saw Roman was still in the corner of the room, quietly observing the nightly ritual.

"Would you like to have a drink with me in the drawing room?" she asked, then wondered what had made her ask this.

"I would," he answered simply, and followed her downstairs.

When they were settled, her with some sweet wine and he with a tumbler of brandy, she said, "Thank you for tonight. Andrew had a wonderful time."

"And you? Did you enjoy yourself?"

"Other than fearing my heart would give way when you were on that Dandy Horse, I enjoyed it, yes."

"You didn't expect to."

"Why do you say that?"

"Because of me. I daresay if you had attended the pleasure gardens with Luci and the most hallowed 'Uncle

David' it would have been a more relaxing time. Andrew certainly would have enjoyed it better."

"You mustn't blame him. He will come round in time."

"Do you think so?" His look was penetrating.

She didn't say anything because she really wasn't certain of anything. Roman's coming into their lives had turned everything into a twist. She didn't recognize what was normal any longer.

She would have never thought her son to be the petulant type, and yet he was absolutely immovable in his reticence with Roman. Whatever he felt against the man, he felt it deeply and nothing seemed to be able to budge him.

And herself . . . that was the biggest surprise of all. She could not understand her changed attitude toward Roman. Maybe it was simply that the thing she feared most had happened, so she needn't be afraid of him any longer. He knew her worst secret, and he had done none of the things she had dreamed he might.

She had expected him to be brutal. And that, she had to admit to herself, had been unfair. She had judged him wrongly. The man had not only shown patience—and just exactly where had Roman learned patience?—he'd shown sensitivity. In fact, he had been so deft in his charm, she was stunned that her son could withstand its effects.

She certainly was not able to.

Roman swirled the brandy, peering at her over the glass. "You see him to bed each night? You don't have a nurse do it?"

"Sometimes when I have to go out in the evening, I have the nurse do it, but if I am at home I do it. I enjoy it. Don't forget, I didn't have a nurse for the last five years. These duties were mine."

"Did you resent it?"

"Not in the least. Why would a mother resent tending her own child?"

She should have known better and realized immediately that she had blundered onto a sore spot she knew well enough. His mother had neglected the care of her children cruelly.

Waving her hand, she tried to make light of it. "My mother tended me, as you know. I always expected to take care of my own children. What I didn't expect was to come into money, but I am not going to allow that to change me."

"Yet you've changed so much."

"Have I? I suppose I am older." She felt a tad self-conscious thinking how she must compare to his memories of her. She ducked her head, concentrating on her wine.

It was her favorite, a sweet, fruity blend imported from Germany, but it tasted like vinegar at this moment. She wasn't in the mood for it. She put it aside.

"You are much improved," he said in a matter-of-fact voice. "Come, don't pretend you don't know it, for if you have a mirror you have surely taken note that the years have been kind to you. Maturity has deepened your looks. You used to be pretty. Now you are beautiful."

She picked up her wine again, just for something to do. "Thank you. Your compliments are unnecessary."

"Do you think I am seducing you?"

"No." She looked up, her face instantly heating with a flush of embarrassment. "Of course not."

"Then I must increase my efforts. I am trying to seduce you." The slow smile that claimed his face was pure sin. "Surely you know I still want you. I believe I've been rather obvious about it."

She hated herself for growing flustered. "You are not! You forget, I know when you are bent on seduction."

"Don't be so quick to think you know me, Trista. Much time has passed, and many things have changed. You and I are not the same green youths that we were."

"So, you are seducing me." She tried to sound droll, not excited. Which she was, despite herself.

"Well, right now I am enjoying the fact that my son did not bolt in terror when he saw me, and he even allowed me to approach him. I believe the Dandy Horse was a stroke of brilliance. Sometimes I think I am a genius."

"You are too modest."

"I have never been burdened by that attribute. You cannot have forgotten how shameless I am."

"Ah. I recall it now."

"So, I am basking in my success, enjoying this brandy and your company. And hoping for further developments."

Her heart gave one giddy leap and began to thump more emphatically. She jerked her chin up and tried to appear unfazed. "Leading to my bed?"

"Or the carpet. It appears accommodating enough."

She was so shocked that she laughed when she should have sent him a prim scowl. But that had always been her failing. His rakish behavior had the power to amuse her, disarm her, charm her. Yes, that was it, that slow melting feeling that was too delicious to resist.

"No one laughs at my jokes the way you do," he observed. "And it is such a wonderful laugh, by the way. No, people mistake my sarcasm constantly. They think I am serious when I am merely being self-deprecating, or they think me outlandish."

"You are outlandish."

"And brazen?"

"That of course. Do not appear so pleased. It is not a compliment."

"It has stood me in good stead. Take the night we first kissed, for example. I recall how I teased you that night. I said unforgivably bold things. I was testing you, waiting to see how you would react. Would you be shocked and slap me for the devil I was? Would you demur, giving a token rebuff yet encouraging me at the same time? And trust your oppositional soul, you did neither. You stared at me outright, as if daring me. I swear you had my pride on the line so that I had to dredge up the courage to pursue you or slink off in humiliation and never show my face again."

It was true. She'd been wanting him to kiss her for so long. When the hero of her childhood had come home a grown man and noticed she'd become a woman, she had welcomed his flirtation.

His smile spread lazily over his handsome face. "I was rather clumsy about it, as I recall. I kept creeping closer, and you'd retreat, but you never broke eye contact, and that only encouraged me. That was very wicked of you. One must never encourage me."

Her pulse was racing. He was in pursuit, and this was Roman at his most dangerous, most exhilarating. "But you managed to close the distance," she said.

His eyes narrowed. "You let me."

She had. "And then you just stood there," she whispered, angling a look at him that teased, although she hardly understood the sultry impulse to do so, "talking and talking and talking until I thought you would never shut up and do it."

"And in the end, when I leaned down to kiss you, you all but leaped into my arms."

She realized she was smiling, caught herself, and turned away. "I don't think we should be talking like this."

"Have you taken any other lovers?" he asked bluntly.

"No," she replied with a glib toss of her head, "have you?"

"No one of sustained interest."

"In six years, you've found no one that amused you, not even a bit?"

"Not a one," he said smoothly.

"Not even any of those ladies you took to Vauxhall?"

"Least of all them." He smiled, and it was a slow, naughty smile. "And they were not ladies."

"And what of the woman for whom you came to the shop to purchase a hat? She must have been special."

He sighed, settling back. "I was waiting for you to ask. I suppose I must explain. The woman was special in only that she possessed a shrill sister who is married to my cousin, and the two of them and Annabelle and I made a convenient foursome for outings. That day, when her hat blew off, said sister began to screech right there in the street at the prospect of the impropriety of her sister going bareheaded. Raymond and I had no choice but to spring into action. No wonder the man drinks. So, we made haste to the nearest milliner, willing to pay ten crowns for a burlap bonnet merely to shut her up."

She laughed. "You made that up."

"Upon my honor, I did not. I'd introduce you to her and let you hear it from her lips, except I no longer see them socially."

She lowered her eyes. Was he telling her that he was not involved with Annabelle any longer?

"My cousin and his wife have returned to Hampshire where they reside."

"And this sister?"

"She was a fine person, just not . . ." The long pause held an air of expectancy. "Right for me," he finished.

He was taunting her. He wanted her to think he was about to say, *She was not you.*

She must not forget how much Roman loved to play.

"This is all so familiar," he said suddenly. "At Whitethorn, we'd spend many nights just so, you and I. I have never had the particular blend of pique and pleasure that always comes in your company."

"It is probably best not to remember Whitethorn."

"Why not?" He downed the rest of his drink. "They were pleasant times. We would argue in the evenings while Grace sulked and Mother stared into space. I think I would have gone mad without you to debate with. We'd get into it so heatedly that we would frighten them away. Off to their beds they'd go, and then, you and I—"

"It is getting late!" she said, standing. "You've finished your drink."

He didn't move. "We would make love."

She stood, transfixed, unable to believe he'd said it.

He put his empty glass down slowly. It made a muted sound. He rose, unfolding himself in an unhurried manner, and stood, very close.

She felt as if her body had been turned to stone, for she could not move. And then he reached for her and she was released.

What was the point of resisting when she knew damned well she was fighting futilely? With a sob of relief, she gave in to the pressures that had been building for hours, for days, for weeks. Everything fell like a massive landslide.

She fell into his arms and he kissed her.

Chapter 11

Trista's bedroom was decorated in rose and yellow. It was full of tasteful fabrics, flounces, pillows, and walnut furnishings carved with graceful lines. It was a woman's room, designed specifically to her tastes, but the moment Roman entered, it became something different. It was not the retreat she had wished to create with all of the carefully planned selections of furnishings and fabric. Now, it became a sumptuous setting for seduction.

She latched the door, holding his gaze as he advanced on her, pushed her back against the wall and kissed her again. His long, hard-muscled frame pressed the length of her, and she thrilled at the feel of him. Her hands slid down his back, pulling at his jacket. With a few adjustments and without breaking the kiss, he maneuvered out of it so that it fell onto the floor.

Now she could feel him. Under the silky softness of his shirt, she felt muscle and sinew and her womb contracted. His scent brought back so much memory, and her head swam insanely.

She breathed his name and he laughed a low rumble of victory. Stepping away, he took her hand and led her, backward step by backward step, to the bed, his eyes never leaving hers. Excitement pulsed through her veins, sparked by this madness that he fed by kissing her palm, and then each one of her fingers. His chest heaved, as if he'd run a marathon, but he took his time.

When the back of his calf bumped the side of the bed, he yanked her to him, and slowly and deliberately, took each finger in his mouth, playing with it against his tongue, before giving each one a small bite.

"If you are hungry, we can visit the kitchens," she said in a rush.

"I believe my appetites will be fed best right here," he replied, and moved swiftly to turn and deposit them on the bed. "Although if you have a penchant for the kitchens, we can try that when we are finished here. There is a sturdy table, I trust."

In the blink of an eye, she found herself on her back, with him leaning over her. "There." He sighed, and grinned like the devil.

"You are quite proud of yourself," she observed wryly.

He sat up and took off her shoes, thumping them noisily to the floor in his rush. Then he removed his. "Indeed, it was a masterful move, although I admit I was slightly concerned in case we missed. It might prove difficult to explain to the physician how we came by our injuries. It had to be timed perfectly, without the smallest allowance for error." He situated himself comfortably next to her. "But it was romantic, wasn't it?"

"Terribly so." She fought the feverish feeling crawling up her spine. "I am quite breathless."

Lowering his lips to her shoulder, he said, "If you think you are breathless now, I cannot wait to see you in a moment or two."

It did not take nearly so long to elicit several gasps when he began to remove her clothing. As he stripped away her gown, his mood shifted away from playfulness and into stark hunger.

His eyes darkened as he gazed at her. Her body was barely

covered by her shift, but it was thin, not the coarse cottons she had worn before, and little was left to the imagination. She crossed her arms over her chest self-consciously as he continued to stare.

"Your breasts are different. Larger, fuller," he said. Gently, he pulled her hands away so that he could see them.

Trista lay under his scrutiny, her breathing rapid and shallow. She wanted to scream for him to touch her. She felt a mingling of shame and excitement at his bold perusal.

His eyes greedily took in all he exposed. He pulled down the shoulders of her chemise until her breasts were bared. Her hands fumbled for his shirt, and he reached to the back of his collar and removed it over his head for her.

Then he reached for her again.

"Your body is different," he said, his voice filled with awe. Like a child with a present, he suddenly tugged on her flimsy garment to get rid of the barrier.

"I want to see you," he said, working swiftly.

Within moments, she lay nude, and his eyes roamed, dark and lingering. Then he smiled. "You are gorgeous. I'd forgotten. How could I have forgotten?"

His mouth lowered to her flat stomach. His hands splayed over the womb that had borne his son, and he kissed her trembling flesh.

She bit her lips, but refused to cry out. The feel of his hands on her was driving her fever higher. She pulled on his trousers. He obliged her, and she took in the sight of him. He was larger, harder, thicker, leaner in all the right places. She came to her knees and faced him as he climbed back into bed.

"Six years," he said, cupping her face in his palm. "It has been six years."

Then he pulled her down on the bed with him, his mouth sealing over hers.

Roman had learned quite a great deal in the intervening years. He was surer of himself, more impatient. Or maybe it was the circumstances, the fact that they had both wanted this from the moment they had set eyes on each other.

He didn't tolerate her modesty, and the strangeness of their being so intimate again after so many years apart dissipated into a haze of sensual pleasure. His clever hands roused her and his mouth bit tiny love bites along her quivering flesh. She reacquainted herself with his body, a man's body that was warm and silken-fleshed and rough all at the same time.

His hands roamed, slowly picking up pace. He muttered something as his mouth found the sensitive peak of one breast. In her belly, the tight coil of pleasure ignited, burning slow and hot like a fuse and her hands grew clumsy, too hurried and needy to be artful.

He, too, became furtive as the tension mounted. Grasping, panting, they wrapped their fingers together, their hands over their heads as he bore down, pressing her into the sinfully silken coverlet. And then he was part of her, and her body came up off the bed, the contact electric, shattering. He cried out, and the sound was her name.

It all came flooding back, as if each intimate stroke rolled them back through years. The feeling of belonging enveloped her, of the rightness of this, reuniting with a part of herself that she'd left with him.

With that thought came the free fall of her climax. It burst over her like razor-sharp points of light. He deepened his penetration, quickening in the final throes of possession until he, too, convulsed, driving harder until he shook with release and came to rest in her arms.

Roman kept his eyes closed, afraid that if he opened them he would find himself in some dream, or a delusion fed by a mind made feverish with pent-up wanting. This was Trista. He had to keep thinking it.

He smelled her scent, fresh and mixed with hints of flowers, spices, and woman, and he thought, *open your eyes, it's all right. It* is *her.*

She spoke. "Are you asleep already?"

He cracked his eyes open. "Thinking."

And there was Trista. She was gorgeous, her face flushed, a fine sheen of perspiration giving her a glow.

"What are you thinking?"

Stretching, he tightened his grip on her waist. "That I like making love to you."

She laid her head on his chest and said, "You cannot fall asleep." She said this lazily, and he wondered if she was dozing herself.

"I will not." Sleep? And miss one moment of this. "I swear."

He'd thought about her so often, replayed the times they'd spent together over and over in his mind. He'd worn out the memories until they'd faded, become unclear and unfocused.

But this was vivid and new.

The even sound of her breathing told him that she'd fallen asleep. He gazed at her, feeling the pull in his chest. How he'd missed her.

Her mouth, slightly open in repose, was cherry-red, luscious, and far too tempting. Her body was invitingly warm along his side, and it fit, softly molded to his shape.

She belonged to him. She had since forever. When he was a child, he'd not understood his wanting. She'd only been a girl. An extraordinary girl, yes, but there had been no identifiable carnality to his perceptions. He only had known that she haunted him. Something about her inflicted tiny wounds to his heart every time he looked at her. He'd thought the answer to his restless feelings was to dominate her, try to bully her.

It was only as a man that he'd recognized the power of his feelings. When he'd returned home from University and seen her again, he'd known then that all of the years he'd fought with her, teased her, consoled her, taught her, that they'd all been a precursor to taking her as a man takes a woman.

It had been a confusing time. He was twenty-four, newly home to the place where he'd spent a miserable childhood and not pleased to be there. He'd been angry in fact, and sullen, which was not an unusual state for the inhabitants of Whitethorn to find him. He'd wished to go off on the Grand Tour instead of coming home, but his father had decided he was needed to take the helm of the family interest.

The old Lord Aylesgarth had wisely forbore mentioning that this was a precursor to requiring Roman's marriage. It was his father's plan to flatter him with his long-withheld attention, lull him into increasing knowledge of the family affairs, followed by responsibilities that had given Roman, for the first time in his life, a sense of purpose, of pride—real pride, not the bluster and swagger he had used in the past to cover his pain.

And Roman had felt, at last, important. He had a purpose now, something worthwhile.

He'd seen Trista again, and they'd fallen in love. And bounty was a fine thing, for he had lived with the knowledge that he was both loved by this woman who'd held his heart forever, and needed by the one man whom he had strived all his life to have notice him.

And then he'd been forced to choose.

Trista had not only failed to understand that choice, she'd *blamed* him. As if he could have changed the course of society. As if he should have stood up to all and sundry and cried, "No, I shall marry Trista Nash and no other, for she is the one I love."

And what if he had? It would have done nothing less than bring ruination to his family. They would have sunk into poverty, perhaps even prison for their debts. His sister, who had never had a thing in her life, would have been cheated of her future. His wife had brought stability, if not happiness.

He'd convinced himself he was the wounded one. Trista had hated him for failing her. But she'd failed him.

Perhaps he would forgive that, forgive her keeping Andrew from him. It might be that he'd forgive her anything, without a shred of pride because it was all still there. The wanting. The insatiable wanting that never went away.

In these six years, it had only burrowed deep, thundering

like a dammed river breaking its gates and flooding him in consuming need.

She shifted, sighing softly in her sleep, and he nudged her a bit to disentangle himself from her. She rolled to her other side, deeply in slumber, stretching her arm out, her fingers flexing like a cat exercising its claws.

He rose and dressed, his limbs heavy and tingling with the languid feel one gets just after sex, only this was much more noticeable, as if his body were protesting each motion that would make them part. As he pulled on his trousers, something fell from the pocket and made a sound that sounded unnaturally loud in the quiet darkness.

He picked up the toy soldier. Holding it, he inspected it for damage. It was the Major Khoury replica of the Horse Guard regiment he'd brought to Andrew on their first day together. His son had rejected it, the gift Roman had selected so carefully, so sure that his son would love it.

This particularly stiff little man, painted face blank and straight body ever at attention, had become something of a talisman for Roman. He'd pocketed it before shoving the box containing his scorned gift aside. Without knowing why, he'd kept it with him.

He ran his finger over it, making certain it was not chipped, and returned it to his pocket.

Giving Trista one more glance, he paused at the door, lingered. He'd see her tomorrow, he promised, and already he felt better. He left, with the perfume of her skin still on him, and the tiniest trace of a shiver still rattling the marrow of his bones.

When Trista awoke, she stretched, running the backs of her hands along the silken sheets. She was aware of a deep-seated feeling in her muscles and a scent. And a loss of some sort.

She opened her eyes and found Roman gone. The clock on the table had it near to three in the morning. Her lamp still burned, but the oil was considerably lower.

Sitting up, she looked about. All trace of Roman had been removed. She sighed. She shouldn't have fallen asleep.

Throwing herself back down on the bed, she went over the interlude in her mind. She felt many things, most of them conflicting. Happiness and fear and embarrassment and joy. Most of all, she marveled that she had not suspected in the least that she would be so vulnerable to him. She'd thought herself very straight on the subject of Roman, Lord Aylesgarth.

It was the damned Dandy Horse.

She'd seen him on that thing, sailing along as proud and cocksure as a bantam rooster, his eyes shining and his heart so blatantly on his sleeve hoping to impress his son, and she'd melted. She fell, hard, and here she was, less than ten hours later, contemplating the situation that had landed her in bed with him.

One would think she'd have learned to resist him by now.

That was the thought she had as she drifted off to sleep again, pleasant thoughts of seeing Roman again sinking down with her into her sleep. She was awakened shortly with a clear, nerve-rattling thought.

She remembered why she had left him six years ago.

They'd argued, and like many of their verbal battles, it had served as foreplay for their lovemaking later. It was something she didn't always like, but always enjoyed.

They'd fallen into bed, drowning out arguments with passion, and when he'd gone, she'd lain just as now until shock had bolted through her. She had realized that she was being lulled by love into something she did not believe in. She was going to become this man's mistress because she was too weak. Too in love, too unwilling to contemplate living without him.

She'd packed a few things that night. By morning she was gone. At first, her plan was to frighten him, make him know she was not going to slip so easily into his plan. She'd make him see what she meant to him.

And then she'd learned she was pregnant, and the little

maneuver to get her way became real. The stakes had become too high.

Maybe she'd overestimated herself.

And it was that thought that was with her now. She'd overestimated herself.

She'd left him before because she understood that a woman of her class could only mean one thing to a man of Roman's class. A mistress. A whore—same thing.

Which is exactly what she was now. He'd offered nothing more.

How many times did one have to sleep with a man before one officially became a mistress? One time? Ten times? Or perhaps twice.

Twice. It was a bona fide affair if it was twice.

She'd come full circle with nothing to show for it. And the damned man had her right where she was six years ago—half in love with him, panting for his touch.

Oh, God. She'd be lucky if it were only half.

She slept no more. When she rose and dressed, she felt very different from the woman she'd been yesterday. It had been like that before. Cold resolve had removed all doubt, all confusion as to what she should do, and it was with mechanical resolve that she laid her plan.

Then and now. It was the same, running together, pulling her back to a place she didn't wish to go.

The past had repeated itself.

That day, Roman returned.

He trotted up the front steps with a spring in his step, flowers clutched in his hand, and a jaunty grin on his face.

He was told that Mrs. Fairhaven was not in.

Leaving the flowers, he dashed a note on his card. No message came, although he expressly instructed Trista to send him word when he might call.

He didn't trot up the steps the following day. It was the hour when morning calls were being conducted all over the city, and he was told that this was precisely where Mrs. Fairhaven was.

He did not leave his card.

He returned the day after. He rapped upon the door, no grin, no flowers, and when the door was opened, he shoved his way in, strode to the back of the house, and found Trista and Michaela Khoury together in the family drawing room.

Thwarted, he stewed, determined to wait out the visitor, but she was invited to tea. Rude or not, he took no hints when it was suggested that the hour was growing late.

He was polite, though barely so. He made conversation with Mrs. Khoury. Trista took to pointedly ignoring him halfway through the visit, and he bided his time.

She couldn't avoid him forever.

With a distressed look at her half sister, Michaela said, "Well, I should be getting back. The major is due home this evening from his trip, and then we must ready the house." She explained to Roman, "We are closing it for the summer. My husband much prefers his country home, and has indulged me coming to London so I may see Mrs. Fairhaven."

He nodded. "His indulgence is to our benefit. It was delightful to meet you."

Despite the circumstances, this was not a lie. Michaela Khoury had been gracious and kind, although she could not have missed the tension boiling in the air.

"You owe me an explanation," he said when Michaela had gone.

Trista pursed her lips. "Please let us not have a scene."

"I think we should please have a scene. It is long overdue."

She made an impatient gesture and stood. He was already on his feet, and he squared off against her. "What happened between now and when I left you Wednesday evening?" he asked sharply, his eyes penetrating.

"I realized what a mistake I'd made. Again."

"Oh, for God's sake. I thought we had established the mistake was running from me."

"Is that what you thought?" She was breathless, incredulous, her eyes snapping at him like ashen flame. "My God, you are unbelievably conceited, not to mention conveniently forgetful. This was all my doing, then—your behavior had nothing to do with it?"

"You told me you regretted not telling me about Andrew."

"Which is a completely different thing than saying I regret not becoming your mistress. I do not regret that decision, and I am not about to reverse it at this late date. I told you when we met again that I will not compromise myself, not for you, nor for anyone."

"Mistress?"

She took a deep breath, apparently trying to start over, this time more in control. "Roman, we have known each other for a very long time, and we've both known that there has been a certain . . . connection. We were children together, and it was an unhappy time for us. We both made each other contented. I found a friend, and you found a family in my mother and me. Naturally, as we grew, we thought we were in love, perhaps mistaking those feelings for something else, but it wasn't strong enough to last, and it died. But we still have this . . . well, it is some sort of shared part, some affection."

He watched her rationalize away, speechless, feeling his heart sinking into quicksand. She was very stiff, almost prim as she spoke.

"You discovered we share a son, and that is a bond that will be with us for the rest of our lives. It was wrong of us to take all of that connectedness into the bedroom. All right, we were curious. It's been a long time, and our history . . ."

His arms crossed over his chest, his right forefinger stroking his upper lip, staring at her, eyes hard and unblinking. It rattled her. He knew this.

She faltered, then squared her shoulders, her voice stronger as she said firmly, "Now that our curiosity has been appeased, we should have a care not to misinterpret that emotion for anything more—"

He uncurled his fingers, pointing at her. "You will not keep me from my son."

It was spoken softly, in an even tone that was nonetheless threatening. He meant it to be.

He was suddenly afraid.

She blinked, as if startled, and then her face creased as if he'd hurt her feelings.

How dare she? She was sitting there after cutting him these last days and now she was explaining things to him as if he were a slow-witted child, and she had the nerve, the unmitigated gall, to act offended.

He narrowed his eyes, concentrating dark thoughts on Trista.

"He is my blood," he said. "I will not go quietly away because you've decided you've overestimated your . . . affection for me. He is my son, and he will know me."

"This is not about Andrew."

"The hell it isn't. In any event, he is all I care about at this point."

He'd forgotten how good it felt to strike out when being hurt yourself. His chest stung, as if he'd been punched on the inside, and it made his voice harsh, rasping.

"You can keep your fickle desires and your twisted woman's logic and all your references about history and curiosity. Did you think I'd fight you on this, throw myself at your feet and beg you to take me into your bed again? I wouldn't waste my time. All I wish from you is that you pose no obstruction to me seeing my son."

She stared at him, and he had a strong impression that she was battling her own emotions.

It gave him pleasure to know this. Misery loves company and suffering is best borne with a companion. He liked hurting her, frightening her. He'd been a bully as a child, a frightened lonely lad who had thought being mean as a good way to even the score. He'd not thought that way for a long, long time, but it came forth now, the deeply satisfying knowledge that the fear in her eyes gave him power.

What feeble comfort, but his pride would not be denied.

"He should be accustomed to our outings, and know now that there is no need to fear me. Send a maid with him if you wish, but it is not necessary for you to accompany us any longer. I will see him the day after next, at which time I will take him for the afternoon and return him after tea."

He strode out, clamping down his self-control. What he really wished to do was shake her, demand to know what she was thinking, why she would cast him from her again.

He damned her a hundred times on his way home, and himself for being a fool twice for the same inconstant woman.

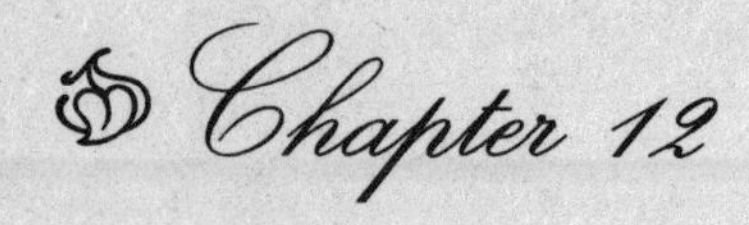

Chapter 12

"I think you should dance," May said to Trista after she turned down the fifth request to take a turn on the parquet.

"I do not feel like dancing," Trista said. She fiddled with her fan, avoiding May's eye.

"Darling, you look beautiful tonight and there are so many interesting people about. Surely you are not bored of the *ton* already."

"No. Just out of sorts tonight. Indeed, I don't know what is the matter with me." She gave her aunt a smile and a squeeze. "Of course I shall apply myself to having a marvelous time. There is no excuse not to. Perhaps I just need a refreshment to shore up my flagging energies."

She sounded so resolute, it touched May, who squeezed in return. "Have a glass of the champagne. It is excellent, and it will shore up a crumbling dike."

May knew exactly what it was that dogged her niece. It was Aylesgarth, that was obvious, although Trista stubbornly refused to discuss the matter. All of May's most clever inquiries had been politely shut down.

Which was maddening. May was consumed with curiosity. She had no idea what had passed between the two of them, but she was certain something momentous had occurred.

She liked Roman. She had a feeling for the man and she thought it admirable that he was not only willing to do his duty by Andrew, he actually was interested in the boy, and looked to deepen the relationship.

She had noticed that Roman had not taken Trista out of late. He had, however, been to see his son, and was beginning to oversee certain matters, such as the changing of his tutor and the selection of some of his activities. This she admired. She would never speak a word against her brother, but it had appalled her when she'd learned how he'd neglected his own offspring. Roman was different from Woolrich in many ways.

Somehow, she wasn't certain Trista understood this.

She sighed, sipping listlessly at the glass of champagne she had taken so that Trista would not imbibe alone and her mind went to another matter of great worry.

Much on her mind was Robert, who was different of late. He'd been testy, impatient. He was positively rude on the subject of Lord Charbonneau, making snide comments about the man and actually seeming angry when he came to call. He couldn't be jealous—that was simply too absurd, Robert jealous of Lord Charbonneau.

"They are so much in love," Trista said.

Starting, Lady May relaxed when she saw Trista was speaking about Michaela and Adrian. "Those two are indeed enviable," May said of the couple smiling into each other's faces.

"It is amazing, I think, that his limp does not appear to trouble him at all at the moment."

"A war wound fades to insignificance when one is young and at a gorgeous ball dancing with someone who can send all other concerns to flight."

She had meant it to sound bright and breathy, but she heard the dull flatness in her own voice and flushed with embarrassment. She wouldn't have anyone know that she, too, was envious of how her dear niece could enjoy publicly the attentions of a doting husband, unencumbered by secrets, which once seemed exciting but now felt like a terrible burden.

She sighed. She simply had to get this ado with Robert sorted out. She was becoming maudlin, and she could never abide maudlin people.

"My dear Lady May," Lord Charbonneau said, coming to her side, pointing a toe, and dipping a long, sweeping bow. His right hand performed a ridiculous flourish.

She smiled in welcome. Charbonneau was a dramatic man, given to gossip and bragging, but at least he was not dull. He could debate on intellectual topics and actually seemed to enjoy it when she voiced her view. Not only did he tolerate her being more intelligent than he, he listened to her without resorting to male smugness. In that respect, he reminded her of Robert, and it was precisely for this reason she had welcomed his company. If he wasn't an ideal companion, at least he was tolerable, even diverting.

And she was lonely when she was out in public. It eased this loneliness to have him dancing in attendance.

"Did you come to beg a dance?" she inquired with a flirtatious smile. Such things came second nature to her.

"If you wish." He deferred to her with an incline of his head. "I do not need to take in the reel. My energy is on the wane this week. Perhaps a touch of the ague."

"And yet you look so well," Trista said, turning to greet him. They liked each other and were always happy to be in each other's company. "Perhaps it is that new waistcoat. Red is such a flattering color."

He blushed, pleased, and returned the compliment, declaring that she looked gorgeous tonight, as indeed she did. The green gown she had chosen, so pale and designed with few froths so as not to spoil the classic design, was a perfect foil for her soft beauty. But her eyes were sad and the sparkling energy that animated her was missing.

Yes, that was the problem with Charbonneau, too, May just now realized. He was bland. No spark.

Trista saw some friends and left them to join them. May

watched her go, saw her happily welcomed into the circle. It seemed to cheer her. It was good to see Trista smile, distracted by the female chatter that enveloped her.

"So, what will it be, Lady May?" Lord Charbonneau asked, drawing her attention back to him. "Cards, a stroll in the gardens?"

"Cards, I think. I've been having the most disastrous luck of late in all-fours and I am anxious to turn it around."

Charbonneau frowned as he led her into the parlor where several tables had been set up for card playing. "I hope you do not lose your head with gambling."

"If you ask if I am reckless in my wagers, I can assure you I am not. But it is thrilling, is it not, to feel that particular tingling when you know something is right, as if fate is whispering in your ear. And though the odds are stacked against you, you simply must see it to the end, ignore the risk and focus on the gain."

Charbonneau frowned disapprovingly. "I do not enjoy wagering. I don't think I am lucky. One must have some knack for good fortune to enjoy games of chance."

She was suddenly impatient with him. "Then sit by my side and for heaven's sake, do not speak so ill. It will jinx my luck."

Taking the chair to her right, he pushed it a bit away from the table to indicate he should not be dealt in. May made pleasant conversation with the other players.

Her luck was good, and she began to play in earnest. Charbonneau drifted away and the player to her left was replaced by an older man whom she barely noticed. She eagerly awaited her cards as they were dealt to the players.

When she felt someone's eyes upon her, she raised her gaze inquiringly to the man who had just been dealt his hand. His shoulders were hunched, his gray hair hanging in his face in a most unbecoming fashion.

May's heart stopped.

Dark brown eyes rimmed with blackest lashes pinned her, each nestled deeply under a slash of brow that forked over a strong, aquiline nose.

It was . . . it was Robert.

She must have reacted, the surprise and joy catching her off guard so that she only recalled her surroundings when he twitched a warning frown at her.

Not knowing what else to do, she jerked her head to study her cards. Whereas the card game had provided adequate distraction only a moment ago, she was suddenly unable to comprehend what it was her eyes were seeing. Random thoughts jumbled in her head as she tried to concentrate.

"It is to you," the woman beside her said gently, and May looked up to find the entire table waiting for her to place her bet.

She flustered, and this drew some notice, for she was known for her poise and unflappability.

Without thinking, she pushed a pile of coins to the center of the table.

She dared a look to Robert.

"Feeling lucky this evening are you?" he said. He'd made his voice low, heavy, with a gruffness that wasn't in his usual tone. It was part of the disguise.

It was remarkable how he had transformed himself. His hair had been grayed, his skin looked sallow, his eyes sunken by dark circles. His hair, usually sleek, appeared wiry. His slender, elegant frame looked heavier. He had padded his middle so that he appeared paunchy.

But that elegant mouth was unmarred. His eyes snapped brightly with mischief, and he was absolutely the most gorgeous thing, even paunchy and gray and sallow, that she had ever set eyes upon.

She shivered, suddenly excited by the danger. "Tonight, a certain modicum of recklessness seems in order," she replied.

His eyes flickered over her, giving her a perusal that was definitely suggestive. She warmed at the explicit sensuality of the look. Her heart hammered, the blood rushed through her veins. The intolerable excitement drove up her temperature.

She was beginning to come back to herself now that the shock was wearing off, ready and willing to play if it was a game Robert had in mind. The smile she gave him was her best come-hither signal, and he returned the gesture in kind.

"Lord Carstairs?"

He attended to his cards at the prod.

May marveled. He masqueraded as a fictitious Lord Carstairs. This . . . disguise. It was so subtle, it amazed her. Had she not loved every line of his face, treasured the exact color of his eyes, the shape of his nose, the way his arrogance rode the high bridge of it, and if she'd not played sensually with the full mouth more times than she could count, she might have been fooled.

He played his turn, then leaned forward on an elbow.

"There is a saying. You probably heard it. It says that when one is lucky in cards, they are then unlucky in love."

"I have not found that to be true." Their eye contact sent bolts of reaction through her.

Someone coughed, drawing their attention.

"My lord, your draw," one of the players said.

Robert pushed a pile of coins to the center of the table. Lady May tried to concentrate on her cards and managed to come up with a play. She had a good head for cards usually but as she expected this to be a throwaway hand, she made a modest wager.

She had just completed her turn when she felt something under the table. She stifled the startled cry that almost erupted at the feeling of Robert's hand on her thigh. Even through layers of silk, she could feel his heat.

She looked at him, and he simply smoldered. She found her stays were much too tight. He said something under his breath, gave her thigh a last squeeze, and smoothly slipped back into a congenial mode to disguise what had just transpired.

She grew impatient with cards, and just when she thought she would scream from the frustration of the pretense, he asked her to dance. She had never danced with Robert, and she loved to dance.

Battling the building pressure in her throat, she accepted, and was led onto the floor. The musicians did a suspiciously abrupt ending, stranding the dancers for a moment before a waltz was struck up.

"You arranged that," she whispered.

"I had to. I cannot recall any of those silly steps of the quadrille or any other." He swirled her about in a deliriously artful move. "But I love the waltz."

She laughed gaily. "You dance divinely for an over-aged man with a sagging middle."

"I am made young again for you."

"While that is extraordinarily flattering, I rather think you are enjoying this little adventure."

His eyes sparkled. He kept his expression completely the same while lifting his eyes and scanning the room so subtly that if she didn't know him so well, she might have missed the significance.

He was watching the room. He didn't forget his ruse, not for a single step. Robert was not a clumsy man, and yet he plodded rather than glided through the waltz, and that was part of the playacting. It was a flawless performance.

"You've done this before." She watched his expression. It didn't change, didn't give anything away.

"Danced? Why, yes."

"No. Disguised yourself. You aren't at all nervous."

"Of course I am. I would be a fool not to be nervous. I would be a bigger fool to flounder while in the midst of the party by showing it."

"Why did you do it?"

His look was enigmatic. "I don't suppose I cared very much for you stepping out so often with that blasted Charbonneau fellow."

"You *were* jealous?" She was incredulous. She had dismissed the thought as ridiculous when it had occurred to her.

He gave a lofty look. "Jealous only that the man can publicly romance you."

"And so you decided to do so as well."

"You do not seem displeased."

"I do not believe I ever knew you to be so . . . devious." She pronounced the last word with relish.

He chuckled, and she laughed, enjoying him too much to worry about the details. He gave her a whirl, foregoing his studied plodding for just one punctuating moment of gracefulness, and it was then that she spied Lord Charbonneau watching them. He was frowning.

It didn't trouble her. She was having too much fun, and she didn't think of him again. It was too exhilarating to have Robert with her like this. Suddenly, the party took on a new meaning. It was great fun.

They danced only a bit more, strolled for a space among the manicured gardens, and chatted with some of her friends who were curious about her strange escort for the evening.

Robert made it his business to appear disagreeable. She thought it adorable, the ruse as thin as gossamer, but indeed, others seemed not only to be eager to put a distance between them, they barely noticed him. And that, she was intelligent enough to realize, was the object all along.

They laughed about it on the way home. He could imitate each and every brand of snub so expertly that her sides ached. He had her breathless, from joy and from kisses. They fell into her bed, their hands clumsy and quick with passion, still apt to burst unpredictably throughout the night into hysterical laughter at a particularly smart moment, or foolish one.

It was exhilarating. She could not recall the last time she had had so exciting a time.

They exhausted themselves with making love. Later, when the candles had gutted themselves and all was quiet, May spoke very softly into the darkness.

"Who are you, Robert?"

She had asked the question many times as he'd slept by her side.

This was the first time she said it when she knew him to be awake. But she still got no answer.

* * *

*Andrew sat in the parlor, waiting for Lord Aylesgarth to ar*rive. In his hand was the old, chipped wooden toy boat Uncle David had given him long ago. He turned it over and over again. It bothered Lord Aylesgarth when he saw the old toy, but it was Andrew's favorite. It made him feel safe. He loved it.

Lord Aylesgarth had presented him with much finer ships. One was a meticulous replica of a Spanish galleon, complete with bristling masts and a tiny mullioned window at the aft cabin. Mama had made a big fuss over it and said it had cost a great deal of money. Andrew supposed it was very interesting, but it wasn't special, not like his old boat.

He'd been given smaller toys as well, stuffed toys and mechanical wonders that performed when wound with a shiny key. Lord Aylesgarth had even purchased a carved pony head on a stick for pretend riding.

But he didn't like these playthings. He didn't like Lord Aylesgarth.

Uncle David and Aunt Luci had tried to talk to him about it. He couldn't tell them—and he wouldn't even if he could—but there were no words to say. It was all feeling. A huge, hard, prickly feeling in his throat when he saw him.

All he knew was that Lord Aylesgarth had made Mama cry. And then . . . he'd made Mama smile. That had been even more upsetting. The truth was, he was awfully frightened of Lord Aylesgarth—not that he thought for a moment that the big man with the wide shoulders and strange, slightly sad smile would harm him. It was not that kind of frightened. There was something about him, as if he assumed command of things so smoothly when he went into a place. And when he came into a place where Mama was, she changed.

When he was about, Mama saw nothing but him. She behaved differently, and Andrew did not like that.

It wasn't fair. He didn't belong with them; he wasn't their family.

Now Mama didn't see Lord Aylesgarth any longer, which was good, although Andrew didn't know why he still had to go on outings if she no longer wished to be Lord Aylesgarth's friend.

Most of the time, however, he *did* like the things they did. Sometimes they visited Lady Grace. Andrew liked her very much. She always had a toffee for him, and she didn't get all nervous and fidgety around Aylesgarth the way other women were always doing—including Mama. Lady Grace liked Lord Aylesgarth, but she spoke sharply to him, arguing with him on occasion—which they both seemed to think was fine—and Andrew thought that was amusing.

And Lord Aylesgarth was nice to him. He never yelled back at Lady Grace, or at Andrew when he was rude. He just let Andrew alone for a while, keeping his distance, his presence immutable and silent. In a way, Andrew *did* like him, and this was very confusing because mostly he wished that the man would just go away.

He heard the coach pull up to the front of the house. Mama appeared in the doorway, her face drawn and her smile false.

This was why he disliked the man. Seeing the effect of his arrival on Mama made the butterflies in his stomach twirl.

"Lord Aylesgarth is here," she said unnecessarily.

Her face was full of understanding. She knew he wanted to stay here with her. He wanted Uncle David to take him to see the ships, not Lord Aylesgarth.

But it would do no good to argue with Mama. She never let him beg off on these outings.

It wasn't fair.

He slid off the seat, stuffing the old, beaten toy into his pocket. The rap upon the door was like a death knell.

Mama grew flustered, her face getting all pink and her hands suddenly fluttering around like a pair of nervous birds. Andrew's mouth went tight, his eyes taking in her reaction.

"There he is. Come." Mama's voice was strange. Sort of high and all breathy, like his was after he raced up the stairs.

Did Mama like Lord Aylesgarth? Or did she hate him as much as Andrew did?

He just couldn't understand.

John Footman showed in the caller. Mama drew Andrew forward, her hand lightly on Andrew's shoulder. He didn't hang back, but neither did he go eagerly.

Aylesgarth was so much taller than Uncle David. It was always startling to Andrew how large he was. He was dark, with lots of hair on his head, where Uncle David had none. His face was handsome but not warm. There was something about him that made you almost want to admire him.

He smiled guardedly at Andrew, and Andrew ducked his head. He was forced to be polite when he really wanted to tell the man to go away!

Mama asked, "Will you be returning before or after tea?"

Lord Aylesgarth didn't look at Mama. He fiddled with his gloves, his nose in the air, and a quality to his voice that, had he the vocabulary, Andrew would have described as disdainful.

"We will take tea together at a hotel." To Andrew, he said, "Lady Grace is in my carriage, waiting for us. She is to accompany us today."

Andrew nodded, barely registering this pleasant news. He watched his mother anxiously.

Mama forced a smile and said that sounded grand. She seemed so sad, and at that moment Andrew wanted to shout at Lord Aylesgarth, but he wasn't quite certain what the man had done wrong. Somehow, he had upset Mama again.

Which is exactly why he disliked the man so much.

When he returned home that evening, he told Mama that the outing had been pleasant, but he did not make much of the exciting events. Lord Aylesgarth had taken him *aboard* a ship. It seemed he owned some ships or something like that, and all the people at the docks treated him with such respect, and despite himself Andrew had been filled with wonder.

Mama thanked Aylesgarth, their manner as polite and stiff as always. And then something very interesting happened. A man came to the door. He was a friend of Lady

May's—Andrew had been presented to him before. He was a lord, and his name always sounded to Andrew to be "charred bones." He wasn't scary, though. He was very pleasant.

He wished Mama could marry him, Andrew thought as all of the grown-ups shuffled around in the hall. Of course, he had already wished she could marry Uncle David, but Uncle David was already married to Aunt Luci, so Mama had explained that she couldn't, and that also she didn't love Uncle David in the right way.

But she looked as if she liked Lord Charred Bones. Although he wasn't as tall or as handsome as Lord Aylesgarth, she always smiled at him and they talked very easily, and quite pleasantly. There were no tense undercurrents, no clouds of gloom over everyone's head like there was with Aylesgarth.

Andrew had a startling and decidedly pleasant thought. Maybe they would be in love, and then Lord Aylesgarth would stop coming about and making Mama so unhappy and upset. Mama could marry Lord Charred Bones!

His nursery maid, Nancy, came to take him to bed because Mama was already dressed and ready to go out with Aunt May. Lord Aylesgarth left quickly at this. Andrew heard his gruff farewell as he climbed the stairs behind his nurse.

He just knew Mama was so relieved now that he'd gone.

The idea that Lord Charred Bones might ask her to marry him led him to a dream, a wonderfully happy dream where they all lived together in the house. When he awoke, he told Nancy the dream. Nancy laughed, saying, "La! I think it be Lady May old 'Charred Bones' is after, young master."

That made him angry, and he thought about it for several days. It nagged him. He knew better than to ask about it. Mama always said he should not worry about adult affairs.

But it *was* his affair. He wanted his mother to marry Lord Charred Bones, and he decided Nancy didn't know anything. In his imagination, he convinced himself not only that it *could* happen, but that it was going to happen.

And when Lord Aylesgarth came to take tea with him a week later, bearing a box with five brightly painted figures small enough to stand on the decks of some of his larger ships, he told him the good news about his mother's impending marriage.

Lord Aylesgarth was not pleased.

Chapter 13

Roman sat with his sister, Grace, both silent as they digested the news he had learned that morning. Apparently, Trista was going to wed Lord Charbonneau and move to a splendid house near the sea.

"She cannot mean to remove the child from London," Grace said. She stirred her coffee, the sound grating on Roman's nerves. "She would not dare."

"She is free to take herself or her child wherever she wishes."

"But you are his father."

"Which I cannot acknowledge. If I do, I expose Trista and the child to scandal."

Grace pressed her lips together as she continued to stir vigorously.

"The boy does not deserve that. He deserves my protection." He ran his hands through his hair. "I have been thinking of letting him go. Nothing is coming of our visiting. He has not eased toward me. I cannot understand why he hates me."

"Perhaps she's poisoned his mind against you. It is obvious she said something to make the boy dread the outings."

Roman shook his head. "Trista most certainly would not put Andrew through any anguish for some petty revenge against me."

Grace sniffed. Sometimes, when she got her back up like this, she put him to mind of their mother on her worst days.

"We have to face the fact that she is marrying this man, this Charbonneau, because she cares for him."

"Do not be foolish. She is in love with you. She always has been and always will be."

Roman only wished this were true. He'd thought—and this was so incredibly stupid he cringed to acknowledge it in his most private thoughts—that theirs was unalterable destiny. He flushed, his ears stinging even though only he knew how mad he'd been.

But he'd felt it, hadn't he? He'd seen her look, the softness, the way she had kissed him, made love with him. Then she'd gone cold again.

Destiny. Thank God he had not spoken of it, nor of the insane ideas that had begun to float in his brain, of possibilities that were not more than gossamer-thin delusions.

Grace said, "Or this may be a ruse to make you jealous, prod you into action."

His patience was running out with his sister's antagonism toward Trista. It was old, it was tiresome, and it was unjust.

"Would that it were," he replied. "Trista has never been manipulative. You've harbored these resentments for all these years, but they are unfounded. So, fine, you dislike her, but you cannot accuse her of an elaborate ruse to get her way. It is more like Trista to run, in case you hadn't noticed."

She was poised to run again. The prospect choked him.

He wouldn't see her again. She'd grow old and have other children. The invisible hand on his throat cinched tighter.

"She runs, just as she always did," Grace said as if explaining something to a child, "so that you will follow."

He drew in a long breath, cautioning himself. "Then she might have made herself a bit easier to find, for I searched.

Can you not spare a little sympathy for a woman in her position when you are yourself a woman?"

"I would never be caught in the predicament she is in," she declared pompously.

He sighed, struggling not to lose his temper. "She believed she was in love, a state in which I gather you have never found yourself."

He stung her with that barb, and he felt a momentary jab of regret, but he did not relent. "You know quite well that I had planned to marry her until Father came to Whitethorn."

"You had responsibilities. You made the right choice."

The word made him dizzy, and it struck him then that he had made his own choice. All of this time, he'd blamed his father. He'd blamed Trista for not understanding he'd had no choice.

But he had. He'd chosen to be the good son because he had needed to be a good son. It had come with sacrifice, but it had not been foisted on him. A draconian choice, true, but his to make. No self-pity on that score, not anymore.

Grace said, "She should have understood. But instead snuck off, taking her child, not even telling you of his existence."

"She thought," he said softly, "that perhaps I owed a responsibility to her as well."

"You defend her as if she were some kind of saint—"

Something inside Roman snapped. "Why is it I am forever defending her to you, but never the reverse?"

"I suppose she has never maligned me," Grace challenged, clearly not believing this.

"In fact, dear sister, she has not. She has never, not once, said a word against you. That is our mother's voice telling you that. It was she who was jealous of everyone, but in her mind the world conspired against her. Tell me—who envied her the pitiful, limited life she led? She was ill. Her mind was ill with the melancholy and drink warped her perception. Why you would wish to emulate her I cannot fathom."

He stopped short, knowing at once that he'd gone too far. And yet he didn't regret it.

"Do you really think I am like Mother?" Her voice was barely a whisper.

He clenched his jaw. "There is much inside of me that prompts me to say no, that I misspoke just now, that I did not mean it. But that would be a lie, and, after all, you do not have to ask me what you already know."

He stopped, feeling a surge of control come over him to tamp down his tirade. His shoulders sank. "Grace, I do not wish to hurt you. We should stop this conversation here. I am not really myself, and I did not say the thing properly. If we speak of this, it should not be in anger. I have much on my mind. Andrew . . ."

Andrew would hate him until the end of his days. And Trista would live in happiness with another man. The hand of dread closed over his gut, nearly folded him in half. He was losing his son. He was losing his love.

"I must go." He left without preamble, not wishing to have to contend with what he had wrought with his rush of words.

"Roman—"

"I will speak to you when I can."

"You must think of something. We cannot lose your son. He is dear to us both."

He nodded and left. The blood had gone out of him, leaving him without strength.

Sickness roiled in his gut. He found what he wanted most was to crawl into a hole and never come out.

He had never been helpless before. Obstacles had been mastered. A bad marriage, financial ruin—those things, he had survived. His past had shaped him, made in him many bad things, but some good as well. He was a man who made his own way. He didn't whine about the costs. He fought—God knows he'd fought back all of his life against the vagaries of fate.

So . . . why would he stop now?

The despondency he'd been feeling drained away as that thought rushed energy into every pore.

How had he forgotten who he was?

* * *

The women gathered in the Hyde Park house were divided on the question of Lord Aylesgarth.

Trista sipped tea after an all-female luncheon with her aunt, her half sister, Michaela, and her cousin, Luci. The topic of discussion was Roman, and had been Roman for the entire visit.

This was prompted by a strange and disturbing comment Andrew had made earlier that day to David. He had said he would not be going on outings with Roman any longer. What was worse, this seemed to delight him.

Trista was aware of nothing that indicated Roman meant to stop seeing Andrew regularly. She had sought the advice of the three people closest to her in how to approach her son.

May felt she understood. "He feels Aylesgarth threatens his happy home. He senses the currents between you two, and it frightens him. He doesn't understand what it is that is so powerful that it influences you as it does. You must explain this to him, Trista, dear. But first, you have to admit it to yourself that you still have strong feelings toward the man."

"How do I explain?" Trista felt a welling of despair. She didn't want to think how right her aunt was. She had almost let herself become Roman's paramour. What life would that be—loving a man, and hating him as well, because he had made her less than she wanted to be?

Michaela offered her advice. "You have to give it time," she said. "I know it is horrible right now, but these things have a way of resolving themselves."

Michaela had a mysterious confidence about the entire matter, as if she understood something she was not quite willing to divulge. But, of course, she was madly in love with her husband and those in love were always unaccountably optimistic, so Trista could not put much stock in that.

"And you?" Trista asked Luci, who shrugged and replied, "I have absolutely no idea. I am only happy that I am not in your position."

Honesty at last. Trista laughed, and they all joined her.

That was when John Footman entered. He seemed uncomfortable as he announced the arrival of the Lord of Aylesgarth.

The women looked at each other, ridiculously guilty at being caught talking about the man with him just outside the doorway.

Trista stood. "I will see him in the blue parlor, thank you."

She'd pay five shillings for as many minutes to make repairs on her appearance, but she could not spare the time for her vanity. He, of course, looked wonderful. Her heart gave a sharp, acute ache. She remembered him like this when he'd come in from riding the fells, wind-blown and flushed and so appealing it made her knees shake to look at him.

No. It was a mistake to keep remembering—she had to stop. It broke her focus, made her weak and vulnerable when she needed to be strong.

He didn't bow, merely inclined his head. "Thank you for seeing me."

He was being civil. But there was enormous energy caged in him, roiling just below the surface. He went to a chair and sat, his legs straddled wide.

His face was guarded, his eyes wary and sharp as darts. She felt the skin on the back of her neck prickle.

"Is it something about Andrew?" she asked, taking a seat across from him.

"In a way. I . . ." His brows shot down, forming a look of consternation. He leaned forward, his elbows on his knees. "I am afraid I do not know how to begin."

She folded her hands and placed them on her lap, determined to wait him out.

"First allow me to say that I am aware that what I am about to ask you is absurdly presumptuous."

He flashed her a quick, self-deprecating smile, the way he always did, to make amends when he'd been wicked. He'd plied her with that look too many times to recount.

She took a deep breath, resolving to stay grounded in the present.

He said, "It is a matter of marriage that I wish to speak to you."

Oh, God. He was marrying again.

"Your marriage?" she managed, the words like sand in her dry throat.

He gave her a grin, full of irony. "More yours, I should think. I wish to know if you are in love with Lord Charbonneau."

"Of course not," she replied without thought.

He seemed relieved. That mobile mouth of his twitched into a smile before he recovered himself and became serious again.

"Then you are doing this for other reasons, and I have a good idea what they are. I think perhaps I can change your mind." He got to his feet. "I have come to a realization. It is a simple one, though not altogether obvious. As I can always rely on you to tell me when I am in error, I will assume you will correct me should my reasoning go astray."

She shook her head, confused. "What—?"

He held up an imperious finger. "You do not trust me. But you want me," he stated calmly. "That infuriating mash of excuses you flew at me about a long-deceased friendship and *curiosity* and such—which I am ashamed to say completely had me duped for a spell—was so much rubbish, it is not worth repeating."

She flushed, recoiling into her seat as he bore down upon her. "I know you too well, Trista. If you deny it, it will not persuade me. Time apart has not lessened the way we always understood each other. I know you. I feel the things that go through your mind. What I do not know is why you are willing to wed someone else when you do not love him? Although I can suppose the only explanation is that you wish to escape from me. How can you know me all of these years and think I could allow that to happen?"

He stopped himself, adding a shrug. "I cannot lose you . . . because of Andrew, of course. You know how I feel on this matter. Therefore, your actions have forced me to take drastic measures to ensure that he will not be removed from me.

That is why I am proposing myself as an alternative—and dare I say, an infinitely more desirable one given my paternity over your son. I ask that you consider me instead of Charbonneau."

She felt overwhelmed, struggling to filter through these words that did not make any sense. And she was growing concerned. She knew this look, this tone. He was a force to be reckoned with at these times, and she was in no way capable of matching him in full verbal combat.

"I wish to return home," he stated. "I wish to take Andrew to Whitethorn, show him the house, the lands, the country that is in his blood. Not some shoreline haven, but the land where you were raised, and I ran wild. It is his."

"You are taking Andrew to Whitethorn," she repeated, shock dulling her brain, focusing only on this.

This was it, then. What she had feared. He was taking her son. He was asserting his rights, and she was going to lose Andrew.

She felt slightly dizzy. Her fingers dug into the tufted cushion of the chair.

She'd fight him. She'd never lose Andrew. "You will not take him away from me," she choked.

He looked at her oddly. "I assumed you would wish to return home as well. I want us to go together."

She stood, inflamed suddenly. "How many times will you make me deny you, Roman? I am not, nor will I ever be, your mistress. I gave up everything not once, but twice already—do you think I would succumb now? Or do you imagine blackmailing me with Andrew will gain you what you wish? How in the world do you imagine—"

"I am not asking you to be my mistress," he said suddenly. "I am asking you to be my wife."

She paused, stunned. From the corner of her eye, she saw a movement, but she was too shocked to realize what it was.

He shrugged. "It makes sense, Trista. Think about it. It is a solution that is more palatable than marrying someone you do not wish to just to escape me. You know you have more feeling for me than Charbonneau. We share a common background, we share Whitethorn. We are of a kind, you and I."

His wife.

Marriage?

She kept thinking these words, over and over in her head.

It was, at one time, all she ever wanted. And now?

She could have him. Her husband, hers for the rest of their years together . . . but it was for Andrew he made this sacrifice.

Was it a sacrifice? Her chest felt as if a stone bore down on it. She struggled to think clearly.

He moved closer, sensing her weakness as emotion flooded over her. She felt for the chair behind her, but he was there, suddenly, and his arm went around her waist, supporting her.

"You know it is the correct thing to do. It simplifies things. It is a better solution than Charbonneau."

"There is no Charbonneau," she said in a rush, not certain she could get the words out. She felt breathless. Though confused, she understood clearly enough that he thought she was engaged to Charbonneau. "Andrew told you something about Charbonneau, did he not? I did not understand why he told David . . . It is no matter." She forced herself to meet his eyes. "I am not engaged to Lord Charbonneau. It is Lady May he desires. He and I are merely friends."

His brow creased for only a moment. Then he shrugged. "Then there are less complications in our way—no messy broken engagement or anyone's insulted pride to contend with. The situation must be faced, Trista. For Andrew's sake. How can you argue against the logic, the absolute necessity of us being wed?"

"Yes, of course." She ducked her head and fought for breath. "It is no doubt best for Andrew, and infinitely desirable for us to be . . . married when he learns the truth."

Stepping closer, he took her chin in his hand and tilted her head up so that she would look at him again. "It is a good course of action, Trista. We want each other—and it is not mere *curiosity*. I shall take you home, as my wife, the mistress of Whitethorn. It's what I promised you a long time ago, after all."

If he wasn't holding her, she might have collapsed onto the carpet.

A wolfish grin spread over his face and he chuckled. "Trista," he murmured softly, and began to lower his head to kiss her.

A shout brought both of them up short. They spun round in unison and there, in the doorway, stood Andrew.

His little face was red, his eyes huge and angry. He shouted, "No! She is not going to marry you. You cannot make her. We are going to live by the sea."

They sprang apart, and Trista only had time to take a step toward her son before he dashed forward and without warning, lifted his small foot and kicked Roman squarely in the shin.

The howl of surprise startled them all. Roman folded, clutching his leg.

"Go away!" cried Andrew, his lips trembling.

"Andrew!" Trista yelled, her voice taking on a sharpness it never had before. "How dare you behave like this!"

"I don't want you to go away with him." He lifted his foot again and took aim.

"Stop it! Stop this at once," she said, grabbing his shoulder and yanking him away before he could do any more damage. "You must not behave this way toward your father."

The words were out before she knew what she was saying. Everything stopped.

Andrew's face went blank. His eyes seemed to grow enormous.

It took a moment for Trista to realize what she had said. She gasped, covering her mouth. She stepped back, looking from Roman to the little boy.

Roman was frozen, stricken, his eyes trained on his son. And Andrew was looking at him.

"It's true," Roman said softly to Andrew. "You are my

son." He took a step forward, then halted. "You even look like me. Haven't you noticed?"

Andrew's infuriated gaze shot to Trista. Very slowly, she nodded. "Yes."

He sputtered for a moment and before they could anticipate what he would do, he turned and bolted from the room.

There was crushing silence for a short eternity, broken at last by Roman's softly spoken inquiry. "Well, then, Trista. What do you say to marriage?"

The question had no fathomable answer other than yes. For every reason, but she spoke only of one. "For Andrew's sake, I will marry you."

His eyes were dark, and she faced him defiantly, acting as if her heart were not breaking. His only word in response was a dark, growling, "Excellent."

And so it was agreed.

*"Marriage!" Lady May exclaimed, clapping her hands to-*gether in delight. "This is wonderful news."

"For Andrew's sake," Trista quickly clarified. She looked from May to Michaela. "He wishes to be with his son, of course. It is all very logical."

Luci was troubled. "Is this . . . arrangement acceptable to you?"

"Indeed, it's . . ." Her bravado faltered. Her hand came up in an airy wave of unconcern, but it froze in midair, then dropped. "It is far preferable than having the boy exposed to the world's scorn."

May and Michaela exchanged doubtful looks. Clearing her throat, May said, "But, Trista, dear, you are fond of him. I know you do care for him, don't you?"

Fond of him. She was insanely in love with him. Her heart had not beat once in all these years without her loving him.

"I am fond of him," she allowed in a tame voice, betraying nothing.

"But . . . oh, dear." Michaela looked uncomfortable. "Is he fond . . . What I mean to say is, does he only wish the child, or . . . Dear Trista, I am most concerned that he will treat you well."

Trista looked away, not able to hold those green eyes Michaela was famous for. Aunt May said they were their father's eyes. They saw so much. Things she didn't wish anyone to see.

"He is a good man," she answered, knowing this was not what Michaela was asking. She wished to know if Roman loved her. They were talking around it, using words like *fond* and *care* instead of what they meant, but they all clearly understood what tact would not allow them to say.

She tried to face her sister again, but Michaela's eyes gleamed with hope and she had to look away, for that hope was within her own heart. Michaela had such great love in her life, she wanted no less for Trista. Trista realized this and appreciated it, trying not to think on how it depressed her.

"He wants me because I am Andrew's mother." That much was true. What more she could say on the matter, she hardly knew. "Do not have any worries. He will treat me with the respect my status as his wife deserves."

The concern in her sister's face did not dissipate, as if she sensed Trista's wavering confidence. To bolster the illusion that she was joyous, Trista smiled and laughed. "It will be lovely, you will see."

"I know it will," Aunt May said, patting Michaela's hand, as if to comfort her. She rose and came to Trista and kissed her. "You are to be congratulated. Lord Aylesgarth is quite impressive, my dear. He has my favor. I know this will turn out to be the right choice, Trista. I *feel* it."

But Michaela was not so easily silenced. She asked, "And Andrew is happy?"

Trista's smile froze. She could not lie to them on this account. "He will get used to the idea. In time."

May touched her face affectionately. "You are being evasive, and you should know by now that will simply not work with me. Luci and Michaela, too, are not so easily fooled. What exactly did the child say?"

"Nothing." Trista gave up her pretense of sangfroid. "I

told him he was to have a new father and he said absolutely nothing. Not one single word. I fear he had hopes of my marrying Lord Charbonneau, if you can believe such nonsense, and us living by the sea. That is what prompted this entire thing. He told Lord Aylesgarth, and that was what made Roman propose."

"Oh, dear," Luci groaned. "That child has a troubling imagination. He employs it to avoid thinking about the things he dislikes. He may not be very . . . accepting, then."

Michaela was thoughtful. "Pardon me, but did you say it was for fear of you marrying Lord Charbonneau that Lord Aylesgarth spoke?"

"It was. I am afraid Andrew told him . . . well, not a fib. A hope, I daresay. He wanted me to marry someone else. For some reason he is adamantly opposed to Roman."

Michaela's mood brightened. "Well, that is it, then. The man was jealous." Michaela tossed her head, setting gleaming fat curls bouncing. "Jealousy is a good sign, do you not agree, Aunt May?"

"It is. Oh, let's not fret over this. All will be well." She hurried to the escritoire and pulled out a plumed pen and a sheet of paper. "We must get busy. This is a dreadfully hurried affair. Marriage by special license . . . ah, well, the sooner it is settled, I suppose the better for everyone. Oh, come, Trista, let us be merry about it. And do not worry over the boy. He will come around."

Trista sighed. They both seemed absurdly optimistic, dismissing all her cares. Would it were so simple.

So what if Roman was jealous? He still thought of her as his. Habit, no doubt. And Andrew's silence was far from benign. He hated the idea of the marriage, but he was too resigned to make a tantrum over it because he knew it would not bring him what he wanted.

But she was going to marry Roman, nonetheless, so she made herself cheerful and spoke no more of her concerns.

The business of getting married was accomplished with great speed and little fuss. The ceremony was performed at St. George's in Hanover Square. Luci and Michaela were

Trista's attendants. Grace was there as well as a large gathering of Roman's friends.

There was a grand breakfast afterward. Roman insisted and May had happily conspired to bring it about. The single biggest surprise came when Grace extended the invitation for her home to be used for the affair. It was Roman's house, really, and Trista wondered if this was the reason the place was offered. It was no secret Grace was nearly as disillusioned about the union as Andrew.

The boy had not warmed to the idea in the short interval it took to prepare for the big day. He sat stoically through the ceremony, insisting on holding his uncle David's hand.

He had refused to discuss the matter of Roman's being his father, although Trista had tried many times to explain it to him. He'd once said, "You'll have other babies and forget about me," and Trista had emphatically insisted that this would never be the case. He told her he wished she would marry Uncle David.

Trista asked him, "Why do you fear you will be left behind with Lord Aylesgarth, but not if I marry Uncle David?"

"Because Uncle David loves me," he replied simply.

"Your father loves you," she said.

His eyes had grown luminous, and she saw by the mutinous set of his chin that he wished to say something but was unsure if he should. "Go ahead," she told him.

After a moment, he said, "He doesn't tell good stories."

"Oh, darling, he is simply different, and I'm afraid you are one of those people who dislike it very much when things turn out to be different than what they expected. But change is inevitable, and often happens for the good. You'll be pleased in the end, I promise. We will be happy."

"Are you happy, Mama?" he asked, his voice high and filled with desperate appeal. He needed to be reassured.

Was she happy? Yes. Yes, for she had the man at last who she'd wanted all of her life. And sad because he was marrying her to solidify a claim on this child and not for love of her. It was bitter only because once she had hoped for so much more.

Once she'd had his love, but not his name. Now she would have his name . . . but what of his love?

"I am very happy," she had told Andrew, and he'd relaxed somewhat. She'd held him, and he'd let her. Sometimes he didn't, for it was important above all things to be grown up and some things he had determined big boys did not do. He could be quite insistent about it at times, and then at others he would disregard the entire nonsense and snuggle to her like he used to do when he was in nappies.

This he did now, and she savored the feel of him, small still but growing. He was growing fast.

She was glad at that moment that it had all happened the way it had. If she'd waited much longer to tell him the truth, it might have been worse. As he'd gotten older, he might have hated her for lying to him for so long. He was still young enough to forgive her.

For all of her fretting over her son, she was not immune to the import of the day. She felt as if she floated through it, receiving the well-wishers with a smile and giving appropriate responses, yet all the while acutely aware of Roman.

There was no sign of his being at all the reluctant bridegroom. He was polite to their guests and her family, attentive to her and Andrew, and, if she wasn't being a tad vain to think it, excited. His eyes glowed and his mouth stretched frequently in a ready smile.

When the guests had gone and the servants were busy about their work of putting the house to rights, Trista, Roman, and Andrew took their leave. Upon arriving at the Hyde Park house, Trista had what she thought was an inspiration. Instead of her putting Andrew to bed, she suggested Roman should do it.

Her son did not seem delighted. Roman inclined his head, acquiescing to the suggestion, but he did not seem to think it a good idea either.

Trista peeked in at them later. Andrew was lying in his little cot. Roman seemed so large next to him, seated on a chair and reading stiffly from a children's book. Two things indicated this was not going well—Roman's flat, staccato reading voice, completely devoid of the kind of theatrics David used to great effect and which delighted Andrew so, and the second being the simple fact that the boy was lying with his back turned toward his father.

She crept to her bedroom, and when Roman came in, she put on a cheerful face. "Is Andrew asleep?" she asked brightly.

"I believe so," Roman replied, "although he might have been pretending so that I would leave him in peace."

"He will adjust," she said.

"Things will be better when we are at Whitethorn." He slipped his left hand into his trouser pocket and drew out an object she did not see. He paused a moment. Then he looked up, smiling at her before turning away, the matter put aside.

The mention of Whitethorn had a strange effect upon her.

Whitethorn and Roman. They were one in the same, a part of her past, a part of her now.

She was humbled by the recollections. The mercurial boy, the tender, wild-hearted lover, the quiet, slightly sad man all came to her mind. And the feeling that overrode it all was the elusive knowledge that she had what she had wanted most.

She was his wife, what she'd wanted. Why wasn't it enough?

Roman watched her, and she realized that she'd been standing in the middle of the room, staring at nothing as her thoughts jumbled in her head.

He smiled, approached her, and gently cupped her chin. "If I did not know you so well, I might think you were nervous."

She was no shy bride on her wedding night, though she found it difficult to meet his eye. He might guess the things she'd been thinking, wanting, and it would shame her for him to know she still loved him when he had spoken only of desire.

But he had always known how to get around any show of reticence. His patient kiss melted her, stripping away all thought and bringing her to the most elemental level where the two of them had no doubts, no misunderstandings, no problems. He took her as his wife, and she held him inside her, savoring this moment and forbidding herself to want anything more for a little while.

And it was enough, it was. For a little while.

*The following day, when Roman began to make arrange*ments to leave, Trista protested that it was too soon, but in this he would not be swayed.

He wished to take his family home.

Chapter 14

What surprised Trista most about her first sight of the massive house was that it made her want to weep. She fought the impulse bravely, mindful of the pair of eyes set raptly on her, for Andrew was apprehensive and wary.

Still, it got away from her a bit.

She dabbed at her face with her handkerchief. She smiled at her son, wanting to reassure him. "I'm happy," she explained. "Women are sometimes silly about these things."

He laid his cheek against her arm. Raising her gaze, she found Roman studying them dispassionately. He turned to the window, and watched in silence as the sprawling place grew closer.

In an effort to appear cheery, she said, "The gardens are looking quite green."

"They've a lot of rain in these parts."

"I don't like rain," Andrew said softly.

"Well, the rain's done now," Roman told him, "and it's left behind lovely lawns to run upon and thickets in which to find rabbits, and leagues of countryside where you will discover all sorts of adventures. I know. I found a few here myself when I was your age."

He frowned and a sweep of ridiculously long lashes veiled his eyes again.

The staff lined up outside. Trista alighted and squared her shoulders—why, she was nervous! She approached the house.

She was the mistress of Whitethorn, and that thought thrilled and terrified her. The place of her childhood and of her seduction had grown in her memory to mythical proportions, both too wonderful and too awful to be accurate.

On one side of her was Andrew, shrinking into her skirts. She felt like that, a part of her just as overwhelmed as he was. How ever would she manage being mistress of this great house?

And on the other side of her stood Roman, tall and proud, surveying his domain, a look of peace and pleasure on his face that inspired a similar welling within her own breast.

Yes, she felt like that as well. She was coming home.

The current housekeeper, Mrs. Wells, and the head footman, called John as all head footmen were, stepped up and she greeted them. They called her Lady Aylesgarth. She'd heard it before, of course, but here, on the great stone steps of the house that was now to be hers, she *felt* it for the first time.

Roman's hand cupped her elbow, and when she looked up at him, she found only a kind smile, as if he might guess her emotion. He led her inside.

"This is Whitethorn, Andrew," he said when they stood in the large great hall. A fire glowed a welcome in the massive hearth that was as tall as Trista herself. "This is your home."

Andrew forgot to be sullen for a full minute. He gaped at his surroundings, and it was clear to see he was impressed.

That made Roman smile, and his gaze shifted to Trista, and she smiled, too.

Dinner was a grand affair in the dining room. Roman saw this, frowned, and shifted his place setting so that they were closer. Then, after a moment to think about it, he had Andrew summoned and set a place for him.

"Just on our first night, you understand," he told the boy.

Andrew, still wide-eyed, sat in his chair. Trista laughed, delighted with the idea. The huge chairs with upholstered seats and backs and heavy carvings on the arms dwarfed the child. He looked lost in a giant world.

Roman raised his brows, looking down his long, well-shaped nose at his son. "What do you think of Whitethorn, Andrew?"

"It is very nice, sir."

Roman touched his tongue to his top lip, and Trista knew he was trying not to smile. "Indeed, thank you. It would be seemly if you would address me as 'Father,' now that we are a family."

Andrew's face creased. He seemed quite cross. His head snapped around to Trista. "Must I, Mama?"

She started to say that he did, but Roman spoke first. "I would prefer it, but if you do not wish—"

Trista intervened. "Roman, perhaps if you recollect that our son is in possession of your willfulness, you will see the merit in taking a firm hand. He is to call you Papa, of course."

"Nonsense." He placed his elbows on the table and laced his fingers. "You know nothing of boys. Boys need to be free to choose their own way, they cannot have these things forced upon them."

"On the contrary," she countered. "Boys need strong guidance. Some boys more than others. Now, it is a courtesy that I expect of him, and he understands the necessity of that."

"Manners and courtesy are womanish." He threw Andrew a conspiratorial look, as if sharing exasperation over women. He sat back, sighing, and said to Andrew, "You think the house grand, do you?"

The boy piped up in reply. "My bed is so high I have to climb onto a stool to reach it."

"Have a care not to fall out of it when you are sleeping. I remember that bed."

Andrew looked concerned and nodded. "There are lots of toys up there."

"Did you see the spring horse?"

"That's too babyish for me," Andrew said.

"Of course," Roman replied smoothly. "Perhaps the tin soldiers."

"I have tin soldiers."

"Yes, I recall that you do, quite a number. I brought some to you and you told me you had more than enough and I should return them to the toy shop."

Andrew had the grace to look shamefaced.

Roman asked, "Which toys do you like . . . oh, wait—"

And they finished in unison, "The ships."

"Still determined to be a sailor, are you?"

Andrew answered, "Oh, yes!"

"Ah, then we shall have to visit the lake."

"The lake!"

"Indeed," Roman said. He took his time in elaborating, chewing for a space before saying, "Whitethorn has its own lake, a few of them, actually, but one is really spectacular. Very good for skipping stones, I'd say."

"What about sailing boats?"

Roman nodded, continuing in a pleasant vein. "Indeed. We can sail even regular rowboats on it. Your toy boats would be fine, too. It is very picturesque."

"What is pic-a-rest?"

Trista leaned forward, "Pretty. Now eat."

Pleased, Andrew took the fork in hand and began to address his food, chewing thoughtfully.

After dinner, Andrew was sent upstairs. "Good night, Mama," he said, coming to Trista to give her a kiss. He had Nancy with him, but it seemed to her that he lingered at her side a bit longer than was strictly necessary. It might be that he was a bit afraid.

"How about if I come and see you after you've washed up?"

"Yes, thank you." He hesitated again, then his eyes shifted shyly to Roman. "Good night."

"Good night, Andrew."

He went to Nancy.

Roman was unusually quiet. Trista was restless herself, and she stood up, thinking to find something to do to break the tension. Perhaps there were playing cards in the escritoire. She located some and laid out a hand, then gathered them together when she couldn't concentrate.

"Are you going to see to him, then?" Roman asked.

"In a while," she answered, rising to replace the playing cards.

He was sitting in the chair, not really looking at anything, and it struck her that as momentous as this homecoming was for her, it must be for him as well.

She drew to his side. "It's been kept up beautifully."

"I made certain it was."

"You always loved this house."

He looked at her oddly. "No. I didn't."

She was taken aback.

"But you wished to come back."

His eyes lowered to half-mast. "A wounded animal crawls back to its den to die."

What did he mean—wounded? Die?

He drew in a breath. "I am not that unchanged, I suppose. It was here in this house that absolutely everything of consequence happened, good or ill. So what else would I do, I ask you, but rush here and battle it all at once. No sense dithering about in London." His laugh was low and filled with self-ridicule. "I've never done things by halves, Trista. You know that. Here is where I found what mattered and here is where I lost it. It has seen my happiest moment and even more of my ignominious defeats. Whitethorn witnessed it all."

"But don't you love Whitethorn?" she asked, bewildered.

"I hate it," he said. He rose and stretched, then laughed. "But I will defeat it."

His eyes locked on hers. "I will. Now, you had better go see to Andrew. Whitethorn is an intimidating place, and it is his first night."

* * *

The room that had been prepared for her was the Lady's suite. This brought a slight shock to Trista when Mrs. Wells, who seemed to have taken the transition of Trista becoming her mistress without a stumble, showed her in.

The fact that the housekeeper accepted her put a major worry out of her brain. Mrs. Wells would set the tone for the other servants, many of whom Trista had known when she herself was in service here.

As they puttered about, setting the room to rights, the housekeeper caught Trista up with the news on those in the house—who had married, who had left, who had died, and who had retired.

Listening, Trista looked about her. She was very familiar with these rooms, and the association was not completely pleasant. Her mother could be found here, every day, attending Lady Aylesgarth, and upon her death, Trista herself had spent all her hours by the old woman's bedside, seeing to her duties as her caretaker. She had not been harsh or even demanding, but she had been very depressing.

The place had been aired and freshened, but otherwise, it was exactly as it had been then. As Mrs. Wells lit the lamps for her, Trista thanked her for the effort she had made to effect a welcoming feeling.

"We want you to know we're happy to have you home." Mrs. Wells beamed at her.

Trista gave in to the impulse she'd been resisting and hugged her. Mrs. Wells said good night with a happy smile, and left her to get ready for bed. She was alone for only a moment when Roman knocked, then peeked his head around the door.

"Hello," he said. "How are you getting on?"

She felt an instant surge of relief at seeing him. "Very well," she lied.

"Grace has sent word that she would like to join us here. I said it was a good idea."

She spoke up eagerly. "Perhaps she would prefer this room."

He looked about, and she thought his expression was a

bit baleful. "It would not be proper. It is the mistress's suite. And it is important to set the right tone, especially at first."

"But I do not think these rooms really suit me."

Roman laughed. "What will the servants think if you do not take the Lady's suite? Come now, it will seem less strange in time. You can't have your old room in the attics, can you?"

Roman hovered at the threshold, his eyes tracking her as she went from ornate chair to plush crimson draperies to heavily carved chests with a twist of distaste on her face.

"You will become accustomed to it," he said, but he didn't sound convinced, as if he, too, had doubts. "After all, we came here to confront our ghosts, did we not?"

Her head snapped to look at him. "Did we?"

His reply was a sober look, and she had the feeling he was not really seeing her.

She could not relax here, and yet he had an excellent point about setting the correct tone. It had troubled her no small amount that she might not be accepted by the staff and the neighborhood. It was thoughtful of Roman to arrange for her to be given all the trappings of her new position.

Therefore, she could hardly say she didn't want to stay here. She really was probably being a ninny over all of it. And he was surely correct, she would grow used to it in time and the stilted discomfort that had suddenly seized her would fade.

"I'll leave you then," he said. "Have a pleasant night."

She was terrified, astonishment apparent on her face. She had thought he would wish to stay with her tonight. He'd been so attentive, so amorous since they'd been married. Although nothing had been resolved, bed was the one place she could shed the complexities of what lay between them. She had been awaiting him as she had prowled this room, she just now realized, wanting very badly for that same reassurance she found in his arms.

"Very well," she said in a weak voice that didn't sound at all like hers.

He stepped back and shut the door, sealing himself in the safety of the outer hall.

She wished she had the courage to call him back.

A strange emotion enveloped her as she faced the room alone. Scenes played in her memory of Lady Aylesgarth, of her mother, of herself. When she'd come to this house as a child, it had been a haven from the scourges the world would make against a bastard child, but it had not been a home.

Was it now?

Strangely, despite all of this time and the many profound changes the years had wrought, she still felt like an interloper.

Lord Charbonneau sat with great flourish, his expression pinched and smug. Lady May watched him, a mild, guarded smile in place as her mind quickly assessed that cat-who-ate-the-canary gleam in his eye.

She didn't trust men as a rule. She'd learned that lesson a long, long time ago, and quite bitterly.

But she didn't hate them. In point of fact, she liked their company. Men were infinitely amusing . . . in their place. In the fifteen years since being widowed, only one man had breached the aloofness behind which she had sheltered after Matthew's death.

Robert owned a part of her and it was an exhilarating discovery to want to belong to another in a way she had not ever dreamed. Under other circumstances, it might have been uncomplicated. And yet . . .

And yet there was the past stocked with ghosts and rattling skeletons, both hers and Robert's. Something told her they would only be ignored for so long.

"Dear Lady May," said Charbonneau. He beamed at her, the glimpse of whatever had raised her internal alarm gone now. "You are utterly ravishing. That dress is simply gorgeous. It makes you glow."

"You exaggerate. This is only a simple frock." They

laughed, both sharing the jest, for Lady May did not have in possession anything any person would call a simple frock.

He sat back. "I must thank you for inviting me for tea."

"Your message said that you had some rather peculiar news—quite a scintillating tease, those words. I simply couldn't resist." Her smile was slightly scolding. "Which I am sure you guessed would be the case. Oh, but I have not seen you in so long a time, I thought it right and fitting that we should have tea together, just us, and catch up on all the news."

"Yes. My thoughts exactly, my dear. You have been . . . otherwise occupied." There was a distinct sourness in his tone.

It was then she sensed a cat-and-mouse game, a test of patience. He had something very important to tell her, and he was going to take his time about it. May poured out when the tea tray arrived, pretending interest in the minor peccadilloes of those in their social set. He particularly delighted in relaying the shocking tale of Lady Masterson's son running off with a vicar's daughter.

"Of course, she was well-endowed, in that particular way of women that makes men stupid." He raised his brows and May gave an obligatory giggle. "And so, who could blame him? Oh, dear, and have you heard that Lord and Lady Beckinsdale engaged their seventeen-year-old, Larissa, to the ancient Duke of Henley?"

"That old lecher!"

"Indeed, it is a disgrace. I might pity the chit, but she is so giddy at being a duchess, she doesn't even mind," he said, sinking his teeth into the soft center of an iced cake.

"Of course, there are advantages of marrying someone older. Widowhood, to put a fine point to it. It does have its merits. Not to mention that she will be a duchess and wealthy. Perhaps the girl is not so foolish."

They exchanged smiles, both executing their measure in this crafted small-talk, whiling the time until he worked his way to what he had come for.

He got to it right after his second cup was poured.

"Oh, I almost forgot to mention that I had heard something about that Lord Carstairs for whom you've shown so much fondness of late."

A stab of emotion—resentment laced with fear—jabbed hard at her chest. Of all the things she'd anticipated, she hadn't thought it would be Robert.

"Come, May, you know who I mean. You met him playing cards a few weeks ago?"

"Oh, yes," she said. "I've enjoyed his company several times since. But I hardly call it a fondness."

"Yes. We all noticed you seemed to find his company particularly diverting. It has everyone talking," he said, and it sounded like an admonishment. For the first time, she realized just how deeply his jealousy ran.

Strange, that she hadn't thought of that before. That had been stupid. Lord, she hadn't thought of Charbonneau at all—or anyone else—let alone take into account his feelings. She had simply been having too glorious a time with Robert.

But Charbonneau . . . he had been a friend, merely—surely he'd known that. True, she'd known he wished the relationship to be more, but as she had done with many men before him, she had quickly disabused him of any notions of intimacy. She was so clever at the game by now, a master at turning the tide of the infatuation so that she and the besotted man always parted the best of friends.

The first crawl of apprehension danced along her spine, and she thought that perhaps she'd been foolish in her joy at having Robert and her engage in a spectacular and exciting farce.

It seems it had drawn interest. Instinctively she knew that was dangerous for Robert.

Charbonneau wiped his fingers on a linen napkin. "There is a good deal of gossip about the fellow, you know. It's all rather mysterious, him turning up in society like that, all of a sudden. And you know, the hostesses of the parties he's attended all admit on close questioning that they did not invite him, but his presence was so intriguing and made their soirees such a hit that they didn't admit it."

May felt light-headed and took in a long, deep breath to steady her nerves. The sense of alarm increased.

"It was Lord Camric that noticed this Lord Carstairs as he calls himself bears an uncommon resemblance to a certain noble family. Camric was very good friends with the late Lord Lyles and mentioned that Carstairs bears a strange resemblance to his friend. Alas, as inferred by the usage of the word *late,* his old comrade is dead, so it could not be him."

She laughed, a sharp, rude sound of relief. "Then how does any of this signify?"

"He recollected the son was very similar in appearance to Lord Lyles. His youngest, Marcus."

Her smile faded. "I am familiar with Lord Camric. Surely you cannot put any credence in what he says. He is in his dotage. His memory is gone, and no doubt his eyes are unsure."

"The strange thing about old age, however, is that recent memory is gone, lost in a fog of confusion, but long-distant recollections emerge fresh and keen with just a little prodding. Knowing this, I asked several men of advanced years if they knew Lord Carstairs. He looked to be their age, and I thought perhaps they might recognize him. They also noted the resemblance. Knowing it could not be Lord Lyles, I asked about the son. They affirmed Camric's recollection of a distinct resemblance. Now, is that not most odd?"

He grinned. May was silent, dread gathering around her.

"Indeed, not the strangest, however. Lyles's son, this would be Marcus Roberts—that is the family name, Roberts—is also dead."

He let that pronouncement sit for a moment, then frowned, prodding, "Do you not recall the name? He was that traitor who jumped to his death off London Bridge rather than face punishment for the crime of murder," Charbonneau went on.

"And what does this have to do with Lord Carstairs?"

"The resemblance," Charbonneau said with a smug air.

"But how could such an elderly gentleman as Lord Carstairs have anything to do with Lord Lyles's son? There is a score of years difference in their ages. And what is all this talk of a dead son? I fear I am most confused."

"It would seem a puzzle. But, dear Lady May, I recollected a fellow I knew at University. My age, he was, and of normal appearance, but when I saw him years later I would have sworn he was double his age. No mistake, he looked awful. It's rough living that does it, doesn't it?"

He spread his hands and for the first time May noticed how soft and white they were. She shivered with repulsion.

"And so," he continued, "what if this Roberts, suspected of treason and murder when he ran off, has unduly aged."

"But you said he was dead."

"I said he jumped from the bridge. Curiously enough . . ." He paused, his tone bubbling with unchecked excitement. "I did a bit of checking. They found a body. Drowned. But it was a while after Roberts disappeared, and, well, the river isn't kind. The body was not identifiable, but there was his clothing and a watch that were linked to Roberts, but these things are easily feigned."

"If I am inferring your meaning correctly, you believe Lord Carstairs to be the infamous Marcus Roberts. But this is flawed, sir, as surely there were witnesses of his flight into the river."

"There were, but can we believe them? Marcus Roberts was a crafty one, do not forget. After all, he killed that French count in cold blood."

May was certain the pressure in her head was going to burst a blood vessel. She remembered now—the entire scandal. The French count was a fellow named de Nancier, an aristocrat who had come after the French Revolution to stay with relatives in London. He'd been found with his throat cut.

Robert had done that?

No. Marcus Roberts had. But were the two one in the same?

She gave no indication of her inner thoughts. Donning an

expression of interest, she kept her gaze direct, intent and very, very careful.

"It was a ghastly business. And there was the little girl."

May thought she might lose herself for a moment. The room tilted in one crazy swoop, but, no, it righted herself, and she managed to sound calm as she asked, "Did they attribute that to him?"

"It was never known. The girl said it was a stranger who used her so vilely, and it is widely assumed by her family to have been Roberts. She nearly died, and still bears the injury, poor thing. Her leg was never allowed to set properly."

"It is far-fetched. I must tell you, it is a thin accusation when so much indicates that Marcus Roberts is dead, and it is a serious business to malign Lord Carstairs without anything but such outrageous conjecture."

"It is only a possibility. Of course, I cannot prove it. I merely open the subject to consideration. I cannot help it if people are talking now that Camric has made the association . . ."

He paused effectively, giving May enough time to form a clear picture of how the gossip was fermenting even as they spoke, making it impossible for Robert to appear in public with her again. They didn't know, not for certain, but the talk was enough.

And she was equally certain that Charbonneau had arranged it.

She felt ill. But she was damned if she would allow Charbonneau to see it.

"This is fascinating," she gushed. "Have you confronted Lord Carstairs—or whoever he is with any of this?"

Horrified, Charbonneau replied, "Certainly not. If Camric is correct, why, the man is dangerous. Oh, not a hazard to myself, I dare say, but you've kept such constant company with him, I feared he might target you if indeed he is the savage we suspect."

It was exactly her association with him that had brought Robert into Charbonneau's sights. May felt guilt, and fear. Strong fear.

"Indeed, I will give him a sturdy cut so that he will not mistake me," she assured her guest. "Oh, do not worry, I shall do nothing to indicate it was you who put me wise to the shroud of suspicion around him. I shall simply lose interest. This I do all of the time. Perhaps I can find someone else to amuse me at parties. I suppose Lord Dalrumple will do. He is an earl, after all, and he has been so attentive lately."

He bristled, clearly having planned she would return to him, fall into his arms in gratitude for saving her from social ruination or actual danger. This she knew, and savored his discomfiture. It was spiteful, teasing him like that but she didn't regret it.

"I've upset you," Charbonneau observed in a wheedling tone.

Her mind was working furiously. The best thing to do now was to call off Charbonneau as quickly as possible, and that meant assuring him that his tactics had been effective.

"Oh, dear. If what you say is true, it is rather disconcerting to think I have been keeping company with such a man."

Charbonneau leaned forward, and for a moment all of his chilling joy at what he had wrought showed on his face. "But you shall not be doing so in the future. You will not see Lord Carstairs again. I hesitated to bring this matter to your attention, but fears for your safety precluded all other consideration."

How she would have liked to slap him. For Robert's sake, she lowered her eyes, knowing exactly how to look placid and demure. "No, I certainly shall not."

Chapter 15

Jason Knightsbridge gazed at Whitethorn and felt a welling of emotions he couldn't name. He'd spent half his youth here, climbing in and out of windows, running down the servants' stairs, or sneaking up them to Roman's rooms. He and the son of this house had been two of a kind in their boyhood days—unrepentant hellions, scourges upon the hamlets nestled in these parts, as mischievous as boys could be and not find themselves behind the bars of a gaol.

He'd had a good home, not like what Roman had had to contend with, and it had driven his mother to distraction why he would act so outrageously when he'd been taught better. His old Gran used to say it was just a devil in him. That, he often thought, was true. He had a need to run, to feel the rush of a thrill at a prank, to taste the wildness of a life outside ordered life, interminable lessons, monotonous chores, and quiet evenings by the fire.

Once at a fair, a wizened gypsy woman had looked at him and told him his soul was on a quest. He'd laughed at that. But she'd turned out to be right. She probably said that to half her customers, but in his case, it had been exactly on the mark. He'd found that quest . . . or it had found him.

He adjusted his collar, thinking that perhaps he should remove it, just for this first meeting, then thought better of it. For all he knew, Roman had already been informed that his childhood partner in crime had taken over the parsonage.

He raised the knocker and squared his shoulders. The hair he'd pulled into a queue at the nape of his neck tickled the spot between his shoulder blades as his thoughts brushed over the question that had been uppermost in his mind all morning.

Would Grace be here?

He caught himself and scowled at his foolishness. And what difference would it make if she were? She had no use for him. He might be a parson, quite reformed from the young scamp he'd been in his youth, but his new status did not redeem him from the fact that she could not abide him. All may be equal in the eyes of God, but the country life was an ordered life, where everyone knew their place.

Hers was the delicate young lady of the big country house, and his was the wastrel she had always looked upon with thinly masked distaste. He knew it was a defensive dislike on her part. He had stolen her brother, taken him off on raids and adventure, and they'd ditched the pampered princess. Oh, yes, she'd fairly detested him for all of the abandonment throughout the years.

It was unfortunate that he'd glimpsed something in her he hadn't been able to forget in the years she'd been gone. Most of all he remembered those large eyes that were like dark windows to depths that had intrigued him enough to still wonder after all this time what secret thoughts they held. The child he and Roman had regarded as no more than a pest for so many years had grown up into a remarkable woman, and he'd only realized her quiet force and unstated beauty just before she'd left Whitethorn to follow Roman to the City.

"Reverend Knightsbridge," the old butler said pleasantly. He was a parishioner and active member of the small church Jason tended on the other side of the hills.

Jason removed his hat. "Williams, it is good to see you. So, this is the front door."

"Come in, sir." The servant chuckled. "Is it the first time you've seen it, then?"

"I am quite familiar with the kitchen gardens, many spots of which are ideal for throwing stones at window panes to certain rooms, and with the service entrances where one might sneak inside when one is not supposed to, but it is the first time I've been at the front door. It is rather a nice door. Oak, I should think."

They laughed, and Jason ran his hand over his thick gold hair, finding himself nervous. "Will you ask if Lord Aylesgarth will see me?"

After it was determined that the master was at home—which meant Roman would see him—Jason was shown into the library.

"My God!" Roman roared, seeing his collar. "You are a priest?"

"A humble parson," Jason said, laughing. "No more remarkable than you. Lord Aylesgarth and master of Whitethorn. I always knew you would inherit, of course, but it is quite a different thing in actuality."

"The hell with all of that," Roman said, striding forward in that definite way he always had, as if doubt never plagued him. He shook Jason's hand with a vigorous pump. "I am glad to see you. I had thought to write you, but then it went the way of all my best intentions."

Jason grinned. "I cannot believe you've come home. And married to Trista Nash, of all things, after so much time. It is wonderful."

Roman gave him an arch look. "Oh. It is too marvelous to be believed."

Picking up on the sarcasm, Jason said, "In trouble again, are you?"

"I fear I've rushed in where angels fear to tread."

"It was your habit of old."

"Yes, well, some things, I fear, do not change," Roman stated drolly. He spread his hands wide. "I don't know if what I require is a drink or a parson."

Jason said, "Why not both?"

They sat comfortably, Roman demanding to know how the devil he wound up a man of God.

"It just came to me one day. As I'd never had any ambition, I didn't wish to learn a trade. I used to like to read. I probably never told you, ashamed because I thought you would call it womanish. It wasn't something hellions did."

"No, indeed, it would have been an unforgivable disgrace. Too quiet a pastime. Hellions like we were, they prefer to let crabby Mrs. Fitzbert's hens out at three in the morning, making a ruckus to wake the dead."

"Or steal old Mr. Henshaw's laundry and hang it out of the church belfry."

They guffawed, recalling some of their more hilarious mischief, then caught themselves. "Oh, that was wrong," Jason said, his lips still twitching.

Roman cleared his throat. "Absolutely. We should have been given the switch."

"Remember when Kenly over in the village tried to do just that?"

They burst into laughter again.

"Stay for luncheon, will you," Roman said. "Trista will have my hide if she doesn't get to visit with you."

They went for a walk around the grounds. Roman asked about the current happenings in the neighborhood, amazed at the thorough and thoughtful discourse his old friend gave on the community. It was quite a change from their wild days when they had cared for no one but themselves.

When they returned to the house, they ordered refreshments and removed their coats.

"Time has altered some things, but others remain the same," Jason observed. "Here we are, grown men, and look at us. No one could have dreamed you would return to preside over the family seat."

"And you would be wearing a collar," interjected Roman.

"Yet you and Trista are still together. Tell me, is she changed as well?"

Roman avoided Jason's gaze. "She is beautiful. She is full of generosity and energy. But she is different. Life has altered her as well." He pursed his lips, looking moody. "She . . . we have a son."

He paused for Jason to digest this before adding, "He is five years of age. The official story is that Trista married a Captain Fairhaven who sired the boy. It was what he believed up until a few months ago. This captain is a complete fiction. Trista was never married, but I do not wish to expose this. Therefore, we've agreed on a compromise. I will adopt Andrew legally and raise him, with only our immediate family knowing the truth. Anyone else who suspects the truth can be damned, but this is the only manner in which to put things to rights as best I can."

Jason watched his old friend. They hadn't seen each other for six years or more. And yet, it had seemed to him as if they hadn't missed a day in their friendship. "A son. And Trista as your wife. It must please you, then, that things are working in your favor after long last."

"Working in my favor? Man, I am adrift as I never was. I cannot seem to understand why she married me. I fear it is because I forced her."

"Forced her? What the devil—?"

"For the boy," he clarified impatiently. "And the child cannot stand the sight of me, a condition that is not improving since I implemented the brilliant idea of bringing everyone here to this damned place. I feel it closing in on me, reminding me of some rather unpleasant things I'd as soon forget."

Jason rose, strolled to the window, and pretended to look out. "The lawns are in excellent condition. The house looks as good as it ever has."

"That is why I employ as many servants as I do, to keep the house and the lawns in top form."

"An odd thing for a man to spend well-earned coin upon when he detests a place. After Trista left, you said you hated Whitethorn, and when you were of age, that you would go away and never return."

"I did say that."

Jason angled his head to look at his old friend. "Why did you come back?"

Roman made a face, full of hesitation, opened his mouth, then shrugged instead of speaking.

"Do not shirk on me now," said Jason. "You've been amazingly candid to this point."

"I am not shirking," Roman said crossly.

Ah, Jason thought with an inner smile. The pride was intact. One had only to needle it just a bit to get the predictable response.

Roman took a moment. "I don't think I really know why I wanted to. Or I needed to. I just . . . felt it. And it was quite unmistakably urgent." He admitted these last two words grudgingly and his look turned sheepish. "This may sound utterly insane, but I thought if Trista and I had any way of getting past what happened, we had to come back here and face it."

His hands scrubbed his face and he laughed. "I spent my entire life at Whitethorn wishing to be quit of this place, and yet here I am when I don't know what else to do."

Jason said, "Like a father wolf marshalling his straying pack back to the den."

Roman gave him a serious look. "I mean to win her. You know, I will do anything to bring that about."

"But you have her."

His eyes clouded. "I have her less now than I ever did. It cannot be forgotten that I gave her away for a dowry."

"It was duty."

Roman scowled. "As if that matters."

"It matters. Your family needed you."

"So they could continue to refurbish an already overdone house and have the latest frills from Paris and stay connected to the best circles?"

Jason paused. "I didn't know you felt used."

Roman looked at him, seeming a little astonished. "I did?"

Jason shrugged. He wasn't the world's most accomplished person in understanding the pathways of the heart. Now, the soul, that was his domain. He had a knack for faith, for inspiring belief in others at time of trouble.

"I think I did it for myself as well," Roman said after a

moment. His voice was slow, thoughtful, in the manner of someone discovering something for the first time. "I should admit that. I'd almost come to terms with the fact that my father was never going to regard me as anything more than a pet he might visit once in a while, play with, then leave to get on with the other more salient aspects of life. And then he came here, wanting me to take my place as a man, beside him. He said I was of age. I was so thrilled, so full of myself. God, I was stupid."

"Trista changed everything."

"Yes. Trista made everything so much better, and then, so much worse. The situation was . . . impossible. I lost badly." He made a harsh sound and shrugged. "Which I deserved. I never thought she would leave me. I can hardly fathom my own arrogance."

"You had great fortune in her," Jason said. "She was for you from the day she arrived, that solemn little thing in the tattered dresses."

Roman smiled quietly, his eyes lowering as his thoughts turned inward. He pulled himself roughly out of reflection after only a moment, donning a quick smile.

"And what of you—a parson. I have to hear this tale."

Jason made a dismissive gesture. He never spoke of his transformation from rascal to reverend, but he could hardly refuse when his normally reticent friend had been so forthcoming.

"Strangely enough, there is little drama in it. I was raising hell, as usual, for a good two years after you left Whitethorn. It got lonely for a while when you were first gone, but a new set of cronies and a whole lot of gin made it bearable. My horse threw me one night on the way home from the tavern, and the other fellows were too drunk to notice. I broke my leg, and lay there. When I sobered up, it was a hell of a fright. I was not discovered for two days."

Roman's eyebrows twitched. As it had been when Roman spoke of Trista, there was no need to go into maudlin details. He would not explain about the effects of those days and nights alone in the wilderness, in excruciating pain. He had thought he was going to die, and die horribly, slowly, and all alone. He had thought it so incredibly stupid a way to go, when he had people who loved him.

But Roman would guess all of it, fill in what he would not say. Jason didn't have to put into words the physical pain, the self-examination, recrimination, regrets, and, finally, penance, that had brought him to a surreal sense of peace as he awaited death.

Roman said, "So that was it, then." He said it softly, and Jason knew he understood.

"That was it. It just made sense after that to go to the church."

"That," Roman said with an admiring light in his eye, "is an absolute miracle. So they can happen. And have you wed?"

Jason's smile drifted away from him. "No. Only one miracle so far." He shrugged, hated himself for not being able to resist, and then asked, "How is Grace? Did you see her in London?"

"I told her to come back to Whitethorn, to make it up to her so that she wouldn't think I was leaving her behind, and she's gone and taken me up on it. She arrives in a few days' time. I suppose she is anxious to be home. She has not been back in years."

"Four years." He caught himself, and shrugged, as if he were not acutely aware of how long she'd been gone.

"When she followed me to London after the death of my wife, I thought it was a good idea, but the city didn't suit her. She, more than I, longed to return to Whitethorn, but of course she would not return unless I agreed to accompany her. And I never wished to, before now."

"She did not marry."

"She . . . city society did not seem to her liking. She kept to herself . . . and no, she did not marry."

"Grace always depended on you very much."

"Perhaps too much. I suppose that is why she persists in her dislike of Trista. She behaves as if it is some grand contest between the two, where there can only be one winner. At least Andrew loves her. Perhaps it will help ease him into the change. He is still rather resistant to the whole idea of having to leave London. I do not believe he likes it here very much. He was fond of this uncle . . ."

Jason knew Roman would not discuss his problems, but he couldn't disguise them. He wore them on every line of his face for a fleeting moment before he composed his features and let the subject drop.

Roman called in the footman and with a wink at Jason, told him, "Inform Lady Aylesgarth that the parson will be having luncheon with us." To Jason, he said, "Come, let us go and see what she says about that collar you are wearing."

The tactic of surprise was effective in rendering Trista speechless with delight once they walked into the dining hall. She'd been standing stiffly, being Lady Aylesgarth, dressed soberly yet elegantly, but when she saw him, her eyes went from his face to his collar and back again to his face. "Jason!" she exclaimed, launching herself at him.

He embraced her, peeling back her arms sooner than she wished once he caught sight of Roman's frown. "It is unimaginably wonderful to see you, Trista. What a beautiful woman you've become!"

It was true. Trista had been lovely, from childhood through the years that were typically awkward, and as a young woman the blossom began to unfold. But now, she was mature, her face full of mobile emotion, her eyes shining unabashedly with the same enthusiasm she'd given to everything that interested her, and everyone she loved.

"And you—you are a parson!" She swept her hand toward his collar. "How?"

He laughed. "Don't sound so surprised. Surely I wasn't that wicked, was I?"

"You were awful. I recollect the time you stole my muff and my hands froze on the way to church."

"Ah, I had forgotten. Now I shall have to add that to my penance."

She cast a look to Roman, who beamed back at her, and

Jason caught it, caught the energy, and saw what he'd always seen between them.

No wonder Grace felt the outcast, competing with Trista for her brother's attention. It was as if no one else existed in the entire world. Even the prickliness that characterized their current manner toward each other—this he had picked up immediately in the restraint they demonstrated—it was unmistakably there, potent, real, and throbbing with a life all of its own.

They spent the rest of the afternoon remembering and laughing, with little eating done in between despite the fact that luncheon lasted three hours.

Andrew was called down and Jason gaped at the small face, so much like Roman's in so many details. He noted the closeness the boy displayed to his mother, who beamed with pride at showing him off, as well as the wary looks he shot to a reserved Roman, and he recalled what Roman had said about the boy not liking him.

He felt a moment of disquiet. He was a man of faith, and in that vein he had enormous belief in the goodness and rightness of God in the lives of himself and his fellow men.

But if that were so, he wondered fleetingly, then how can it be that these two—three with the child now in the thick of it—who loved so deeply could be so stricken? All right, Roman was lousy with the sin of pride, and perhaps that was the matter, but should it make a misery of all of that phenomenal goodness?

When he took his leave, he gave his friend a bracing slap on the back. "I'll pray for you," he told him, jerking his head toward Trista.

Roman scowled, but murmured something under his breath that sounded suspiciously like, "Thank you."

Grace arrived along with a spring storm that ripped viciously over the fells. She entered Whitethorn a bit worse for the drenching she received in the forecourt and in a foul mood.

Trista's fuss over her wet condition when she crossed the threshold to the front hall was met with a bored look.

"You needn't go on so," she said after suffering a stiff embrace. "It is only water."

But when Andrew shot forward eagerly, shouting, "Aunt Grace!" he was given a warm reception.

She hugged him to her, then extended her arms so that she might view him better. "Hello, young man," she said with fondness in her voice.

Andrew beamed. "Hello. I'm glad you've come. Do you want to come and see my nursery?"

"Let me dry off and see if I can manage to have a cup of tea served to me, and I will come and visit your wonderful nursery."

"Come right inside," Trista said, flushing at the implication that her hospitality had been lacking. "Of course we shall order tea."

Grace swept into the library, ignoring Trista's gesture for her to follow her to the parlor. "John, have Mrs. Graves bring tea in here. Is there a fire lit?" She glanced over her shoulder to Trista, who followed. "Where is my brother?"

"He is in the stables showing off some new horses he's had sent from London . . ."

Trista trailed off, for Grace had begun speaking with Andrew. "No, no," she said, "you come and sit with Aunt Grace and tell me all about your stay here. Do you like it?"

"It's big," Andrew said, screwing up his little face. Grace sat in one of the heavy, masculine chairs, and held her arm out for Andrew to come by her side, which he readily did.

"Of course it is big. It is a great estate, and you are now part of one of the finest and most important families in all of England. This house shall be yours one day, and you shall grow up in it to know all of its secrets, which I shall tell you. I was a little girl here, and rather lonely"—this with an almost imperceptible jerk of her gaze to touch Trista briefly—"and I learned all of the secrets, so I can teach them to you."

Andrew bounced up and down and clasped his hands together. "Will you?"

"Oh, of course," she said, "but the person to ask, of course, is your father. He ran wild in these parts for years as a boy. He had a secret place he'd go to, and he'd roam—"

Trista sat. "Andrew does not roam the countryside."

"It is an interesting place. He must be allowed to explore it. Roman used to love to do so."

"I don't think Andrew will be feeling the same need to wander the forests and fells," Trista said.

Grace gave her a lofty look. "Boys need to wander. It is their nature."

"*My* son," Trista asserted, "does not have any call to traipsing about on his own like some gypsy when he is unaccustomed to country life."

Grace's look was arch. "I was suggesting his father show him his old haunts. I thought they might be of interest to him, but, of course, if you object . . ."

Trista's retort was drowned out by Andrew's loud and impassioned protests that he very much wished to be shown the wonders of the countryside.

With an effort to get control of the conversation, Trista said, "But Roman already has taken him to the lake. Andrew can skip a rock three times now."

"Four," the boy said.

"Four."

But Grace only sniffed. "The boy must learn that there is more complexity in his father than a mere trick with rocks." Not giving Trista a chance to respond, she turned once again to Andrew. "There is much about these parts that your father knows. He had wonderful adventures here. Why, he'd be gone for days and days, and come home with tales of the wild things he had done."

The boy was thoughtful, as if considering this new attraction. "Really?"

"Oh, yes. You should ask him sometime, I'm certain he'd love to tell you."

Trista would have very much liked to wipe the smug satisfaction off Grace's face, but she had to admit she had been bested quite soundly. By enticing Andrew with these delectable mysteries, she had effectively hooked the boy into an interest in his father, which had no doubt been her goal.

That and to vex Trista.

Millie, a maid, wheeled the tray in, smiling a greeting to Grace.

"Why, it is good to see you," Grace said in a particular tone of commanding pleasantness Trista had not yet mastered.

"Good day, miss," Millie said. Without a glance at Trista, the maid brought the tray directly to Grace.

"You look marvelous, Millie. Did I hear you've been engaged?"

"Yes, miss," Millie said proudly. "To Patrick, who's just been made head groom over at the grange. Lord Tenfry says he depends on him terribly."

Trista frowned. She hadn't known this.

Grace smiled. "Well, congratulations. I hope that doesn't mean that you will be leaving us."

Us? Trista felt the world settle around the room, encompassing Grace and even Andrew, who looked at his aunt with the same fondness in his face as when he looked at his aunt May, or cousin Luci and the most adored Uncle David. "Us" were Aylesgarths.

Trista was lawfully an Aylesgarth, but somehow she didn't think she was included in that "us."

Roman entered, Jason beside him. They were deep in conversation.

"Those are fine horses, I'll admit it," Jason was saying.

"It's what I was telling you. You must go to Carson's, there is no place else like it for purchasing—Grace! You've arrived early."

Grace smiled sublimely at her brother, holding out her hand. It was a ridiculous formality, but she seemed to relish it, and he performed his duty with aplomb.

Trista watched sourly.

"You thought to leave me behind in London," she sniffed, trotting out the old petulance that made her so tedious as a child. "I tell you, I was bereft to think my only relative abandoned me for some flighty—Jason?"

Her airy diatribe cut off as she gaped at the parson. She must have only just noticed it was him with whom Roman conversed. "Jason Knightsbridge?"

"Hello, Grace," he said, bowing formally.

"My God!" she exclaimed. Her face flushed. "You have . . . you are . . . you . . ."

"You have grown into the beautiful woman you promised to be when I last saw you." Jason's words were spoken quietly, but with a hint of awe of which no one besides Trista seemed to take any notice.

Roman grinned and bounced on his heels. "I believe my sister is undone by the fact that our childhood friend is now a man of the cloth."

Grace raised her brows loftily. "He was no friend of mine. A miscreant in miniature when he was a boy, and I am not fooled in the least by that ridiculous ornament."

"My collar?" Jason asked. Trista saw his back draw tight and his gaze narrowed ever so slightly.

"Come, Grace," Roman countered good-naturedly, "Jason here has turned over a new leaf."

"I refuse to believe it." She peered down at her nephew. "Do not under any circumstances allow this pretender to spiritual fortitude lead you astray, my boy."

Trista had been having a difficult time struggling with her self-control, and at this point she lost it utterly.

"That is unforgivably rude. And please do not presume to instruct my son." She rose and placed a protective hand on Andrew's shoulder. "I am his mother, and I will determine what company is fit for him to keep."

"And I suppose you approve?" Her tone was full of mockery.

"Yes, in fact, I endorse the reverend's influence over some others whom Andrew favors."

Her meaning, clearly given and clearly taken, turned Grace's face white.

Roman stepped forward and steered his wife back to her seat. "Did you have Mrs. Jones prepare Grace's old room?"

"That is already done and you know it," Trista hissed, turning on him. "Do you doubt I can execute so simple a task?"

"Not in front of the boy!" he said in an urgent undertone, and Trista was shocked at herself. A glance at Andrew told her that indeed the child sat bemused by the gales of conflict buffeting about the room.

She sat down, sobered to realize she had gotten so heated. She was ashamed of herself.

Grace's hatred was an old one. She had always felt excluded by Roman's attraction to her and saw Trista as a rival. But why did she dislike Jason so much? She didn't recall Grace having a hatred for him when they were children. But by her high color and spiny attitude with him just now, he was chief on her list of insufferables.

"Well, I suppose you will want tea." Grace spoke with haughtiness, assuming the role of hostess once again.

Trista, whom Roman had only just managed to sooth into taking her seat, shot up again.

In the delicate play of manners that constituted the society in which both of them were meticulously versed, the gauntlet had clearly been thrown by Grace: a challenge to power. A small slight had huge implications, and a lapse in etiquette could be deeply significant. Such as now.

But Trista wasn't of this world. She was a servant, the daughter of a servant and the forgotten by-blow of an unrepentant rake. It was of this Grace wished to remind her.

And it was working. She felt her civility slipping away from her. It was only the realization of how ridiculous she would seem shouting, "This is my house now, I am mistress of Whitethorn, and I will offer tea!" that stopped her from another outburst.

Instead of the intemperate behavior in which she would have dearly liked to indulge, she said in a calm tone, "Come, Andrew, I will see you back to the nursery."

"Let him stay," Roman said magnanimously. "Now that

all of the surprises are out of the way, we shall all take our seats and have a very pleasant tea."

Trista stared at him for a heartbeat, then shook her head. Dear, dunderheaded Roman, who never understood that some things could not be mastered by sheer determination. No, he was always too wrapped up in his own confidence to take proper note of a full-blown hurricane right in his own parlor.

"I'd like to stay, Mama," Andrew said, in a tentative voice. He was a tad more perceptive than his hopeless father, but not enough to rouse himself to her side.

She hated the sharp stab of betrayal she felt.

"Of course," she said after only a moment's hesitation, "you may stay. You have missed your aunt. If you will excuse me, however, I wished to get some letters written this morning for Michaela and Aunt May."

She went out the door, thinking to head up to her room when Jason called to her.

Wanting only retreat, she paused, reluctant to look the handsome parson in the eye.

"Come down," he urged, his foot on the bottom step. "Take a walk with me on the lawns. Or . . . Roman said you were overseeing the restoration of the gardens. Why don't you show me."

"I do not think I shall make a very good hostess today, Reverend."

"By God, if you call me that again I shall never speak to you," he stated flatly. "I have been Jason Knightsbridge to you and ever shall remain. And I do not require hostessing, I simply require your companionship."

She shifted from one foot to the other as she sought some excuse. As she could find none, she descended the stairs and picked out a straw hat she kept by the door. Then she led him out through the east parlor.

They walked in the sunshine for a bit, their only exchange Jason asking her if she would like him to fetch her a parasol. She declined.

"Would it be presumptuous if I asked about you and Roman?"

"Yes."

He fell silent. They walked on a bit more.

She said, "Would it be presumptuous if I asked why Grace has a dislike of you?"

"Not at all. Ask away. I have no idea."

"Is it simply that she dislikes anyone who takes Roman's time?"

"A plausible theory, but consider Andrew. She seems to get on quite well with him."

He grunted. Then he said, "You should not let her get you in a swoon, you know."

"Grace?"

"Yes. It is what she is after."

"It seems we are not exactly favorites with her, you and me."

He made a movement of his shoulders, a kind of shrug that was half executed. "Her roar is like a kitten's hiss. It tells more of her feelings of fear than of anger."

"I wish I were more understanding. She gets under my skin." Trista sighed. "Why must things be so difficult?"

"I take it we are not just speaking of Grace."

She knew he meant Roman. She gave him a look that admitted what she would not say.

"If I were speaking to one of my flock," he said, his grin twisted wryly, "I would say that difficulties arrive when one is resisting . . . oh, different people call it different things—God's plan, fate, destiny . . ."

She looked at him, astonished to hear something akin to preaching coming from the man who once, with Roman, let three mud-soaked pigs loose in pinched-faced Mrs. Gibbons's parlor.

"You think that my destiny is here?"

Jason smiled at her and shrugged.

Chapter 16

Grace was seething.

First, that . . . *woman.* That usurper, that spoiled, ignorant, grasping . . . well, there were names for people like that, but being a lady of the first cut, Grace didn't even so much as *think* it.

But it rhymed with "witch."

She hated Trista Nash . . . Fairhaven . . . whatever her name was.

Aylesgarth. It was Aylesgarth now.

Resentment gripped her like a merciless fist.

In her room, Grace paced, her footsteps heavy. The unfairness, the humiliation seized her, squeezed her, nearly bursting her heart. How could Trista always win—always! Without fail, at every turn she prevailed and Grace was left to watch, empty-handed and aching.

Sinking onto the bed, she covered her eyes with fists. Trista . . . a nemesis she had never been able to conquer. It had come so easy to her, all the things Grace had ever wanted. Trista was nothing, a *bastard* child, for God's sake, sired by an infamous reprobate, a servant . . . how could she have so much?

It was humiliating to recall how Roman had pulled her aside to speak to her. He had told her that she was going to have to accept the fact that Trista was mistress of Whitethorn.

When she replied that she was not certain she could do so, he'd said, "Then leave her house." His voice had been soft, with not a hint of anger in it, but it was strong.

"Leave my home?"

"This is her home now. She is my wife. She is Lady Aylesgarth."

"You always preferred her!" Grace flung. "It was always Trista in your blood, in your brain. You never gave a thought to me—"

She had cut off, realizing how petulant she sounded. Why could she never say it right? It was so petty when put into mere words, and so potent when it ate at her heart.

He had finished the matter by stating, "You have to make peace with this, Grace, or you must leave."

She should have known this was how it would be. He still belonged to Trista, first and foremost.

Of all the wrongs Grace felt Trista had done to her, this was by far the worst. For some unthinkably cruel taunt of the fates, Trista had, from the moment she had stepped foot in this house, an extraordinary connection to her brother.

All right. She regretted the little scene she'd orchestrated in the library. She couldn't blame it on Trista. She had been rude.

She was most remorseful that poor little Andrew had been so bewildered. Roman sent him off to the nursery directly after Trista made her dramatic exit, but he'd been disturbed. Grace wished she could have held him, comforted him. She genuinely loved the child. It was the first time she'd ever been close to one, and she found it sparked a possessive yearning in her she'd never experienced before.

In a way, it only added to her pain. She wondered if she'd ever be a mother. She had never wanted to be before. She'd seen marriage as an undesirable arrangement and favored her independence. However, she liked the idea of a child all of a sudden. And perhaps, if she had a man, she wouldn't be so sensitive to the attentions of her brother to his wife, which was where, she had to admit, they belonged.

For some insane reason, she thought of Jason Knightsbridge. And that air of trustworthiness that he wore as distinctly as the collar around his neck. She was aware of a picking up of her heartbeat.

She had no liking for Jason. He'd been Roman's friend, a wild and ungovernable boy. He'd never wished anything to do with her.

Except once. He had visited her after Trista had run off and Roman had left for the city, saying that he wished to be her *friend.* She had been insulted—he deigned to notice her now that all of the more interesting folk had departed? She had turned him away and not thought of him in years.

Now he was posing as a reverend, of all the preposterous things! Well, he looked ridiculous. Parsons were supposed to be slight, academic-looking fellows. He . . . well, he looked as if he'd just ridden off the fells, his face darkened by sun, his hair streaked gold. He wore it absurdly long. And what parson worth his salt strode around with a body that took up so much space? Those shoulders alone could eclipse half of the alter with him standing in front of the congregation. No doubt attendance by wide-eyed misses trebled since he took over the parsonage.

She resolutely turned her thoughts away from Jason Knightsbridge. She had enough to concern herself with without wasting her energy on that man.

She was home again. She'd come full circle.

She began to arrange her belongings in her room. The glow from the lamps was cheerful as she moved, putting things where they belonged. She tried to hum softly to dispel the silence. When she was finished, she looked about her.

It looked like her room again. Just like it had all of her childhood.

Out of the blue, one piercing memory came to her, of her mother lying in her bed, her head wobbly, her breath reeking of gin. She had cupped Grace's chin in her hand, her fingers biting into tender flesh. It was in those most dangerous days following her father's departure from their yearly visit. Mother had drunk herself into a stupor, rousing herself to look at her daughter and say, "No one wants us, Gracie."

And that was fairly well the truth.

Given her mastery of the social graces, Lady May should have been able to think of something clever and subtle in how she could approach Robert about Charbonneau's accusations.

This was not the case. She found herself waiting anxiously for his arrival all evening, pacing and tapping her foot and nibbling at her nails, which was a habit she thought she had vanquished when she was twelve. The moment he strode through her door, she stopped him in his tracks by saying, "Charbonneau believes you are Marcus Roberts."

He didn't react strongly, only paused a moment, then entered the room. He sat, looked for the tumbler that she usually had at the ready for him—it was on the table to his left—and sighed.

"I am Marcus Roberts."

May had expected this, but it still knocked the wind from her.

"Yes, *the* Marcus Roberts who was named a traitor and a murderer for the death of Count de Nuncier. You wonder if I killed him? I did. I did it in the manner of a spy, which was my trade at the time, a silent and swift method of slitting open his throat."

He spoke plainly, as if this was an ordinary skill one might possess and discuss in parlor conversation.

"If you think I am horrified, you are wrong," May said, her own manner just as dispassionate as his.

"Then you are a fool. It is a grave thing when someone takes another's life."

"Are you saying then that you regret doing it?"

That stopped him. His eyes slipped away to some spot of memory May couldn't see. "No. I do not regret it."

"Then tell me why you killed him."

He paused, caught in a silent debate. Eventually, he seemed to come to some conclusion. He took his drink with him to a seat and began to speak.

"I was a spy for his majesty during the war. My specialty was blackmail. I was part of a team of men who investigated the excesses of prominent men in France. Once these were discovered, they were useful in extorting their loyalty. It was a simple matter to convince a man with sins to turn traitor in order to protect his secrets. I am afraid we had little scruples. We were fighting a war, after all."

May waited as he drew in a breath, preparing himself to tell the rest. "Some of these men were easy prey for us. Their sins were of a nature too beastly to repeat. I know you are a woman of the world, May, but there are things that exist on this earth that would make even you swoon to learn of them."

His eyes darkened, as if some bitter memory shadowed them. "And I realized, you see, that the problem with blackmail is that the person who is committing heinous acts is afraid of discovery, so he will pay anything, do anything, betray anyone to keep from discovery—a fact that was useful to us—but *he does not stop.* In effect, we protected these men, and they continued their crimes.

"I was told not to concern myself with this, that my business was to advance intelligence for king and country. Murdered women or missing French children were not my concern."

May's hand crept to her mouth, covering it.

"One man in particular had predilections that chilled even a seasoned and cynical man like myself. He was convinced to turn against France, but then this was discovered, and he was smuggled out of the country and into England. He came to reside in London, to a branch of his family who welcomed him. Of course, he was hailed as a hero for all the help he'd given his majesty during the war. He was given protection."

He became immersed in thought. "They were afraid of him, actually, for he knew too many of our dirty little secrets—he'd been involved in half of them. My insistence that he was a danger went unheeded. I couldn't let it go. I was obsessed with him, watching closely for a sign that he would resume his crimes."

"And he did," May said quietly.

"The child of the family who took him in. She was a little girl of ten. He must have thought her dead and attempted to dispose of the body, but she was found soon enough that she survived. A wound to her leg had turned gangrenous, however. It had to be amputated."

There was a long silence. Then Robert said simply, "I killed de Nuncier the next night."

May let out the breath she hadn't realized she'd been holding.

"I didn't lie about it to my superiors," Robert went on, "but I never expected to be betrayed. The deputy minister was a man named Cavett. He was ruthlessly ambitious, and he didn't like me. I was a loose end, perhaps a bit wild, ungovernable, and I knew where the skeletons were buried. He gave me up to the authorities for the murder of de Nuncier. But, of course, I was not to be allowed to go to a trial, where I might say something Cavett did not wish me to say. I was held briefly in seclusion, and then I was allowed to 'escape,' which meant I was escorted to the London Bridge where I was to have been thrown over."

May's fingers pressed her temple. "But they did not?"

"Oh, they did. Cavett was a megalomaniac, and nobody dared cross him. He was hated, too, however, and I had a few friends in strategic places and some modifications were made to the original plan. I was taken to a low spot and allowed to jump from the bridge. It was a relatively safe distance, and technically, they had 'thrown' me from the bridge. Marcus Roberts was not heard from again. The matter was put to rest."

"You gave up everything."

"It was a fair trade in order to live."

"And then what did you do?"

"I'd operated in France for the duration of the war, so

hiding was a skill I had long since mastered. The first thing to do was to get out of the city, which I did. A rule of covert movement was to be as unseen as possible. I knew that nobles do not look at servants. One excellent way to disguise oneself was to pose as a servant."

"But didn't your friends, your family . . . I mean, they could have helped you to have the truth known."

"I thought my family might be of service, which was a singularly stupid idea as we had never been close or even remotely fond of each other. I made my way to their country estate, found a position at a neighbor's stable, and set out to make out what the lay of things were. It became immediately apparent that my parents and siblings were anxious to distance themselves from me. As far as they were concerned, I was a disgrace to the family. I suspected they would turn me in, or perhaps put a ball in me instead of going through the dredging up of another public scandal, then dump my body in the Wye to protect their social position. So, I was on my own. I didn't wish to contact my friends for fear of reprisal against them, so I worked and I plotted and I dreamed of a way to get even."

"Did you?"

"Nature took care of it for me. Cavett choked to death on a chicken bone one night, and I found I could live with that. I found I could live with most of it. The hard work of my new life suited me, and I didn't have a family any longer. I liked working with my hands. Through hard labor, I was able to slough off the bitterness. In time, I didn't miss my old life, strangely enough. I was content."

She had been drawn to that air of complete self-possession and satisfaction with himself that he now described. May understood that so much of what she loved about him was his confidence, this unshakable knowledge of what he wanted. It was modest, but powerful. He had achieved something men with power and riches had not come close to claiming for themselves. He had liked his life.

Yet there had always been a sadness in him as well. She now understood that, too.

"And the little girl?" she asked softly.

He smiled wryly, acknowledging how well she knew him. "Of course I felt responsible for that girl. Ann Nesbit was her name."

Here he drew in a labored breath, and May wanted to go to him, touch him and comfort him. But she found she could not move.

"When it was safe to return, I transferred my business to London. It was a good move financially, but I was also driven to find out what had happened to that girl. If I had acted sooner, she would have been spared."

"Oh, Robert—"

"She recovered, although she was a cripple. She's grown now, almost seventeen, and engaged to be married."

"A good man?" She knew he would have checked this.

He nodded. "It is a love match. She is happy."

May peered at him, and to her surprise, he shifted as if made uncomfortable by her scrutiny. He was not at peace with Ann Nesbit, but he wanted her to think he was. "And you?" she asked. "Have you found peace?"

"And I . . . well, I found you." His eyes rested on her, and they were warm with his fathomless affection. "Lucky me, I was what you were looking for at the time. An affair with an uncomplicated man of lower class who could be your intellectual equal without making any claims someone of more substantial position would wish to make, it was exactly what the worldly and very sensual widow required."

"In the beginning, yes," May replied.

"Now I have become anything but that. There can be no greater complications than those I live."

"And now those are in jeopardy of being revealed. Because of me."

"Oh, no, darling May, it is because of me. Because I wished not to be trapped in this identity I'd fashioned for myself. I wished to be a man who could take you to a ball, who could converse wittily among your friends and see you sparkle the way you do when you are in your element. I told you before that we should be contented with the half-life of secret lovers, but I wasn't. I wanted all of you, and so it was I who made a grave error of judgment because I wanted . . . more."

He shrugged, and gave her a guilty look that appeared startlingly impish for a man of his years. "I forgot the first and foremost rule of disguise was to be a person no one looks at. As your escort, how could I avoid notice? I miscalculated Charbonneau's interest in you, and therefore in me. That made him *look* at me, and I know better than to ever allow that."

"And this you did for me."

"You think too highly of me. I did it because I was *jealous*."

He laughed at her pleased face. This seemed to break the tension around them and he came to her, taking her face in his large, work-callused hands. "I am in this predicament of my own accord, darling." He paused reflectively. "Which, perhaps, is where I wished to be. Perhaps I am ready to face my demons."

"But I am not!" she declared.

"Don't be afraid," he said kindly.

She jerked away. "How like a man. Do you think you can dispel danger merely by telling me not to be afraid? As if your command of the world is so great, so complete, that nothing can affect us if you don't wish it to."

He was puzzled. "May?"

"The people who wish to kill you, they are gone, but the world would string you up for a traitor if you were ever found out. And now, thanks to our foolishness—*together*—there is a distinct likelihood that you are now ripe for discovery. But why should I worry? It is so silly of me to think anything horrible might happen when the world thinks you a ravager of children and a treasonous murderer. Anyone who revealed you, caught you, killed you even outside the realm of justice would be lauded as a hero."

The ache in her stomach felt like a snake tightening itself into a smaller and smaller knot of despair. She felt ill.

"May, be still."

"I am angry, Robert. Of course I am angry. Look at this—what has happened. But that is not the worst of it. Oh, Robert, I am frightened. I am so frightened!"

She had never been more so, not even when she was fighting for her own life as a young bride with a drunken husband towering over her, fists clenched, and all traces of love gone from his beautiful eyes. This was much more terrifying than Matthew, even Matthew at his worst.

Matthew. Her secret.

It brought down her temper a bit to be reminded that she, too, hid from her past.

He sensed her shift of mood and tried to touch her again. She was not ready to admit he was right. She threw off his hand. "I could lose you," she blurted. Whirling upon him, she jabbed her finger at the air. "And do not tell me that it is not going to happen in that insufferably reasonable tone you employ when you are trying to placate me. It is patronizing. It is demeaning. I could lose you, Marcus Roberts."

His head jerked, as if she'd slapped him. Marcus Roberts—his name. Then he smiled, but it was a sad, resigned smile. Doing the most a man of his ilk could ever manage to admit, that he was wrong and she was right, he nodded.

She went to him then, without reservation, and grasped him to her with frantic hands. He kissed her, and they clung to each other for a very long time.

*Roman was feeling sorry for himself. Sitting alone in the li*brary late one night, he pondered what a mess he'd made of it all.

Grace hated Trista. She disliked Jason, too, which puzzled him. She was adamant, and he could get no sensible reason from her as to why.

Andrew couldn't abide him still. The move to Whitethorn had done nothing to alleviate the tension between them.

Trista . . . well, Trista was tense and skittish and he couldn't seem to get anything right with her, but she didn't seem to mind Jason at all. . . .

In fact, she had appeared quite easy in his company as they strolled the grounds and chatted, no doubt Jason listening oh-so-patiently and with the infinite sympathy as she detailed her woes. Oh, God, he was jealous of Jason.

He should have been the one to go after Trista when she'd fled that day, smooth her feathers. But he had had to stay and smooth Grace's. That had not worked.

And the boy. The boy was driving him insane.

Why didn't his son like him? Was he so horrible?

He doused the lamps, all but for the one he took with him, and climbed the stairs. At the top, he paused. Every bone in him wanted to turn right, down the corridor to the mistress's room. He wanted Trista.

This, however, he did not do. He wondered that his pride would be so resolute against doing what he most wanted. Useless thing, pride, he thought, turning left.

What insane impulse, throbbing urgently in his gut, had led him to bring everyone back here?

To make it right. That's what had driven him home. But it was so much worse.

The thing he could not settle in his mind was the wondering why she had married him. The sex, surely. The sex he could no longer help himself to because all the other unanswered questions got in the way.

Trista would do anything for her son. Even marry the boy's father.

His mind betrayed him, straying down this path. He was no longer a youth, defeated by the miseries of this house, damn it. He would not be bested.

He turned about and headed to Trista's bedroom, determined to overcome this pall here and now. He would have been flayed alive rather than admit it to anyone, but he was frightened. Lord save him from this disgraceful apprehension, but his hand shook as the light skittered wildly across the carpet and threw itself garishly against her door.

It still remained in his mind's eye his mother's door.

He froze.

"Come here, Roman. Come closer, I cannot see you."

She couldn't see him because the room was closed up, draperies drawn tight, lamps burning low, because the light hurt her eyes, she said.

"Don't shrink away. Why do you shrink away from me? Don't you love Mother?"

He shrank from her because she reeked of spirits, and the smell made him sick from fumes and loss.

"You are a bad boy. You come here now. What—do you think you are better than me, just as your father does? Is that why you run off all the time? You run away from me just like he does!"

Yes. Yes!

His one fist slammed into his open palm as he squeezed his eyes tightly shut, willing the images away.

He had to get this behind him.

The intensity of these feelings, which had gripped him the first time he had crossed the threshold of the Lady's suite, had not lessened with time, as he'd hoped. He'd cursed himself seventy times seven times since for the impulse that had made him insist Trista take the room. It was the mistress of the house's room. She needed to know—and everyone needed to know—that she, once a servant, was now the lady of the house.

That put him in mind of Grace, who would never accept such a thing and that reminded him of the mess everything was in.

He squared his shoulders. He would not give in to this bleak mood. He laid his hands on the door, then his cheek. "Trista," he called out softly. He did not go inside, nor did he even try the knob to see if the door was locked or opened to him, should he chance by.

No answer came. She was asleep, then. He felt disappointment.

This ridiculous situation could not be allowed to go on any longer. But he was not foolish enough to think he could do it here, where the shadows from the past were thickest. Not the place, then, nor the time. He was tired, not at his best.

He left, but a resolve began to form in his breast. This

house was long overdue for a healthy airing to make room for the happiness he so wished could settle into the cracks and fissures, breathe new life into its creaking woods, cleansing and purifying, chasing away all of the shadows.

And with that thought, riding with him into sleep and awake the next morning, he felt much better.

He had a direction, at least.

*The news that the Lord of Aylesgarth was once again in res-*idence at Whitethorn brought everyone in the district out on Sunday. The small church of St. Alvin was bursting at its seams, stuffed with curiosity seekers aiming to get a glimpse of the prodigal lord returned.

Not only was he more breathlessly handsome than he had been as a young man, the ladies whispered behind rapidly fluttering fans, but he was as bold as always, unrepentant after his long reign as the holy terror of the neighborhood and then his abruptly leaving these parts, which had been a high insult to those who frowned on fast living in the city.

And now he brings his wife—and that part of it had to be the most shocking. They, of course, remembered Trista Nash. Everyone was over the top, buzzing frantically that he'd married one of his servants!

Trista walked into the church with Andrew's small hand clutched in hers, her other firmly holding on to Roman's arm. She was acutely aware of what was in the minds of those around her. Rows of people stared without apology, their silence following her up the center aisle as she and her family headed for the Aylesgarth family pew.

"There will be a host of sore necks come tomorrow, with all of this craning." Roman spoke under his breath, then broke out in a brash smile as he met the stares head-on. "Wave, darling."

Trista remembered most of them, although she had no friends among them. When she'd lived at Whitethorn, she and her mother had kept to themselves. It was partly natural, for a governess's place is always the gray region between lord and servant, and partly because Judith's time was nearly completely taken up in later years with tending Roman's mother, which left no time for recreation or socializing.

Trista had made some friends as a girl and younger woman, but they'd left to marry, and, of course, the ladies of the neighborhood had never socialized with a governess's daughter and paid companion, so those who were now her social equals were strangers to her.

Not friendly ones, either, she thought. Not a one of them so much as inclined their head at her.

Grace had no such troubles. She chatted as they made their way to the family pew, drawing Andrew with her to present him to the local matrons, who surveyed him with approval. If they noted the resemblance to Roman—which, to Trista's eyes, was as obvious as the nose on his face—they did not seem scandalized.

Roman seemed pleased at his sister. Trista gave him a strange look. "See how comfortable she is," he said, jerking his chin to indicate Grace as she moved easily among the crowd. "Being home is doing her good."

This made him very happy and without further explanation, he pulled her on ahead of Grace and Andrew.

Trista wished she was above the burning resentment that grabbed hold of her. She should be pleased that Grace, who rarely took time out from her self-pity to think about another person, was interested in making a smooth presentation for Andrew. And yet, she was thinking that it should have been *her* place.

Roman squeezed her arm as he steered her to her seat. "Let her do it. It will please her, and it seems to be successful."

She was surprised he had read her thoughts so effectively. Roman had never been known for extraordinary sensitivity.

"You are annoyed," he prodded.

She pressed her lips tight. "I will not make complaint of your sister."

"Oh, go ahead. She makes plenty of complaints about you."

Shocked, she gaped for a moment before whispering a repressive, "Roman!"

"Did you think otherwise?"

Trista sputtered for a moment, then gave up. "Well, I do admit, I am vexed with her. It must seem odd to everyone that she is introducing him about when we are right here. It is my place. Your place," she reminded him, "as his father."

"Yes, but they hate me," he replied blandly, "and you were a paid servant. There is bound to be resentment. Do not worry. You know they are not going to take to this marriage at first, but they will come round in time."

A surge of irrational possessiveness took hold of her. "You know she is determined to assert herself as lady of Whitethorn."

"Yes, yes. I have already told her to stop that. Please do not pester me."

She was stunned. "Pester you? I couldn't care less how many teas she orders or what else she does in the house. But I am not being overly sensitive to observe that taking over in public like this is not a small slight. It is rather humiliating, which I think was precisely her purpose."

"Liar," he said, then threw her a grin to take away the sting. "The ordering the tea bothered you as well."

"Why do you insist on being tiresome?" she chided, and marveled how she sounded like an old hen, scolding him so. But he only grinned broadly at her, his eyes dancing with the fire that made him irresistible. "You do not care," she accused.

"I never cared what others thought. Why should it surprise you?"

She sat back in her seat with a huff of exasperation, staring straight ahead. "Oh, never mind."

When his voice came again, it was close to her ear, a mere whisper. "And so your color is returned, and you've quite lost that awful self-consciousness you were displaying earlier. I know you, Trista, and the cure for your nerves is a small measure of spleen."

"You are despicable," she whispered softly.

"You say it like an endearment."

"It is one of your finer points," she offered with a shrug, biting her lips together as his soft chuckles floated over to her.

The opening hymn began, and Jason entered. She was surprised to see him looking so solemn, and . . . well, like a parson. He seemed remarkably at home up on the pulpit.

Looking to her left, Trista saw how Roman watched his friend. There was pride in his face. But on his other side, Grace sat smoldering at Jason.

The sermon was delightful. Without seeming to expend much effort, Jason was entertaining and poignant in turns, citing quotes and stories to make his point. Andrew, who usually fidgeted terribly in church, paid attention in patches, smiling at some of the puns and, at one point, laughing so loudly that Trista had to touch his knee to get him to tone it down a bit.

"But it was funny, Mama," he protested in a loud whisper.

"Yes, it was, but we are, after all, in church."

And to her amazement, he glanced up at his father, who shrugged with a grin, giving Andrew the silent signal that his mother might be correct, but he was in complete sympathy with the boy.

Andrew returned a look of disgust, complete simpatico between the two males.

Trista groaned softly. So it was going to be like that, was it?

Roman's face shone with pleasure, and he gave her his bawdiest wink. She knew his emotions ran deep at this, the smallest of signs that his son might not regard him as an enemy any longer.

She kept her face composed in lines of exasperation. Anything else would disappoint him. But inside, her heart sang.

Chapter 17

When the service was concluded, Trista grew wary again. Now was the time that the congregation filed out of the church and clustered about the steps and front lawns to socialize.

Once out of the pew, Grace rushed past, making fast for the carriage only to be waylaid by a group of young ladies who welcomed her with loud exclamations. Roman stood to watch.

"What is it?" Trista asked.

"Grace. She is sometimes . . . nervous in these situations."

"She was not nervous when we entered."

Roman looked puzzled. "Indeed, she did seem quite at ease. Perhaps she is feeling better. Perhaps . . ."

"Better? Was she ill today?"

His eyes sparkled. "Nothing that fresh country air didn't seem to cure. She is home. She is in her element. Perhaps I was not so wrong after all in having her come here."

"We should go greet Jason," she said, pointing to a cluster of people by the foot of the steps leading out of the church.

"Nonsense. Waiting in crowds is maddening."

"He is your friend, and you are the lord in these parts. People will be expecting it."

"We'll see him later, and I'll tell him he was marvelous. He is coming to the house for dinner." He pushed her past the crowd, determined not to get caught. "He *was* marvelous, though, didn't you think? Quite surprised me. I was actually moved at some of the parts."

"Dare I hold out hope that he shall redeem you? Ah, but I am asking too much, even for a man of Jason's talents. He would have to be a veritable miracle worker."

He took the tease good-naturedly, for there was no tartness in her voice.

There were some children racing about on the side of the church house, engaged in a game of tag. Trista was aware that Andrew had been watching them.

"Would you like to go and meet them?" Trista asked him.

She knew he would, but a look of fear took over his face. "No, thank you."

Roman bent to speak to his son. "They are the children of the local landowners here, Andrew. They are probably as anxious to meet you as you are to meet them. I am sure they would like to play with you. It would take only a moment's awkwardness to introduce you, then you would be fine."

Andrew frowned more tightly and shrank back into his mother's skirts. Roman straightened, and she could see from his expression that he was deeply disappointed his camaraderie with Andrew had not lasted very long.

"Well, then," he pronounced, engaging Trista's gaze, "we shall have a small afternoon fete, so that Andrew might meet his neighbors."

Trista felt a surge of dizzying anxiety take her over. She would have to play hostess to the children's parents, a chore she did not welcome. She harbored no illusions about how she would be received by the country gentry. It would be as Roman said—slow, grudging, and perhaps never quite complete.

But Andrew must have friends. "Of course," she agreed.

She stopped short at seeing a sturdy-boned woman advancing upon them. There was no mistaking the determined look in her eye, nor the direct stride that brought her unerringly to cut off their path.

"Dame Bately," Trista said.

She remembered the woman quite distinctly. Her mother had taken her to church when they lived here, and Dame Bately had made very distinct overtures of friendship. Judith had been mistrustful whether it was true liking on the dame's part or if she were so curious about the great house that she saw a channel for gossip by befriending the pretty young governess.

Although Trista's mother had kept her distance, Dame Bately was always pleasant and never took offense. In later years, Trista thought that perhaps her mother had been wrong about her.

However, Dame Bately's look now was anything but friendly. Her eyebrows were drawn down into a point over her nose. She managed a smile, but the severe nature of her gaze belied any true welcome.

"Trista Nash," she said in that booming, imperious voice of hers.

Roman interjected a wide shoulder between them. "May I present Lady Aylesgarth, my wife, Dame Bately."

"Get out of the way, I can't see the girl," Dame Bately said imperiously, waving a hand upon which rested a monstrous signet ring. "You are a no-account scoundrel, and I never did understand why you would waste all your opportunity running around the neighborhood thinking up ways to nettle your neighbors."

"I've reformed," Roman told her solemnly. "I hardly ever do such things anymore."

Her arrogance cracked just for a moment. Her mouth twisted, not quite a smile. Then she waved the signet ring at him again. Roman stepped aside with a flourish. Trista stared at him in bemusement. How could he so easily surrender her to Dame Bately?

"Now, I can see you." She moved uncomfortably close.

"Judith's girl . . ." She mused as she looked Trista over, her rheumy eyes quick. "You're still lovely, I'll give you that. Done well for yourself, I've heard. Woolrich's brat? Ah, I knew him. Fellow was full of fun, he was, but not a responsible bone in him. Scoundrel, he was."

Her gaze darted to Roman, as if to silently add, "Just like you."

He smiled back and nodded, in full approval.

"Dame Bately," said Trista, "have you met my wife's son, Andrew?"

Her gaze didn't leave Trista's face. "You are still lovely. More so. Ah . . . Impure beauty fades, but true spirit enhances one's looks as the years advance . . ."

Trista looked to Roman nervously. The unspoken question of Mrs. Bately's sanity hung in the air.

But the old woman was done with her cryptic musings. She looked at the boy—who blinked back at the large commanding figure—and pronounced, "He's got a fine look about him. He'll make a good Aylesgarth." She sniffed and turned to Roman. "So, is this a sign of things to come?"

"You mean . . ."

"I mean, young Aylesgarth, that you are back in residence in that house that has waited many years to see a family inside it once again. You done running about London or are you going back there like your father did?"

The mood was charged in an instant. Roman let the words stand for a moment, taking his time before he replied. "I do not intend for any of what passed for acceptable behavior in the past to continue at Whitethorn. I am here, with my wife and my new son. When and if I leave to 'run about' London, it shall be in no way similar to how my father conducted himself. After all, both my wife and new son enjoy running around London, as well." With a twinkling glance to Andrew, he added, "Preferrably on a velocipede."

"A what? Oh, never mind. Well, I'm glad to see you've finally done right. I've never liked you, not since you and that scoundrel in there dressed my nanny goat in the freshly washed unmentionables that had been left hanging out to dry." Her eyes took a moment to appraise him anew. "But you've finally had the sense to marry this girl, so there must be some good in you."

"Your esteem has touched my heart," Roman assured her, "and inspired me to heights of goodness I heretofore had never imagined."

Her stern expression broke just for a moment. "You've a wit about you, something I've never imagined. I thought you deficient in the head as a boy. Why else would you be so bent on causing chaos, going missing for days on end. Judith believed in you, but I thought her a sentimental fool because you were so beautiful. Still are. But you've discovered your brain."

"It was a momentous day."

She did smile at that. "I dare say," she muttered. "I'm done with you. Got to tell the others about you. I will admit you've passed muster."

Her words were grudging, but she lost her battle with her smile when Roman took her hand and bent over it, and kissed the signet ring. "Be kind," he begged her.

"Impertinent rascal," she muttered, moving away before she gave up any more of her sternness. The knot of anxious women to which she headed tried not to look excited that she was finally on her way with the report.

"We used to call her Batty Bately," Roman said with fondness in his voice, watching her go. "Your mother gave me a right proper chewing out when we dressed up her goat. Even made me feel bad."

"Why did you do it? And all of the other things you used to do? They were never dangerous to anyone, never really destructive, but simply a nuisance."

He pursed his lips. "Well, I suppose I could come up with something very sensible, some logic that might persuade you that it was not pure wickedness, but the truth of it was, I was bored and there were times . . ."

She saw his eyelids drop, the way his nostrils flared, and she put a hand on his arm.

"There were times," he continued, "when I felt quite

mean. Like hurting would feel good. I couldn't harm a living thing, of course, so I reveled in being an unparalleled nuisance. It felt good to put a bit of chaos in the world."

"Well, you were a holy terror."

He made a pouting face, as if he were disappointed not to receive a more nurturing sort of response. "Not all the time."

"No," she said reassuringly, smiling at the way he pretended to relax at this. "No, not all the time. You could be quite charming when you wished, which I supposed saved you from a thrashing or two."

"Nearly all. My mother didn't have the stomach for it. She made the head groom do it, but he was a softhearted man. One or two whacks were about all he could manage."

"The fool," she mused lightly, "for had he been made of sterner stuff, the neighborhood would have fared better."

He nodded bleakly. "Or at least old Batty Bately."

"Oh, Roman, you are Lord Aylesgarth now. It is Dame Bately."

He kissed her fingers, his gaze grabbing hers. "What a good thing it is that I have you to remind me."

And despite herself—for she knew it was all silliness, this nonsense Roman was so good at playing so as to beguile a person clear out of their heart—she felt herself glow.

Grace was shocked to see Jason in the center hallway.

"What are you doing here?" she said. She fluttered her hands to the sheer scrap of embroidered lawn she had tucked into her bodice and drew it higher.

He responded with a droll lift of his eyebrows. "I am invited for dinner."

She wished she had known so she might have made certain to be scarce.

Tossing her head, she said, "Well, they are in there." She jerked her head in the direction of the parlor. "Trista and Roman."

"Where were you going?" he asked. His eyes were very intent on her. He made her nervous. Was it the collar? Or his eyes? They were gray, she noticed for the first time. A soft gray, as if a finely spun web lay over disks of dark sapphire blue.

"To my room."

"Running away?" He grinned, a dangerously charming grin. "From me?"

"Of course not. How immodest to think so highly of yourself. I am . . . I am out of sorts."

"You did not enjoy the sermon today. Tell me, what was it you did not like?"

"I thought it a fine sermon."

"You frowned the entire time. Come. Tell me what you thought."

"Why should you wish to hear my opinion?" she asked. He had moved closer, and without realizing it, she had retreated a step or two.

"I would have you think well of me. I cannot comprehend why it is you do not. I seem to make you very angry. And not just me. Trista riles you, doesn't she? I trust you have not come to Whitethorn with thoughts of interfering with Roman's marriage."

"No," she replied heatedly, and she was sincere. "I would not do such a thing. You would think the worst of me, wouldn't you?"

"Quite the contrary," he said with an enigmatic look. "I always see the best in you. Even if I did not say so."

She paused, wondering if he had meant to compliment her. It was such a strange thing, inferring that he had noticed her. But that was exactly the problem. He had never noticed her.

"I am glad to hear you have accepted Trista. You will only make trouble for yourself. Your brother cares deeply for you, but it is possible to press him too far."

Her heart pounded. Was this why he was paying her so much attention—for Trista's benefit? "Why, thank you so much for your good counsel, but I do warn you to proceed at your own hazard. I am not a tame little lamb searching for a shepherd."

"You mock me because I am a pastor. Is that what annoys

you so much? You have an antipathy for men in religious service?"

She pulled a face and whirled, heading for the stairs. She was three risers up when he trotted up behind her and said, "I will have an answer first."

She turned. He had one foot on the first step, his hand braced on his knee, waiting for her answer. The earnestness in his eyes caught her unawares.

"Very well. It is not your collar . . . per se. And it is not a new condition between us . . . this *antipathy.* I never liked you, Jason. And you never liked me, so do not pretend now to be some saintly pastor with a benign smile and patience for everyone. You had no care for me for many years. You were a devil, simply put, and now you are just bursting with caring for everyone."

"So you think I am a hypocrite?" That brought him up short, and she was disconcerted to feel a pang of remorse that she had scored a hit.

She said, "I think you were a selfish boy, and a snob."

He spread his hands. She noticed they were large, rough-looking, not gentleman's hands. Or parson's. "I am the snob? Your memory is faulty, dear Grace. Do you forget when I offered you friendship years ago? You turned me out because I was a commoner. You were off to London, you said, to fancy parties and much more important people than my humble self."

"I-I did not mean that," she said, feeling abashed at hearing her own words thrown back at her. She had said that to him, it was true, but it was only to cover her hurt.

She pointed her finger at him. "And I only said that because you . . . well, *you* were the snob. I was always beneath your notice until you lost all your other diversions. You ignored me and then suddenly, when I was the only one left, I merited your *friendship.* Well, I wished you to know that I was not going to faint in appreciation that you had noticed me."

"Ah. I see. I had hurt you." He sighed. "Allow me to enlighten you. Yes, I ignored you," he explained patiently, "because you were a *girl*. Observe your nephew one of these days and see the horror on his face when you mention the opposite sex. I was rather late in desiring to have *friendships* with the opposite gender." His gaze dropped. "And when I did notice you . . . it was exactly for the same reason. Because you were a girl."

Her heart bumped against her chest with a sensation that was somewhere between pleasure and pain. She fought against it, fearing it. "There was one night when you came for Roman. You threw the rocks up to his window, and I heard him leave. I followed. I did not let him see me, but I could not be alone. I was afraid, still . . . you see, I used to hate to sleep alone and I had crawled in that night to sleep with him. He would let me, if I didn't disturb him too much. Roman told you he could not run with you that night. And do you know what you said?"

He lowered his eyes. His body shifted slightly. "I do not remember," he replied quietly. "But I know what I must have said."

"You said, 'She's a silly baby. It will do her good to get over her fright on her own.' You persuaded him to go. And he left with you."

He didn't respond for a long time. "Poor Grace, it is true we were cruel to you, both of us. I was a cad, a callow boy without proper manners or care. I don't know why I was like that. I suppose I never thought of anyone else's feelings. My mother often accused me of that sin in those days. Seeing this from your point of view, I suppose you do have cause to hate me."

Her skipping heart dove downward, landing in her womb. She wanted to tell him she didn't hate him. Not hate. But she couldn't forgive him, not so easily.

He appeared suddenly uncomfortable. "I deeply regret that, Grace. But I must speak to you about Trista." He cleared his throat. "She is going to need your help. She has much to overcome in establishing herself here in the district. She is not as strong as you might think."

"And she is not as fragile as you seem to think."

He considered her for a long moment. "What a small heart you have to refuse to help her. Has she done anything to hurt you? Or did she just exist?"

She looked away, and her eyes stung. She blinked rapidly to dispel the gathering tears. She was embarrassed suddenly; not at all proud to be defending herself on this matter.

He said, "None of us were perfect when we were children, least of all me, but it is sad to see that you most of all have not overcome those times that were so unhappy for you."

She lost the fight. Tears splashed onto her cheeks. Raising her finger, she jabbed it at him. "Just because you are a parson now, do not presume to preach to me on my faults. I don't need any guidance from you, *Reverend*."

His manner changed abruptly. "You are angry, and I accept that you have a right to be. Roman and Trista and I—we all failed you, it seems. When are you going to stop punishing us all?"

"Did I hit a nerve?"

His face clouded, and his voice deepened to a strident tone. "There is only one raw nerve in this hallway, and I believe it belongs to you."

There! She'd made him angry. For some reason, this gave her bitter satisfaction.

It would drive him away.

He seemed like he might leave, and she realized with a start that she didn't wish him to. She waited while he seemed to be making up his mind.

"Grace," he said then, "is it that you felt no one ever loved you?"

She gasped. She wanted to slap him, but her hands would not obey her will. She stood quite still, watching him for any signs that he was mocking her, but his tone was infinitely gentle.

And then some desperate impulse rushed to the surface. "Yes," she blurted. "If you must know, then, yes. No one ever did, and it is not self-pity to say so. There, Parson, what clever Bible reference do you have that can take care of that?"

"I have no cure," he readily admitted, "only a question."

She blinked, startled. "A question?"

He stepped forward, and she had to brace herself to keep from shrinking away from the kind concern etched in the lines of his face. "Grace Aylesgarth: When did you ever let them?"

He left her breathless and gaping, frozen and wildly furious so that by the time she heard the door to the parlor where Roman and Trista awaited their dinner guest open and close, she had not moved a muscle.

It was pouring in London. May stood by her carriage, letting the rain soak her and resolutely ignoring the imploring glances from her maid.

She had come to see Ann Nesbit.

A young girl exited the house. She was saying, "It is not raining, George. At least not much. Simply everyone is out and it would be a shame to stay inside."

She was roughly twelve years old or so, pretty with blond ringlets that bounced when she walked. She spotted May. "Oh. Hello."

May donned a smile, and came forward. "Hello," she said, and the girl gave her a huge, open grin. "Do you live here?"

"Yes. I'm Olivia Nesbit. Who are you? Did you get caught in the rain?"

Lady May introduced herself and the girl asked, "Are you a friend of Ann's?"

"Ann Nesbit? Is she your sister?"

"My cousin. I live with her. She said I might since her house is grand and Papa is always working."

"She sounds kind."

"Oh, she is," young Olivia assured her. "And when she marries, she said I can stay on, that I am not to be turned out. Papa didn't expect that. He wept when Ann told him. Imagine!"

"Imagine Ann's generosity or your Papa's sentiment?"

She seemed confused for a moment then shrugged. "Both, I suppose. Did you wish to see her? Is that why you've come?"

"I have. I am Lady May Hayworth. Here is my card."

The girl squinted at the script. "My! I'll give it to her."

She turned and started up the steps, but stopped only after a few and wheeled around suddenly, as if struck by some inspirational idea. "Are you the one who sends the money?"

Lady May blinked in surprise. "Pardon me?"

"Are you . . ." The girl stopped, the hopeful light fading from her eyes and she appeared acutely embarrassed. She stammered, flustered as she stated again that she would give the card to her cousin and hurried inside the open doorway.

No sooner had she gone inside the house when an elderly woman with a cloud of white hair appeared, and caught sight of May. "My stars, has that wicked child left you standing in the rain? Please forgive us, my lady, and come in, come in."

May entered the hall and waited until Ann arrived, which was not a long interval.

She walked slowly into the hall with the aid of a pair of crutches. Ann had a pleasant but cautious smile on her face. She said, "My lady. How may I help you?"

"Thank you for seeing me," May said. "I am certain you must think this quite strange."

"Come inside," Ann said, her voice cultured but not clipped as the upper class affected to demonstrate their exclusivity in their speech. She was pleasant-faced, not beautiful but subdued and radiant with the blessing of an exceptional complexion and pretty eyes. May followed her lead, and they took their time settling into a formal salon just off the main entrance.

"May I offer you refreshment?" Ann said politely.

"No, thank you. I do not think I will be staying that long." May glanced uncertainly at Olivia. "May I speak with you privately?"

Olivia was not so well-mannered to hide her disappointment when Ann, after a moment's hesitation, ordered her from the room.

"First please allow me to assure you that it is not my intention to cause you any distress," May began. Ann inclined her head in acknowledgment and May continued. "I recently became aware of some facts about a person dear to me. Those facts involve an incident that includes you. It is, however, in the name of a just and noble cause that I broach what is undoubtedly a very painful subject for you."

"I am afraid I do not understand." Ann's voice was cooler now. May guessed that despite her denial, Ann had some inkling of May's purpose.

"Circumstances force me to risk being rude in order to be direct. I am referring to the unfortunate events that led to your injury when you were a girl."

The hardening of the woman's eyes, the fresh flare of panic and fear, made May speak faster. "The man you accused, Marcus Roberts—"

Ann's face was alarmingly red, her voice so hollow the words she spoke sounded as if they were wrung out of a well. "You dare ask me such a thing."

"Marcus Roberts was not the man who harmed you. De Nuncier did what you blamed Roberts for."

The face that was red went ghostly pale. Her eyes shone and her chin quivered as her hands felt for the arms of her chair and gripped them until her knuckles turned white. She said two words so faintly, they were barely audible. May thought they were, "I didn't."

May said, "The man, Marcus Roberts, killed de Nuncier, and for that he was almost murdered himself."

Ann winced. "Oh, God," she said absently, then her eyes focused. "Almost murdered—you said, 'almost murdered.' Does that mean . . ."

"He is alive."

May nodded. Ann's face dissolved. "My God."

Giving her a moment to digest this, May sat in the quiet. The room was well-appointed, comfortable without being rich. Suddenly, the strange question Olivia had asked came back to her.

She snapped her head back to Ann. "He is the one sending the money, Ann. Marcus Roberts, son of Lord Lyles."

The woman appeared stricken, and then the fear returned, played on her face as she struggled to remain calm. "Why would you say such a thing? How could it be him?"

"He survived with his guilt—a guilt over you, for he had known the monster de Nuncier before the count came to this country. He blamed himself for the harm that befell you at de Nuncier's hands."

She seemed to fight with herself, wanting to protest. Her body was rigid, full of fury. And then she halted, her posture going limp.

Her words were a long time in coming. "My father," she said in a whisper, "was so thrilled to have the count live with us. It elevated us. Everyone was enamored of the French nobles migrating from the continent. It made us important."

"Did he know it was de Nuncier who attacked you?"

She didn't answer, just lowered her face and stayed there, frozen for a long time. "I didn't tell him. I did not think he would believe me. He thought so highly of the count."

"So you blamed Marcus Roberts."

"No! It was not I! I never accused him. But I did not tell the truth because I was afraid. I know it was wrong, but I hardly knew what else to do. I was a child, and I believed people would call me wicked."

There was nothing about her that begged understanding. Nor was she defiant. She spoke the words plainly, without any emotion.

May leaned forward. "It is like that, for children, isn't it? No one listens."

"Father was incensed when he learned Roberts killed de Nuncier. It was the end of his passage into the *ton*. When Roberts was named the killer, he became convinced it was he who had attacked me as well. The facts were not examined too closely. People's emotions were too high for rational thought. There was an outcry, there was a villain to blame, the villain died in a cowardly act of escape, and then all of the sudden it was over. It was easy to forget. We had peace and that was all that mattered."

"But, when the monies appeared in your accounts . . . did you never suspect that it came from him?"

"From a dead man? I thought of a thousand scenarios, but never that one. When the money from our inheritance began to dwindle, we thought we might have to sell the house, but suddenly the taxes were paid and our solicitor informed us there was a stipend for living expenses. The funds have arrived regularly since then, and when I took in Olivia, they increased in proportion. Whomever this benefactor is, he has taken great pains to remain anonymous, for I have tried to find his identity."

Ann's face creased into a frown, and she swallowed with some difficulty. "And now you tell me the man I had a part in wrongfully accusing of a horrible crime is the one who has done all of this good in my life? Why should he? Why would he repay my wrong with such goodness?"

May's eyes glistened so that Ann's image swam momentarily. "If you knew him, you would understand."

Ann ducked her head again, going into another stillness as before. After a moment, she said, "Then he forgives me, do you think?"

"Oh, my dear, if only you could understand that it is he who craves forgiveness from you. If you can find such a thing in your heart, then I would ask you to give it."

Ann was incredulous. "I will, if you ask it in his behalf. But in truth there is nothing to forgive."

Laughing, May's joy and relief made her giddy. "Of course not, of course, but as an engaged woman you are aware, of course, that men rarely see things as plainly as they are. They have to save the world, and failing that, they suffer. Indulge me, please, because of the man who has done so much good for you."

Ann nodded. "Oh, I shall, I promise you. How extraordinary for you to come here like this."

"Well, I was determined, and I have my ways of getting what I wish," May admitted with a certain amount of pride.

"You love him very much, I see."

May felt that swelling feeling, felt it block her air and choke her throat. "Oh, very, very much, yes."

Trista awoke with a small cry, sitting up and peering into the darkness, unsure for a moment where she was.

Lady Aylesgarth's room . . . no, her room.

Lying back, she sighed, the tiredness pulling at her. Her face was wet, and she realized she'd been crying in her sleep. Her dream had been of Roman.

Oh, yes, she thought as a soft sigh escaped her. She'd dreamed of the time when they'd been young lovers, of the time he'd taken her with him and showed her the places he'd used to hide when he'd been a boy. She had felt so happy, so complete.

And then she had awakened.

She climbed out of bed. Her eyes had adjusted a bit to the darkness, but it did not chase her mood to see the familiar around her. This room oppressed her. She'd stayed here to please Roman, but it was making her have these dreadful nightmares, full of sadness and frustration.

The dream had left her feeling bereft. The emptiness inside her was restless. She slipped out of the room, finding herself in the hall without knowing exactly what it was she was planning to do. Heading for the back of the hall, she climbed the narrow staircase where the walls were whitewashed and rough, not graced with delicately dyed fabric. The banister was plain wood, uncarved, and there were no treads on the risers, for these were the servants' stairs.

She had raced up and down these stairs so many times, she knew them as completely as she knew her own son's face. Her feet found the rhythm of the risers and she moved upward, to the attics to find her old bedroom.

On the threshold she paused, then pushed open the door and stepped inside. She looked into the darkness.

Not having brought a candle with her, she felt foolish, but

she stepped into the room in any case, feeling better even though the inky black concealed everything from her.

The cot had a real mattress, which Mama had arranged for her, and it was still here, stripped bare of linens. The table she had used, the row of pegs on the wall, and the shelves, three of them, that had housed all of her worldly possessions at one time. The pretty curtains still hung in the small square window high up on the sill.

On wintry nights, that window had bristled with frost, and her breath had puffed out white. She'd huddled in the coverlets and later she'd been warmed by a large, naked masculine form that had somehow fit into that narrow space with her.

Well, they'd managed it by squeezing very close together, although neither had minded the rather squashing accommodations.

That memory made her smile.

"Trista?"

She whirled with a gasp.

Roman stood in the doorway. "What is it? What is wrong?"

She gave a small cry and clutched her chest. "My God, Roman. I didn't hear you."

He entered. "Are you all right?" He looked about the room, "What are you doing here?"

She let her eyes wander. "Do you remember this place?"

He paused. "Of course I do." His voice was rough.

She began a tight circle, concentrating on each corner. "I remember you coming here to me. You would stand, just like that, in the doorway and call to me to see if I was awake."

If the moon was brighter she might be able to see his face. Or perhaps it was best it stayed in shadow. She might die of shame if she had to look at him.

"I was frightened in your mother's room," she blurted.

"It's your room."

She made a helpless gesture with her hands and stood there.

He said, "It is all right."

"Yes, I know it is. I'm just . . ."

"Trista," he said. "Why are you here?"

"I don't know." But she lied. She had wanted the past. She had wanted things to be as they'd been when they'd been happy and loved each other in this room.

She was absolutely sure she didn't speak any of these thoughts aloud, and yet he said her name again and came to take her in his arms.

She moved, too, and found herself where she had been so often. He smelled familiar and wonderful.

"Trista," he said, murmuring against her temple, his lips caressing her flesh.

She made to answer, but his mouth smothered the shape of his name on her lips, his kiss filling her so that she did not need to speak it. She felt it all through her. Roman.

She felt herself bending, molding her body to arch under the power of his. Roman could touch her, thrill her, but it had been years since he'd kissed her like this. It was not simply physical desire, but emotional. It called forth something deep and clamoring that she'd held back forever.

He took her bottom lip between his teeth, nibbling lightly. His breath fanned across her mouth. "Come to my—"

"No. Here." She pulled at him.

"Here?"

"Here. Like before. Make it like before."

He reacted. A gruff, primitive sound escaped him. He crushed her to him again. "Yes. It's what I want. Like before, all over again."

She took his hand and put it to her breast, her body jolting with the contact. Beneath his palm, her breast grew tender, swollen and hot, aching. He kissed her hard, his tongue mating with hers.

His hands worked off her night rail. His touch was so silky light, she shivered. She closed her eyes, and her head fell back.

His mouth settled in the curve of her neck, just below her ear. His hand, so light, so delicately stirring, traced the contour of her breast as his tongue flicked lightly along her mouth. His hands did things that left her breathless, so weak she didn't think she could stand.

She reached for him, and he caught her hand. He laid her back, his breathing the only sound in the darkness to blend with the shirring of skin along the bare canvas mattress. Her back made contact with the rough material. It was cold, shocking. His mouth was hot on her skin. She felt him tug at his clothes, unsheathing the heat of his body so that when he lay on her, it was like being pressed under a fire-hot brand.

He slid down her body with leisurely strokes of his tongue, touching her, teasing her, rousing her to panting expectation until she squirmed. Then his mouth settled on her, his tongue lashing alive pleasure, and she arched, climaxing immediately.

Floating on the dreamy spirals, she felt him shift, felt his flesh hot and hard against her thigh. She felt languorous, intoxicated and full of sultry mischief.

She sat up, surprising him. So taken aback was he that when she prodded him with one slim hand on his chest, he complied and lay back.

She straddled him, looking down at the fine masculine form, large and rippling with sinew and muscle. She leaned back, her hands on his thighs, reveling that it added to his excitement to watch her.

What it was that made her so bold, she did not know, but it felt glorious. She had the power of a woman, the power to surrender herself and command her man with her sensuality. He murmured something she didn't catch, but the tone was unmistakably impatient.

Ah, but she wanted to experiment. She wanted to do all the forbidden things she feared to do.

Her hands came up his thigh, and he muttered a strangled oath. She liked it, liked that he could do nothing with her atop him. His hands reached for her and she slapped them away.

Then she cupped both hands around the shaft of flesh and

she saw him react. She squeezed him and his hips rose as a ragged gasp tore from the back of his throat.

She rose up and his hands grasped her hips expecting her to sheath herself over him. They'd done that before. But she pulled away, and his arms flailed for a moment before he saw what she meant to do.

Bending, she pressed her mouth against the flesh above his navel. Then she followed the line of increasingly coarse hair to the core of him. He nearly came off the bed.

But he loved it. She could tell it was as glorious for him as it had been when he'd favored her with the same intimate kiss.

"Inside you," he said. His strong hands repositioned them. He entered her urgently, with a rough, delicious surge. Her fingers curled into the hard flesh of his back. He stared at her, and she could watch every nuance of sensation as he lost himself in slow degrees until he shattered into completeness.

He moved to a more comfortable position, and she curled tightly against his side. His hand moved up and down her side, very warm. It felt wonderful. Trista closed her eyes and breathed in deeply, then let out the breath in a whoosh.

"What?" he murmured. His voice was thick from their pleasure.

She could feel all the memories they'd made in this room gather around them now, succoring them in a cocoon of shared love. No shadows now.

The heartache of the past faded. It was pale now as a weak shade, fading, slipping away to be lost.

She suddenly recalled all the beauty there was to be remembered.

Chapter 18

"We still fit in this bed," Trista purred.

Roman stretched. "Not comfortably."

"Snugly," she replied.

"Which has its attraction."

She laughed, then grew serious. "My bed is more accommodating."

His head fell forward in defeat, nestling into her shoulder. "Oh, God, this is humiliating. I could not bring myself to visit you in that room."

She popped up onto her elbow to stare at him. "What?"

He grimaced, making a play of his embarrassment. "It was too . . ."

"Too much like her. I know. I hate it as well."

"Why didn't you tell me?"

"You were adamant that I stay there—the lady of the house and all of that."

"But I thought you would like it. It has a gorgeous view and a spacious dressing area."

"Well . . . it is a nice enough room—"

"Nice enough? God, woman, that place cost a fortune. I know, because I had the bills to pay for years afterward."

She sighed. "It is very rich, and I am certain it is the utmost in taste and elegance. But it is just . . . so . . ." She made an expressive gesture with her hand. "Red," she finished at last.

"Well, red is kingly. Expensive."

"Gaudy," she supplied.

"I do not . . . It feels wrong, like I am wiping out her memory if I change her room. It was *her* place, the only place she ever stayed, I . . ."

"Roman," she said, returning to her elbow to stare at him, "you just finished saying you couldn't bear to step foot in the room. Why keep it as a shrine to unhappy memories? Surely, you can bear to put them to rest."

His eyes drifted away and he took a deep, long breath. "I wish I hadn't hated her. I wanted to love her. Sometimes, I thought I did."

"Of course you did, she was your mother."

"I think I wanted to save her. I thought if she was better, then my father would come home, and stay."

"I know how much you admired your father."

"Too much."

"Why too much?"

He chewed on this for a while. "Because he cost me everything. He cost me you, and you were everything to me." There was a protracted pause. "When I was a boy, I'd run off, each time determined to never return to this house. But you brought me back every time. I'd think, 'What is Trista doing? Is Grace picking on her too much? Is she missing me?' and I'd come back."

"And I would await you, patient because I knew . . ."

Had she been about to betray herself? She could not tell him she had always known he would return for they had a connection distance and time could not sever.

"Maybe we should not talk about this," she said, losing courage. It was not time yet. The past was a quagmire, of times of happiness and so much regret. And she was still not sure of him. Oh, it felt wonderful to be held in his arms, to be like this, but she still knew nothing of his feelings for her.

They had known great passion, a bond that went soul-deep. Was that why he kept talking about their years together? Was his fondness caught up in a time that had had its moment, then slipped behind them only to be kept alive in tumultuous memory?

This was what she wanted so badly to know. She knew what she had been to him once. And now she was his wife. She had no idea what that meant. Was she to be a wife, as his first wife had been? Oh, surely, more fondly than that, but this was not a man who felt marriage meant love. She of all people knew that. He'd have kept her for a dalliance and vows to another woman would not have stopped him.

And now she was the one he was bound to, but bound by what? Legality, a shared child, convention.

How sad it made her to think that was all it was. So many others would be contented with that. Perhaps she should be, as well.

She had to try harder not to allow her feelings to interfere with a perfectly reasonable arrangement.

At her protracted silence, he said, "I suppose we should redecorate your bedroom. It should be as the present Lady Aylesgarth requires."

She thanked him, but her thoughts had dampened her mood, so that the tone of her appreciation roused his interest. "Are you quite well?" he asked.

If she said that she was not, she would humiliate herself. So she smiled and assured him that she could not be better. It pained her to lie to him.

"You what*?" Robert thundered.*

The look on his face would have cowed any other sane person, but Lady May was not feeling sane at the moment. She was delirious with joy.

"I went to see Ann Nesbit!" She was very pleased with herself. "And she told me everything. She admitted it was de Nuncier! Robert—I know I can convince her to clear you."

He was incredulous. May ignored the less than ecstatic

expression. "I told her you were the one sending the money."

His tanned face paled.

"It is you isn't it?" May practically crowed.

"How did you . . . ?"

"I did not know, actually," she said. "Her young cousin let it slip that there was someone sending money. She thought I might be their mysterious benefactress. It put me keen to a mystery, but I confess it was not difficult to decipher, knowing you as I do."

"And you told them?" Up until now, Robert had maintained a controlled manner. But now his voice thundered.

May blinked. "Why, of course."

He looked like a different man. His nostrils were curled, his lips pulled into a tight line. His voice had lowered to a deep, grating whisper. "You told them it was me, Marcus Roberts, who sent them the money?"

"Yes," May said in a small voice. "But it was after I had her admit that it wasn't you who assaulted her. I told her—"

"Who gave you permission to meddle in my affairs? What gives you the right?"

She tried to laugh. "My, my, Robert, you are taking this all the wrong way. I meant no harm."

"Did you think you understood this matter better than I? Did you think I was perhaps not intelligent enough to see what was to be done, but you—clever, wise, and oh-so-charming Lady May Hayworth—needs to rush in and make it all better? What arrogance."

"Arrogance?" Her chin came up. "I wanted to help."

"You didn't trust me!" he shouted, the sound booming around the walls and leaving her gaping.

"The servants—"

"I don't give a damn!" he said again, not compromising on his volume. "I don't give a damn about the servants!" He shoved his hands through his hair, leaving it sticking up in gray-streaked spikes. "You rush off and blithely announce to Ann Nesbit, 'Oh, yes, I know Marcus Roberts. He's a dear friend of mine, and he's sending you money because he's acknowledging his guilt.' How could you be so . . . high-handed?"

She was ready to shoot a retort right back at him, but she hesitated. "Why are you so angry?"

"Because, you little fool, you've put yourself in danger. Why do you think I've not declared my identity? There is still a price on my head, and you . . . May, the danger I care about is not for me. Don't you understand, you've made it clear that I am known to you?"

She tried to scoff, but the seriousness on his face stopped her. "Do you really think so?"

"It is a possibility." He paced. "The last thing I expected from you was that you would turn into a meddling female." He whirled and headed for the door. "I have to find out what I can. I still have some contacts."

Then he was gone, without so much as a farewell or a thank-you. She stopped herself from calling him back. The first and foremost emotion that registered at the moment, once her fears began to retreat to brood in the back of her brain, was indignation.

He had refused to allow her to explain. Ann Nesbit would never do anything to harm him. He simply did not understand, had not been there in Ann's parlor, heard the things she said and felt the true gratitude coming from lips trembling with emotion.

He had accused her of not trusting him, but it was he who did not trust her. And he had accused her of meddling—of arrogance! Well, she might have meddled, just a little, but she had done good, she was sure of it.

But in time, May began to doubt she'd done the right thing. What if her rash confrontation *had* stirred the hornet's nest, as Robert feared?

In the following days, Robert's continued absence, an uncharacteristic thing since he'd never been one for a grudge, left her alone with these mounting thoughts of dread. She had no diversions. Trista had gone to Whitethorn, of course, and Michaela and Adrian left for their country home. It was poor luck that she would find herself alone at this particular time when she most needed her family members.

They were much in her thoughts, however, especially Andrew and Trista. Her first letter from Whitethorn arrived. It was cheerful, but it was not difficult to guess that returning to the home of her youth was proving more bitter than sweet for her niece. Not only that, Andrew was not adjusting well.

May sat down at her pretty escritoire, determined to put the matter of Robert . . . Marcus out of her mind, and dipped her quill. She dashed off a quick message, and sent it out right away. Then she swept upstairs and informed her maid that she wished her to pack her trunks immediately. She was leaving for Whitethorn.

She needed her family, and it might be that they might need her. It was good to know someone did.

Roman received Trista's request to meet him in the library. He entered to find her frowning over a letter.

She held up the foolscap. "I've a letter from my aunt. She wishes to visit."

"That is fine," he said, relieved this was all.

She gnawed on her lip. "In fact, she says that my reading of this letter should find her well on her way."

"Ah." He was startled.

"Do you mind very much?"

"Not at all. The woman likes me, which besides indicating that she is an excellent judge of character, means that she is always welcome in my home."

Trista smiled, then glanced down at the letter, her amusement wilting into worry.

"Let me see that," he said. Trista did not intend to offer it to him, but when he tugged on it with a soft, "May I?" she didn't object.

He perused it. "She does indeed seem subtly troubled. Do you have any idea why?"

She shook her head.

"Do not worry," he told her, folding the letter and putting

it aside. He came to her, gently touching her cheek. "We shall take very good care of her when she arrives. It is good she came to us. If there is trouble, she should seek out her family. And that is me as well as you, now. And I know Andrew will cheer her."

She looked up at him, her eyes wide and full of happiness. "Thank you for being so kind."

"You think so? You've accused me of being a beast to you when we were children. And now you see me as kind. Dare I hope you've allowed I've changed?"

"Not at all. You are the same. The kindness was in you always. I remember the doll you patched together for me."

He searched a moment, then found the memory. He squeezed his eyes shut and winced, declaring, "Oh, Lord, it was hideous."

She laughed. Idly, she strode to the letter, picking it up again to read it one more time. "I hope it is nothing too terrible that has her overset."

He plucked the paper from her a second time and put it aside. "It shall do you no good to worry over it. You will see her soon enough and straighten the matter out. Until then, I might know something that could get your mind off this, if you've a mind to trust me."

"What?" she laughed, bemused.

"Someplace I know you would like. Will you come with me?"

His eyes danced and she loved it when he was like this. "Is this one of your secret places?"

He gave her a look that admitted it was. "I vowed never to betray their location. However, if we should walk and find an interesting place, that would not be untoward."

How could she resist? "I'll fetch Andrew."

"No." He caught her as she started out of the room. "Just you and I."

This stunned her. She'd gotten used to the idea that the first and foremost priority to Roman was his son. "Are you certain?"

"I want to take you. Just you." He pulled her closer, his hands lingering on her shoulders. "All right?"

She said, "All right. I'll go fetch my shawl."

He brought round the pony trap and she laughed when she saw him on it. Then he produced a wide straw hat and they proceeded out of the forecourt and down the carriageway at a stately pace.

"Where is your phaeton and fine team?" she asked, amused.

"They would not like where we are going, the horses I mean. As for the phaeton, it is a sturdy conveyance we need, and this one is it."

"I daresay Annabelle and Raymond and his wife . . . what was her name? Oh, bother. In any case, they would no doubt be astonished to see the urbane man of Town right now—driving a trap in a straw hat!"

He squinted, as if against the sun, although the wide brim of the hat shaded his face. "You know she was never anything important."

"Who?"

He grinned. "You know well who. Annabelle."

"Are you telling me that I should not be jealous of her?"

"Indeed, that is what I am saying."

"Then I will be reassured if you promise you will not be jealous of Jason."

"Jason! Are you serious? Me, jealous of him?" He snapped the reigns irritably.

"You were put out he came to speak with me the day Grace arrived and I left the parlor abruptly. Admit it."

"Jealous of Jason, that will be the day. Good Lord I am not—all right, it is a bargain."

He abandoned his protestations so abruptly, and with such a rakishly charming surrender that it made her laugh. He gave her a long look over his shoulder. "I was not really jealous, of course. The man is a parson, you know."

"I know it."

"And you are a good woman."

She shot him a sideways look loaded with her best flirtatious smile. "Why, thank you."

"You are welcome, and besides, the both of you know that I would do despicable and painful things to anyone who ever touched you in any way. Besides me, of course."

"Oh, really?" She couldn't keep the undertone of laughter from her voice. "Well, that is certainly a robust deterrent."

"And since neither you nor Jason is a fool, then I know I am quite safe from being cuckolded. No need to be jealous, then, you see. It is merely a matter of logic."

She looked up at him. "You are smug. Insufferably smug."

He tapped his temple with his forefinger. "Logic," he repeated.

"Smug," she muttered, but the smile played on her lips for a long while.

But when she saw where he'd taken her, her smile faltered.

Not that she was not pleased, she was. Deeply. But she was overcome, as well.

He watched her carefully.

This was the place they'd come many times when they'd been in love. So many days, spent here, filled with long, endless hours of talking, telling each other absolutely every secret thing in their heart.

It was meant for romance, this place. It was isolated, for one. And it was physically imposing. Boulders of large, flat shale were piled into a tower they used to climb upon, to sit in the sun. In the distance was the lake, and around them the forest nestled beneath the fells. The river was far off, coiling along the floor of the fertile valley, but visible from here through clusters of trees and over farmhouse roofs.

"But you've brought me here before. We . . ." They'd made love up there.

"I was not supposed to show this place to anyone, ever. But when it became difficult for us to find time alone, I brought you here, but I pretended I happened upon it."

Her eyes sought his. "Do you remember?"

"I've never forgotten. Not a single moment," he said. "Come on, then. We have a climb."

He was down from the cart and already on his way to her side to help her out before she could protest.

Climb?

It was peculiar, how the power of this place grabbed her like a silk scarf about her neck. A little frightening, but sensuous and soft. It felt good.

She had run with her hair down, dressed in her chemise and petticoats, feet bare to better grip the rocks as she clamored like an urchin over them. And he had looked like a pirate, standing tall on the topmost rock, his billowing shirt open and his boots scuffed from the climb, making her laugh with his ridiculous claims at all he could see as he surveyed the homes of their neighbors.

She felt him touch her face, and realized she was smiling. His thumb brushed along her bottom lip. "We were so happy here."

She nodded.

His smile deepened as his head came up to catch the flight of a memory passing over his mind. "God. You used to laugh with your whole soul."

She closed her eyes, but the assault on her senses didn't abate. It was not so much the physical attributes of this place, how the familiar vistas unearthing long-neglected remembrance, but the feel of it that soaked into her pores and burrowed into her heart.

"I wonder if you laugh like that any longer."

She shrugged. "I suppose Andrew can make me laugh like that."

His tone tensed. "He is your joy."

"He is so like you. Yes, he gives me joy."

She could feel him staring at her. "I used to miss you so much," she said before she lost her courage. "I'd look at him and be so angry at you for not being there to see how wonderful he was."

How could she blurt out such a thing? she thought and immediately wanted to turn away, but he would not let her.

He held her, and in a moment she was glad she had spoken. Her chest felt lighter.

There were things she needed for him to know.

"I hate that you took him away from me," he said softly. "But I'm glad he was with you. It makes me feel connected to you those years when we were apart."

She stared and stared, not knowing what to say.

"I think," he said carefully, softly, "you must find a way to forgive me."

She gaped, shocked at this. It was he who must forgive her.

Before she could ask what he meant, he took off his coat. Then, to her amazement, he began to climb the pile of rocks. She shaded her eyes and watched him as he scaled quickly up the boulders. He paused, his knee bent, shoulders thrown back, the wind lifting his hair and he threw her his most rakish grin. "Coming?"

"I am wearing a dress."

"So take it off. Like you used to."

"I am not a heathen."

He threw his head back and laughed. "Oh, yes you are. Come on."

She cursed him—which only made him laugh louder—and bent down to unlace her shoes. Her stockings were fine and apt to tear, so she removed them as well.

Then she took off her dress and followed him in her underclothes.

The rock was cold and rough against the soles of her feet. She squinted up at him, holding her hand over her eyes to shield them from the sun's glare.

Roman had climbed to a height that looked dizzying from here.

"You are not afraid, are you?" he taunted.

"You are being utterly foolish."

"And you, madam, are a coward."

"Damn you!" She hitched her petticoats and tucked them into a rather unsightly knot, leaving her legs bare from the knees down. Gingerly she climbed on the first rise.

"Have you forgotten how easy it is?" he coaxed. "There is a pattern."

She recalled that now. She searched and found the next step, and the next.

Feeling very good about herself, she clamored up the side, concentrating on how to advance on each boulder. Heights hadn't bothered her as a child, but now she couldn't bear the thought of her distance from terra firma. If she did not look down and did not look up, she could put the roiling of her insides out of her mind.

She was startled when she landed on a larger rise, and Roman was waiting there for her. His arm caught her around the waist, and he pulled her to him. "I've got you," he said, and almost as an afterthought, he bent his head to seal a kiss over her parted lips.

"So say it," she required when he had pulled away.

"Say what?"

"That I am marvelously brave." She threw her chin up and challenged him.

"But you are not at the top yet," he replied, and turned to take three steep steps away from her. She followed, noticing that he paused to keep an eye on her, watching carefully as she copied his path.

"Did you think I could not do it on my own?" she asked him between breaths.

"Not at all." Damn him, he wasn't even winded. "I simply missed your company."

Hand in hand, he guided her to the top. When they reached it, he stood beaming at her, feeling triumphant and clever.

She was exhilarated as well. His smile was full of pride. "Now, I will say it. You are marvelously brave." He took a step toward her. "And not just for climbing these rocks. Sometimes bravery is just foolishness with flair. No, I'd say your most stellar act of courage was something far more dangerous."

The wind was sharper here. She had the strangest idea

that the whirling air wrapped around them and pulled them closer.

"You married me."

She laughed. He touched her hair where it fell loose from her pins and floated around her face, tucking it into place. He smiled when it worked loose and the wind played with it again. "And pray tell why does that make me brave?"

"Because you knew what you were getting."

"I'd say that made me very clever."

He smiled, watching her closely.

"That pleases you, you arrogant lout," she accused.

"It *was* a compliment. I think. Was it not meant to please?"

"Yes, yes, it was a compliment." She nudged him. "Now you can compliment me."

"I already did. I said you were very brave."

"And clever . . ."

"*You* said you were clever."

"You must agree."

"Very well, you are clever."

"I forgive you," she said suddenly.

The playfulness vanished. He stood, his face suddenly a mask. Then it collapsed into a grimace, as if he could not accept this. "Do not do that."

"What?"

"You give it away too cheaply. What do you forgive?"

"That you were an ignorant fool who threw away the best thing that ever happened to him."

He considered this and a smile came over his face. "You are an odd bird, Lady Aylesgarth. You offer me solace and then attack." He laughed. "But quite on point. I was wrong to marry Therese. It ultimately brought no happiness to anyone."

She bowed her head. "And it is time for me to tell you how sorry I am for my . . . Roman I was wrong for what I did. I mean Andrew, for taking him away, not telling you. Not giving you a chance, at least, or choice to be a father to him."

Turning her face up to him, her eyes were pleading. His

gaze moved restlessly over each feature. The tension in him was palpable, and it connected to the same in her. "Did you do it out of spite?"

"No!" she replied heatedly.

He nodded, a half-smile curling on his lips. "I forgive you," he said. "But I was not certain you forgave yourself."

She swallowed hard, wanting to take this in. But his forgiveness was not enough.

Her sin lived in the sullen expression of her child when he looked at his father, one that was growing more and more solid every day. Instead of abating, Andrew's tensions with his father had increased lately.

It would not truly be finished between them until Andrew loved him.

He moved forward to close the distance she had put between them. "Who knows, Trista, perhaps you were right. I can pretend that it would have made a difference if I'd known of his existence, but what if I'd not done things differently? I was so self-important, so focused on this 'duty,' and when you refused to become my mistress, it was I who felt betrayed by you. How dare you not know that this was my moment, the one I'd been waiting for. My father needed me. He wanted me." He broke off with a sigh.

She settled close, laying her cheek against the crisp lawn of his shirt, warmed by the beating heart underneath.

He leaned back, peering at her. "Maybe we simply did our best. Can you live with that?"

"Our best was not very good," she began. "We botched it very thoroughly."

"But we were so . . . well, stupid. Young, flawed, full of ourselves."

She laughed again. "Yes. I hate to admit it, but yes. I thought that the world was a place where ideals existed without compromise."

"And pride reigned."

"Ah . . . pride." She sighed pensively.

He shrugged. "No one is perfect."

Trista threw her head back and gave herself into the silliness of playing with Roman. His hands caught her hair, pulling gently until the pins fell out and her golden hair fell in a cascade of curls down her back.

"Yes," he mused, studying her like one would a painting, with his eyes alight with a strange intensity. "That is exactly how I remember you laughing. With your entire soul, and pure joy, unrestrained, pouring out of you and into the very air so that I could breathe it in and feel it, too."

The last of her laughter hiccupped in her throat. "When did you become a poet?" she asked in wonder.

"When I became inspired."

She wanted badly to tell him that she loved him. This was the moment. Where were the words, why had they deserted her?

His gaze locked with hers, holding it for a moment, and she told herself that he knew. "Do you think we are too old to make love up here like we used to?" he asked.

"Of course we are. I cannot imagine anything more undignified. You are Lord Aylesgarth, and I a wife, and mother. And besides, the rock is hard and we have a nice bed at home."

His look was purposefully oblique. "So . . . you are saying what, precisely?"

"That you are insane if you think I am going to remove my clothing and lie on this rock."

He began to sink to his knees, pulling her down with him. "Then I shall bay at the moon in the throes of this insanity, for that is exactly what I mean to do."

Chapter 19

In the nursery at Whitethorn, Andrew nibbled unenthusiastically at his tea biscuit. His nursemaid kept glancing at him, a soft smile on her face, but her eyes were sharp.

Nancy was a bit like Mama. She always knew when he was sad.

He'd gone downstairs to find some toys he'd left in the parlor, and he'd overheard Papa telling Mama he was taking her to a special place, and when Mama wished to fetch him, Andrew, Papa had said no.

This had filled Andrew with strong feelings. He'd run up to the nursery. He hadn't been able to forget that his papa had said no. Nancy always knew when he was upset. She didn't know why, but she wanted to. She kept asking him questions and watching him all the time with that worried expression.

"Come on now," she said, rushing forward. "You can have more cream in your tea. You'd like that, wouldn't you? Nice and sweet and creamy. There?"

"All right," he said, but it was just to make her happy. He didn't want his biscuit, and he didn't want to drink his tea. He didn't think he could. His stomach felt tight.

Nancy poured more cream in his mug and stirred, smiling hopefully. "There, that's better. Now . . . how about a walk after you have your rest?"

He shrugged. "Yes, please."

She hunkered down and smoothed his hair out of his face. This was something Mama always did. He wanted his mama right now, and though he loved Nancy and knew she loved him, she was no substitute for what his heart wished.

"You're just a wee bit tired, I suppose," she said, feeling his brow for fever. Satisfied, she let out a speculative sigh. "A good rest will set you to rights, I'll wager."

She left him to do a bit of tidying up of the nursery. When she glanced over, Andrew pretended to take a sip of his tea and munch his biscuit. This reassured her, and she soon left him to fetch the freshly laundered linens for his bed. He was to have a lie-down until she came back, after he finished his tea.

He dumped his tea into the chamber pot and threw his biscuit out the window. Then he climbed into bed and pulled the coverlet over himself.

He closed his eyes, thinking of Mama and Papa. His little heart thumped hard in his chest.

Andrew squeezed his eyes together, wanting to sleep so that he would stop thinking about it. They'd never before left him out of an outing. In fact, he'd gone on every one, even the ones he had not wished to go on in the beginning.

He tried to remember what Mama said, about always loving him, and that Papa loved him more than anything. He did not believe that. His mother's love, he felt every moment, strong and steady. But his father, he did not know about yet.

Papa was pleasant to Andrew, even fun to be with. But he had eyes only for Mama, and Andrew was certain it was her Papa loved, not him.

That could be why he did not wish to have Andrew with them today. Maybe the fears he'd had were correct. Maybe Papa just wished to take Mama away.

It hurt to think this, because he'd just begun to like him.

Papa knew things Mama did not. He also had a wonderful sense of adventure, even mischief, that was fun and shocking in a way that he had to admit delighted him almost always. And Mama did not mind it when they did things she normally would not approve of, not when Papa gave her one of those looks that made her blush.

He'd almost gotten used to those looks. He'd had to; it was happening more and more. In time, he'd begun to relax. He began to think that Mama looking at Papa like that and Papa looking at Mama did not mean he was going to be forgotten.

But they'd forgotten him today. He'd been left out. On purpose.

Maybe they would wish him to go back to London. He could live with Aunt Luci and Uncle David.

He found, however, that the prospect of being with his uncle David was not as thrilling as it once had been. He still loved him, and missed him very much, yes, but he was getting used to things here, sort of . . . well, liking having a papa after all. He wasn't a sea captain, of course, but he was interesting and amusing and Andrew could not help but admire him. The people at church had thought him fine, and if the other boys would be his friends as Papa planned, it might be very nice to live at Whitethorn instead of sailing the seas on a great ship.

Maybe, he should not have been so mean to Papa in the beginning. But he couldn't help it! Besides, he had not seemed to mind. Which had been very frustrating at the time, but now Andrew was grateful.

A thought made him burrow deeper between his coverlet. His little body began to shake.

Maybe Papa did mind after all.

Trista was pouring over the household accounts when Grace breezed in. She stopped short, seeming shocked to find Trista in the study.

Trista said, "If you are looking for your brother, he and

Jason are riding the estate at the moment. He said they would be gone a good part of the day."

"Oh, bother." Grace stood awkwardly for a moment.

"You can sit if you like. I was just about to take a break." Trista stretched. She was feeling tired, and her body ached from being hunched over the ledgers. "I'm having a difficult time deciphering the accounting system Mrs. Benbury has been using."

With a hand braced at the small of her back, she walked carefully to a chair. Grace watched her.

"Age," Trista told her, relaxing into a seat. "Would you mind ringing for some tea?"

"I wouldn't want to appear too presumptuous." Grace picked up the bell, looking not at all pleased to be stuck with Trista when she'd been looking for Roman.

"I do not wish to keep you," Trista said, "although I think it is about time we iron a few things out between us, don't you?"

This apparently was a distasteful notion. Grace frowned fiercely and changed the subject. "I cannot believe he is doing such a feudal thing as riding the lands. Father used to do that when he'd come home for a visit. He said it excited the workers, made them feel singled out and appreciated, but he said it like it was a grand lark. The poor dolts didn't have a clue that he cared less about them than he did us. It rather put into perspective the trinkets he brought with him and the token bounce on the knee twice a year."

"I realize things were very trying for you in the past, Grace," Trista began carefully, "and that is what makes this so difficult. This was an unhappy home for you and Roman."

"But not for you. You had your mother."

"She was very fond of you and of Roman. We have a troubled past, you and I, but it is the present to contend with."

"Yes, and you've quite won the day. Mistress of Whitethorn, wife to Roman, and mother of his son and heir."

"And you are beloved sister to my husband and aunt to

my son, two individuals I hold most dear. I would like very much for us to find a way to get along better."

Grace made a face of displeasure. "I have gotten the message quite clearly and have not interfered. Have I done anything to slight you since I received a dressing down from your admirers?"

"Admirers?"

"Roman. And Jason." She choked on the last name.

"I am sorry about that. They should not have interfered." But she found it sweet that Roman had defended her. "I shall handle my own battles."

"Yes," Grace mused, her voice filled with mocking drama. "Capable, indefatigable Trista. Is there anything you cannot do?"

"I cannot seem to make you like me," Trista said. "And I've tried nearly all of my life."

The statement gave Grace pause. She blinked, then her eyes narrowed, as if she sensed a trick. "Isn't it enough that you have Roman at your feet, and Jason, too, it seems? Must you be adored by everyone?"

"No. I wanted a friendship with you, another female. We were girls together, and we could have shared a special bond. You did not wish it, however, and I accepted that without any malice. I still would like to if you could ever manage to make yourself pleasant every once in a while. You are family."

"Oh, please. Do not pretend that you *care* about me. You are doing this only for Roman and Andrew."

"Of course I am. What is wrong with that? I am trying to make peace between us for their sakes. If not for them, I would not give an arrogant, mean-spirited, petty, embittered person such as yourself the time of day."

Grace's mouth snapped shut with an audible click. She appraised Trista. "And if you hadn't given birth to an adorable replica of my brother and then married that brother, I would count myself well rid of you."

"I understand."

Grace stopped, surveyed her opponent. "We do not have to be friends."

"We've managed well enough this far," Trista agreed with a shrug.

Grace smiled slowly. "Well, at least we understand each other."

Trista nodded pleasantly. "Perfectly. Ah, here is the tea. Are you certain you will not join me?"

Grace took a seat, folded her hands, and waited. Trista raised a brow inquisitively. Acting supremely unconcerned, Grace waited as Trista poured out.

"Now," Grace said as she sat back with the cup just handed to her, "we have to discuss the matter of Andrew and introducing him to the neighborhood boys."

"I am arranging an afternoon party here at the house."

"That could prove interesting. It could also prove disastrous. Let us not be obscure about the circumstances involved here. You were once a servant in this house. Now you wish to be accepted as its mistress. This needs to be handled delicately."

"Do you think I am not 'capable' enough?" Trista asked archly. "You had such confidence in me only a moment ago."

"I was speaking from frustration. The truth is in this instance you are at a disadvantage." She sipped her tea while Trista stewed. It was nothing she didn't know already, but Grace made no secret of liking having something to gloat upon. "I, however, am in a position to help. Our less enlightened neighbors might think to snub you, but they would not refuse an invitation for a party which we *both* sponsor.

"I offer only for Andrew, of course," Grace added quickly. "He must be made to be contented here, and if we present a united front to the gossips, they will have no cause to cut the family. We must make it unthinkable for them to refuse the invitation. The family shall show its support of you, and therefore they must accept you as Lady Aylesgarth."

Although it stung, Trista had to admit it was all true. "It

would make a considerable difference to have you involved. I thank you for your willingness to put your efforts into this."

"Yes, well, let us not get all misty-eyed over it. It's simply a party—for Andrew's sake."

Trista inclined her head. "Of course."

She fussed at her gown. "I mean, it isn't as if we have agreed to undergo some major ongoing project, such as building a new wing of the house."

"Oh!" Trista exclaimed. "But I am redecorating my rooms and am quite overwhelmed with all of the choices I need to make. You wouldn't happen to have an eye for color, would you?"

"What? You are redoing my mother's rooms?" Grace went stiff. "They were done over for her, and at great cost. They are lovely as they are, and I shall certainly not lift a finger to change them."

"Then it is a good thing that I have arrived when I did," said a new voice. "It appears I am just in time to save the day. I am excellent at redoing room décor."

"Aunt May!" Trista cried, jumping up to fling herself into the arms of the petite woman who breezed into the room in a cloud of feathers.

May laughed. "Ah, I told the footman not to announce me. I wanted to take you off guard. I see I did. Oh, dear," she added when Trista squeezed her a tad too hard.

"I missed you," Trista said, "and I know Andrew did, too. He will be thrilled."

"Then fetch him immediately so that I can give him the good news that I have arrived. I notice you have not included your new husband in those you anticipate being happy to see me."

"Nonsense. Roman will be delighted. He was happy that you were coming when I showed him your letter."

She patted Trista's hand and turned to Grace. "Hello, Lady Grace. It is good to see you again."

"Grace and I were just planning a party," Trista explained.

May clapped her hands together. At the muffled sound, she removed her gloves. "Then it is actually true about me arriving in the nick of time. I happen to be excellent at parties as well."

"Yes, Aunt May, but Grace should take the lead on this," Trista said nervously as May sat down. Aunt May had a tendency to take charge.

May smiled at her niece, giving her a look of keen understanding. "Grace, then you must tell me the rules. Every neighborhood has rules, and as our expert, you must help us outsiders to understand them."

Grace was cautious, but soon was coaxed into talking. As she relaxed, she became quite glib, and had them in giggles at the petty dramas she described.

Once May assessed that Grace knew her society, she relaxed. She was not up to her usual take-charge tactics. The vigor was out of her, her mind occupied, caught in knots over Robert—one moment she was furious with him, then the next she was equally furious with herself and finding that she could not blame him for taking her to task.

She could not bear it if she had done anything to bring harm to Robert. She'd sooner take the punishment on herself—he had to know that.

That was what anguished her the most, the worry. And the waiting. If what she had done in seeking out Ann Nesbit had been a terrible mistake, she would see the ill effects soon.

Trista noticed her aunt was less bright, less cheerful than usual. Indeed, the fact that she had not taken over the party planning—for her aunt loved parties—was enough to indicate all was not well. When May excused herself to go to see Andrew before heading to her room for a rest and to freshen herself for the evening, Trista thought to follow her. But her aunt really did look tired, and she thought it best to leave her to a quick nap. They could talk later.

She continued to work with Grace, amazed how enthusiastic her sister-in-law had become, scribbling down a thorough list of guests and the particulars on refreshments and entertainments they had brainstormed together.

It was not long before the men entered. Grace glanced up from her note-taking and observed dryly, "The lord of the manor has returned from roaming his lands to survey his domain. Have the piglet killed and roasted, pile high the trenchers, and tap a keg of mulled ale. It is time for all in the hall to feast."

Roman gave Trista a quick kiss on her forehead.

"Grace and I are planning the party," Trista told him.

"The one for Andrew," Grace put in quickly, shooting a nervous glance at Jason, whose brows had shot up at this.

"Is it going to be some kind of medieval feast?" Roman asked, bewildered.

Trista laughed, looked to Grace, who caught her eye and laughed too. "No, no. Grace had said she thought it feudal that you'd ride out . . . oh, I'll explain later. Aunt May is upstairs. She arrived a few hours ago."

"Ah. I shall look forward to seeing her." Roman circled to the table where he kept decanted spirits. "It is good of you, Grace, to lend your skill. We appreciate it. Jason, what is your poison?"

"Two fingers of scotch." He took a seat, smiling at Grace. "A party . . . well."

Grace gave him a withering look, for he was unapologetically gloating. "So that Andrew might make friends."

"If you'll excuse me," Trista said, standing. "Speaking of Andrew, I'd like to spend the late afternoon with him before I dress for dinner."

"But I've only just arrived home!" declared Roman, disappointed. "Now you are running off."

"It is not my fault that you were gone all day. Come with me, then."

Roman shrugged. "Right. Here, Jason." He handed the scotch to his friend. "I'll be back directly."

Before either Grace or Jason could protest—and Grace would dearly have liked to—they were left alone in the library as Roman and Trista swept out, already talking animatedly between themselves. Their laughter floated back.

Grace made to get up. "If you will excuse me. I have to . . . rest. And change for dinner."

"Tired again, are you? You must call the physician about this weak condition that comes over you whenever I come into the house."

"You are baiting me," she replied calmly. "I do not think that is very commendable behavior for a parson."

"I have a few sins still left in me." The light in his eyes burned mischief. And something else that touched off the most delicious of shivers. "After all, I am a man of flesh and blood. Not a saint."

Her voice was rusty. "Won't your congregation find themselves disappointed to learn this?"

"I am trusting you to keep my secret." He held up a long, slender finger and pointed it at her slyly. "And I will keep yours."

"But I do not have a secret." She paused. "At least none that you know."

"I know that you are not as cold as you pretend to be. Your help with this party proves it. Dare I hope that some of our last conversation made an impression?" He threw this last out to deliberately taunt her, a thin ruse.

Which nonetheless worked.

"Ridiculous. I was bored. And it is for the benefit—"

"Of Andrew, whom you adore, yes, I heard you before. You made such a point of it, twice in fact, that I could not fail to miss the emphasis. Although I do not doubt you are bored here in the country." He made an expansive gesture with his hand. "I am sure you find it tiresome after your exciting years in London, enjoying the social set."

Grace stiffened. "Never mind," she said irritably and stalked to the window where she stared out, her arms drawn up around herself.

There was a long silence as he watched her, his brows creased in thought. "Grace?"

"I hate that you wear that collar."

He nodded, and came to stand with her. "I know."

"Why are you so patient with me?" she asked. "Is it because it is your duty? As *parson*?"

He thought about this for a moment. "You try so hard to frighten everyone away, don't you?"

"Then why don't you go away?" she said, but it was without venom.

"I know you too well and for too long. You cannot hide from me."

"What do you see, then?" She looked at him openly, her face unmasked of all pretense. He thought he saw just the briefest flash of hope.

He said simply, "Your heart."

She was overcome, but not displeased. She seemed to be doing battle with herself. Then she came to a decision. Nervously, she said, "It is probably a sin to lie to a parson."

"It is a sin to lie. Period."

She dropped her gaze. "You will probably hear of it sooner or later. What you said just now about parties and the gay life of society in London, I . . . I lived a quiet life in the city. I did not attend parties. It was quite the opposite."

"You do not mean to tell me you never gave the Town scene a whirl."

"I did, of course, when I first arrived, but then I found the people so very . . . I do not think I was meant for the city."

"Then why stay?" he asked.

She met his eyes boldly, refusing to cower. "Because I could not bear to come back here. I could not bear it here, this house. Alone."

He drew his head slowly from side to side. "No. You would not have been alone."

She looked away, her face flushing scarlet.

It was silly, really, that she had never thought of coming home to him. Perhaps it was because for so many years, he had never thought of her.

Jason slipped his hand over her elbow. His fingers were strong, warm through the thin cotton of her dress. "Tell me why you were not happy in London."

"The people were . . . different. I did not know them, and I found it very difficult to speak with them. At social gatherings, I never knew what to say. They were sophisticated, part of the *bon ton,* and I was a simple country girl. I must have seemed like an idiot to them."

"You could never seem like an idiot."

She cut him off, holding up a hand to ward off the words of comfort he was ready to proffer. "It does not matter if it was true or not that they thought ill of me. It is what I believed, and I could not be convinced otherwise. Do you know how many times Roman tried? What was worse, I knew that I *was* wrong. But there was this horrible fear that came over me whenever I had to face them, and I could not control it, not with my will or with reason, and I stopped going. When I'd meet people during errand-running or day outings, they'd ask where I'd gotten to and that they had been wondering about me. I was mortified. Soon, I could not go out at all."

"My God, Grace." He moved closer. She could smell the masculine spiciness of him. It was pleasant enough to make her the tiniest bit dizzy.

Whirling to face him, she said, "There. That should make you happy. The spoiled little rich girl is not so smug and superior after all." She could feel the hot tears stinging her eyes. Damn, she *would not* cry in front of him again. "And all along, you had it in reverse. A snob, you call me, when it seems to me that it is I who am always coming up short. How is that for a snob?"

She was halfway to the door when he bolted ahead of her, slamming his hand onto the paneled wall to keep her from leaving.

Out of breath, she refused to look at him. "I do not know why I confided this to you," she said. "If you do have some unfair power to make people tell you their failings, some training in disarming people and exposing them at their weakest, then I think it is wretchedly unfair of you to let it loose on people without giving them warning."

"Grace," he whispered. She closed her eyes against the

thrill that went through her at her softly spoken name. "You wanted to tell me."

And so she had. She felt relief, even as fresh eddies of panic and rich self-loathing began to weigh down her limbs.

She forced herself to face him. His handsomeness, that impenetrable solidness and the dark currents of his virility nearly took her breath away. She was too vulnerable for him right now. She tried to turn, but he caught her chin in his free hand and held her face. His eyes searched it, and she blinked back, aware that she didn't want to hide anything from him any longer.

And then, bless her, Lady May Hayworth swept into the room, posing a perfect opportunity for Grace to break away. She did so without artistry, hardly caring about Lady May's pretty astonishment, or the dark scowl on Jason Knightbridge's face.

Lady May took the opportunity of finding Trista alone over breakfast the following morning to confide in her. She told her everything about Robert.

Trista laid down her fork, no longer interested in eating. "So, the man I met at our home, Robert . . . er . . ."

"Carsons. He is this Marcus Roberts. Yes, he really is a stable keeper and sells carriages, just as I said. It is how we met. That is what he does for a living presently."

"But . . . he's also a spy?"

"Was a spy." May tapped her cheek with her finger, deep in thought. "You know, it makes so much sense. There was always something very . . . covertly exciting about Robert."

Roman entered. He smiled pleasantly, and Trista and May exchanged looks of uncertainty.

Roman frowned, sensing the tension.

May explained, "I was just telling Trista about a particular problem I am having."

"Anything I can help with?" he asked, taking his seat and unfolding his napkin.

"He is . . . well, more than a friend actually. If it would

not be a bother, I would rather appreciate your take on the matter."

"No bother." He grinned, piling his plate high with eggs.

He listened intently as May repeated her story, following up with a few questions. He was particularly insightful regarding Miss Nesbit.

"She has guilt," he said, his eyes narrowed in concentration. "She is not completely hardened against Marcus Roberts, and she did not deny that she'd lied."

"Oh, no. She was relieved to finally get this burden from her," May agreed.

"Then she may be persuaded to testify to these truths."

May was uncertain. "It is one thing to tell me privately of how the truths got confused, for I do believe she was just a hurt child who did not have the strength to contradict the adults who were fashioning these lies, but quite another to go public."

"And yet, as long as she does not tell the truth, he is a hunted man, especially now. Would she be willing to send a man to his death to protect herself from embarrassment?"

"Well, I don't know, I am sure," May said, somewhat taken aback by this slant on things. "I only spoke with her the one time." She smiled, looking at Roman with hope shining in her face. "Perhaps she could be persuaded."

Roman reached out and took her hand. "We could pay a visit to her, you and I. Between us, we might be able to get her to see a way through this."

Trista watched May's hand grasp desperate hold of her husband's. She felt a poignant jab of pride at him. He looked so large, so commanding and capable next to petite Aunt May, and it obviously comforted May that he was willing to help.

"It is a good idea," she said. "Let's do it. After the party, we shall come up with a plan."

"Yes," Trista said. "We'll all go to London. Andrew can visit Luci and David. I will tell him."

After that, the day took on a kind of glow. They were trapped inside by a deluge of rain, but decided to make the most of it. They played parlor games and at Roman's persuasion, sat down to several different types of card games, in which Roman proved impossibly competitive, which made Trista and May so angry they combined their efforts to defeat him. This caused him to sulk for a short time and swear vengeance. Jason came by for tea, and was pressed into a foursome of renewed card playing.

Trista noted that Jason seemed restless. He kept looking to the door, as if waiting for someone else. Perhaps he wished to speak with Grace, although she couldn't be sorry that Roman's sister chose to keep to herself. She was feeling too fine to test the truce between them, and should Grace be in one of her more caustic moods, Trista had no doubts that this truce would be shattered.

As it was, they laughed until their sides ached in the cozy confines of the parlor, which took on quite a different aspect from the days of old when it was dusty, unused, and deathly quiet. But Trista didn't muse too long on the past, not today, when they were all having so much fun.

At tea, Andrew was brought in after his lessons had concluded, and Trista was disappointed in his reaction when she told him what she would have thought would have been good news: that he was going to visit his uncle David and aunt Luci very soon.

Instead of the joyful response she was anticipating, Andrew grew pale. He threw a vicious look at his father.

Trista tried to speak to him, but he pulled away when she drew him to her and she let him go. She'd speak to him later.

She sighed, content to let the matter wait. Her gaze fell on Jason and Roman, who were shouting good-naturedly about some point of contention regarding a wager they had made on the turn of the cards. She smiled, chuckling at them.

Aunt May motioned Andrew from Trista's side, cuddling him close as she spoke in low tones to him, and Andrew seemed to relax.

Perhaps no day could be absolutely perfect, but today . . . today had come quite close.

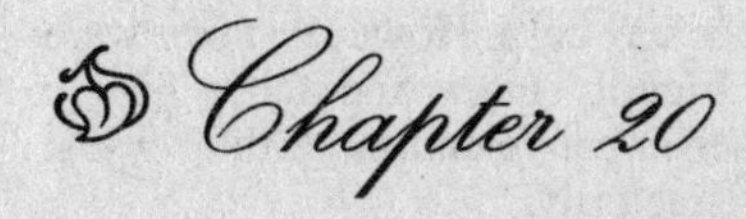

The shouts of children playing were loud enough to challenge the small orchestra tuning their instruments on the terrace. Watching a threesome of boys race by, Trista peered up at Roman and smiled. "I would say the afternoon was a success."

A screech of strings made Roman wince, then turn to glare at the violinist. "We shall see."

He grabbed Grace, who was strolling by with a cup of punch in her hand. "Where did you find the orchestra?" he asked her.

"In a waterfront public house," she shot, but then smiled rather mischievously. She turned to Trista. "Andrew appears happy. It is good to see him thus. He's been rather glum lately. Have you noticed?"

"I had, yes, Grace. I am glad he is having so much fun at the party. Hide-and-seek is one of his favorite games."

"Indeed, I know it as I've been forced to crouch behind the wardrobe in the nursery on several occasions when he's pressed me into playing with him."

Trista indicated the boys who were now running down the terrace steps and making for the garden. "Your efforts have not only made for a wonderful party, they have got you a reprieve now that he has boys his own age to play with."

"And what of you?" Grace asked. Her eyes were sharp on Trista. "Are you having a good time as well?"

It surprised her, this concern. Shrugging, Trista said, "I am not quite certain." Although no one had openly snubbed her, some people were cool, but she didn't mind terribly about that. Those whom had been so were invariably the type she cared little about in any case. However, there were a significant number of friendly faces and those people seemed eager to engage her in conversation. "I think I just might weather the day satisfactorily."

Grace smiled, relieved, and Trista thought she might have misjudged her earlier snappishness. Perhaps she was nervous, too. Roman had mentioned she tended to be uncomfortable in large gatherings, and had been watchful at church and other times she'd been out socially.

Trista leaned close to her husband, telling him, "Dame Bately has been adorably militant about my title. She booms it out in that loud voice of hers, then glares at people as if daring them to flinch."

"Adorably militant?" Roman mused. "What a strange pairing of descriptors, and yet apt."

The three of them turned to watch the older woman who was just now marching about with the women in her clique trailing behind her, like a queen with her attendants in tow.

Grace watched her. "She is quite a force to be reckoned with."

"As are you," Roman said, sweeping his hand to their surroundings with one hand, the other raising his glass in a toast. "You've managed quite a party."

She blushed with pleasure, making her exceptionally beautiful for a moment. "It was not all my doing."

"Oh, come, Grace," Roman said wickedly, "modesty does not become you, especially false modesty."

"Ah," said Jason, coming up just then, "am I too late to give my compliments to the hostesses?"

"Why thank you," Trista beamed. "I am just glad that people actually came."

Grace excused herself. Jason stared after her a moment and excused himself as well, then headed straight for her.

"Who do you think will prevail?" Trista mused lightly, observing the two.

"My sister is stubborn."

"Jason is determined."

He drew her arm through his and stared down at her, his eyes twinkling. "Then I will have to put my money on love."

Trista's heart stopped. It was such a winsome thing for a man such as Roman to say.

Her fingers curled tight into the hard muscle of his arm. Her smile trembled. He simply stared at her, giving no hint of any deeper meaning.

She said, "Indeed."

Jason caught up to Grace near the refreshment table.

"Why are you following me?" she asked him, annoyed.

"Because you have been avoiding me." His reply was casual. "And because I want to dance with you."

"I am not going to dance. I am far too busy. Now, please excuse me, I have guests to see to."

"I am a guest," he said cheerfully.

Her response was a dark look.

"You know," said Jason, "you cannot do that quite like before. Your humor is visible, in the lines around your eyes and your mouth turns up in the corners just the tiniest bit. Now, come, enjoy the party. Trista must take it from here."

"I didn't do it for Trista. Or for Roman."

He rolled his eyes. "I know . . . Andrew. The only male who claims your heart."

They both glanced over at the happy boy, surrounded by the flushed faces of his new friends. Jason leaned close, speaking softly in her ear. "Isn't he a little young for you? Now that he has found some playmates his own age, you might do the same. Now, take a walk with me."

He grabbed her hand and led her off to the west lawn.

There were a few people there, and a knot of youngsters lounged around a few scattered blankets talking among themselves. She didn't put up much more of a struggle beyond a token protest, even when he headed away from the others.

"Now, be honest," he said once they had distanced themselves, "it feels good."

"What?" She thought he meant the warm, strong hand enveloping hers.

"Doing something kind for someone else."

She sighed. "Am I in for another sermon on the merits of good deeds?"

"No, merely an observation. You look happy. There's a change in you, Grace. I thought a great deal about what you told me the last time we spoke, of your fears in London. I wanted so many times to call on you and talk more. But I see my concern was not needed. You seem more contented today than I have ever seen you."

"It is a party," she said, "it is supposed to make people happy."

"You liked helping Trista, didn't you?"

"Oh, bother—I knew you couldn't resist a lecture!"

He jerked his chin up, giving her an appraising look that said he was having none of her argument. "Admit it—liking her is better than tormenting her."

"I most certainly did not *ever* torment her."

His eyebrows climbed and he gave a soft, scolding laugh. "Remember, it is a sin to lie to a parson."

"And what of you?" she challenged. "Is it not a sin to drag young women off to private places when they are needed to oversee important social events?"

"I shall check my Bible when I get home and let you know." He pretended to be very sincere to tease her, and it did make her smile. She quickly sobered her expression.

He touched her cheek, where there had been a flash of dimple. "Why do you hate to smile for me?"

"I do not hate it." The way his fingertip brushed her skin was maddeningly distracting. She did not brush it away, though. "You are being silly, and I just do not want to encourage you."

He shook his head. His eyes were locked on hers, and they burned hot as they held her fast. "What do you think would happen if you encouraged me?"

"I . . . you . . ." She couldn't think worth anything with him touching her like that.

Swallowing hard, she backed away. "I have to get back to the party. Really. If I am seen sneaking off, it will be all the gossip."

"I will take you back," he said, his voice even and reasonable, "if you will promise to dance with me. After all, I am a lonely bachelor, a country parson . . ."

"Lonely? Oh, I doubt that very much. I have never met a more popular parson. All the eligible women of the congregation make calf-eyes at you during the entire service, so don't plead the lonely fellow to me."

"I have an excellent view of the fluttering eyelashes from the pulpit, thank you very much, as well as a larder stuffed with their culinary offerings. But, I wish to dance with *you*. And I want your promise that you will do so."

"Oh, very well." She sounded exasperated, but her stomach fluttered like a mad butterfly and she had the urge to laugh with pleasure. "May I return to my party, now?" she said crisply.

He grinned, and she knew he was not fooled at all. "It is not your party. That is what makes your generous help with this afternoon's festivities all the more admirable. You've designed it so that all the credit goes to Trista."

She narrowed her eyes. "I can change my mind about that dance. . . ."

His hands flew up in surrender. "Then I retract my observation."

She did laugh then, and it was somehow not such a traitorous thing.

He took her back to the party, releasing her to make the rounds among the guests. She could see after a quick check that Andrew was having a dandy of a time. His face was flushed from laughing. Or running. Probably both.

When the dancing started after a hearty supper, Grace scanned the crowd anxiously for Jason. When she spotted him, her heart fell like a lead ball to her feet. His gaze was fixed on her as he made his way through the guests, his expression one of intense determination.

He was coming to collect his dance.

They did not speak. He crooked his elbow to her and she slipped her fingers over the pulsing warmth of muscled arm. They went to the floor.

The dance was a stately promenade, one she had always found boring before. But it took on a different dimension with Jason staring pointedly at her the entire time, the hot look making her flush, a fine sweat breaking out over her skin.

"Come with me again," he asked tightly when they were finished.

Her heart leaped. "I . . ."

He did not wait for an answer, but led her out. She went along like a pliant pup, too bewildered to feel her limbs. Instead of taking her across the lawns as he had done before, they headed inside. She did not resist until he pulled her into a deserted room.

"I will not go in there," she said weakly.

"Oh, yes you will," he growled, reaching for her. With a tug, he brought her momentum around and she landed squarely in his arms.

"Is this something parsons are known to do? Manhandle women?" she asked breathlessly, mortified at how her voice betrayed her excitement.

His eyes moved over her face, which was very close to his own. "No, but men do."

She opened her mouth and he stopped her words with a kiss.

It was so shocking, so unexpected, so *good* she forgot to resist. He wasn't holding her so tightly she could not have escaped had she wished. But that was the key—*if* she had wished.

She had no desire to stop the kiss or to move away from his broad-framed body. The taste, the texture of his soft lips, the scent of man and the sound of their breathing growing more rapid, more shallow, filled up each and every sense.

He let her go only enough to break the kiss. Her eyelids drifted open to find him studying her.

"Come, Grace, it is time to tell me what you feel. I've pursued you, and you've obligingly fled so that I could play the great male hunter. Now, I'm changing the rules. Tell me that you want this as much as I do. Tell me you liked my kiss."

She gave a small squeal of mortification, but he held her fast.

"I need to hear something from you, Grace. Even a man of the cloth needs something more than faith at a crucial moment like this."

Trembling, she remained in his arms, frozen and wanting. And suddenly she didn't want to do this again, push him away because she was afraid to do what she really wanted to do. And that was kiss him again, tell him what he wanted—were those words in her?

Yes. They were in her, yes, but they had no voice.

He let her go, stepping away to brush off his coat and smooth the lines of his jacket. It was a good jacket, not fine but well cut and he looked good in it. She had never thought to ask about his circumstances, but he had never appeared as anything less than Roman's equal in all the times she'd seen them together. He might not have the bloodlines or the fortune, but he held his own among his noble flock.

She saw his expression hardening in degrees and there was an absolute certainty in her that he would not do this again. He would not chase her or scold her or insist she favor him with a dance. She'd had a chance to speak, and she had not.

Oh, God, she could not.

Opening her mouth, she managed the only thing she could. "Yes."

He stopped, giving her a sharp look. "What?"

"I did."

He was puzzled for a moment. *Oh, God, Jason, don't make me say it.*

I liked your kiss.

He understood, staring at her, then softening. "All right then." He smiled. "I hope that did not overtax you too much."

She couldn't help it, she laughed sheepishly. It was such a relief that he was not angry.

"Perhaps we should take things a bit slower." He lifted a lock of hair and smoothed it for her. "I shall take my leave now. You can get back to your duties."

She nodded. She had disappointed him. He was being kind, but her stingy heart had left him unsatisfied.

She wished she could tell him she was sorry.

*Roman's problems began the moment he woke up that morn-*ing to find himself alone in bed. He'd gotten used to having Trista beside him since she'd moved into his suite until the redecorating on her room was finished.

He rang for his valet to come and shave him, and when Barrett entered, he asked, "Have you seen your mistress this morning?"

The slender, white-haired man, as persnickety about his own appearance as he was about his master's, shook his head curtly as he consulted the contents of Roman's wardrobe. He pulled out a deep teal coat. "This, with the brown pants, I think, and that cream shirt."

Roman waved his hand, indicating that Barrett was to do whatever he wished. He understood the need to look neat, well-tailored, and carefully pressed, but he himself had no patience for such nonsense. He was clever enough to find a man who was.

Barrett did, however, have an annoying tendency to fuss with the cravat. After five tries, all of which Roman considered perfectly acceptable, Roman snatched the necktie out of his hands and did it himself while he strode downstairs.

He found Trista in the morning room with Andrew.

"Hello, darling," he said, giving her a kiss on the forehead. "Hello, Andrew."

His son glared at him with suspicion in his eye.

He looked back to Trista. "Is everything all right?"

"Fine. Just a nightmare last night."

"Mama!" Andrew cried.

"I promised I would not tell anyone what the nightmare was about." She explained to Roman, "It was the only way he would tell me." She turned a stern look back to Andrew. "But I did not say I would keep the matter from your father. I will never keep secrets from him."

Mother and son wore the same bullish expression as they faced each other across the table.

Roman laid a hand on his son's shoulder, preparing to say something to diffuse the situation. He had no sooner drawn a breath than Andrew threw off his hand, stood up, and fled the room.

Roman stared after him. "Perhaps I should speak with him." He sank into a seat, reclining as an old weariness took over his body.

"He's been so happy since the party with his friends." Trista stood, her hands clasped at her waist. "He had a bad dream last night. I think he was embarrassed because he wanted me to stay with him and that makes him fearful of acting like a baby. He likes you to think well of him. That has to be what has him out of sorts. Let me speak to him."

Roman stared at the door through which Andrew had disappeared. "I did not hear you rise in the night."

"I slept lightly, I suppose. A mother's watchfulness. I heard Nancy come to the door to my suite and went out to meet her."

"But why did you not wake me?"

She seemed bemused. "Because Andrew had asked for me."

"Of course." Andrew had never needed his papa for comforting.

In fact, the changes he had hoped were progress merely indicated that Andrew had learned to tolerate the situation. He had no need, no admiration, no shared interests with Roman.

His hand slipped into his pocket, closing around the carved wooden soldier. He carried it with him all the time, tucked in secret. He could not say why.

The barriers that kept him from his family were still there. He was a man who had trouble accepting limitations. Trista called it bullying, and perhaps she was correct. But he did not wish to press Andrew. The kind of affection he yearned for from the boy could not be demanded. What was he to do, then? In this one aspect of his life, he was afraid and uncertain, utterly out of his element.

"He seems angry with me again. Perhaps I have neglected him. I have been a bit preoccupied with seeing to my duties as lord."

Trista laughed, coming to stand beside him. "Grace thinks that is feudal."

"Father thought it important," he defended. Then he stopped. "It was neglected for too long."

She slipped her hands over his shoulders. "You are taking this very seriously. Coming home."

"It should have been different," he said.

"I used to think you loved Whitethorn because you gave me up for it, and then you said that you hated it. Now I do not know what to think."

"I did hate it. Because it wasn't what it should be. And yet, Trista, when I brought us back here, it was instinct. And then Jason was here, and a pastor, no less, and it *fit.* I mean, it should be ridiculous, but it wasn't at all. I saw how things could be different. I mean, if Jason Knightsbridge can wear a collar, then anything is possible."

They laughed. Trista gave him a small shove to admonish him. Grabbing her fist, he kissed it. "Don't pretend you can't see how different things are. Even Grace."

Trista slipped her hands down over his chest. "But not Andrew."

"No. Not Andrew." He sighed and laid his head against her stomach.

He might have been arrogant, defying the demons of Whitethorn by attempting to bring happiness into the place, and damn if he was not still afraid that no matter what headway he made to resolving his troubles, those baying fiends would get him in the end.

They always had before.

A footman entered, executing a crisp click of his heels. Trista moved away smoothly and Roman stood.

"My lord, there is a Lord Marcus Roberts here to see Lady May. I thought I should inform you as the man . . ." He struggled uncomfortably with the right words. "I was not certain he was who he said. His clothing . . ."

Trista looked to Roman, who replied to the footman, "Show him in to the library, Tom. I will see him privately."

But Marcus Roberts did not intend to go quietly into a conference with Roman. When he reached the library, Roman was told by a sheepish maid that Tom was still with the uncooperative visitor in the hallway. He was still demanding to see Lady May.

Roman found a man of slightly taller build than himself, but of the rangy kind, with gray salt in his hair and lines around his eyes and mouth that spoke of a pleasant nature, which was, at this moment, not in evidence. Although he wore the garb of a working man, it did not diminish him in the least. He was every bit the aristocrat, eying his host with an air of comfort and implacable authority.

He spoke first. "I shall tell you what I told your housekeeper and footman. I will speak to Lady May. Tell her Robert wishes to see her."

Roman assessed quickly that nothing short of violence was going to divert him. "Lady May may not be in," Roman replied shrewdly. It was accepted that if one did not wish to receive a guest, one had only to say you were not at home, no matter how obvious a lie it might be.

Holding up some news clipping, he said, "She will wish to be home to discuss these."

"Robert?" Lady May said. Roman turned to see Trista and her aunt standing at the foot of the stairs. She must have fetched her right away.

May was not frightened at all. In fact, she appeared unabashedly delighted, and Roman relaxed. "Robert. What are you—?"

"I've come to take . . . to show you these articles," Roberts said. He had the air of a man who rarely felt ill at ease, but was feeling so now.

He moved almost jerkily, thrusting out the hand holding the printed papers. Roman threw up a restraining arm, almost for show since he didn't feel any sense of threat from the other man, but Lord Roberts threw it off easily in a flash of fluid action that surprised his host.

Roman let him go, as May was rushing toward the man. He could see the way of it. But he kept a close watch.

"May," Roberts said softly. He did not seem the slightest bit inhibited by Trista and Roman gawking at him as he took the petite blonde in his arms, speaking softly in his rough voice. "It's over. She told everything."

May jerked back, wide-eyed. "Who . . . no . . . oh, Robert—Ann Nesbit *told*?"

Robert laughed. The sound was startling, diffusing the charge in the air instantly. "And you will never believe *whom* she told."

May was puzzled. "I can't imagine. . . ."

"Lawrence Flatbush."

Roman exchanged looks with Trista, but she seemed no more able to comprehend this than he. For some reason, the name of the premiere reporter who liked to write lurid and provocative stories for a major London newspaper broke the older couple into gales of laughter.

"Oh, but Robert, you hate him!"

"I daresay he's growing on me. And you yourself have argued his influence. He does get the Town talking. Look at this."

Stepping up to the couple as Robert rifled through the papers he'd brought, Roman placed a hand on Robert's shoulder, a gentler hand, and this time he did not shove it off.

"Perhaps," Roman said softly, "you may wish to have some privacy."

May smiled appreciatively at Roman, stopping to give him a small kiss on the cheek before taking Robert's hand and leading him into the library. She closed the door.

Looking to Trista, Roman threw his hands up in the air. "One would think the master of this house would know what is going on within its walls. I, however, do not possess a clue."

Trista smiled and sidled up to him. "Oh, Roman, do not be so feudal."

Chapter 21

The beauty of being the kind of person no one notices, Grace thought as she led her horse out of the stall, is that one can slip off at any time, and no one is the wiser. It gave her enormous freedom. She didn't have to answer to anyone, never had to explain. It was brilliant being alone. She very much preferred it.

Grace bowed her head, her forehead pressed to the withers of the bay mare she was planning to take out for a ride. Yes, keenly independent, that was her. She could do anything.

She could not love.

A hiccup of grief surprised her. She was *not* feeling sorry for herself. Grabbing a saddle from the tack room, she resolved to manage the thing herself. She wanted to be riding, with the wind in her face and distance behind her.

"My lady, can I help you?" It was one of the stable workers. His polite request jolted her out of her thoughts with a squeak.

"Yes, I was . . . I thought I would ride to visit some friends."

He bobbed his head. "Let me get that for you."

Bless him and his tact, he didn't act as if she were daft, wrestling with the tack. She had needed to feel competent, capable, different from the shy, insecure creature she had turned into somehow.

"Wait just a moment, and I'll get Rob to go with you," the man said when he was finished.

"No. Do not trouble him. I'll be fine. I've been riding these fells since I was a girl. And . . . I prefer to be alone."

She led the horse out of the stables. Country life was much more manageable, much more free. The strict constraints she'd known in London were not so tight here at home. Here she knew the life, knew who she was.

Oh, but she didn't—not anymore. She wanted to be more. Only, she didn't know how to do it.

At the door of the stables, she was surprised to see Andrew.

"I want to run away," he told her. "Can you take me?"

It struck her as the best idea she'd heard in a long time.

The first thing Robert did when he and May were alone was to kiss her. She melted into him, but he set her firmly from him after a few moments. "Sit," he commanded, and she did so, somewhat dazed.

He sat opposite and handed her one of the newspaper clippings. "This one arrived with a note from Ann. Here." He added a handwritten paper to the pile.

May read quickly. "Oh, Robert, she is so grateful to you."

His jaw worked as he nodded. She reached out to him and grasped his hand. "She knows it was you who saved her."

Clearing his throat, he tapped the article. "Read what Flatbush says."

May took a moment to scan the article. She cried out, her hands fluttering excitedly. "He says you are a hero."

"Not that. Read on. He made some inquiries in the ministry and there is no record of my having worked there."

May was confused. "Is that good?"

"The deputy minister had to have expunged those files to cover for his mistake. Everything about me is gone."

"If the records are lost, then there is no proof that you killed de Nuncier."

"Yet I did so, and I will tell the truth if I am brought to trial. In the article, Ann Nesbit names me as de Nuncier's murderer."

"But she admits it saved her life and she even says . . . oh, look, Flatbush pulled out his best to make this point—that you saved other innocents. He's even got some witnesses who knew him in France, and they say he was a monster. There will be no trial, there can't be. You don't convict someone who kills to save another's life."

"No. You are correct. I doubt that there will be legal repercussions of this. I am daring to think, darling, that this might all be over at last."

May beamed at him, her eyes welling with tears.

"Here now, what is this," Robert said, coming to kneel before her. "This is happy news."

"I am happy. Oh, Robert, I thought I'd done a terrible thing. You were so angry. But I was desperate with the thought that if anything had happened to you—"

"No, no, love, I was not angry. It is just . . . Lord, May, when you live as I have, with not a soul to think about and no one to care for you, you get used to it. I was just shocked, that is all, and perhaps a bit put out. I never wanted you tainted by any of that. I was afraid you had brought harm to yourself by admitting to Ann Nesbit that you knew me."

"But I would not have done so if I had not known she would be sympathetic," May told him. "I am not a young girl, Robert, I am a woman of the world. I do know people."

Robert smiled. "So you do. What an extraordinary woman you are. No wonder I fell in love with you."

May could not speak for a long moment. "You love me?"

"Of course. And you love me."

"Yes . . . You knew?"

"I've always known how I felt about you. But I couldn't claim you, not as I was. How could I speak of anything inside when I was effectively lying to you about my very identity?"

She pushed away the nagging reminder that she, too, had lied to him. A lie of omission was still a lie. "Should I call you Marcus now?"

"I am not sure. Would you like to?"

She thought about it for a moment. "I've gotten used to Robert. When we are out in public, I can call you Lord Roberts, and perhaps Marcus when we are with our close friends."

"We do not have close friends, May."

"We will. I intend to make you fully part of my life. You are a nobleman, and you are my love, so I will expect that you will comport yourself as a proper peer who is in love with me should."

He grinned. "It will be my pleasure, my Lady May. And I will reap all the rewards that a proper gentleman deserves."

She arched her brow in interest. "Such as?"

He smiled and pulled her close. "No more basement windows."

Trista's arrival in the library won Roman a reprieve from the house ledgers he'd been working on for the better part of the morning.

"You've come to rescue me," he said cheerfully, shoving the books away. "What a tedious task. My father's man of affairs and his staff do an excellent job. However, I must develop some proficiency in overseeing their duties. We feudal lords need to keep our eye on things."

She laughed softly. Trista felt that warm, melting feeling that he could always make her feel. It had not dissipated with time, but grown stronger. She loved him now more than she ever had, but not, she knew, as much as she would. Each day brought a deepening feeling of security, comfort, and love so full and bright it didn't seem possible one heart could hold so much and not burst.

"I have something important I need to speak to you about." She took his hand. "Roman. I am going to tell you something, and I want you to promise to tell me the truth. I need to know your honest reaction, not what you think you ought—"

"Is there some trouble?"

"No, it is not trouble." She hoped it was not. Bracing herself, she said, "I wish to call the doctor in to consult. I've noticed recently some changes and I think . . . well, I think I might be with child."

He blinked. Otherwise he did not move. "With child?"

She realized now that he was not displeased, but simply in shock. "If I am, does it make you happy?"

"Happy?"

"Roman, you must say something other than repeating my last word back to—"

He grabbed her, hugging her close and then quickly releasing her. "I . . . God, I didn't mean to . . ." He stared down at her flat stomach.

She laughed. He was absolutely stupid over the news, and that had to be a good sign. "You are going to be impossible about this, aren't you?"

"Did I hurt you?" he demanded.

"No. You will not harm me if you hold me. In fact, I demand you hold me."

He did so, and his arms were gentle. She asked him, "You are pleased about the baby?"

"I am delirious."

She smiled, surprised to find her cheeks wet.

"What am I thinking, you must sit down." He pulled back and rushed her to a chair, which he all but shoved her into in his eagerness for her to be off her feet. She would have popped back up as she did not appreciate him manhandling her, even if it was with the best of intentions, but he knelt before her, his face full of such earnest happiness mixed with anxiety that she could not upset him further.

"Roman," she said sternly, "you must not fuss."

"I am not fussing. You shouldn't have been standing. Everyone knows that a pregnant woman must not exert herself."

"I can stand. I can walk. I can do anything I used to. Please, I've been through this before. It is not the affliction some make it out to be. I will be fatigued, it is true. But if you act like an idiot every time I step a toe to the floor, then it will drive me mad. And insane mothers are not good for babies."

This at first alarmed him. He didn't seem to know she was joking. But he came to himself, and smiled sheepishly.

Her heart flipped. How utterly wonderful Roman looked when he smiled that way. She laid a hand on his cheek. "We go through the having of this child together."

A ghost of sadness drifted across his face. He had missed so much with Andrew. It still haunted him.

The pulse of warm flesh under her palm kindled a sweet awareness of the hardness of his jaw, the smoothly shaven cheek. By night, it would be rough with growth and the feel of it against her own cheek would be of a different texture. But now, it was silk. "Andrew loves you."

His eyes lowered. He didn't believe her. "And he knows you love him," she said softly.

"I want things to be right with him, before we . . . I am happy about the child, believe me, Trista, but . . ."

"It will turn out all right. It is new. So much has happened so quickly, but in time, it will sort out."

"You are not as convinced as you wish me to believe. You are worried as well."

She could not lie to him. "A mother always worries. It just comes with the position. Andrew has much to be happy about, he will see this. Maybe he only misses Luci and David. He will cheer when he visits them."

She realized too late that it was the wrong thing to say. Roman straightened suddenly. She wanted to pull him back, but all of the words spilling from her mouth seemed to be the wrong ones and she thought it best she hold her peace.

"No more of this." Roman braced a smile. "We have happy news today. The best news."

She eyed him with a wry lift to one brow. "May I rise now? I would like you to hold me again."

He offered her his hand and pulled her up. "You may stand."

She smirked. "Thank you, my liege."

May entered then, Lord Roberts with her. "There you are," she said. "I've been looking for you. I do not believe the proper introductions have been made."

She presented Lord Roberts to them formally, and he bowed. "Excuse my sudden appearance," he murmured. "I believe Lady May told you the rather unusual circumstances in which I find myself."

"We know something of it, yes," Roman said. "Come and sit. Would you care for brandy?"

"Be a darling, would you, Roman, and pour some wine for me," said May. "Trista, where is Andrew? He was not in the nursery. I wanted him to join us."

"Why, he is with Nancy."

"He is not. Nancy was tidying up when I looked in."

Trista frowned. "Excuse me." She went to find her housekeeper, locating Mrs. Wells in her office going over the ordering.

"No, ma'am, I don't know where they are," Mrs. Wells said, coming to her feet. She had the same disquiet on her face that Trista felt. "But I'll have James and Frances have a look round."

She returned to the drawing room without a word of her worries, saying only that Andrew would be along presently. But three quarters of an hour later brought the housekeeper to the door. "My lady, I must speak with you."

Roman laid a restraining hand on Trista's arm to keep her with him. "What is it, Mrs. Wells?"

"Nancy said that the boy went to see his aunt. He had seen her from his room and she suspects he went to join her in the stables. But Joseph said he saw Lady Grace out for a ride. He saddled the horse for her and she went alone, to visit friends, she said."

"Then where is Andrew?" Trista heard the sharpness in her voice. It had risen an octave.

"Steven found this," Mrs. Wells said, passing a paper to her.

It was a picture drawn by Andrew of himself. It read, "I love you." The figure was smiling and waving.

Roman took it from her. She looked at him, desperately hoping he would find some other meaning. He went pale.

Trista felt her legs go weak. "I think," Trista whispered fearfully, "he's gone off."

Roman glared at her, as if the utterance were somehow treasonous. "What do you mean? Gone where?"

Lord Roberts said, "You do not mean you think he's run away?"

"He can only write a few words. He would try to tell us in a picture what he planned." Trista looked at each of them in turn, hoping they would convince her she was wrong.

Roman tossed the picture aside. "I am going out to look for him. Mrs. Wells, send someone to the parsonage. Ask the reverend to come at once."

"Why—?" Trista began, but he cut her off, saying, "Oh, God, Trista, no, not that. He is my closest friend. I would have him by my side, to help me look."

He barked out more instructions as he made for the hall.

"I will come with you," Lord Roberts called after him. "I do not know the lands hereabouts, but I can pair with you and be an extra set of eyes."

Roman nodded gratefully and disappeared up the stairs. He returned speedily, dressed for riding.

He paused before leaving, taking Trista's hands. "Think about the baby," he said to her softly, "and try not to worry. I will bring him home. I swear I will."

Trista only nodded. May put a protective arm about her shoulders as Roman released her. "Shush, now and do not worry. Roman will find him."

"Yes," Trista said, drawing herself up with an effort. "He knows these fells. He knows them better than anyone, he and Jason together. And Lord Robert. They will bring Andrew home."

Chapter 22

For Roman, the wildness of the fells, the long, open stretches high above the homes of the village and outlying farms had once been a refuge. Now, they were a landscape of terrors as he and his servants, along with Jason and Lord Roberts, rode them league by league in search of Andrew.

He had taken these paths too many times to count, ridden while he laughed, and at times, fought not to cry. He'd never ridden like this, with his heart in his throat.

"Do you think he's headed into the woods?" Jason shouted over the thunder of their horses.

"Let us check the crags first," Roman responded. He turned to his other side. Lord Roberts sat his horse like an expert, holding the reigns with one hand. Roman gestured to the left, where they would inspect the tumble of huge boulders where he'd camped many times. It was a logical place for Andrew to seek shelter.

They raced over the fell, the hoof beats deafening. Roman's eyes scanned constantly as his mind worked with feverish rapidity, thinking of where Andrew could have gone.

The crags showed no sign of anyone having been there

in a long time. Roman circled it twice, dismounted, and climbed in and out of the jumble of rock. He took them next to the woods, to the places he knew, all of them in turn as his heart began to twist with growing anxiety.

The sun was low, and the shadows it cast long, as he emerged from the woods. Jason cantered up beside him. "Let us go back to Whitethorn," he said.

Roman turned a murderous look on him. Jason said hurriedly, "They might have had word."

Shaking his head, Roman reared his horse away from home. "Trista would have sent someone to me, to tell me. We head north."

It was nearly dawn when Trista heard the trample of boots coming through the front door. She ran, shouting, "Roman, he is home!"

She flew straight to him and he caught her. "He came in late, after ten. I wanted to send someone out to tell you, but we had to wait for first light. We didn't know where you were."

"Is he harmed?" he barked. "Is he all right?"

"He is fine. He is completely fine. He is upstairs."

"No, Mama, I am here," a small voice said. They turned to see Andrew standing at the bottom of the stairs, looking tiny in the vast hall.

Roman broke away and went two steps toward him, then stopped. She knew Roman was struggling to remain calm, but his emotions were raw and he'd ridden all night. He was probably battling with the understandable dilemma of whether to spank the child or kiss him.

"Do you know what you put your mother through, running off like that?" he inquired. He sounded stern. Andrew had never heard him speak like this. Roman had always tread softly with his son before.

"No, sir. I mean, yes, sir. I did not mean to."

"Where did you go?" Roman demanded.

"He was with me, Roman," Grace said, coming out of the

drawing room where Trista, May, and she had been sitting up during the night waiting.

Behind her, Trista heard the sharp intake of breath. It came from Jason. He moved to her side.

Grace said, "I should have left word, but I did not think to be out this long. The horse—"

Roman turned on her, his look feral. "What in the name of hell did you think you were doing with my son?"

"Roman, no, let her explain." Trista tried to intervene. Roman shook his head, waving his hand to quiet her.

"This is between me and my sister, Trista. She breeds unhappiness in this house to favor the bitterness she feels toward us all." Turning back to Grace, who stood stricken at the vehemence of her brother's anger, he lowered his voice to a growl. "For the girl you were, innocent and hurt, and the ignorant boy that I once was, I tolerated you. I tried to help you, to understand your selfishness, your tantrums, and your spoiled—"

Trista cut him off, her voice ringing with authority. "It was Grace who brought him back. There was an accident."

Roman hardly heard her. "Do you know what your irresponsible lark left us thinking, worried like mad?"

"I am sorry," Grace cried. "I know you've been out of your mind. I didn't think—"

"I know what you thought of—yourself. I am done with you—Andrew!"

He turned away from Grace to the boy racing up the steps. He started after him, then stopped, shoving his hands through his hair, realizing he'd probably frightened him away.

Trista laid her hand on his arm. "I will go speak to him for you."

He let her take three steps before he spoke, his voice strong and sharp. "You will not interfere."

She stopped, turning to stare incredulously at him.

He pointed to her. "I have done what you wished, filtered my actions through your permission thinking it was you who knew him best, you to better advise me, but it has come to nothing in the end. I should not have depended on you to do what I should have done."

May stepped forward. "You should probably not be saying these things after the night you had."

"Forgive me," Roman told her tersely, "but I am done with women's advice."

"Roman," Jason tried, but was silenced by his friend's look.

Trista faced her husband. "You blame me?"

Roman shook his head. "This is not for you, Trista. This is Andrew, and me. It should have been all along. If I am a bully, then so be it." Grimly, he set out, adding, "My son and I have a great deal to say to each other. It is time I began to act as a father to him."

After Roman left, Trista after him, the men who had gone with Roman to search for Andrew drifted away. Grace saw Lady May come up to a distinguished-looking older gentleman she did not recognize. She knew from Trista this was Lord Marcus Roberts.

Her shoulders felt impossibly heavy. She'd been up all night, worrying about Roman, knowing her thoughtlessness had caused such a crisis. . . .

She headed for the stairs. She was so tired.

"Grace," Jason called.

Bracing herself, Grace paused. "I suppose you have to have your say," she said wearily. "Was there anything Roman left out? That I think of no one's needs but my own? Ah. I believe he mentioned that. That I am without a doubt the most irresponsible person in existence . . . yes, he rather wore that one out. I am afraid he left nothing original for you to lecture me about, Reverend, so you will have to content yourself with repeating the nearly exhausted subject of my depravity . . . or was it stupidity?"

"Do you argue that you do not deserve every bit of the tongue-lashing you received?" he asked quietly. "Not for evil intentions, but for the fact that the man is wrung down to his last frayed nerve?"

She turned. "I may have." Her eyes filled despite her earlier calm. Looking at Jason was always her undoing. He was staring at her with a directness that always seemed to pierce her.

"I thought only to take him for a little ride," she told him, "to talk to him, calm him down. We spoke, and I was so caught up in trying to help him that we went out farther than I had seen. The horse went lame, and we had to walk home."

"You should have said this to Roman."

"He would not hear it."

"He thought you'd gone to your friend's, and that Andrew was out alone. You should have let someone know what you were about."

"Yes." She frowned, rubbing two fingers against a throbbing temple. "I realize now. I did not mean for all of this wretched scene. It does not escape me, the irony that I've striven to sew chaos on more than one occasion. And yet there was no malice in me this time. No matter what I intend, I never seem to be able to have it turn out well."

"Then it must be that you have a talent for botching things," he observed wryly.

She looked at him in surprise. "Isn't a parson supposed to comfort people?"

He came to her, his eyes holding a challenge. "I have comfort for you Grace, but I did not think you would take it."

She wanted to lower her eyes, but something in his expression made that an act of cowardice. "Are you offering comfort?"

"I have strong arms and an understanding heart. Is this what you want? If it is, you shall have to be brave enough to claim it. Are you brave, Grace?"

"Yes!" She sobbed the word before pride could snatch it from her lips. "Yes, Jason, I do want to be brave."

"Then come." He held his arms out and she fell into them. He held her tight and close. She lay her head on his shoulder, feeling how strong and substantial this was.

"He will never forgive me," she said.

"He is exhausted, reeling from the ordeal, and as I recall, your brother is a brute on an empty stomach. He will reconcile with you."

She snuffled a bit as he cuddled her to him again. "Do you offer this sort of comfort to all of your congregation?" she asked.

"Only the ones I suspect are in love with me."

Pulling back sharply, she saw he was smiling softly, no mockery apparent. "And do not deny it, Grace. Remember . . ."

"It is a sin to lie to a parson."

He grinned, and then he kissed her.

For a long moment she was contented in his arms, the feel of him so close, and all her fears that had had her trapped for so long began to fall away. It was time. She loved him.

She could love.

She smiled at him, touched his face. "I am in love with you, Jason. And I like your kisses."

His smile twitched. "There's my brave girl."

He kissed her, and she fell gratefully into the safety of his warmth. This was home, she realized, not a place, like Whitethorn or any other building, but the love and patience and complete acceptance Jason had given her.

When the kiss ended, she tilted her head to gaze up at him. "And you are a most excellent parson. I like your sermons. And . . ."

"Yes, Grace?" His eyes were soft. That didn't frighten her anymore. It felt safe. And the way he looked at her opened her heart to endless possibility.

"And I am going to take great joy in making you very, very happy for the rest of your life."

"Are you proposing?" he asked, aghast.

"No." She blushed. "I shall leave that to you, of course. But just so you know, I will accept."

When Roman arrived in the nursery, he found a distraught Nancy.

"He's barricaded himself inside," Nancy said.

"He's afraid." Trista came in behind him. "Roman, you've frightened him."

"Yes, I know," Roman replied, unaffected. He eyed the door.

"You are not going to break it, are you?" Trista cried.

"I might if he does not come out of his own accord. And if it troubles you to be here, then you must leave, for I will not be put off again."

Nancy squeaked as Roman rapped hard on the door until it shook on its hinges. "Come out here, now, young man!" he said loudly. "Believe me, you do not want to defy me. I swear to you I will not hesitate to take you over my knee."

"Roman!"

"Stay out of this, Trista." His voice was calm now, resonating with authority as he turned to the door. "If he has a fear of me or if he dislikes the idea of a live father in his life rather than a fantasy, then we shall have it out of him now and we shall put it to rights. Andrew, if you do not come out here now, I will consider you to be willfully disobedient. . . ."

He broke off as a small face dominated by wide, fearful eyes appeared in the doorway. "Mama?" he squeaked.

"You may run to your mama for comfort when I am through with you. Now answer me, boy. Did you intend to run away?"

Andrew opened and closed his mouth, clearly terrified. "Yes, sir," he managed.

Roman's jaw worked as he considered him for a moment before asking, "I will know why."

Andrew's eyes slid to Trista.

"Do not look to your mother. I am speaking to you."

His gaze snapped back to the tall, imposing figure. His little chest was rising and falling quickly and Roman knew he was very close to sobbing.

"You shouted at Aunt Grace."

"I know. I was overset at the moment. I was out all night looking for you. I thought you were by yourself on the fells in the night. I was nearly mad with worry."

Andrew blinked. His voice was small. "We had an accident with the horse and had to walk home."

"Did you intend to run away? You left a picture."

The thickly lashed lids lowered. He said nothing.

"Answer me, Andrew. Did you wish to flee from me . . . us?" He gentled his tone, but it still demanded compliance. "You may speak to me without fear. I shall not punish you for what you say. Tell me. Why did you wish to leave Whitethorn?"

"I didn't wish to go! You made me!" Andrew blurted. "You were going to send me away!"

Roman was taken aback in surprise. "Send you away? Wherever did you get that idea?"

"Mama said we were going to London. I am to live with Uncle David and Aunt Luci."

"What?" Trista gasped. "Andrew, no, that is not true. You misunderstood."

Roman cut her off, "I know you do not like it here, but it is where you will stay. And I know you wish to live with your uncle David, but you will not. That part of your life is done, though it may pain you to face this."

Andrew hiccuped, his face confused. His lips pressed together.

Then Roman realized what the boy had said. "You thought I was going to send you away. It upset you." Roman pondered the closed face. "I assure you, nothing could be further from the truth. You are my son, *my* son, Andrew. I would never send you away from me."

Andrew was trembling. Roman's arms ached to reach for him, but he would only shrink away.

"Like it or not," he continued, "it is my blood in your veins, my temper that you turn against me now, and my face set in such mutinous lines that you wear. This home is yours, vast and drafty though it is. When I die, it will be your home to raise your children. It is all yours, Andrew, because you . . . you are mine. Nothing, nothing will separate us."

This had some effect on him. Andrew's beleaguered expression began to relax. His chin warbled and the tight line of his mouth softened.

Falling on his knee, Roman held the little boy by the shoulders. "Do you know what I thought when I found you missing? Do you know what torment went through my mind, thinking of all that could happen to a little boy alone on the fells? I know the dangers, I ran wild out there all my childhood because I hated this house. I've tried, Andrew, tried with everything in me to make this a house my son would not wish to run from."

Andrew watched him, fascinated. Roman barely saw him.

"As I rode last night I tormented myself with wondering how I had failed you so that you would flee me as I fled my own parents. I tried to make things different here, to show you how welcome and needed you were, but you never seemed to understand that I love you."

"You love Mama," Andrew said, but his voice was uneven and his lips trembled and there was hope in his eyes.

"And you. And the brothers and sisters that will come after you. How can you not know how precious you are to me?"

Roman had to stop because tears had come to his eyes and to his throat, and both stung. He tried to breathe in, to clear the clogged emotions, but the breath hitched and he felt a scalding, shameful heat on his cheek.

"Papa," Andrew said, his eyes wide with wonder and fear, "why are you crying?"

Shaking his head, Roman told him, "I am not crying. Men do not weep, even at times of great emotion." He paused, then snatched the small, chubby hand with five neat dimples at each knuckle and pressed it to his lips. "Well, perhaps they do, when their relief is very great. I was terrified, you see."

"Why?"

"Because," he whispered roughly, "I was so afraid I would not see you again."

"And that would make you so sad?"

Roman nodded. "Unspeakably."

Andrew looked up at Trista, weeping softly behind Roman, then looked back down at his father. "I didn't want to go."

"Good. That is very good. Because, you see, nothing is any good without you here with us, Andrew. We need you."

Andrew took a long time to digest this, staring at his father, his strong, powerful father, kneeling before him, kissing his hand with a strange, scratchy sound in his voice and his eyelashes wet and forming dark stars around shimmering eyes. He touched the wetness on the whisker-roughened face with wonder and concern.

Then the little boy surged forward suddenly, throwing his small, thin arms about Roman's thick neck and holding tight. "I'm sorry, Papa. I'm sorry!"

Roman lowered his face to the fragrance of open air and softness captured in his son's silky hair. His hands grasped the small, trembling body. "All right. All right," he crooned, closing his eyes to contain the emotion that threatened to spill.

"I love you, Papa. I don't want to leave you or Mama."

"It is all right," he said softly. For the first time, Roman held his first-born child.

Chapter 23

Roman knew his weaknesses well. That was why, with so much to set to rights, he concentrated on consuming a large meal to cease the insistent cramping of his stomach. After that, he went to sleep to clear his head and renew himself. It was not avoidance, but preparation.

Trista used to say that when his stomach growled, *he* growled. He ate a hearty meal when he awoke, for good measure.

Then, he thought, he would consider the next phase of the battle.

For that is what it seemed to him. Battles, continuous battles. Respites were brief and infrequent before the next foray began. Which was exactly his weary thought when Grace sent word that she would like to see him.

He was not set in his mind on the matter of his sister. After he had gotten the entire story from Andrew, he had known he owed her an apology. And yet he did not regret much of what he said. He wished he had not said it in such a way. It pained him to see her still caught in pain, disgruntled, and disagreeable.

He instructed that she come to him in the library, and as

he waited, he considered and discarded a few score of ways to approach her.

When she entered, he was shocked by her appearance. She was not sullen or wild-eyed with fury as he'd thought she'd be. She was calm, perhaps a bit nervous. She looked lovely, he realized. She was a fair creature, with silky dark hair and a glowing complexion. It had been a long time since he'd seen her so pretty, and he realized it was the air about her. She seemed unfettered by troubles.

She spoke before he could. "Roman, please accept my deepest regrets for not thinking to leave notice with someone when I took Andrew with me. There is no excuse for this omission. I cannot fathom what you endured when we were gone."

All his carefully planned and unsatisfactory phrases deserted him. "You've caught me unawares. I was prepared to be the one to say I was sorry. I accused you wrongly. Andrew has explained what happened."

She smiled. "You were overwrought. I know Andrew is your heart. And what you said was fair. Or it was. I do not wish it to be so any longer. What is more, I know you refrained from telling me the truth for a long time."

"This is strange," said Roman. "I'd expected you to make me crawl. I was prepared to do so to make amends. You . . . you are very different," Roman observed.

"It seems all at once that the whole world is different."

He returned her smile, peering at her strangely. "And of course, you are welcome to stay at Whitethorn. It is your home."

"No. I'll be moving to the parsonage." She laughed, this time with outright glee at his look of consternation. "You see, Jason and I are to marry. Oh, he hasn't asked me yet. He may wish to speak to you about it first—tradition and all that."

This was certainly a shock, and left Roman sputtering.

She laughed lightly. It had been forever since he'd heard her laugh like that. "You have enough to cope with now. We can talk later. Happy news for a change, Roman. Imagine."

"Yes. Yes. It is wonderful to see you contented, Grace. Wonderful, really. You cannot know what it means to me."

She took his hands. "I know you care for me. I want to thank you, Roman. You've been a good brother. You helped me in London. You let me come home, and I did not make it easy for you. And you have tried so hard to make up to me about the past. I want you to know that you no longer have to. I love Jason, and I am to have my own house, my own life. I am happy, Roman."

"That means a great deal to me," he said sincerely.

She smiled. "I know. You always had a good heart. Please tell me that you are happy, as well."

He paused. "I intend to be."

Grace said, "Ah. I have no doubts. That indomitable will of yours . . ."

"I have learned, sister," he said carefully, "that sometimes wanting something badly, even with a will of iron, is not enough."

She placed a hand on his chest, flat over his heart. "I know you have all it takes to win. Heart and will, and, of course . . ." She paused, raising her brows thoughtfully. "Well, love," she finished.

In the small bedroom in the attic, where once Trista Nash had been a girl, Roman placed the last of the items back on the shelf and surveyed his work.

He tried to remember, thinking if it was the same. It had to be perfect.

The sound of a shoe scraping on the bare floor brought Roman around with a start. He was chagrined to find his wife standing in the doorway.

"Roman? Mrs. Wells said she'd seen you come up here. What are you . . . ?" Slowly she entered the room, looking around in awe. "Roman . . . what did you do?"

He spread his hands helplessly, fighting the deep disappointment. He had wanted the stage to be perfect for what he had to say to his wife.

"It was supposed to be a surprise," he said, trying to make his voice light.

She was silent as she took everything in. "These are all of my belongings. Everything I owned when I left Whitethorn."

He waved a dusty hand at the shelves. "I tried to put them back the way they were. I couldn't remember, though."

"You saved them?"

"Did you think I would destroy them?"

"I didn't think that, no. I just imagined the servants would clear out the room." She touched a hand-embroidered pillow. "My mother made this for me. Where did you find all of this?"

"It was in one of the attics, tucked way back under the eaves. I had it packed up and put away when you left."

She walked swiftly to the shelf and took down the doll he'd just placed. It was the one he'd repaired so badly for her.

She held it as tenderly as she would a baby. He traced a finger over the cracked face. "I wanted to make it right for you."

When she turned to him, her eyes were filled with tears. "Roman."

He held up one finger and pressed it against her lips. "I want to make this right, too. I should not have said those things I said. I would not hurt you."

She shook her head quickly. "No. No, Roman, we must always speak the truth to each other. I did interfere. I meant to make things better, but I got in the way. I suppose it was my guilt for what I'd done. I thought I had to be the one to make it right between you and Andrew. What I should have done is trusted you."

"I was not always trustworthy, but I shall never make that mistake again. I will never allow anything to come between us again, Trista. You know you've been everything that was important in my life, and if I lost my way, then I've paid for it. I intend to make things better for you and me. There is so much I want you to know." He spread his arms out. "I want to tell you, and I want to show you."

"Is that why you did this?" She gazed about her again. "Why?"

"I began the project a few days ago. At the time, I thought I intended it to be for you, to tell you what I could not. But I think it was really for me." Roman took the doll and examined the ruined face. "I loved this room. I loved you, so I loved coming here, and all those quiet times, talking and making love. We were so happy. How could I have not seen that this room held the only happiness I'd known? I think the entire wish to come home to Whitethorn was to be back here, right here in this room."

She grabbed his hands, staring up into his face. "I know why you hated Whitethorn for once it was filled with unhappiness, but you brought us home and changed the memories. You made us a family."

"The love I feel for you is so different than the one we shared in this room," she said. "Then, we were young, immature, and to some extent selfish, because we were so unformed. Now, the feeling is larger. It needs more than this room. It needs the whole house."

He grinned at her, pressing his forehead to hers. "It was I who was to have made a speech."

"Do not cheat me. Tell me."

"Only that I love you. Inadequate words to describe the feeling in me that only you can bring. It is so much love that I fear I will expire from it. You are in me, Trista, forever. There will never be a day when you are not in my mind and in my heart, when you are all of my life. You and Andrew, the family we will make, it is all I've ever wanted."

She came into his arms, kissing him. He held her, closing his eyes to savor this moment. "You get used to doing without something, even something as vital as love and it doesn't seem entirely possible when you find it."

She pulled back and took his hand in hers. "My darling, it is within your grasp."

He went to slip his hand around her waist. "Yes. I feel it."

The doll she held in his other hand got in the way. He had forgotten about it. He caught Trista's eye and grinned. He placed the doll back on the shelf.

"There," he said softly. "She's home."

Epilogue

Trista laid the letter down on her lap. Under the bright sun, she sheltered comfortably under her parasol. In front of her, her husband and son were shouting encouragement to each other.

"Brilliant!" Andrew declared, and Roman laughed with him, handing him a new stone, giving him a few pointers, then stepping away so that Andrew could set himself before letting loose with that particular flick that sent the small missile hopping across the surface of the lake.

The next stone skipped seven times. The two males whooped with self-congratulatory glee.

"I am going to find more stones!" Andrew declared.

Roman came back to the blanket and sat while Andrew scouted the riverbank for appropriate ammunition.

"How is London?" Roman asked, indicating the letter.

"Aunt May says they are being received everywhere. It seems Lord Roberts is currently one of the Town's leading heroes. All that worry for nothing."

"The *ton* is fickle. They loved Brummel, and kept him in their bosom even when his debts had him at the gates of debtor's prison. If they like you, they will embrace you."

"Did they embrace you?"

"Of course. I was considered a rake, of course. Not with good reason, but sometimes when a man doesn't make a spectacle of himself paying court to this debutante or that one, he gets a certain reputation as being aloof. Aloof, therefore, a rake."

Trista gazed at him. "You never paid court to a lady? Why not?"

"Because I never found a woman with which I wished to do so." He turned on his side and made to lean on his elbow, but a wince of pain brought him up and digging in his pocket.

He withdrew a toy soldier. He flipped it absently over his fingers and then under, as he spoke. "I already had met the love of my life, so there was no point, was there?"

"Why did you not tell me that when we met?"

"Why didn't you tell me there was no Captain Fairhaven and you'd never even thought of looking at another man since me?"

Trista opened her mouth, then closed it and gave him a look that made him laugh.

"That particular expression brings me to mind of my sister in days past, although I've seen nothing but smiles from her since she's begun tormenting Jason over the parsonage."

"Oh, Roman, even you cannot begrudge her wanting to make the place over. It was the worst sort of bachelor house—she showed me. Books piled from floor to ceiling."

"So?"

"So, what happens when their children come along? The wedding is only a month away."

Roman chuckled. "I'll wager she'll have the house done over completely by then. You know my sister."

"Yes, the Aylesgarth indomitable will. It runs in the family."

"Papa, see!" Andrew dumped his bounty on the blanket. Trista tsked and brushed away the dirt that came along with four nicely rounded and flatly shaped stones.

"Ah." Roman nodded as he perused them with approval. "These are excellent."

"What is that?" Andrew asked, taking the soldier out of Roman's hand.

Roman looked to Trista and smiled. "Something I was keeping for you."

"It is a Horse Guard. Like Uncle Adrian. Brilliant! He will sail on the ship I brought. Oh. We can skip the stones if you like, though."

"Do what you will," Roman said easily. "I will sit here and keep your mother company."

Andrew frowned. "Do not sit out in the sun too long, Mama. You do not wish the baby to get overly warm."

Trista laughed and promised to have a care.

When they were alone again, Andrew busily readying his ship to set sail on the lake, Roman moved over closer to Trista and laid his head on her lap. She placed her hand on his forehead and smoothed the hair from his brow.

"You are not going to skip more stones?" Trista inquired.

He looked up at the sky, at the clouds scooting quickly across the azure expanse. The wind moved over them, stirring the air slightly. The sun climbed high, igniting scents baked up from the earth to fill him with the aromas of all of the life around him, and the slightest hint of Trista that was unmistakable whenever he was within arm's breadth of her.

He adjusted himself more comfortably and closed his eyes. "I'll just stay right here."

Trista smiled.

Turn the page for a special preview of
Jacqueline Navin's next novel in the
Mayfair Brides series

The Beauty of Bond Street

Coming soon from Berkley Sensation!

Prologue

"I believe I liked it better when I was your secret lover," Lord Marcus Roberts said to Lady May Ellinsworth Hayworth as he flipped through the papers. It was a Tuesday morning, a rather typical day. They sat in companionable silence in the sunlit coziness of her informal drawing room.

May sighed, frowning through the spectacles perched on the end of her nose at the delicate embroidery upon which she was working. "That was because all you did was sneak into my boudoir at night."

"Which I enjoyed," he admitted. "And the adventure of sneaking into the Hyde Park house after the chimney fire . . . well, at least it was something to look forward to."

She smiled, remembering their trysts when she was staying with her niece while her house was being refurbished. It *did* have an element of adventure.

"You did nothing but complain. 'I am too old for this,' you kept saying, and, Robert, you are only six and forty." She leveled a well-manicured finger at him. "And if you say that is old, then beware, for I am only two years younger."

His name was Marcus Roberts, and he was a peer, but she still called him by the name he had used when he'd posed as a commoner and seduced her. With rough hands and silken kisses, he'd made her fall in love with a stable master.

"But you look a score my junior," he replied with a diplomatic sparkle in his eye.

She smiled into his darkly handsome face. "It was so lovely when it was just the two of us in our own world."

"And now," he said, pulling a face as he snapped the paper to fold it neatly, "we have to be respectable."

"I thought you liked spending leisurely hours with me. And, after all, it was you who came out in public first. That disguise . . ." She fell into laughter, which he observed impassively. She smoothed the pink feathers frothing around her neck and composed herself. "You said you did it so that you would be able to squire me about in public."

"See, then, it is your fault. You drove me mad, running about with that silly lord who was in love with you. I had to do something."

"You risked everything for me. And I love you for it."

He pretended not to love her sweet declaration, but his bluster lost some of its blow. "But we lost our privacy. Now I must depart and dress for the evening in a few hours. You will go upstairs and bathe—without me, which I find intolerably bothersome. And then I must return to escort you to the rout tonight. It is all so much work."

"I see." She lowered her head to her needlework again, her lips tightly twitching. She had a good idea where this conversation was headed.

"If you would but marry me—"

"Aha, now we have the meat of it. This is your ploy." She put down her embroidery and stood. Her petite frame was slender, wrapped in a stunning gown of silk in pink, her favorite color. "We have been through this. Can you not accept and be happy with how things are?"

"No," he countered sharply. "I am most dissatisfied."

She saw he was not in a mood to be charmed. Crossing to the jumble of supplies strewn over the settee, she fetched some threads out of her sewing box and turned the topic of conversation. "You are coming tonight to Hasting's rout, are you not?"

"I shall," he said with a suffering tone. "Although I would rather not. I did not miss society when I was out of it."

She paused as she tried to thread her needle. "But—"

He held up a hand. "Do not trouble to explain. I know you must go for Sophie's sake, and I am not meaning to make complaint."

"It is her first large gathering, a debut of sorts." She returned to her seat. "When I bring one of my brother's children into society, I feel close to him. With the two others, I could look into their faces and see him. I admit, it is a bit more difficult with Sophie. Perhaps because she is so beautiful. Oh, Robert, she is going to make a terrific splash. She just needs to relax. Loosen her stiffness. She is so . . . formal. Once she is over her nerves, I am confident she will do fine." She frowned, and her concentration slipped, causing her to prick her finger. She made a small exclamation, putting it immediately to her mouth.

Robert came to his feet. "Let me do that," he said, and took her hand and begun to suck the tip of her finger.

"You are naughty. I must go . . ."

"Upstairs?"

"We cannot . . . Sophie . . . is . . . My maid will be looking for me soon to dress my . . . hair . . . I . . ."

She could hear the breathy weakness in her own voice. After all this time together, he could still do this to her.

Tiny jolts of excitement shot from the slender finger he was now plying with his tongue.

"Stop! You are wicked."

"I thought you'd forgotten. You've been so wrapped up with your latest protégé."

"You cannot be jealous," she scolded, taking her hand back so that she might claim the normal functioning of her heart.

"May, darling, you know I would never make issue with any of your efforts to reunite yourself with your family. I know what it means to you, and I mean to help you in all ways possible." He grimaced and added, "Even if it means going to Hasting's rout tonight."

She softened. "I know you love me, and I know you understand, Robert. But admit it, you do not like Sophie. I can tell it. You are not the same as you were when I was first getting to know Michaela and Trista."

He thought on this a moment. "I have no objection to Sophie. It is only that she seems to frustrate you. It is in you I sense some discontent with her."

She'd been looking for the young woman for more than a year. Her solicitors had sent out letters. No response was ever heard, and she had begun to give up hope. When Sophie Kent had suddenly appeared at the solicitor's office five months ago, explaining that her mother, Millicent Anderson, recently died, and she was now free to respond to Lady May's inquiries, May had been overjoyed.

But unlike the other young women whom May had welcomed into the fold, she had not been able to draw close to Sophie, foster a friendship. Sophie was pleasant, and most appreciative—too appreciative—of all May provided. Her manners were flawless and she was very compliant and eager to please. But she was cold in some way. She held herself back, reserving herself—May could not put her finger on what it was.

"All right," she conceded, "I am a bit . . . oh, the word would be disappointed. She is a lovely girl, and I am truly fond of her. But she is so remote. So guarded."

"Poor May. You give so much, and you certainly have a right to expect a like return. But Sophie . . . well, her life might have been a hard one, making it difficult for her to be open with someone until she knows them for a long time."

She allowed him to lead her to the settee, clearing away the jumble she'd torn out of her sewing box. She curled comfortably beside him. If a servant were to come in, it would be unseemly, but really, when had she cared for such things?

She lay her head on his shoulder. "How is it you always know just the right thing to say to soothe me?"

He wrapped his arms around her. "Because I love you." Tucking her close to his side, he said, "Come now, I do not wish you to worry on Sophie. No doubt she will come round in time."

"Perhaps." There was an interval of silence. "You feel it, too, with her, do you not, Robert?"

He considered this. "To my mind it seems . . . as if she is hiding something."

May twisted in his arms and looked up at him, a slight tremor of disquiet tickling across her skin. "Can you always tell if a woman is hiding something?"

"I have rather keen senses. From all those years as a spy, you understand. It gives one a preternatural sense about things."

His stare seemed a bit too intense, and a ripple of uncertainty fluttered in her heart. May asked, "What do you propose we should do?"

"What else is there to do?" he replied. "She will confide in you when she knows it is safe, that you will not stand against her no matter what. When you love someone, then nothing can break that, May. So, I suppose there is nothing to do but wait patiently for trust to grow."

Was he only only speaking of her newly found niece? She grew silent, wondering if her suspicions that Robert knew of her own secret were founded in anything but a restless conscience.

She longed to tell him. What a relief it would be to unburden the past. He himself had possessed secrets. It was she herself who had helped him expose his true identity and clear his name. He had trusted her . . .

But, no, her circumstances were far different. Robert had been a hero, a man who had done a great thing to protect an innocent. He'd sacrificed for honor, for some ultimate good. She could claim no such thing.

Some secrets could not be born, not even with love.

They were interrupted at that moment by a sharp rap. The

pocket doors were opened and Johnson, dressed smartly in his footman's livery, entered the room.

May straightened, giving her servant her attention.

"Madam, pardon me for intruding so abruptly." He was flustered, which was unlike Johnson. "It is a matter of utmost urgency. A man just arrived with a most disturbing request, and bade me give it to you with all haste. He is waiting in the hall. He begs speak with you."

He produced a letter, holding it out for her on the salver she used for her correspondence. The fact that he'd taken the time to observe this formality seemed incongruous to his manner.

May picked up the letter and read swiftly. She handed it to Robert and turned to Johnson. "Bring Lord Farnsworth to me."

Robert looked up after reading the missive. "Gideon?"

May called after Johnson. "And fetch the surgeon at once!"

The servant went out swiftly, returning with a rather bedraggled dandy with a worried face and a wrung hat between his clenched fists. May stepped forward, forgoing all courtesies.

"Is he hurt badly?"

"Yes, my lady, he is. I have come to you in all desperation. I dare not take him to hospital."

"Good God, no!"

"But we have only bachelor's quarters in St. James."

Robert stepped forward. "Is his injury mortal?"

"I know not. But it is grave. Please, you must understand this. When the disaster occurred, my thought was of you, as he mentioned he'd seen you just last month, and spoke of you so highly and with a fondness I'd scarce heard from him before. I believe you are related although I do not know how."

"My dead husband's brother," May clarified in a rush, "and beloved to me, although we have barely kept in touch, however, these years past. I spoke to him only recently at

Lady Hernshaw's soiree." She brushed aside the explanation when she realized she was babbling a bit from the shock.

"He did not wish to come here. He was . . . I think it was humiliating for him to beg charity, but, my lady, I hardly know where else to take him."

Shifting to a tone of authority, she said, "Of course, you did the exact correct thing. He must be here, with family. Have him brought here at once, but in secrecy. Dueling, in case you did not know Mr. Farnsworth, is not legal. He could be arrested, as could you for serving as second. Bring him through the mews, then in the servant's entrance. And do not worry yourself that he will protest. You must tell him that I insist, if he gives you any trouble over it."

"In any event, he is in no position to argue," Robert said, placing a comforting hand on Lady May's shoulder. "I will go with Mr. Farnsworth, my lady, and fetch my lord to you. Do not make yourself anxious. He will be brought here, I assure you."

The command in his tone reassured her. She grasped his hands, holding his gaze for a moment to communicate to him her thanks. She had come not only to love this man, but also to depend on him in a strange way. She was a strong woman in her own right, but she did not object to his taking charge and comforting her at times when she needed it. She had come to know it was not weakness to lean into a man, draw comfort from him, and relinquish a tiring grip on the matters that pressed upon her.

When he was gone, she thought of Gideon, of how he had looked when she'd seen him last. He had possessed a devil-may-care air, a grin filled with wickedness and eyes full of such sadness . . . She thought, then, of him small and staring at her with those same impossibly gorgeous eyes filled with adulation. Inevitably, she came to remember Matthew, and her heart gave a painful wrench.

She reflected how strange it was to have thought of her bitter secret only moments ago and have the one living reminder of it soon to land on her doorstep.

Chapter 1

Sophie Kent's first thought when she heard running footsteps, shouts, and then the low, urgent voices was that they'd come for her.

Poised frozen in the midst of the exquisitely furnished room that was her bedchamber here at Lady May Hayworth's ultra-fashionable home on Park Lane, she waited for the pounding of feet on the stairs, a signal that the magistrate and his constables were about to burst in and announce that she'd been caught dead to rights impersonating a person of quality.

The sounds died down, fading into a quiet she thought ominous. Not the constable, then, nor the magistrate. In degrees, her breathing came normally. She sat calmly at the dressing and schooled her thoughts away from anxieties.

She had her toilette to make for tonight's rout, her first large party. She took in a deep nourishing breath. Now *there* was anxiety. She was to enter society proper tonight. The *beau monde*—the beautiful world she had always watched, envied, craved.

She was still in her wrapper, her hair loose and long, twirling haphazardly around her shoulders in a golden cascade, awaiting the attention of her dressers, the first of whom entered just then, breathless and waving her hands excitedly.

"So sorry, miss," Sally said. "My lady is late for her toilette. There is a to-do."

"Oh?" Sophie told herself not to be alarmed. So there was something going on in the house. Her heart beat crazily against all the logic she could muster. "I hope it was not bad news."

"I wouldn't have a clue, miss," said Sally with enough of a pout to communicate how dearly she would have liked one. "I left word to be called when my lady is ready for me, but I thought we could get started."

Jeannie, the other maid, came in just then and set about setting out Sophie's clothing. "The gold brocade, miss?" she asked.

"No, Jeannie. That one. Aunt May picked it for tonight."

It never rolled off her tongue. *Aunt May*. Because it was a lie.

Jeannie pulled out an eggshell sheath embroidered with white. Lace and pearls were used sparingly to compliment the dress's elegant simplicity.

Sally chatted as she worked. "She rushed back to the mews with Lord Roberts. He was the one giving orders because my lady was too tearful to do it. It could be a horse, I suppose. She loves animals as much as she does people."

Although she knew that one should never indulge in gossip with the servants, she could not help herself. "The mews. What was she doing there?"

Jeannie frowned at her as she fussed over the dress. The sisters were as different as two people could be. Jeannie was quiet, proper, while Sally was friendly and open.

"It surely has the mistress overset, whatever it is," Sally said. Sally pushed hairpins in with merciless force. Sophie forbore under the rough handling, knowing the skilled maid made the results worth it. "She has such a big heart. For the world I wouldn't wish her troubles."

Jeannie rolled her eyes. "I heard cook mention something

to Mrs. Hanover to ready a room. I think they are bringing someone in. A man."

Sally gaped amazed at her sister. "You did? Well, why didn't you say so before? It's no harm we mean in talking about it, but concern. And curiosity," she added with a giggle.

"Was someone injured?" Sophie asked.

"I don't know, miss. I don't think we should be saying all this," Jeannie said as she searched for the correct pair of stockings. She clearly regretted her breaking of the code. "My lady might not like it."

"Don't be such a stick, Jeannie," Sally said petulantly, and yanked on Sophie's hair.

"It's just I don't want to look disloyal to my lady," Jeannie explained.

"No one could ever accuse you of that," Sophie said, indulging in a regrettable tendency to have the last word. "Lady May would certainly understand our worrying after her when such extraordinary happenings are going on in her home."

Jeannie pursed her lips as she opened the paint box and selected some rouge powder and tint for Sophie's mouth.

"Thank you, but no," Sophie said in the nicest way she could manage.

Regarding her with open disdain, Jeannie balked. "You will be peculiar if you are not enhanced. All the other women will be."

Sophie did not like wearing the cosmetics. True, they looked exceedingly smart on Lady May, elevating her fair prettiness to absolute glamour. However, the overly flushed cheeks on a rice-powdered pallor, replete with reddened lips that were achieved by the use of these crimson pots, reminded her too much of her mother and her aunts. As dear as they were, she wanted nothing of their trappings, nothing to remind her of the empty, lonely lives they had lived.

"I think the pink for my lips, then," Sophie said, trying to be accommodating.

Jeannie glanced at the dress laid out on the bed. She saw

at once Sophie's suggestion for less color was a good one. Pressing her lips together, she assembled the correct shades and began to dab them on.

"A light hand, please," Sophie cautioned, and Jeannie nodded curtly.

If there was one thing Sophie knew, as the daughter of an actress and courtesan, it was how to create an alluring effect. Her mother, Aunt Linnie, and Aunt Millie had been renowned in their days, enjoying a significant amount of acclaim. Many a man had felt privileged to have one of the talented beauties grace his bed.

This had led to a string of wealthy "protectors" and a gay life. But when age stole their looks, the adulation faded and the premier demimonde had moved on to younger, fresher faces and they had been all but forgotten.

The three women had moved in together to Aunt Millicent's house, a tidy townhouse in Fitzroy Square, and Sophie, the only surviving child among them, had been their pet. All three were equally her mother. She had mourned each one as they had fallen ill and died. First Aunt Linnie, who was petite and rather vapid but sweet as a child, then Mother, who had been distant and vaguely bitter at the loneliness of her later years. The last to go was wise, strong Aunt Millie, who had succumbed to influenza last fall. With her passing, Sophie had been left penniless, defenseless, and quite alone.

"These shoes, miss?" Jeannie asked.

Sophie barely looked at the slippers. "Yes, please."

She would have gladly taken employment, but without money, a home, nor the meanest prospect for a respectable life—who would hire her or take her into service? She was far too comely to work as a governess or companion. She was too educated to be considered for employment as a servant or shopkeeper's assistant.

The dire situation became abysmally apparent when Lord Terrance, who had been Aunt Millicent's protector and owned the house in Fitzroy Square, had come after the funeral to visit Sophie. He'd been gentle, even apologetic, that she was to be put out of her home. No doubt he'd felt obliged to offer her a generous portion for her to remain in the house, but it was not charity he offered.

She could remain, yes, but as his mistress. It was a kindly offer, probably made more from pity than lust, but Sophie understood clearly that he would still have availed himself of what he had purchased. It was simply the way it was done.

Sophie flinched at the memory of that humiliating interview.

"Did I hurt you, miss?"

Hurt? She was immune to hurt. The final humiliation had been that afternoon, comfortably seated with the kindly Lord Terrance, serving him tea and hearing him propose so logically, so calmly that she become his mistress.

She'd thought—*How had I ever thought to avoid this? It is my future, my destiny. It was my mother's life, Aunt Linnie and Aunt Millie's life. They had thought it a fine way for a woman to make her way in the world. Only I had wanted better. But I am not better than this.*

She'd nearly cried right in front of the good man as he waited patiently for her answer.

"Miss? Are you angry with me? Did I pull too hard?"

"No. No, Sally. It's fine. I was just . . . oh, woolgathering."

"I'll try to have a care," Sally promised.

She tamped down anger that had come with these memories. On the heels of the despair that had nearly carried her away, she'd grown furious, and that had sustained her. She was not angry at Lord Terrance, nor her aunts. They were simply who they were, doing what they thought right. She'd been angry at no one in particular. At life, perhaps, or fate.

In any event, it had vitalized her. It had made her determined to survive. She'd determined very clearly at that moment she would do anything in her power to change her destiny. She would not live the life of a whore.

It was a crude way of putting it, but it was, after all, what she was used to hearing. It was what the others had called her mother and aunts away from their hearing, but not from hers. It was what the children called her mother, what the ladies who passed them on the street hissed just loud enough for her to hear.

Oh, Aunt Linnie liked the term "courtesan." Practical Aunt Millicent had said they were mistresses, a fine tradition and not dishonorable in the least. Mother had clung to her having been an actress, stating there was no disgrace in being a fashionable demimonde.

But there had been deep disgrace these women had chosen not to acknowledge. Sophie had felt it every day of her life.

"Jeannie," Sally said, "Please bring me the curling tongs from the fire."

Sophie braced herself. She dared not breathe while Sally tortured her locks into tamed ringlets. It was ironic, really, that she submitted herself to these machinations to catch a man when she'd spent so many years avoiding them. But then, this time, she was after marriage.

Many of the men who had come to gatherings at her aunt's home had offered to seduce her and keep her well for the privilege. She was not the kind of woman, from the kind of background, the kind of family, to whom these swaggering sticks offered marriage. She had refused all of them. But now . . . now it was completely different. She had become a lady of quality for the price of a lie.

She had done what she had to survive. It was not such a sin, then, was it? In an ivory box where Aunt Millie had kept important papers, she'd found the birth and death notices of Millicent's daughter, and three letters of inquiry from solicitors in the service of one Lady May Haworth requesting that she contact them regarding the daughter born to Millicent Anderson of the late Earl of Woolrich.

That poor child, Sophie knew, had died in infancy. Sophie's mother had once told her the two of them would have been of an age. She recalled it clearly because she had so desperately wished that the child had lived so that she would have one friend who did not hate her for her low birth.

Sophie had seen her chance, then. She took the letter. Stole it? Borrowed it. She'd presented herself to the solicitors as Millicent's daughter.

"All right, miss, now let me put these pearls in . . ." Sally frowned at her creation, calculating the right spot in the artful arrangement of curls for ornamentation.

Sophie's fingers toyed idly with the expensive bottles glittering like prisms on the vanity as she ticked off the commandments she'd broken. Thou shalt not steal. Thou shalt not bear false witness.

Thou shalt not covet thy neighbor's wealthy aunt with a tidy inheritance all ready and waiting for just the right girl, of which you are not, but you could be . . . you could, with some clever artifice and a bit of luck . . . since the right one had died all those years ago and would not suffer for the lie in any case.

Ah, but her falseness ate at her.

She sighed, and looked at the mirror again. Such a pretty face, Mama had always said, holding her chin to keep her still so that she could admire the beauty she'd produced. Sophie was her jewel. She cooed over the almond eyes of pale aqua, the straight, fine nose, and the sculpted cheekbones. She sighed in pride and envy at the full lips. Her evenly spaced white teeth encouraged her mother to beg her smile more often, and add a beguiling twinkle to her eye when she did so to captivate a man. They'd been excited to see her settled with a wealthy protector. An earl, a duke!

"Do you have a chill?" Jeannie asked.

"No," she said quickly.

A shawl was fetched for her anyway.

She refused to think on these things any longer. She had work to do—that was how she thought of tonight. She had one season—this was all her conscience would allow her to take advantage of Lady May—to make the best marriage possible. It was not a mistress she sought to be, but a wife. A respectable wife of a well-bred man of good standing.

That was how she was going to make certain *her* children would be welcomed by good families. They would not be hissed at on the street, nor cruelly cut by others at their church school. They would be invited with the other children to each other's houses for tea and playtime. Her sons would sit in the drawing rooms of polite society and go to school and be well thought of among the quality. Her daughters would dance at assemblies and not be shunned or, worse, propositioned. They would not draw the lustful eyes of young men who thought them an easy tumble for the fact of who their mother was and what she had been.

The world did not dare hurl insults or make rude comments or sneer at anyone who was tied to an important family. The rich, the powerful were immune to all she had endured.

One season. And when she was wed, she would find a way to repay May for every pence she'd taken from her.

She closed her eyes, vowing this silently. Even if she never learned the truth, as Sophie was determined she never would, then at least Sophie's principles would be satisfied.

"Well, open your eyes, miss. Do you not like it?" asked Sally.

Sophie obeyed, and stared at her reflection. Her beauty surprised her. She was used to her face, used to the reaction it got, but Sally had outdone herself. What she saw surpassed all Sophie's hopes to make a good impression on this most important of evenings.

She rose and went to Jeannie, who, with Sally, held out the dress. She slipped into it, her body beginning to hum with excitement. She felt it, like a charge in the air, the way the air snaps before a bolt of lightening hits nearby.

Moments later, George, one of the footmen, knocked on the door to give her the startling news that their evening's outing was canceled.

Sophie was immediately transformed into a state of concern. Her first and only thought was of Lady May.

She forgot the sensation of only a moment ago of electricity in the air. About tonight holding her destiny.

May gazed at Gideon Hayworth, the Earl of Ashford, and thought him as beautiful as Lucifer in repose. Her throat constricted. Feelings clashed inside her. She was overcome by memories, of love, of self-recrimination, and, above all, of fear.

His blond hair was as pale as wheat, curling rakishly in a style so effortlessly fashionable it made her ache at his fine beauty. His head had been covered in fat curls when he'd been a boy, always tousled and unkempt.

Nothing else of the boyish Gideon remained. His body was hard, the body of a man. He was devoid of his shirt, for it had been in tatters and the surgeon's assistant had had to cut it away. Gideon had been carefully washed; and his right hand, arm, and shoulder were bandaged, as well as a good portion of his head on that side.

He'd been dueling this morning. Pistols at dawn, somewhere in the park, by Lord Farsworth's report. The pan had been overloaded, which had been the fault of Mr. Farnsworth, who had beaten his breast and pulled his hair at the mistake. When Gideon had shot—aimed wide as all his shots were, for he was no stranger to the challenge of honor and never shot to hit his target, only that honor be satisfied by the entire barbaric ritual being played out to the end—the gun had misfired. The powder exploded, seriously injuring him.

The smell of charred flesh and hair had been replaced by the acrid smell of the medicines the surgeon had used to paint the wounds after he'd cleaned them. He was not bleeding his patient, which May had insisted upon. She could not tolerate leeches. She would rather die of that bad blood than endure those things affixed to her skin, and she could not consent to submitting Gideon to such treatment. The surgeon, a serious fellow with wiry white hair and a full beard named Daley, had relented with trepidation.

Her willpower gave out, and she reached out a hand to his sweating brow and touched him. He felt clammy.

Gideon's eyelids fluttered open, revealing vivid green irises. She was startled at the familiarity of them. They had been lit with a wicked gleam for as long as she'd known him. But his eyes appeared flat now. His mouth had a whiteness about it.

"Rest," she told him. "I know you are in pain."

He shook his head as if to deny this, but said nothing.

"Dr. Daley just left. You were sleeping." Unconscious. It had frightened her to death how he had lingered in unnatural slumber. "He says you will make a good recovery if you behave."

His mouth twitched as if he appreciated the unlikeliness of his doing such a foreign thing as behaving.

His mouth began to work, and she tried to shush him, but he spoke in a tired, husky voice. "I used to dream this."

She leaned forward. "What?"

"When I had to go away—after Matthew died—I dreamed I'd wake up and you would be there. And then you'd take me with you."

She recoiled. Her emotions damned painfully in her throat, preventing speech. Patting his hand, she could only nod, and in a moment it was all too much—seeing him, touching him, having him sleeping and looking so much like the little boy she had loved.

She rose. "I shall not stay with you if you insist on speaking. It is not good for your recovery. The surgeon said rest. I will leave you."

His hand closed over her wrist with surprising strength. She pulled away, fighting a dizzying feeling of drowning.

"No . . . don't go." He could barely make the words and his eyelid was already falling to pull him back into the sleep induced by the sedative Daley had administered.

"Rest well, I shall return," she managed. This seemed to relax him, or else the drug took hold, for his grip loosened and May extricated herself and fled from the room.

Gideon's eyes fluttered. "Don't go," he whispered, and his loose hold on consciousness slipped. He fell fitfully into sleep.